'A timely, terrifying, hear[...]
Chris Whitaker, author of *We Begin at the End*

'*Delicate Condition* is the feminist update to *Rosemary's Baby* we all needed – a twisty page-turner with unsettling details and crackling writing that's also a timely critique of sexism in modern medicine'
Andrea Bartz, author of *We Were Never Here*

'One to be read by all women, everywhere. I could not put it down'
Lisa Hall, author of *Between You And Me*

'Heartbreakingly visceral, eerie and intense, reading *Delicate Condition* is feeling, with every new turn of the page, what it's like for your body to no longer be your own. A spooky, devour-in-one-sitting story that's guaranteed to have everyone talking'
Leah Konen, author of *One White Lie*

'Pitch black horror meets smart psychological thriller in this fantastically moreish debut. I devoured it, feeling simultaneously sick and thrilled. And that ending ... just perfect'
S.J.I. Holliday, author of *The Deaths of December*

'What a thrilling, visceral read. So dark, and very fast paced'
Heather Darwent, author of *The Things We Do To Our Friends*

'So many reader emotions, I didn't know who to trust; if anyone! *Delicate Condition* is a thriller, a horror, a mystery and it's lingering in my mind, an after-effect of a chilling read'
J.M. Hewitt, author of *The Life She Wants*

'A darkly visceral and magically evocative novel. You won't be able to put this one down until you've absorbed every last terrifying word'
Sarah Lawton, author of *All The Little Things*

'Fabulously original. A deeply unsettling read that plays on women's darkest fears of pregnancy'
Gemma Rogers, author of *The Secret*

'A suspenseful, visceral read, where the supernatural meets some terrifying truths of motherhood. You won't be able to put it down. I loved it'
A.J. Elwood, author of *The Cottingley Cuckoo*

'Both disturbing and unrelentingly captivating, *Delicate Condition* grabbed me and didn't let go until its final page'
Darcy Coates, author of *The Haunting of Ashburn House*

'A frightening, propulsive read brimming with brutal truths about motherhood, autonomy and the everyday horror of not being believed. This twisty horror thriller will have you guessing until the staggering end'
Rachel Harrison, author of *Cackle*

'I've never read anything like it before. Phenomenal, and an important read'
Louise Mullins, author of *One Night Only*

'A visceral rallying cry against the horrors of medical gaslighting, our culture's indifference to birthing people's pain, and the complete terror of creating and sustaining life. Beautifully written, unbearably tense and deeply scary'
Katie Gutierrez, author of *More Than You'll Ever Know*

'*Delicate Condition* paints an unyielding and heart-wrenching portrait of pregnancy that reaches like a clawed hand inside your chest. I could not put it down'
Katrina Monroe, author of *Graveyard of Lost Children*

DELICATE CONDITION

DANIELLE VALENTINE

 VIPER

Delicate Condition contains scenes of miscarriage and childbirth, as well as cancer survival and implied animal endangerment.

First published in Great Britain in 2023 by
VIPER, part of Serpent's Tail,
an imprint of Profile Books Ltd
29 Cloth Fair
London
EC1A 7JQ
www.serpentstail.com

First published in the United States by Sourcebooks Landmark,
an imprint of Sourcebooks

Internal design © 2023 by Sourcebooks
Internal Design by Laura Boren/Sourcebooks

10 9 8 7 6 5 4 3 2 1

Printed and bound in Great Britain by Clays Ltd, Elcograf S.p.A.

The moral right of the author has been asserted.

A CIP catalogue record for this book is available from the British Library.

Hardback ISBN 978 1 80081 832 3
Trade paperback ISBN 978 1 80081 835 4
eISBN 978 1 80081 834 7

FSC
www.fsc.org
MIX
Paper from
responsible sources
FSC® C018072

*For everyone who's experienced
pregnancy, child loss, infertility or labor.
And for the people who believed
them when they said it hurt.*

Unto the woman he said,

I will greatly multiply thy pain and thy conception;

in pain thou shalt bring forth children...

Genesis 3:16, ASV

PROLOGUE

ALL MOTHERS HAVE ONE THING IN COMMON: PAIN.

Maybe that's why there are so many superstitions surrounding pregnancy. Don't go to a cemetery or your child will die young. Circling birds are bad luck. Avoid large bodies of water if you don't want to miscarry. Wear a closed loop around your neck and your baby will be strangled by their umbilical cord. I think we all believe, somewhere deep in our bones, that darkness is fickle and easily placated with small gifts. My favorite superstition is the one that says more women deliver during a full moon than at any other time of the month. Transforming into mothers instead of wolves. Howling like wild things.

I thought my birth story would be one of the easy ones. After everything I'd gone through to get my little pink plus sign, my big fat positive, I thought the universe owed me something. Until that night, at least. The night she climbed into my bed.

I was already drifting when the mattress shifted beneath me, so I'd barely noticed the arm snaking around my waist, the hand hovering near my belly. The part of my brain that was still conscious assumed the arm belonged to my husband. But then she moved in closer, her thin hips pressing into me from behind, and gradually, I became aware of how she felt against me, how her body was narrower than my husband's, lighter. Hair rose on the back of my neck, but I was still too asleep to move.

Then, I heard her voice in my ear, that one whispered word: "*Baby.*"

That's when I became aware, suddenly and with complete certainty, that my husband wasn't the one in bed with me. I'd screamed and scrambled to my feet, but it was dark, and she ran out the door and down the stairs before I could get a good look at her.

It wasn't until later that I realized my only picture of our unborn baby was gone too. She'd taken it from my bedside table while I was sleeping.

I think that's when I knew that things were going to get bad. It felt like a sign, an omen. Weren't there old wives' tales about what would happen to your baby if his picture was stolen? I thought of the terrible stories I used to love when I was young, stories of fairies who took children from their cribs and replaced them with babies made of wood, of witches who promised wishes in exchange for firstborn children, of predatory birds snatching babies and flying far away. Stories told by women and mothers. Stories no one believed anymore.

I didn't know this then, but the truth is there's no such thing as an uncomplicated pregnancy. We all give something up in exchange for our babies. Nearly everyone on this planet was welcomed by the sounds of a woman screaming.

DAY 14

Egg retrieval

1

MY HUSBAND NEVER CALLED ME. I ALWAYS JOKED THAT THIS
was because he didn't know how to use his phone, that he was the
only tech bro in the world who still had an iPhone in the single digits.
But, that morning, Dex called three times—at 6:55, 7:01, and 7:02—
which was how I knew something was very wrong.

I'd been in the shower, water spray in my face, my ears, blocking
the sound of the phone vibrating on the marble counter. After, I stood
dripping on the tile, looking down at those three calls and thinking
all the normal, horrible things you think when your husband calls
you so many times in a row: that the tiny plane he'd been on this
morning had crashed or was crashing, that he was dead, dying, that
he'd called to say goodbye, but I'd missed him and I'd never hear his
voice again. A part of me even thought maybe I deserved it, that
things were going too well, that I was overdue for some trauma.

"Where the hell are you?" he snapped when I called him back at
7:04 a.m. His normally low, easygoing voice sounded irritated, which
weirdly made me feel a flutter of relief. He wouldn't snap at me if he
was dying.

"I'm getting dressed now. Why? What's wrong?" My abdomen was killing me. I folded the waistband of my yoga pants down while we talked, unable to avoid catching sight of the bruises from my injections. There were three of them, each as dark as a streak of mud, the width of a handprint on my softly bloated lower belly. As if there was something inside of me, some creature pressing its hands right up against the underside of my skin, trying to get out.

"You're still at home?" Dex asked. Definitely irritated. "You know you were supposed to be here an hour before the appointment, right?"

I felt a skip of paranoia but reminded myself that I'd planned this morning down to the last minute, the last second. I'd spoken with Cora, the receptionist at the Riverside fertility clinic, just yesterday morning and confirmed I'd gotten the time right. I'd set three alarms. The traffic wasn't bad, and my friend Georgia—the only person I knew who owned a car in the city—had just texted to let me know she was on her way over to pick me up. All I had to do was throw on some clothes and head out. I had plenty of time.

"It should take me less than an hour to get there. I'm walking out the door in fifteen minutes."

"The appointment *starts* at eight, Anna. You were supposed to be here ten minutes ago."

A cold gripping panic washed over me as I counted the hours back in my head, thinking *no, no, no*. "No...I wrote down the time I was supposed to be at the clinic in my calendar." I tried to remember the exact time Cora had told me when I called, but it was no use. The only way I'd been able to keep all the times and dates straight was by putting them in my online calendar. This appointment was the only thing on my schedule, other than Dex's flight from San Francisco. I'd double-checked it before I went to bed last night. *Triple* checked it. I'd written the reminder in all-caps. GET TO CLINIC BY 8 AM!!!

"You must've written it down wrong," Dex insisted.

"No," I said. "I'm sure I didn't."

"Obviously you did, since you were supposed to be here at *seven*. Jesus, Anna, we talked about...never mind. How soon can you get here?"

I didn't answer right away. I couldn't have made such an obvious mistake, such a *dumb* mistake. I'd been on the IVF roller coaster for a while. I knew better.

This morning was my egg retrieval surgery, arguably the most important appointment in the entire IVF cycle. Perfect timing was crucial, otherwise I risked losing my chance—which meant starting over at the beginning. Going back to weeks of birth control and two, then three injections every single day, to bruises the size of fists on my abdomen, my thighs, to daily visits to the clinic for blood work and ultrasounds.

I'd already been through that part twice. This third round had taken everything from me, every reserve of strength I had left. I needed it to work.

"I'm leaving now," I told Dex. He sighed, and I could tell he'd moved his mouth away from the phone, hoping I wouldn't hear his frustration. I pictured him waiting for me in the Riverside Clinic lobby, jet-lagged in the dark jeans and pressed white shirt he always wore to meet investors, his leather overnight bag at his feet. He'd had to fly all night to make it in time for the 8 a.m. appointment, and he never could sleep on planes. And he was supposed to give sperm today, so he couldn't take an Ambien or even have a glass of wine. He was probably exhausted.

"Anna—" he started, but I hung up before he could tell me it was hopeless, that I was already too late. I was going to figure this out.

You couldn't get anywhere quickly in New York City, especially not from Brooklyn Heights, where we lived. And the Riverside Clinic was all the way in the Upper West Side, at least a forty-five-minute drive by car, and that was only if there was no traffic. This might be one of those rare times when the subway was faster—only forty minutes if I could catch the express.

I had to waste precious seconds digging through my dresser for the only pair of jeans that still fit me, hesitating a beat before grabbing a real bra with an underwire. I was an actor. Until recently, I was best known for a role I did in my teens on a beloved culty television show called *Spellbound* that was canceled after only two seasons. Since then, I've mostly worked as a character actor, playing the quirky best friend through my twenties, then transitioning to the frumpy housewife in my thirties, but almost never the lead. People tended to recognize my face, but they often couldn't quite place whether it was from a film or their daughter's preschool pickup. If they did realize I was an actor, I was always "that girl from that show; you'd know her if you saw her."

That all changed earlier this year, when my most recent project, an art house film called *The Auteur*, exploded into mainstream success. I'd just gotten back from a months-long press tour promoting it, which meant more photos of my face in people's feeds, more clips and GIFs circulating on social media. It was surreal and amazing—but it meant no more walking around the city without putting on a real bra.

A few minutes later, I somehow managed to fight past the dogs to get outside and lock the door.

I was distracted. Distracted enough that, the first time I saw her, she barely made an impression. She was a shadow at the corner of my eye, and I'd glanced over at her, squinting against the sun, as I pulled the front door shut and jerked my key in the lock. There were always people around in New York City, crying in public and breaking up on crowded street corners and making out on subways. I doubt I'd have noticed her if it wasn't for the blue baseball cap pulled low over her forehead, the giant sunglasses hiding half her face. It looked like what the really famous actors wore when they were hoping not to be noticed. Not actors like me, but like Jennifer Lawrence or Siobhan Walsh, the ones who couldn't step out their doors without being accosted.

She'd been staring at something on the sidewalk, transfixed. But then she looked up and saw me and immediately turned around, head ducked, walking briskly away.

I saw what she'd been staring at as I ran down the sidewalk, right past the spot where she'd been standing. It was a bird's nest. Someone must've knocked it out of a tree because it had crashed to the sidewalk, bits of straw and sticks scattered everywhere, a single blue egg smashed open, spilling yolk and a half-formed embryo on the concrete.

I hurried away, stomach churning.

2

THE NEXT FORTY MINUTES PASSED LIKE A MONTAGE: ONE second, I was running down Henry Street, tote bag slapping my hip, and then I was jerking my Metro card out of my wallet and tripping down the stairs—because of course I'd trip. Then, finally, I was jogging up the steps on 163rd Street, thinking, *Please don't let it be too late, please God, I'll do anything.*

In my hurry, I raced past a poster of my own face at the top of the subway stairs. It was a poster from *The Auteur*, my character peering mournfully out a car window, crow's-feet creasing the skin around my eyes, my hair tangled and wild. A single review floated above my head, just one word: *Masterful*.

If the circumstances had been different, I might've pulled out my phone and taken a quick photo. It was still so strange to see a poster of my own face in public like this—evidence that the work I'd been doing for twenty years meant something to someone outside my own family and friends. I would never get used to it.

But I didn't have time for that now. It was already 7:47 a.m. I should've been changing into a gown, waiting in the operating room, making small talk with my anesthesiologist.

I wouldn't forgive myself if I messed this up, not after all the time I'd wasted in my twenties and thirties. I'd thought I was being so smart, focusing on my career before worrying about marriage and kids. And then, one day, I woke up and I was thirty-six years old, and time was officially running out. I'd never thought of myself as the kind of woman who needed a man and kids to have a full life, but the thing was, I didn't have a full life without them either. My dirty secret was that I wanted more. I wanted a husband to wake me up with coffee on my birthday, a kid to shove a silly handmade card into my face. I wanted a family.

The universe must've heard my wish because that was the year I met Dexter Harding at a suicide prevention organization's walk. He was older, in his forties, divorced. He'd gone on a dorky rant about the best way to knot your hiking boots (you needed to use something called a "surgeon's knot," which I still didn't know how to tie), he'd been confident enough to ask for my number, and he'd made me laugh. I'd known, right after our first conversation, that he was it for me.

We started dating the next week, became engaged over the holidays, and got married just eight months after the night we met.

We started trying that night when—giddy with champagne—we'd decided to just skip the condom and "see what happened." That was years ago. It made me feel incredibly naïve that I'd ever believed it would be that simple.

Dex was waiting on the sidewalk outside of the Riverside Clinic when I finally arrived. He was short and slender, but in incredibly good shape, with long, lean muscles and broad shoulders—the kind of guy you expected to run into on a deserted trail deep in the woods, or teaching ski lessons at some mountain chalet, not standing outside a bougie fertility clinic in Manhattan.

He'd stuck his hands into his pockets, and he was trying to look casual, but his dark hair was sticking up in sweaty spikes, giving him away. I could picture him running his hand through it, anxious, waiting for me.

It was 7:55. I was sweating, gasping for breath. "Am I too late?"

"You were supposed to be here an hour ago," Dex said. He hated to be late. "I don't understand how you could—"

"I know," I said, interrupting him. "I'm so mad at myself just... Please, tell me we can still do this." He still looked pretty annoyed, so I added another desperate "*Please*."

With that, he softened. "I think it's going to be okay," he grumbled. "I spoke with Dr. Hill, and I convinced her to get you into an operating room now. But you have to hurry."

I exhaled, relieved. I was new to Dr. Carla Hill's practice, but she was supposed to be a "miracle worker" according to our friend Talia. I was desperate for her to like me.

"I'm so sorry," I said.

"It's fine, I took care of it." Dex squeezed my fingers, and I noticed that the sleepless night had carved hollows into his cheeks, leaving his skin sallow and gray. My husband wasn't conventionally attractive, but in my opinion, he was very handsome, with his strong jaw and rich brown eyes. True, his hair was perpetually too shaggy, and his face had a rugged look to it on account of his Scottish ancestry and crooked nose (which—he'd told me drunkenly, on our third date—he'd broken falling down the stairs at his parents' house in Somerville, not hiking the Salkantay Trail, as he let people believe), but I thought the flaws added interest to his features, setting him apart from a sea of generic Manhattan businessmen and LA actors. I couldn't help picturing a baby with Dex's dark eyes, his lopsided smile. The image cracked me open inside, and I had to push it away. The Riverside Clinic was chic and modern-looking. Floral wallpaper covered the wall behind the receptionist desk, the leaves of the flowers coordinating perfectly with the pastel green chairs in the waiting room. Maternal artwork hung from the other three walls: watercolor women breastfeeding perfect newborns, sketchy outlines of pregnant women gazing lovingly down at their swollen bellies. I felt a deep longing looking at those pictures. That's what I wanted, just that. Why did it have to be so hard?

One or two people discreetly glanced at my face as we headed across the lobby, quickly looking away again. I felt an intense burst of anxiety. I couldn't figure out if I wanted to laugh at how absurd it was, being recognized here, or if I wanted to cry. It was strange, this feeling. I mean, I'd craved this kind of attention for almost two decades, hadn't I? It came with success; it's what being an actor was. But this was different from what I'd expected. It was...*meaner*. Before *The Auteur*, if people realized I was an actor at all, they'd smile or wave or ask me to take a selfie like I was someone they knew, a friend, even. Now, they nudged their neighbors and whispered behind their hands and snapped covert pics when I wasn't looking. It made me think of the crueler things some fans had said about me online, things about the wrinkles around my eyes, or my hair, which was already starting to gray. Things designed to cut me down, as though people were offended by the fact that a woman my age could still be successful. It made me feel exposed, raw.

We were ushered into a small, mirrored room, and I avoided my reflection as I undressed. I was given an IV of something called "twilight anesthesia," which made me feel spacey and light-headed.

"You feeling okay?" Dex was crouched by my hospital bed, holding my hand.

"Fine," I murmured. "Sleepy."

"It's going to happen this time. I can feel it." He kissed my knuckles and my forehead and said, in a quieter voice, "It's going to be really hard. We're going to have to work at this all the time, but I want to do that because I want you."

I smiled. He was trying to do the line from *The Notebook*. It was a joke, because Dex never watched movies, not even famous ones. I'd spent our first few months together quoting romantic comedies at him and he had no idea—he thought I was just clever. When he figured out my game, he started doing it, too, trying to find the most obscure lines, the ones I wouldn't guess right away.

"The line is, 'We're going to have to work at this *every day*,'" I corrected him.

His cell phone buzzed in his pocket, distracting him for a moment. He took it out and frowned down at the screen, then stuck it back in his pocket without answering. "Nah, it's *all the time*."

I was sure I was right, but it didn't matter. "You should answer your cell phone," I murmured, slurring a bit. "Could be important."

"What could be more important than this?" he asked, a smile in his voice.

Then, because I suppose I couldn't let it go after all: "The quote is *every day*."

"It's not," he insisted. He really hated being wrong.

And then I was wheeled away from him, into an OR, my legs placed in stirrups as I waited for the doctor. I stared at a crack running through the ceiling, drifting in and out, in and out.

As my head went loopy, I thought about how, when I was six years old, I'd asked my mom how babies were made. She'd always been the kind of mom who refused to dumb anything down. There were no cute stories about storks, no picture books with our bodies detailed in brilliant primary colors. She took me to the library, and we found a book on reproduction, and then she plopped me in the middle of the biology section, grad students stepping around us, over us, as she explained about eggs and sperm, and what happens when a man and a woman love each other very much. It took me decades to understand that this too was a fairy tale.

I heard a door open, and then there was the sudden flurry of activity that meant Dr. Hill had arrived. I said one final prayer—*please let this work please*—and then my eyes fluttered, a sudden wave of exhaustion overtaking me.

3

"MS. ALCOTT... MS. ALCOTT, CAN YOU HEAR MY VOICE...?"

"Mmm," I murmured. My eyelids felt sticky. It took all my strength to work them open and focus on the face swimming in front of me. It was creased and wizened, the face of a fairy godmother in a story, the one who would offer the heroine anything she wanted so long as she completed these three tasks: my IVF doctor, Carla Hill.

I tried to lift my head, but the bed dipped and swayed beneath me, so I dropped it back onto my pillow. I was in the recovery room, long and narrow, with a single window on the far side. Dex was crouched on a folding chair beside me.

"Hey," he said, taking my hand. "How are you feeling?"

I tried to answer, but I couldn't. I let my eyes close again. The voices I heard sounded far away, saying something about how I was still on a lot of drugs, but they were going to wear off soon. Nothing to worry about.

"Anna dear, I'm going to need your attention for just a moment," Dr. Hill was saying. "I have a few questions for you."

She always called me *dear* and *darling* and *sweetheart*. It made me feel like she was my grandmother, or maybe like she was one of those old-fashioned family doctors making house calls, carrying a beaten leather doctor's bag, practically part of the family.

"S'okay," I murmured.

"What's your full name?"

"An...na... Vic...Victory..." I was looking for *Victoria*, but my tongue felt so massive, I was having a hard time twisting it around all those consonants. "Anna Alcott."

"Close enough, dear. And do you know today's date?"

For a second my brain was a complete blank. Time had no meaning. It was a white nothingness that we were all floating in, like a soup. And then, "Oh...uh...October"—only I made October sound more like *augdober*—"October five."

"Very good." Dr. Hill patted my hand. "Great. I'm going to let you go back to resting, but I wanted to pop in to let you know that today went well. We retrieved nine eggs."

"Nine?" I repeated, groggy, wondering if I'd misheard her. It was such a small number. *Nine*. "That's... that's bad, right?"

"I'm very happy with this," Dr. Hill insisted, but I thought I noticed a weariness in her eyes. She probably thought I was one of those women who relied too much on Google, believing the fertility message boards over the people with the actual medical degrees. She patted my hand. "Just trust the process, dear."

I nodded, making myself picture the walls of her office, covered in photos of beaming women holding fat, happy babies, their eyes watching me whenever I sat in the chair in front of her desk.

Trust her, they all seemed to be saying. *She's a miracle worker! Just look at us.*

I swallowed the rest of my questions as Dr. Hill produced a small black tablet and tapped something onto the screen. "I'm sending a prescription for progesterone suppositories to the pharmacy. Remember, they need to be refrigerated. That part's very important."

"Refrigerated," I repeated. I licked my lips and asked, as clearly as I could manage, "Will I feel any pain?"

"You may experience some discomfort as you come off anesthesia, but nothing more than you can handle. You can take a low-dose aspirin if it gets to be too much."

She told me to get some rest and that she'd call with an update in the morning, and then she ambled out into the hall, on her way to some other recovery room, some other hopeful couple.

I closed my eyes and tried to make myself feel more optimistic. My part was over, for a little while at least. But I was having a hard time staying positive. The rush of emotion sweeping over me was too distracting. Without meaning to, I thought about some of the meaner tweets strangers have sent me since *The Auteur* premiered—things like *When did Anna Victoria Alcott become ancient* and *Who would want to screw that old bitch?* Horrible things. All because I didn't look exactly like I did when I was in my twenties, playing some other, much more beautiful actor's doting best friend.

I *was* getting older. That was just a fact. Maybe I was too old for this. I pictured the eggs inside of my body like they were grapes gone bad. Sour, rotten fruit, skin bruised and fuzzy with mold, caving in on themselves. Maybe what I was doing was selfish.

I swallowed, feeling guilt and failure and disappointment all rolled into one.

"Hey, this is good news," Dex said, squeezing my hand. "It's like she said; we only need one."

That part, at least, was true. We only needed one.

Within an hour the drugs had worn off, and in two, a nurse was telling me I was okay to travel. I had all-over body aches as the general anesthetic left my muscles. I felt delicate, almost breakable. It was as though someone had reached into my body and gotten my internal organs twisted between their hands, wringing me out like a dish towel. When I asked a nurse if it was normal, she assured me that some achiness was to be expected and offered to get me some water as I waited in the lobby while Dex went outside to meet the car.

I tried to breathe through it. *If this works all the pain will have been worth it*, I told myself.

The receptionist, Cora, was in her mid-twenties and pretty in the way that every New York woman seemed to be pretty: confident and casually chic, with clear skin and no makeup, dark hair and eyes. There was only one other women in the waiting room with me, a pregnant brunette with her face hidden behind a well-worn copy of *Vogue*. A photograph of my friend Siobhan Walsh stared back at me from the cover, her eyes narrowed, lips pursed, oozing cool.

It must've been an old magazine. Siobhan hadn't done any press since her last film, which was years ago. She'd been a nineties "it" girl, working with Scorsese and Fincher back when I was still hustling for guest appearances on daytime soaps. She'd been nominated for her first Oscar before she was old enough to drink and won the damn thing two years later, famously beating out Meryl and Gwyneth. I'd lost count of how many magazine covers I'd seen her on, how many articles I'd read about her, how many famous, beautiful men she'd been photographed with. I used to fantasize, not about being her, but about having her as an older sister. I imagined her taking me under her wing, teaching me how to wear lipstick and tie a silk scarf and charm a casting agent. Maybe it's because I grew up without a mom or any siblings, but I was always yearning for a close female relationship, a role model.

Or maybe it was just *her*. Siobhan Walsh. I'd been watching her movies since I was a kid, just like the rest of the world. She has one of those personalities that oozes off the screen, no matter what character she's actually playing. I think everyone in America either wanted her to be their very best friend or their lover.

When I finally met her, I was so nervous my hands shook, and I wound up spilling tea all over myself. I was mortified. I expected her to say a polite goodbye and then get far away from me, fast. Instead, she'd insisted on switching shirts with me, claiming the accident had been her fault, that she'd surprised me. She'd dragged me into the bathroom despite my protests, and she didn't leave until our shirts were switched and I'd gotten rid of every last bit of tea and mortification. It had been exactly what I'd imagined having a sister might be like.

My phone rang, jerking me out of the memory. I checked the screen and saw the number of my publicist, Emily Chapman. I considered it for a moment, then hit the button to ignore. I was too groggy from the drugs to talk now. I started shuffling through the stack of magazines on the table next to me and felt a little jolt of excitement when

I spotted last month's issue of *Rolling Stone*. I wasn't on the cover, but a smaller headline in the lower left-hand corner read: *Anna Victoria Alcott Wants You to Know What a Real Woman Looks Like.*

The headline didn't sit right with me, even though they'd taken it directly from a quote I'd given. I'd meant I wasn't going to dye my hair and Botox away the wrinkles that had started to crawl across my face. At the time it'd felt like I was part of a larger conversation about women's aging bodies. I even told this story about how I'd stood up to a studio exec who'd asked me to consider a face lift because "no one would believe your costar is going to have sex with a woman your age." My male costar, by the way, was ten years older than I was.

But, looking at the magazine now, I worried that it sounded like I was passing judgment on women who *did* do those things, saying they weren't "real" somehow. It bothered me that I couldn't get the tone right, even when it meant so much to me.

The door to the clinic swung open, a screech of hinges followed by a sudden burst of autumn air. Figuring Dex had probably flagged a car by now, I stood, cringing as I started outside, accidentally bumping into the woman who'd just come in.

"I'm so sorry," I said, glancing at her. She wasn't the type of woman I usually saw in the clinic. She was much older, her hair completely gray, deep lines around her wide unblinking eyes. In her sixties, at least.

I heard Cora call out from the receptionist desk, "Ms. Preecher, you know you're not allowed—"

The woman didn't seem to have registered that she'd spoken. She blinked, staring at me.

"*You.*" She was pointing at me now. "I know you... You're Anna Victoria Alcott, right? From *The Auteur*?"

I smiled, flattered, and said, "Thank you for watching."

But then her eyes traveled across my face, and my shoulders tensed. The downside of jumping into a conversation about how we view aging women is that everyone thinks they have the right to talk about it with you. And I didn't have the emotional reserves to field questions about my age right now. I wanted to be at home, holding a cup of tea, with a hot water bottle pressed to my swollen abdomen.

"I'm so sorry, but my husband's waiting," I said, gingerly moving past her.

"Wait!" she said, but I was already out the door. It was colder outside than I'd expected it to be, so cold that the dry winter air seemed to suck all the moisture from my face, leaving the skin around my eyes tight, my nostrils stiff. Luckily, Dex was just at the corner, waving at a big, black SUV that had just pulled to a stop.

"Dex!" I called, raising my arm.

That's when I heard it, a soft *click,* the shutter release sound a phone made when you took a picture. When I looked around, the woman from the clinic—*Ms. Preecher*—was hurrying down the street shoving her phone into her pocket, intentionally not looking at me.

4

HAD SHE TAKEN MY PICTURE?

I felt dumbfounded. Normally, I'd have been delighted to take a picture with a fan, but I was outside my IVF clinic—she might've even gotten part of the sign in the shot. And it was somehow worse that she'd taken it when I hadn't realized I was being photographed, like she'd captured something intimate, vulnerable. I didn't like knowing that a stranger might have a picture of that moment.

I started to turn around, thinking I might run after her and ask her to please delete the photo, offer to take a selfie with her instead, but I was distracted by another woman standing across the street, looking my way.

She was wearing a blue baseball cap and big sunglasses. It was the same cap-and-sunglasses combo I'd seen outside my townhouse back in Brooklyn. The same *woman* I'd seen back in Brooklyn.

I froze, feeling a prickle of unease. It was weird to see her again, all the way up here. Could she have...*followed* me all the way from Brooklyn?

Heat flared in my face the second the thought entered my head.

God I was self-important. Of course, this stranger hadn't followed me all the way from Brooklyn. I wasn't Rihanna. It's just that the woman who'd snapped my picture had gotten into my head, made me paranoid. This was New York City—people took the same subway lines, the same exits, went to the same coffee shops and offices. You were always crossing paths with the same people here—it was inevitable in a place this crowded.

I gave the woman one last look, then quickly walked away.

By that evening, my abdomen was so bloated that walking was difficult and deep breaths were almost impossible. The aspirin helped some, though not enough. I spent an hour scouring message boards to see if it was safe to take anything stronger, but nothing had been approved for use during IVF. Eventually, I gave up.

I tried to distract myself by cleaning out the spare room, which we'd been using as an office and storage space since we moved in two years ago. I told myself I was just trying to keep busy, but the truth was, I was excited. Eventually, hopefully, this room would become a nursery. We'd paint the walls purple or blue or green, and we'd buy a tiny dresser and bookshelf and crib, and hang colorful art. I felt a shiver, anticipating it.

I was sorting through a box of old *Spellbound* paraphernalia while Dex hovered in the doorway talking about Thanksgiving plans, how he wanted to visit his parents in Massachusetts, even though we'd already agreed to fly out to Burbank to spend the long weekend with my dad and stepmother. I was nodding at the right times, trying to pay attention, but I was distracted. I hadn't even seen some of this *Spellbound* stuff in twenty years.

Dex was saying that his sister, Arlo, was bringing her new girl-friend with her this year, when I moved a huge box out of the way and found a surfboard leaning against the wall: my Teen Choice Award from 2008.

I smiled. I got it my first season of *Spellbound,* the only award I was ever even nominated for. I was only nineteen, and Summer Day was my first role ever. Accepting that award, I'd been so sure it was going to be my big break. I felt naïve now, remembering that, but at the time it'd seemed inevitable.

There were a lot of reasons it hadn't worked out. The network bungled our schedule, and the reviews were brutal and a little sexist. But it had been my fault too. I'd been too young for the responsibility of carrying a show, too shy to promote myself at press events, too inexperienced to deal with agents and managers. When *Spellbound* was canceled before our second season aired, it was impossible not to feel as though I was the one who'd failed, not the show.

After that, I told myself I'd never take success for granted again. I spent the next twenty years accepting every role I was offered, playing sisters and coworkers and best friends. I worked harder than anyone else I knew, vowing that when I got a second chance, I'd be ready for it. But years passed, and then decades, and though I was always able to find steady work, that breakout role never came again. Not until now.

My phone rang, snapping me back to the room. I grabbed it off the floor and glanced at the screen: my publicist, Emily, again.

"I have to take this. It's Emily," I told Dex.

The smile that had been plastered over Dex's face as he talked about his family faded. "Can't you call her back? We're in the middle of something."

I shook my head. "Sorry, I already ignored a call from her earlier. I should really see what she needs." I turned my back on his faint frown as I brought the phone to my ear. "Hey, Em."

"Anna, hi! I'm so glad I was able to reach you." Emily was from London originally, and she had the kind of chic British accent that made everything she said sound cool. I pictured her in her normal uniform: a black blazer thrown over a white T-shirt, perfectly slouchy jeans and kitten heels, all of it topped off with rectangular black glasses, glossy black hair always pulled into an efficient ponytail. California casual at its chicest. I'd been with Emily's firm since my teenage *Spellbound* days, but Emily had only taken me on as a client two years ago, after my last publicist, Catherine, had retired.

"Listen," Emily said, her voice crisp but pleasant, as usual. "I wanted to touch base to make sure Friday's meet and greet is still on your radar."

"I have another meet and greet?" I paused, trying to remember whether Emily had mentioned this to me before now. Possibly not. There had been a lot going on lately. When I first accepted my role in *The Auteur*, everyone involved had believed it was going to be the kind of film that made the rounds at indie theaters and film festivals for a few months before quietly fading into the background—a role I could be proud of but by no means one that was going to rocket me into the A-list. I even remember confidently telling Dex that I was going to take a break from acting when it was all over. I'd been working since I was nineteen years old, and I wanted to step back and focus on building our family.

Suffice it to say, none of us were prepared for what happened two months ago at the Toronto Film Festival, when *The Auteur* surprised absolutely everyone by winning the People's Choice Award. Since then, it's been an all-out effort as the studio has tried to make up for months of Academy Award campaigning. I'd been flying back and forth between New York and Los Angeles for private screenings and meet and greets, attending every luncheon and awards ceremony and gala Emily could get me invited to, living the life of a movie star for the first time in my career. All of a sudden, I was having my hair and makeup styled by the biggest celebrity artists, designers who never knew my name were offering to create gorgeous couture gowns for me to wear when I walked down red carpets, and I was photographed standing alongside the most beautiful people in the world. Leonardo DiCaprio said he loved my movie last week. *Leonardo DiCaprio.* I had a poster of his face on my wall when I was thirteen.

And I started getting interest from directors I'd spent my entire life idolizing. A few days ago, Emily forwarded me a script from Sofia Coppola. I remember laughing out loud when it hit my inbox, thinking how weird it was that this was happening to me *now*, when I was just starting to consider stepping back. I wasn't feeling sorry for myself or anything like that. It was just surreal, like *huh, life can be so weird.*

Of course, the timing has been a little less than ideal. I wouldn't have started IVF if I'd known I was going to be so busy or spend so much time traveling. But women with much more stressful, challenging careers than mine do IVF. I had no right to complain.

"Oh, also, we were able to book you on Seth Meyers," Emily was telling me now. "It's Thursday the twenty-eighth. Do you think you can make that work?"

For a second, I was too dumbfounded to speak. I'd never done *Late Night* before. I'd cheered for plenty of costars who did the late-night circuits to promote our films—but I'd never been invited myself. "Really?"

"Yes, really," Emily said, laughing. "You're having a moment, Anna. How many times do I have to tell you?"

I felt a shot of giddiness, which quickly morphed into anxiety. The timing was going to be tricky. Depending on what happened with the egg retrieval, I could be back in the clinic for surgery within a week or two, and I wasn't sure what recovery time would be like, if it would make sense for me to do a talk show.

But this was Seth Meyers. I've loved him since he was on *Saturday Night Live*.

"I can make it work," I told her, hoping it was true. From the corner of my eye, I noticed Dex's frown deepening.

"Fantastic. I'll send you an invite to remind you to block off the date in your calendar. Or do you want me to just log on and create the appointment myself?"

Emily had been booking so many events for me lately that I finally caved and gave her the password to my calendar. It was easier for both of us that way. "That would be great," I told her. "Thank you."

"Whatever you need. You're my biggest client right now, and this is going to be the most important few months of your career," Emily said. "I know this took us all off guard, but it's going to be great, I can feel it. Until February, I eat, sleep, and breathe Anna Victoria Alcott. This is everything we've worked for."

Emily had never made a secret of how hungry she was. Ambition radiated off of her like a pheromone. I knew this was just as big of a deal for her as it was for me.

"Have you given any more thought to LA?" she asked. Emily wanted me to consider moving out to LA for a month or two during the Academy's peak voting season, so I could attend press events and red carpets at a moment's notice. I'd told her I'd consider it, figuring I'd wait to give her an answer until after I found out whether this IVF round had worked.

"I haven't decided," I said. "I'm still waiting to see how things pan out."

"Right," she said, clocking what I meant. "Of course." Emily knew I was doing IVF. I'd mentioned it to her the last time we got dinner to explain why I wasn't getting a drink, and though I hadn't brought it up again, we both knew what I meant when I said "waiting to see how things pan out."

"I know Oscar campaigning can be a slog," she added, "but I promise we're in the home stretch. Just a few more months of work could change your entire life."

A prick of anxiety moved through me. She had no idea how true her words were.

Dex had gone to the kitchen for a snack while I was on the phone, and he was bent over the fridge when I walked in behind him. "What's Emily calling about now? Some new party she wants you to go to?" His voice was clipped, the word *party* coming out like it was something frivolous. I flinched.

"They're not *just* parties," I said, defensive.

He glanced up at me. "You know I didn't mean it like that."

I swallowed. I knew he didn't. He'd always been supportive of my career. It was just tricky that this was happening now. We'd been so busy over the last few months that we'd barely even seen each other. Timing was never on my side.

"What is it?" he asked, closing the fridge. "Is something wrong?"

"Of course not!" I forced a smile. "Everything's great."

Dex raised an eyebrow, not believing me. It was one of the things I'd first loved about him, how he always seemed to know when I was just saying I was okay to make other people feel better. Lately, though, I've felt an undercurrent of frustration whenever he's pushed me like this. Isn't it enough for me to *say* I'm okay? Do I really have to go the extra mile to make sure he believes me too?

"I feel like an asshole for complaining about anything," I hedged.

"But…?" he urged.

I rubbed the bridge of my nose. "Maybe I'm…a little overwhelmed. There's a lot going on right now. I wish this wasn't all happening at the same time."

"Me too," he said, and I felt another flare of defensiveness before he continued. "But we'll get through it. In my experience, the baby stuff is hard for everyone."

In his experience? I looked up at him, frowning. Was he just talking about us? Or was it something else, some other experience he hadn't mentioned to me?

Dex had been married once before, to a French Lebanese professor living in London named Adeline Jouda. He never really talked about her. The only thing he'd ever told me was they'd gotten married too quickly and then split when they realized they wanted different things.

I looked her up online once. She was gorgeous, impossibly tall and thin, with yards of dark hair and the most perfect lips I'd ever seen outside of a makeup ad. I couldn't tell what "different things" they could've wanted from scanning the little information that was visible on her private Facebook and Instagram pages, but Dex had once mentioned she wasn't very interested in children, so I thought maybe that had something to do with it. Dex wanted a family, and Adeline didn't.

Now, though, something about the knowing tone of his voice when he'd said, "In my experience," made me wonder if there was something else, something he hadn't told me. He made it sound like he'd been through this before, but he'd never said anything like that to me before ever.

I looked at him. "Did you and Adeline ever try to get pregnant?"

His answer came fast. "No."

I felt my stomach tilt. "Really?"

"Kids just weren't in the cards for us." A muscle in Dex's jaw clenched. He wasn't looking at me. After a moment, he added, "Addy made it clear that she wasn't interested in being pregnant."

Addy. I'd never heard him call his ex that.

Dex and I didn't do secrets. We've technically only known each other for a little over two years, but that had never seemed to matter because we'd always talked about everything. I felt like he understood me better than anyone else in my life, and vice versa. But Adeline had always been a tricky subject. I'd noticed that every time I've tried to ask him about his previous marriage, we'd always somehow get off subject. And now, hearing him call her *Addy*, just made me more aware that there was this whole phase of his life that I didn't understand, an entire person who knew things about him that I would never know.

I cleared my throat. "Was that why—?"

"Anna?" Dex asked, interrupting me. "Did you leave these out?"

Dex didn't get seriously annoyed a lot but, when he did, his voice would get very slow and deep, like I was a toddler who'd done something wrong. I turned, seeing a pharmacy bag of progesterone suppositories sitting on the counter, the bright red **REFRIGERATE IMMEDIATELY** sticker seeming to glare at me.

I stared at them, frowning. "I put those in the fridge last night." I had a perfectly clear memory of opening the fridge and putting that bag on the shelf next to the oat milk.

Dex stared at me, then dropped his gaze, his mouth a thin line, neither smiling nor frowning.

"I *did*," I said again, a little sharper than I meant to. It seemed unfair that he just assumed I was the one who'd made the mistake.

"It's fine," Dex said, though I could tell he was biting back his irritation. "You're on a ton of meds right now, you have a lot on your mind, this kind of thing was bound to happen. At least these don't have to be taken at a specific time, like the last ones did."

I felt something anxious work its way through me as Dex picked up the bag and chucked it into the garbage. He was talking about the bottle of Lupron I'd left out a month ago. Lupron was an incredibly expensive fertility treatment that always had to be kept under twenty-five degrees and taken at *very* precise times throughout the day in order to work. I'd left a bottle of it out overnight and it'd been ruined. Dex and I had to make an emergency trip to the pharmacy, calling the clinic on the way so Dr. Hill could rush a new prescription, so we wouldn't miss taking the shot at the right time.

I swallowed, taking his point. If I was absent-minded enough to leave that out, why not this?

"I'll handle it. I can probably call Dr. Hill and get her to send a new prescription through tonight," Dex said, squeezing my shoulder.

I stayed in the kitchen for a few minutes after he'd left, going over everything I'd done the night before, searching for gaps in my memory. I couldn't think of any, but that's the thing about not being able to remember something, isn't it? You don't *know* that you're not remembering. The picture in your head feels like the truth, even if it's a lie.

It bothered me, that I couldn't trust my own memory. How much more was I going to be expected to sacrifice to make this happen? I'd already given my body, my hormones, my time. And now, it seemed, my mind.

And I wasn't even pregnant yet.

IO PREECHER, 1987

IO NEVER MET THE BIOLOGICAL PARENTS. SHE THOUGHT THAT was strange, but her friend May told her it was pretty normal, given the situation. May said the real parents didn't want to meet the women they paid to be their surrogates, that it made it harder for them to pretend the baby was theirs.

How it worked was, the parents arranged for Io to come into Manhattan to a sterile-looking clinic on the thirty-ninth floor of a high-rise in Midtown. A doctor came into her room, told her to get undressed and lie back on the table, and then she'd inseminated her. It was that fast. It felt a little like going in for her annual except that, afterward, she had to lie on her back with her feet in the air for around thirty or forty-five minutes.

To be honest, it wasn't what Io had in mind when May told her she should consider a job being a surrogate. May said she'd been a surrogate the year before, and the couple she'd given the baby to had paid her ten grand, which was more money than Io had ever had at one time. Ten grand could do a lot of things. It could buy a car and put a down payment on an apartment in a good part of town. It could really change her life. And May said there might be other benefits too, things Io could only dream of.

"What kind of benefits?" Io had wanted to know.

But all May would say was, "Just wait. I'm not supposed to be the one who tells you."

Io bristled. She didn't like the secrecy. May had grown up poor as dirt, just like Io had. As far as she could tell, this was just rich people trying to buy the things they couldn't get themselves, like always. Trying to buy life. Telling people like her and May that they'll do things for them, if only they'll give them what they want.

But ten grand was a lot of money, and May said the job was *easy*. She said these people were motivated, that all they wanted was someone young and healthy.

"And obviously the most important thing is that you're—" But May had stopped herself and paused before saying, "*Determined*. The most important thing is that you're determined to be a good mother while you're pregnant, you know? They want you to eat right and exercise, so the baby comes out healthy. You're so lucky they chose you."

Io didn't know, then, how difficult that last part was going to be. She'd thought the hardest part of the whole thing was going to be the pain of labor and, after, giving the baby up. It turned out that part wasn't bad at all. No, the really hard part came before, during the pregnancy. No one had ever told Io that pregnancy was going to be like that. They never told her that her skin would get so dry it felt like it might split open, or that her teeth would bleed whenever she brushed them, that the pain in her hips would get so bad she wouldn't be able to sleep.

And then there were the cravings. Oh God, the cravings. She still had nightmares about them and, after, when she woke up, she'd fumble around in the dark, groping for her stomach, half expecting to find it full and round, the baby still inside of her, the nightmare following her into real life. When she felt flat belly and loose skin, she actually sobbed in relief. *Thank God.*

Thank God it was over.

Sometimes, when the nightmares got really bad, Io would think about what May had said: *You're so lucky.*

Io knew she was lucky. People with two good legs were lucky too, but that didn't mean it wouldn't hurt if one of those legs got caught in a bear trap. The things that made you lucky could also be the things that made you suffer. Io wished people would stop telling women they should be grateful for their suffering instead of trying to help them with it.

And then there was the other thing May hadn't said. Because Io knew that *determined* wasn't the word she'd meant to use. She didn't see May anymore, not since May started talking crazy, but it sounded more like May had been about to say *desperate.*

The most important thing is that you're *desperate.*

DAYS 17–21

Embryo transfer

5

I MADE DEX BRING HIS CELL BECAUSE I WAS PRETTY SURE mine wasn't working. But when he called me as a test, my phone buzzed to life in my hand, his sunburnt face smiling from the photograph that filled the screen. So much for that theory.

We were waiting on our daily update call from Dr. Hill. It was after six, long past office hours, and we usually got a call from the clinic by now, my heart vibrating against my rib cage the second I heard Cora's familiar vocal fry telling us to please hold.

I couldn't help thinking it was a bad sign. This call was the big one, the one letting us know whether any of our embryos were of a high enough quality to transfer back into my body. I was so nervous I was making myself sick.

Dex squeezed my hand as we walked, and I offered him a wan smile. The sun had drifted low in the sky, turning everything dusky gold as we made our way down the brownstone-lined street. We were meeting up with Frank and Talia, the CFO and the CEO of Dex's company, respectively. Our first social event in weeks.

I used to live for nights like this, used to love how the city glittered like a jewel on the other side of the East River, just visible here and there through the blowing fall leaves, and how the slightly percussive sound of my heels on cobblestones was a kind of music, bracelets jingling on my wrists like an accompanying tambourine. I could never understand how I'd gotten so lucky, how my life was so beautiful.

Now, my eyes kept drifting to the children's drawings taped behind apartment windows, the folded-up strollers leaning against the front doors of brownstones. I felt a deep, yearning ache. I thought about how our four little embryos were all alone in a lab somewhere in the city, Dex's and my DNA desperately trying to come together, to form a whole person. It seemed impossible, a magic trick.

"Are you going to be okay?" Dex asked, glancing at me.

"I don't know," I said honestly. "I can't stop obsessing about this call. I feel like I'm going to be the worst dinner guest ever."

Dex didn't seem to be listening. "You'll feel better once we get there," he said.

I wasn't so sure. My feet already hurt, and my belly was too bloated for the skirt I had on, even though it was a size larger than what I usually wore.

Dex was the one who'd wanted to go out tonight. He said it would be a good distraction, and, I don't know, maybe he was right. I'd spent the last three days lounging on the couch in my sweats with the dogs, falling asleep before nine. Even though it always started relaxing enough, it usually ended with me glued to the phone, doom scrolling fertility boards, texting with Siobhan to obsess about odds while she tried to lighten the mood by sending me TikToks of dancing cats and cheesy affirmations.

Dex must've seen the hesitation on my face because he said, "If it gets bad, just use our code phrase."

Now I smiled for real. He'd been distant over the past few months, moody. I couldn't blame him. The IVF stuff had been hard on us both. But he'd gotten warmer since the retrieval. I felt like the Dex I knew and loved was coming back to me.

The code phrase was a remnant from early in our relationship. We'd decided that, whenever one of us wanted to leave someplace early, all we had to do was say, "I crapped my pants." We'd reasoned it was perfect because code words were always so obvious, but this was embarrassing enough that no one would think it was a lie. I should mention that we were very drunk at the time.

"I don't want to be the one to crap my pants," I said.

"Well, I can crap my pants, but we're going to have to come up with, like, a signal, so I know to do it."

"You want a code word for our code phrase?"

"Maybe you can just text me."

I smiled and shook my head. As long as Dex and I were doing this together, everything was going to be okay.

I stopped walking and lifted my face to his for a kiss. As I turned my head, I noticed a slim figure from the corner of my eye: a woman in a blue baseball cap peering out from behind a tree just a few steps away, silently watching us. My heartbeat kicked, my body recognizing the threat a moment before my brain. I jerked away from Dex, my hand flying to my mouth. My breath was dry and harsh in my throat.

But, as my breathing settled, I realized that the thing I'd seen wasn't a woman; it was a child's baseball cap. Someone must've found it on the sidewalk and hung it from the tree branch so its owner could find it more easily. It was dangling, nodding slightly in the wind. Perfectly harmless.

Dex put a hand on my shoulder. "Anna? What is it? Are you okay?"

I blinked, my heart still thumping loudly in my chest, then smiled at him, trying to laugh at myself. It was a hat hanging from a tree for Christ's sake. Not a person.

"Sorry," I told Dex. "Just my eyes playing tricks on me."

―――――――――

Minutes later, Dex pushed the restaurant door open, and we stepped inside a dark, crowded room, immediately engulfed by Friday night Brooklyn sounds: animated voices and clattering silverware and clinking wineglasses. I could see Frank waiting at the bar, a heavy pour of bourbon already sloshing around a crystal cocktail glass, his girlfriend, Bianca, slumped against the bar next to him, grumpily staring at her phone.

Frank was a typical finance guy in slicked hair and pin-striped suits, his jokes always uncomfortably close to being sexist. He found us over the crowd of people, and his face broke into a sharky smile. "Dex! Anna!" he barked, waving.

I hovered just inside the door, thinking that maybe this had been a mistake. This place was so much worse than I'd expected it to be, small and dark and filled with people who looked like trendy influencers. Young people made me feel like what I was doing was ludicrous. I was way too old to be a new mother. I pictured cobwebs growing inside my uterus, my eggs all dried out, decrepit.

A hostess came over to lead us to our table, big smile plastered over her youthful face as she asked for our reservation. I felt something vibrate in my clutch.

"Sorry...just...I'll be a second." I dug my phone out of my bag, hands shaking a little. It was Dr. Hill. It had to be Dr. Hill.

My stomach lodged itself in my throat until the screen blinked to life. But it was just a text, some spam thing asking me whether I know how to satisfy my lady.

"Anna?" Dex said, frowning.

"Sorry," I murmured, but I was still staring at the phone screen, offended. It seemed like a particular slap in the face that I was getting texts about medication to help men have erections while waiting for news from my doctor. I wanted to show it to Dex, say something about how nice it would be to live in a world where we knew as much about how to help women get pregnant as we did about how to help men get erections. But he'd already turned to wave at Frank, so I shoved the phone back into my purse, ignoring it. "Yeah, I'm fine."

I told Dex I'd meet him at the table and slipped into the bathroom to pull myself together.

I switched a faucet on and brought a handful of water to my mouth, to my neck. I felt sick to my stomach. The progesterone suppositories were supposed to make you bloated, but I hadn't expected it to be like this. It was like I was already a few months pregnant, dealing with morning sickness. Or what I imagined morning sickness must feel like, something between a hangover and the first day of my period. My waistband dug into my belly so badly that it hurt to breathe, and then, when I did manage to inhale, my stomach would twist, acid burning up the back of my throat. I felt like I was constantly on the verge of throwing up.

I switched off the faucet, took one look at my reflection, and felt a wave of embarrassment. I looked ridiculous. Even if my skirt wasn't too small, it was completely wrong for this restaurant. The oversized, brightly colored flowers were garish, ludicrously out of place next to all this concrete and steel, and my white shirt was already wrinkled and—now that I was looking at it closely—had some sort of tea or coffee stain on the collar. I was pathetic. I closed my eyes and forced myself to inhale through my nose.

After a second of this, I crouched down to peer under the stalls, and when I was sure I was alone, I pulled out my phone and called Siobhan.

"What if there's something wrong with my eggs?" I asked as soon as she answered. Siobhan and I had stopped doing pleasant small talk about two days after we'd met. "Like, what if they all hatch and they're really spiders?"

"Oh. Well then." Siobhan's voice was low and crinkly, like she'd been sleeping, which was weird since it wasn't even seven yet. As always, hearing it sparked a deep nostalgia in me, the same feeling I might get talking to a childhood friend or beloved relative. We might have only known each other a short time, but I'd been watching her on-screen since I was a teenager. Her voice was as familiar as my own.

I could easily picture her leaning against one of the windows of her sprawling industrial Williamsburg loft, streetlights striping her luminous skin, tiny, faded tattoos on all her fingers. Scent of patchouli hanging around her, French hip-hop playing on her old record player. At the height of her fame back in the nineties, she'd looked exactly the way I'd always wanted to look: tiny and casually stunning, with waist-length tangled black hair and huge dark eyes. Completely, effortlessly herself, the kind of woman who knew where to find the best secret bars in Paris, who perfumeries named signature scents after, who had a lover on every continent.

But that was back when we were both younger and invincible. Siobhan was older now, hardened from her years-long battle with breast cancer. She was going to be okay, the cancer had been in remission for a while, but treatment had been hell. I'd met her at an acupuncturist in Brooklyn just a few months after she'd had surgery to remove another lump from her breast. She'd been in the middle of a round of chemotherapy and had told me that most of her friends had distanced themselves, that they couldn't stomach so much illness. I wasn't surprised. It wasn't the same at all, but I'd had similar experiences while going through IVF. People who I'd thought were close friends had stopped calling and texting, had found other, more fun people to get dinner with. Some people couldn't face the more intense parts of life.

In any case, I didn't like to think of Siobhan dealing with treatment alone, so I'd taken it upon myself to be there for her whenever I could. I'd brought Popsicles to her chemo appointments and hung out with her while she smoked medical-grade marijuana, which was the only thing that eased the pain of her treatments. I was with her when she decided to shave her head. I can still remember watching all that beautiful hair—hair I'd coveted for most of my life—drop to the ground, leaving only peach fuzz and pink scalp.

In return, Siobhan made sure I always knew I could talk to her about what was going on with IVF, that I could call her day or night to complain or freak out. Even my friends who'd been through this themselves hadn't offered as much. We'd bonded over how sick we were of our country's medical system, how frustrating it was to deal with doctors who didn't see the problem with a model that didn't put enough funding into researching anything considered a "women's issue."

Siobhan blew a breath into the phone, bringing my drifting mind back to the bathroom. "Wouldn't that, technically, mean the IVF stuff has worked? You wanted to be a mother, and you would, in fact, be a mother."

"A mother to *spiders*."

"Hey, a baby's a baby."

I cracked a smile. "You're such a bitch." But this was why I'd called her. She always knew when to make me feel better and when to make me laugh.

"Look," Siobhan said now, all serious. "If you need help raising your creepy little spider babies, you know I'll be there for you. I'll love those spiders like they crawled out of my own uterus."

I felt those words in the center of my chest. She wasn't exaggerating. She'd already warned me that she planned on spoiling the hell out of my kid. And her words made me realize something else was true. *I* would love this baby, no matter what. I didn't have to worry.

"Yeah, me too," I said, feeling better. Clearing my throat, I added, "You know how, in old fairy tales, the women are always having to make some horrible exchange to get pregnant? I keep thinking about what I would exchange. Or I guess, what I wouldn't exchange. And the answer is nothing. I would pay any price if it meant I got to be a mother."

"Okay," Siobhan said, playing along. "So, the Devil appears right now and says, 'Hey girl—'"

"The Devil talks like a bad pickup artist?"

"Of course. He says, 'Hey girl, I'll give you a baby tomorrow, but in exchange I want your soul for eternity.' What do you do?"

I didn't even have to think about it. "I'd want to know where to sign."

I meant it too. It scared me how much I meant it. Siobhan must've heard the sincerity in my voice because she breathed, "I get it."

I could picture her nodding on the other end of the phone. We'd had similar conversations when things had gotten dark with her diagnosis. I could still remember her telling me she'd give anything, *do* anything, for just a few more years. I'd felt so bad that I could do nothing to help her.

"But," Siobhan said, "I don't think it'll come to that. If this round doesn't work, the offer to meet my friends from the birthing center still stands, whenever you're ready." Siobhan always seemed to have a friend you should meet, no matter what the problem was. In this case, it was her friends who ran a birthing center in Brooklyn. She took me once, but it looked more like a yoga studio or a cult, so I told her I was going to stick with my doctor. But that was two rounds of IVF ago.

"It's helpful to remember there are still options outside of modern medicine," she continued. "Midwives have been helping women give birth since before doctors existed."

"Yeah," I said, meeting my eyes in the mirror. I could practically hear the *tick tick tick* of a clock inside my head. Soon, I would be forty, the dreaded age when a woman's chances of getting pregnant snapped in half.

Stop, I wanted to say. *Stop, it's going too fast.*

Closing my eyes, I added, "You don't think it's selfish to keep doing this?"

"Selfish? I don't follow."

"I'm just starting to feel like maybe it shouldn't be this hard. That it's unnatural for me to force it. It comes so easily for everyone else."

"Yeah? Like who?" When I didn't answer right away, Siobhan added, "I think easy pregnancies only exist on TV. In real life, everyone's dealing with something."

But why, I wanted to know. I felt a sudden rush of anger and found myself craving one of Siobhan's rants about our sexist medical system. *Why did everyone have to deal with something?* People have been giving birth since the beginning of the human race. Shouldn't we know how to do it by now?

But Dex was waiting for me back in the restaurant, so instead I exhaled and said, "Yeah. Maybe you're right."

"Don't give up. I know how badly you want this. And if you ever need my help for anything, please, just say the word."

It touched me, that Siobhan was willing to offer up her connections, her resources, to help me. It made me wish there was something I could ask her for. I remembered how bad it felt to sit by and watch her suffer, knowing nothing I did would help.

"Thank you," I said. "And I promise, I'll talk to your friends at the birthing center if this round doesn't work out."

"Good. And for the record, I think you're going to be an *amazing* mother." Siobhan had never had biological children, but she'd adopted two kids, both grown now, with her ex-husband. The compliment meant a lot, coming from her.

"Thank you."

"I'd want you to be my mom."

I laughed. "I love you too."

———

I was slipping my phone back into my bag when the bathroom door opened behind me, and Dex's other business partner, Talia, walked in. "Oh good, there you are. Are you hiding from Frank and Bianca too?"

"Why?" I asked, wrinkling my nose. "Have they been awful?"

"Bickering nonstop since I got here." Talia leaned close to the mirror, running her thumb along the bottom of her mouth to fix her lipstick. I glanced at her reflection, taking in her flawless dark-brown skin, a pixie cut forming short spikes behind heavily pierced ears. "They spent the last fifteen minutes arguing about whether or not Bianca likes tomatoes."

"Yikes." I smiled. I adored Talia. She was impossible to describe, a mess of contradictions. She seemed on the surface to be this perfectly put-together business powerhouse, but you couldn't talk to her for more than thirty seconds without hearing all about her passions for astrology and skincare. She'd known Dex and Frank since they were all in college, and to hear Dex talk about her, she was completely brilliant, one of those people who could speak confidently on every subject, who'd read every book, been to every city.

She was also one of Dex's ex-wife's closest friends, a detail that had left me completely terrified to meet her. I'd put it off for months, worried Talia would hate me on sight out of loyalty, that she was secretly working with Adeline to break me and Dex up, that she would spend the entire night comparing the two of us and sending Dex dark looks whenever I didn't measure up. A silly fear perhaps, but I couldn't help it.

But she'd surprised me by taking an instant, almost ridiculous liking to me. We bonded over the fact that we were both Libras who liked to drink tequila, and she'd ended the night by recommending an adaptogen that she swore would give me the best sex of my life. I doubted we'd ever be as close as she was with Adeline, but at least she didn't seem to be actively plotting my downfall.

"I've heard them have this argument enough times that I could perform it as a one-woman show," Talia was saying now. "First, Bianca insists that she doesn't like tomatoes, and then Frank points out this one time five years ago when she ate tomatoes in a salad or something, and then Bianca will say that it doesn't count because those were *sun-dried* tomatoes, and on and on until blood starts coming out of my ears." Talia shook her head, eyes meeting mine in the mirror. "Like, what's the deal, Frank? Do you think she's *lying* to you about the tomatoes? Or do you think she's just too stupid to know what she likes and what she doesn't?"

I glanced at Talia, in her low-cut emerald jumpsuit and expensive shoes, I couldn't help wondering how she managed to look so put together, so effortless. She was in her forties, and she and her partner, Keagan who, somehow, worked even more hours than she did, had been going through IVF for even longer than Dex and I had. And they'd had the added complication of needing to find a sperm donor as Keagan was transgender. Yet she never let the stress show. I wanted to know her trick.

"Maybe the tomatoes are a metaphor," I said.

"Oh, they're a metaphor, all right. I love Frank like a brother, but he can be so *controlling.*" Talia shook her head. "It's like I always tell Adeline—" and then she stopped, abruptly, probably realizing a second too late who she was talking to.

For a moment I didn't say anything, too stunned by the sound of Adeline's name coming out of her mouth. Talia never brought her up. It was as though we'd all made a silent agreement to pretend she wasn't still part of Talia's life.

I found myself going still and quiet, strangely curious to know what Talia always told Adeline. Was it something about her relationship with Dex? Had Dex been controlling when they were together? Did Adeline like tomatoes? Even the smallest detail felt like an unexpected gift.

As though reading my mind, Talia cleared her throat and said, "Sorry. I shouldn't have mentioned her."

"It's okay," I said.

"Actually, it's not," Talia said. She was chewing her lip, not looking at me. After a moment, she said, "I know it's a little strange that I'm still friends with both of them after...well, everything. But I decided when they split that I didn't want to give either of them up. Adeline's been a good friend to me, the best friend I've had. And Dex...Dex is my *family.* I've known him and Frank since college, we own a business together. He's always going to be a part of my life, no matter what."

"I know that."

"I'm just trying to explain..." She hesitated, pinching the bridge of her nose, before adding, "The only way I've been able to make it work is by keeping them completely separate. I don't talk about her with him, I don't talk about him with her. And I never talk about their past, not ever." She looked at me, smiling slightly. "We all deserve a second chance, right?"

I frowned, wanting to know what she meant by that. Second chance? Did she just mean their marriage, that they both deserved a second chance at love? Or was it more than that. Had one of them done something? Screwed up, somehow?

"You know, we should probably get back—they're all waiting for us to order." She was bent over her purse now, packing her things up a little too quickly. "You coming?"

"Yeah, I'll be right out."

After Talia left, I checked my voicemail again, just to make sure Dr. Hill hadn't called. She hadn't. I considered calling the clinic, then talked myself out of it. Patience.

It wasn't until I stuck my phone back into my bag and washed my hands that I noticed a pair of scuffed, black boots just visible below the door in the very last stall in the bathroom. I had a weird, split-second thought that someone had left their shoes in here, that I should get them and bring them up front.

And then the boots *moved,* and I startled, realizing someone was in here with me, that she'd been in here this whole time. But…I'd looked under the stalls, hadn't I? Had she lifted her boots up? Why would someone do that?

I waited for another minute, pretending to double-check my makeup. But the boots didn't move again.

Finally, chilled, I left to join my friends.

6

WALKING BACK OUT INTO THE RESTAURANT, I FELT SELF-conscious, again, wondering if anyone else could see the stain on my shirt as I scanned the crowd for my table. They were sitting near the window, Frank and Talia angled toward each other, drinking bourbon, while Keagan tried to engage a bored-looking Bianca in conversation. I didn't realize Dex was talking to someone on the phone until he stood and started cutting across the room toward me. And then I froze.

It was Dr. Hill. It had to be, otherwise Dex never would've answered his phone in public. He wouldn't have answered his phone *period*.

Oh God.

I couldn't move.

Dex led me outside with a hand at my elbow, not saying a word. When we were alone on the sidewalk, he said, the phone tilted away from his mouth, "It's Dr. Hill. She said she's been trying to call you for the last hour..."

I frowned, confused. "She hasn't, I've been checking my phone every five seconds."

Dex looked like he was going to argue with me, then decided against it. "Well, I've got her now. Let me put her on speaker."

Dr. Hill's folksy voice cut through the quiet of the night. "Good evening, Mr. Harding, Ms. Alcott. How are we doing tonight?"

"We're not too bad, thanks," Dex answered, glancing at me. I couldn't say a word. I didn't want to delay the news any further with small talk. I just wanted to know.

She might've given some reason for calling so late but, if she did, I didn't hear it. I was listening for the only words that mattered, the words that would change our lives: whether any of our embryos had survived, whether we'd be able to move forward with a transfer.

And then, finally, "We have an embryo still developing, which is fantastic news," Dr. Hill said. "It's of excellent quality, so the odds that it will be viable are very good. We're going to go ahead and move forward with a transfer, day after tomorrow. Congratulations."

I made her repeat herself, so I could be sure I'd heard correctly. I had an embryo still developing. We were going to transfer it back into my body in just two more days. It was happening. Finally, it was happening.

Dex folded me into a hug, and I started to cry.

———

Later that night, in bed, I stared at the appointment I'd made on my phone. It was perfectly dark outside, no moon or stars to break up all that black. Our curtainless windows presented a flat surface that was almost like a mirror. I kept catching sight of my own reflection from the corner of my eye.

I'd taken this week and next off work, telling Emily, and my agent and my agent's assistant, that I wouldn't be doing any press until the Seth Meyers interview at the end of the month. For the first time in forever I only had one thing on my calendar. A single entry in a sea of white.

I smiled to myself. Wednesday, 11 a.m., Columbia Medical Center. The day a fertilized egg would be transferred back into my womb. The day my body would finally be given the chance to do what I'd always hoped it could do. Nurture a tiny embryo, grow a child. I pictured myself rubbing a swollen belly while I made tea in the morning, grimacing as I leaned over it to tie my shoes, getting up to use the bathroom two and three times a night. Pregnancy.

My bedside lamp flickered, then buzzed awake again: old building, faulty wiring. I knew I shouldn't let myself hope like this, like it was the only possible future, like it was definitely going to happen. Talia had been through a transfer before, and it hadn't taken. It wasn't a sure thing, even now. But I couldn't help it. I hoped.

We'd never gotten this far before. Every doctor I saw before Dr. Hill told me my body was working perfectly normally, that there was no reason I shouldn't have been able to get pregnant. It was infuriating, knowing there was something wrong and not being able to get anyone to listen.

When Talia told us about Dr. Hill, I finally began to feel a glimmer of hope. She diagnosed me with unexplained infertility and insisted we get started on IVF right away. But even then, it was an uphill battle. Getting to the transfer was like reaching a new level in the process, a chance to become just a little bit pregnant. I'd never even realized you could be "just a little bit" pregnant before but, with IVF, that's exactly what happened. Dr. Hill would transfer our viable egg back into my womb. And then, for two weeks, we'd all wait, crossing our fingers, hoping it implanted in my uterus.

Wind pressed up against our window, making the glass creak. I'd been staring at the little square on my calendar for a long time, memorizing it, and so I saw the exact moment the appointment changed, 11 a.m. smoothly transforming into 12 p.m.

Unexpected shock moved through me. I was suddenly wide awake, frowning.

The *hell...?*

It was a glitch. A problem with my phone's calendar app. It had to be. I closed out of the appointment, opened it again, sure it would reload with the time corrected.

12 pm, the appointment read.

I chewed my lip. Maybe I was just tired, my eyesight blurry from staring at a screen for so long. Or maybe I was remembering the time wrong. Maybe it had been noon all along and I'd just gotten confused, again.

But...no. *No.* Dr. Hill had said eleven. I'd made her say the time again, so I was sure. And I remembered typing the number into my phone, jabbing the *1* key twice. The appointment was at eleven. I *knew* it was at eleven.

I felt a growing panic as I stared down at the screen and allowed myself to consider that maybe there wasn't a problem with my phone or my memory or my eyesight. The appointment had said 11, and then it had changed to 12. It had happened right in front of my eyes. If I was sure I'd inputted the time correctly—which I *was*—then I honestly couldn't explain how this happened.

Unless someone else logged into my calendar and changed it.

A prickle went through me, even as I tried to convince myself

I was being paranoid. But this sort of thing had happened to me before. Ever since *The Auteur* came out, the social media trolls have gotten more intense. There was one, in particular, who called herself *number1crush*. She'd been mocking me relentlessly over the past year, responding to everything I posted, calling me *old lady*, *crypt keeper*, *snake*. I didn't particularly appreciate the bullying, but I could've dealt with it, if that's all it was.

But then she found my address online and began posting Google Earth pictures of my house. She hacked into my personal email account and sent graphic emails to all my contacts. I'd had to close all my accounts and open new ones, change every password, buy expensive security software.

All that was annoying, of course, but the worst part was how it made me feel: violated, unsafe. I stopped trusting certain modes of communication, preferring to talk to people directly or on the phone because it felt safer.

Then, at the end of the summer, when Dex and I were down at Rockaway Beach, Dex trying to teach me how to surf, taking breaks to order tacos from the iconic Tacoway Beach taco stand, I'd posted a pic on Instagram, stupidly not noticing that I'd accidentally included part of the restaurant in the photo.

She'd been the first person to comment: *are you at Rockaway Beach rn???*

And then again, two seconds later: *I'm gonna come find you and tell you what I think of you to your face you snake.*

She hadn't found me that day, thank God, but I still felt a sick shiver, remembering how freaked out I'd been.

My bedside lamp flickered again. This time the sudden flash of light made me flinch, suddenly jumpy. I glanced at our bedroom window, staring into the perfect dark on the other side of the glass. If anyone was standing outside right now, I'd be lit up like I was on a screen. As far as I knew, my harasser had never actually followed me in person. But that was the thing about online harassment—the lines between your internet life and your real one could get so blurry.

I closed out of my calendar app and did a search online for her username, *@number1crush*. She hadn't emailed me or commented on any of my posts in the last week or so, and I'd been desperately hoping that she'd gotten bored and moved on. But maybe she'd just come up with a more effective way to mess with me. She'd already figured out my personal email address. How hard would it be for her to hack into my Google calendar?

It sickened me to imagine her looking through my private appointments. I thought of the smiley emojis I added to events I was excited about, the rows of overenthusiastic exclamation marks. I pictured her poring over it all, laughing at me.

And there were other things too. Private things. Like the detailed instructions I included in event notes telling me when to take which medication and how to store them and any side effects I should watch out for. I frequently included exact addresses for locations I was heading to and phone numbers for new contacts. Sometimes I even added passwords and security codes I didn't want to forget. That calendar said nearly as much about me as a diary. If someone had been reading it, there's no telling how much personal information she had.

With a sinking feeling, I thought about all the appointments I'd messed up. It hadn't just been the retrieval surgery—I'd accidentally taken my trigger shot at the wrong hour, and there were a couple of times when I missed the window for my injections. Dex was always quick to blame it on my bad memory. But what if it hadn't been my fault at all? What if this woman had gone into the calendar after I'd added my appointments and changed the times?

Once I got this idea into my head, I couldn't get it out. How could I have been so careless, leaving personal information like that on the internet, where anyone could hack into it? I should've known better. Nowhere online was safe.

She hadn't posted anything on Instagram, Twitter, or TikTok for the last few days, but there was some sort of long confusing thread on Tumblr. I scrolled all the way to the bottom, trying to see what she was commenting on...

And my heart sunk. It was the photograph of me standing outside on the sidewalk, the Riverside Clinic logo very clear on the glass door behind my head.

I scrolled through the photos, watching myself walk out of the clinic, wave at Dex, and climb into that black SUV. I closed my eyes, feeling like I might throw up.

Number1crush wasn't the one who'd posted the photographs. The way Tumblr nested posts inside other posts had always confused me, but a link beneath the pictures said they were originally uploaded by someone called *preecher_speaks*.

A prickle went through me. I had a vague memory, Cora calling out the name *Ms. Preecher* when that strange woman had come into the clinic. I clicked on her username, and a photo of the woman I'd seen popped up, the name Io Preecher listed below.

I clicked on her username and got to her profile. I don't know what I expected to find, some sort of fan account, maybe? But Io didn't seem to care much about me one way or another. In fact, the photographs she'd taken outside the clinic were the only time she'd posted anything about me at all. All her other posts were strange, rants about the occult and Satan, godless teenagers and the deviant media they consumed. Dead end. Still, she did take that photo. I made a Google alert for her username, so I'd know if she posted anything else, and then I clicked out of her profile and went back to *number1crush*.

This Io Preecher might've taken my photo, but *number1crush* had commented on it. A lot.

this is seriously SICK everyone knows all she cares about is getting famous

like think about this—she's getting pregnant because she needs the attention and she will do literally anything

someone needs to stop her that baby is in so much danger

like omg imagine if that ancient snake had a kid

that baby would be better off never being born

My mouth felt suddenly dry. I read the last comment again, *that baby would be better off never being born.* Were there really people who thought like that? Was that what she was trying to do? Stop me from getting pregnant by screwing with my appointment times? I felt tears gather in the corner of my eyes, anger and fear spreading through me, making my hands shake. I had the sudden urge to hide under my duvet, close my eyes until this all went away.

There was a sudden tap against my bedroom window, sharp enough it made me jump. I jerked my head around, my heart leaping into my throat.

It was just a tree branch, but that didn't stop the nerves from working their way through my gut. I didn't care if I was being paranoid. I couldn't take any chances with something this important.

I went downstairs to look for Dex and found him sitting in the dark, an empty tumbler on the table beside him. He was holding his phone, and he jumped when I said his name.

"Anna…" He rubbed his eyes. "Jesus…I thought you were asleep."

Something about him seemed off. I couldn't tell if it was the rigid set of his shoulders, or just the fact that he'd been drinking alone in the dark. I glanced at his phone. "Were you talking to someone?"

"No…I was playing Scrabble," he added sheepishly. "I couldn't sleep. But you should go up to bed. You need to be well rested. Big day coming up."

"Yeah," I said. I thought of the months of IVF, all the highs and lows and near misses. Dex didn't talk about it much, but I knew it weighed on him. Maybe I didn't need to bring up the stuff about *number1crush* and my appointment times tonight. "Okay, I will. Don't stay up too late, okay?"

He smiled at me sleepily, his face all in shadow. "I won't."

———

I changed all my passwords before I went to bed. Email. Calendar. Computer. Phone. And the next morning, I called Dr. Hill's direct line to change the time of my appointment. She was a little hesitant, telling me I was overreacting, that the security at the clinic was top notch, but I insisted. I didn't want to this woman knowing when I was going in for my procedure; it was too important. I wrote the new time down on a Post-it and stuck in on the fridge.

Tomorrow, ten o'clock.

Post-its, I reasoned, were much harder to tamper with.

7

THE DAY OF THE SURGERY, DEX AND I ARRIVED AT THE HOSPI-
tal an hour and a half early. I changed into a gown and slippers, and
Dr. Hill showed us a picture of our embryo: a black and white petri
dish filled with fuzzy gray shapes.

I stared, awed. Our DNA had come together to form something
that had never existed before. It was unreal, like the terrain of a distant planet that our space shuttles had captured the very first images
of. It was the most beautiful thing I'd ever seen.

"It's the highest possible quality we could've hoped for," Dr. Hill
told us, beaming.

I took out my phone and snapped a picture, even though Dex
worried a photo would jinx it. I couldn't help it. I wanted to remember everything. Every single moment of how our baby was made.

The procedure was fast, painless, and then I was recovering, feeling slow and stupid from the drugs, thanking everyone who walked
past my bed, according to Dex. Doctors. Nurses. Janitors. Dex told
me I was a little embarrassing.

We wouldn't know whether it had worked for another two weeks, but I was sure it had. I swore I could already feel our baby forming inside of me. I was so excited that I printed that little petri dish photograph off my phone so that I could have something to hold on to, something physical, proof that what was happening inside of me was real. I stared at it for hours, perched on the edge of my bed and unable to peel my eyes away from the Rorschach-like splotches of black and white.

Icy rain slapped into my bedroom windows and, somewhere over the East River, there was a deep belly laugh of thunder. I thought about our next-door neighbor's newborn, who I'd held just for a minute or two so her dads could carry a package inside. Her skin had been so, so soft, softer than a puppy's belly. My heart fluttered somewhere deep in my throat, remembering.

It wasn't late, only three in the afternoon, but Dex had gone to pick the dogs up from doggie daycare. The daycare place was only a twenty-minute walk away, but it always took Dex at least an hour to get back. He claimed this was because he felt guilty for leaving them, and that he stopped by a dog park on his way home. In any case, I had the house to myself for a little while. I fell asleep waiting for them to come back, thinking of how our baby's skin might feel, if it would be soft or rough, if it would have those tiny white bumps that babies sometimes had.

Minutes or hours later, I heard the creak of floorboards, the sound of my bedroom door swinging open. *Dex*, I thought, too heavy to move. I drifted deeper as the mattress shifted beneath me, half awake, half asleep. I barely noticed when an arm snaked around my waist, hand hovering near my belly. I was far away, dreaming that I was walking through a big dark house, looking for someone.

Gradually, I became aware of the body pressed against my back, how it was narrower than it should've been, lighter. Hair rose on my neck, but I didn't move. I was still trapped in sleep. In the dream, I began to run, stumbling as I raced down dark halls and dark stairs, around corners and into empty rooms feeling like someone was chasing me.

The smell of cigarette smoke filled my nose. The body moved in closer, thin hips pressing into me from behind. And then there was a voice in my ear, one whispered word.

"*Baby*."

The crashing sound of the storm snapped right off. My eyes opened, alarm bells clanging inside of me as I became aware that Dex wasn't the one in bed with me.

My fear was sudden and complete, blotting out all other emotion, all other thoughts. I scrambled to my feet, my heartbeat slamming in my throat as I whirled around.

A figure hovered in the dark, nothing visible except for the outline of her slight body. I couldn't see her face, couldn't see her clearly at all, but there was something familiar in the shape of her, the way she tilted her head to the side when she looked at me, like a bird. She said nothing, but the soft, rasping sound of her breath in the dark made my skin crawl. The only part of her that I could see clearly in the dim light was her right hand, her fingers curled toward her palm, nails unpolished, a touch overgrown and yellowing.

I remembered the threats *number1crush* had posted online— *someone needs to stop her... that baby would be better off not being born.* Was that what was happening? Had this woman come to stop my baby being born?

I imagined her nails digging into my cheek, the bright pain as they split skin, and I took a single blundering step backward, needing to put as much distance between our two bodies as possible. My eyes skittered around the room, wanting something to throw. There was an antique vase, marble bookends. But what if she had a weapon? A gun? I flashed back on every story I'd ever heard about someone famous being attacked by one of their fans, and everything inside of me went still. Was she here to kill me?

I pressed a hand to my belly, thinking of the embryo that might already be growing inside of me, how I was the only one who could protect it. I felt helpless, woefully unprepared for the enormity of keeping it safe.

"Please." I was trying to sound confident, but my voice came out low and wavering, betraying me. "Please, you can take anything you want. Just go."

The figure stared back at me from the dark. One of her fingers twitched, and I felt it like a slap across the face. I released a desperate, ugly sob.

Go, I thought. *Please.*

The door was right there.

But then she moved, not away from me but *toward* me. Toward my baby. My lungs filled with air, and I felt every primal instinct I'd ever had roar to life, needing to protect my child. I grabbed the nearest thing I could reach—a little stone bust sitting on the bookshelf—and threw it. It crashed into the bedroom door and shattered, but the woman was already out the door and down the stairs. Gone.

8

I WAITED FOR THE POLICE OUTSIDE. I COULDN'T STAND TO BE in that house any longer. It didn't matter how many lights I turned on; the shadows in the corners were all too dark, and I couldn't convince myself that she wasn't still hiding in one of them, waiting for me.

I called Dex fifteen times, but Dex never answered his phone. He didn't even have his voicemail set up; it was just that idiotic robot voice telling me that the number I'd dialed was unavailable. It had been over an hour; he really should be back by now. Eventually, I called the office, thinking he might've stopped by with the dogs, and Talia answered, laughing that she hadn't seen Dex all day.

"Please," I said, unable to keep the fear from my voice. "Can you find him and tell him he needs to come home, now?"

Eventually, a police cruiser rolled up to the curb. I had to stop myself from running up to it, from blubbering and crying. Instead, I took two calming breaths and walked over as coolly as I could manage, hoping she wouldn't notice the way my knees knocked together.

"Are you Anna Alcott?" The cop asked. She was younger than me—thirties, tops.

"Yes"—the name tag on her uniform read *Gia*—"Yes, Gia, I'm Anna. Hi." I was trying for calm, but my voice was thick and shaky, betraying me. I hugged myself, wishing I'd made some tea. I wanted something to hold on to, something warm.

"Why don't you walk me through what happened?"

I told her what I could remember, which wasn't much. Officer Gia listened with her hands at her hips, thumbs hooked into her pockets, nodding every few minutes. When I was done, she asked me if I'd noticed anyone following me over the last few days, if I'd seen anyone strange hanging around, if anyone had threatened me.

"There's this woman who's been harassing me online," I told her. "Her handle is *number1crush*."

She looked skeptical, but I stared at her until she made a note in the corner of her notepad. "How do you know it's a woman?"

I frowned at her. "What?"

"If it's online, it could be anyone, right?"

"Yeah, I guess." I blinked. "But the person who climbed into bed with me was definitely a woman."

"Okay. That all?"

I knew from past experiences that cops never took online harassment seriously. "I think *number1crush* is someone you need to look into," I insisted. "She's been scary in the past, threatening me and posting pictures of my house. I think she even hacked my—"

There was the sudden noise behind me. I yelped and whirled around.

"Hey, it's okay, it's just me." Dex was climbing out of a cab, wrestling to get the dogs over to the curb. He was wearing my pink beanie, which he kept borrowing because he was constantly leaving his hats in cars and cabs.

"Dex," I said, breathing hard. "You scared me." And then I surprised us both by bursting into tears.

"Hey, come here. It's going to be okay." Dex led the dogs up the steps and folded me into a one-armed hug, the dogs leaping up around us, sensing I was upset in the way dogs always could. "It's okay," he murmured into my ear. "It's okay, I'm here now. Everything's going to be okay."

Behind us, Officer Gia made a noise at the back of her throat and said, "Let's take a look inside."

I dried my eyes and led Dex and the police officer inside. Dex put the dogs in the kitchen, and then the three of us went up to the second floor, the scene of the crime. Our bedroom rug was still littered with little shards of stone from the bust I'd thrown. I saw Dex's shoulders stiffen when he noticed. He wrapped an arm around my shoulders and squeezed.

Officer Gia knelt and picked up a small chunk of stone, examining it thoughtfully.

"You get him?" she asked me.

It took me a second to understand what she meant. "What? Oh, no, I didn't hit anyone. And I told you outside, it was a *her*, a woman."

"Too bad." She dropped the broken stone and wiped her hands on her pants, standing again. "I'm not supposed to say that since assault's technically a crime, but I wouldn't have been mad if you had." She tried a smile, joking around with me, which made me instantly, irrationally angry. I didn't want to joke around. I wanted to her to *do* something.

I folded my arms over my chest, hugging myself again. "What happens now? Can you look for her?"

Officer Gia scratched the back of her head. "Well, that depends. Did she take anything?"

It hadn't occurred to me to check. "I don't know."

"Any valuables missing? Jewelry, technology...?"

I scanned the room for a moment before my eyes landed on the empty bedside table. My photograph was missing. I felt the back of my throat constrict.

"Uhm, there was a photograph, on my bedside table. I took it at my doctor's office this morning."

"Can you think of why anyone might want that?"

I tried to think of a real reason, a reason a cop like Gia might take seriously, but I couldn't. I imagined my little baby photo winding up on Tumblr like the pictures of me coming out of the clinic had, *number1crush* posting a string of nasty comments below it about how I didn't deserve to have a baby, how I was much too old, a snake, a crone. I felt a twist inside my gut, right below my belly button.

"I–I guess..." I dropped my arms, trying to calm myself down. "I told you about that woman, the one who's been stalking me online? She posts stuff about me on Tumblr sometimes. Pictures, threats..."

Officer Gia was studying me, nodding. She didn't look very convinced. "Anyone else you can think of that might want to mess with you?"

I opened my mouth, then closed it without saying anything. I honestly didn't know where to start. There were so many people. It happened when you were a public person, but I'd always suspected it happened more when you were known for something like *Spellbound*. It hadn't found much of an audience when it first aired, but Netflix began streaming old episodes around ten years ago, and a new crop of fans discovered Summer Day. I even went to Comic Con a couple of times, back when our old showrunner was playing with the idea of doing a reboot. I'd been kind of surprised by the people there, how they'd followed me around, close enough that I knew they were there, but at just enough of a distance that it didn't make sense to get angry or frustrated with them. They'd always seemed harmless, shy-looking teen girls hanging around outside the bathroom when I went to pee, slumped in a chair in the lounge of my hotel, sitting near the window at whatever coffee shop I stopped in, peeking at me from over the tops of magazines.

But there were more intense fans too. Like the girl on Instagram who'd liked two hundred of my old posts in the span of about ten minutes, or the guy on Facebook who sent me twelve long rambling emails about everything that was going on his life, claiming that he was so sure we'd be best friends, asking if I wanted to meet him.

"You said someone took a picture of you at the clinic," Dex reminded me.

I nodded, thinking about the woman with the gray streaking through her hair, the faint lines around her eyes. "She actually posted the photos online a few days later. Her name is Io Preacher." I glanced at Dex. "But I don't think she really cared about me. She posts a lot of weird stuff online. She seems a little...off."

"And what about your old roommate? What was her name?" Dex frowned slightly. "Ellie something?"

"Ellie *Pratt*." Ellie had been my neighbor, not my roommate. This was when I'd first moved to New York City, almost six years ago, now. She'd lived in the same apartment complex, two doors down and, at first, she'd been completely normal, cool, even. She brought me a plant as a housewarming gift and invited me over for a glass of wine, sending me home with a stack of takeout menus.

But then she got weirdly clingy, finding a reason to stop by my apartment at least once a day, ringing the bell over and over, and even trying the door when I didn't answer right away. And she started dressing like me: same brand of jeans, same very specific clogs that you could only find in a tiny shop in Chinatown. She eventually dyed her hair the same shade of blond as mine, cut it to look just like mine. I still felt a shudder move through me, remembering.

"And that dog walker," Dex added. Oh yes, the dog walker. When I started doing press for *The Auteur*, I'd hired this really sweet guy, Leon Baker, who was in his twenties but looked like he hadn't even been through puberty, to take the dogs out so they wouldn't be stuck inside all day. Leon had been skinny, short, not a single hair growing on his face. I'd actually asked to see his ID, because he'd looked like he was about fourteen. He'd been fantastic for two months— the dogs loved him—until one day, I got home and Peanut Butter was missing. There was no sign of forced entry, no open windows or doors. Everything was exactly the same except my dog was gone.

I'd completely lost my mind. I'd called Leon about fifty times and he hadn't picked up, and then I'd called my friend Georgia and the two of us searched the neighborhood all night. We put up posters and called shelters, and I'd cried so hard I hadn't been able to see straight while Georgia patted my back and told me she was sure he was fine, that we were going to find him, that it would all be okay.

Leon showed up the very next morning, smiling like a deranged clown, Peanut Butter licking his hands. He'd claimed he just wanted to borrow him, that he'd been feeling sad the night before and wanted a warm body to sleep with. That was a year ago. I'd spent a good six months after I'd fired Leon worrying I was going to walk into my house one day and discover that he'd come back and taken Peanut Butter for good.

Officer Gia made me spell Io and Leon and Ellie's names twice, nodding as I repeated the letters. "Okay, thanks, I'll be sure to look into that. Is there anyone else you can think of? Someone strange wandering around the street, maybe? We got a serious homeless population in this city. Once it gets cold, sometimes they start trying doors, hoping for a house no one's living in."

I'd been shaking my head, about to say no, but then I stopped, remembering the woman I'd seen outside my house and, again, up at my doctor's office. I thought of the shoes I saw under the bathroom stall door, the feeling I've had over the last week, like someone's been following me.

But I didn't know how to put that feeling into words without sounding like some diva who'd let fame go to my head. This was New York. Seeing the same person a few times meant nothing. And she hadn't approached me or said anything to me. So maybe I was just being paranoid, seeing threats where there were none. It made more sense to focus on people who'd actually harassed me in the past, instead of sending the cops stumbling in the dark after ghosts.

I shook my head, uneasy but decided. "No. There's no one."

―――――

Days passed. I followed up with Officer Gia every morning but, after the third round of, "I'm sorry, Ms. Alcott, but we just haven't found anything yet," she transferred me to a detective named Michael Wood. Detective Wood had a deep, no-nonsense voice and, the second time I called, he made it clear that I wouldn't have to check in because he would be in touch the moment they had anything new to report. I felt dismissed.

I couldn't tell if he didn't believe me that someone had broken in, or if he just wasn't that concerned. This was Brooklyn, after all. There were real robberies and shootings and drug deals to investigate. I suppose a woman who broke in to steal my baby's photo wasn't exactly the crime of the century.

Dex and I changed the locks and got a new alarm system installed. We stopped taking the dogs to doggie daycare, and I tried to take comfort in the fact that, if this woman broke in again, she was unlikely to get past them, but I still couldn't bring myself to sleep in my own bed. Even after changing the sheets and washing the duvet, I swear I could still smell her there. Dex told me that was impossible, but he hadn't been there; he didn't know what she smelled like.

I tried not to think about her but I just wound up obsessing about whether I was pregnant instead. Dr. Hill had given us strict instructions not to take a test until fourteen days after the implantation, but that didn't stop me from analyzing my body, convinced that everything was a symptom. Two weeks was such a long time to go without knowing whether you were pregnant. Couldn't someone have come up with a better method for figuring this out in the last hundred years or so? Sometimes it felt like the continuation of our species was an ongoing experiment being performed on the backs of women. Or on our wombs.

I kept track of time on a calendar I'd printed off the internet and taped to the front of our refrigerator, big red Sharpie Xs drawn through each passing day. Ten days left, then six, two...

"I got you a present," Dex told me, the morning of. He pulled something out of his pocket. "For luck."

It was a pregnancy test, one of the good, name-brand ones from the drugstore. When you've been trying for as long as we have, you end up testing so frequently that you switch to the cheap paper strips that come a hundred to a box. Buying a good one meant Dex thought this was it. It meant he wanted a memento, something we could take a picture of and tape into a baby book.

I was nervous. "Should we do it now, or...?"

"I have a meeting in five minutes that I really shouldn't be late for," Dex said. "Take the test."

"Okay." I shook out my hands, trying to rid myself of nerves. I peed with the door open for the first time in our entire relationship, and when I was done, neither of us even tried to pretend we could do anything other than stare at the tiny window on that plastic stick, waiting to see if a second line would appear.

"Think pregnant thoughts," Dex said. I barely heard him. Something was happening.

"Dex," I said, breathless, leaning closer. "Is that...?"

"I think so. I think I see it."

The line was so faint it could've been a trick of the light, but as we stared, it grew darker and darker, a watercolor stripe of palest pink.

Proof that I was no longer alone inside my body.

———

Sometimes, when I'm feeling nostalgic, I like to imagine what might've followed that moment if things had gone differently. Dex and I would've anxiously watched my belly grow bigger, looking up which size fruit the baby was that week (a cherry! a pineapple! a watermelon!) There would've been doctor's appointments, Dex holding my hand as we stared at the ultrasound, watching our tiny alien baby float through a sea of black. Look at his toes! His nose! His legs! Then, a baby shower, little onesies in blue or pink and a cake made of diapers, all our friends gathered around us, making bets on the sex, the birth date, the weight. As the months passed, I would've developed a deep connection to the person growing inside me, the kind of connection you read about in cheesy poems on Mother's Day cards. And then, of course, labor. Dex and I timing the contractions, trying to wait as long as possible before going to the hospital. Dex wiping the sweat from my brow as I pushed, telling me I could do it, that I was so strong. The feel of that tiny wriggling body pressed to my chest for the first time, both of us sobbing.

Of course, that's not what happened. But sometimes, when I wake up in the middle of the night and I can't stop my mind from obsessing, wondering if I should have done anything differently, it's nice to imagine that it did.

RAYNA PERKINS, 2018

RAYNA HAD TO WALK PAST THE MAN'S STATUE AT LEAST ONCE every day. It was a nine-foot-tall bronze monstrosity, a white dude standing on an actual pedestal, the etchings to either side calling him *brilliant* and *a philanthropist*, saying his *achievement carried the fame of American surgery throughout the entire world*. Rayna made a point of chewing gum whenever she knew she'd have to make the trek past, just so she had something small and pink and gross she could spit on the man's feet. Her tiny act of rebellion.

Rayna was a medical student. She studied gynecology at Columbia University, so she knew all about that man. She couldn't exactly avoid him, since his name was in every medical textbook. He'd been a surgeon practicing in the mid to late 1800s, and he was known for developing the first successful operation to repair fistulas in the vaginal wall. A lot of Rayna's old white professors liked to say he was some kind of surgical hero. They called him "the father of modern gynecology" and said a lot of very nice things about how his experiments changed the way doctors treated women after pregnancy and *blah, blah, blah*. Rayna waited for those same professors to mention the bodies this man had used, the Black bodies that had made all his groundbreaking experiments possible. They never did, but Rayna wasn't an idiot—she could read between the lines of the story they told. She could see the names history had erased.

Names like Anarcha, Lucy, and Betsey, three of the enslaved women the man bought and operated on without consent, without *anesthesia*. Rayna read about how these women were naked while he operated on them, how they'd been made to perch on their knees on a table while a bunch of other white men in coats stood around watching. She read that the women were strapped down so they couldn't move during the surgery. Back then, white people pretended Black women didn't experience pain, at least not like white women did, so the women wouldn't have been given anything, not even if they'd screamed or cried. Their surgeries took hours, and they would've felt every second.

There were statues of the man who did that to them all over the country. Rayna couldn't stop thinking about all the Black women who had to walk under his shadow to get home and to work and to school. She couldn't stop wondering where Anarcha's and Lucy's and Betsey's statues were.

One day, Rayna walked past the statue and saw that someone had painted the word RACIST across the man's body. When she saw that word, it was like a flame had sparked to life in her chest.

Yes, she thought. *Finally*.

She'd just lifted her hand to her mouth to remove her wad of gum when she saw a flicker at the corner of her eye, movement. She turned on instinct and saw a woman standing on the other side of the street, watching her.

Rayna flinched. And then, when she realized what she was looking at, she stared right back, daring the woman to look away first. But the woman didn't look away. She gazed at her openly, saying nothing. It was a middle-aged blond woman in jeans and a sweatshirt. She didn't seem threatening, but they never did, not until it was too late. Rayna felt a flicker of fear. She kept her gum in her mouth. Just in case.

The protests lasted for days. Rayna came whenever she could make it between classes, joining residents of the bordering neighborhoods who'd been protesting the man since 2011, as well as the younger protestors who carried signs and sometimes even showed up in hospital gowns stained in blood. There were times, even surrounded by all those people, when Rayna was sure someone watching her. She'd feel a flare of heat on the back of her neck, the weight of eyes, always gone when she turned to look. The few times she did catch someone staring at her, it was hard to say for sure that they were doing anything wrong. There was a short young woman dressed all in black, and a much older woman, wrinkled and scowling. Always women, never the same one twice.

And there were other things. No big deal, just the kind of stuff a young, Black woman living alone, tended to notice. The rev of a car engine, moments after she left a bar, like whoever was behind the wheel had been waiting for her; a huddle of women outside the library late at night, too old and not dressed like students, heads whipping around in a crowd of people, looking at her.

Rayna was with the protestors at Central Park, watching and cheering, the day they finally tore that godawful statue down. Someone behind her shouted, "Off with his head!" Others held signs that read, *Believe Black women!*

Yes, Rayna thought. *Yes.*

She was caught up in the energy, and so she didn't pay much attention to the woman standing next to her, an older Black woman who hadn't cheered or shouted, but only watched the statue be removed with a heavy silence, nodding solemnly as it was taken away. When Rayna caught her eye, the woman said, her voice a quiet rumble, "It isn't enough."

"You said it," Rayna murmured, with a rush of affection. The woman reminded her a bit of her mother, something about her heavy gaze, the quiet strength of her voice.

Of course, it wasn't enough. It would never be enough.

It wasn't until Rayna was about to leave, go grab a drink with a few of her friends, that the woman spoke to her again.

"I've been watching you," she said.

And now Rayna felt suddenly cold. Some part of her had been expecting this ever since the day she saw the graffiti on the statue, the day she first realized she was being followed. But she'd always imagined one of the white women approaching her, someone it would've been easier for her to dismiss. She didn't want to dismiss this woman.

She looked around, noticing that her friends had already gone; they must not have realized she wasn't with them.

"It's just you and me, dear," the woman said, seeming to read Rayna's mind.

"What do you want?" Rayna asked. She was starting to feel a little scared, but her voice stayed even. Hearing it, the woman smiled a little wider, like she was impressed with her bravery. Despite herself, Rayna felt a rush of pride.

"We've been looking for girls like you," the woman said.

"Girls like me?" Rayna repeated.

"Healers," the woman clarified. Her brown eyes flashed, something dangerous within them seeming to spark. "We need doctors."

Your baby is as big as a pear

9

IT WASN'T UNTIL JANUARY, A LITTLE OVER TWO MONTHS AFTER that positive pregnancy test, that I first felt the pain, a dull heat in my back, the muscles around my spine tightening.

"Remember to breathe as we get ready to settle into our final resting posture, mamas..." the yoga teacher said, picking her way around the bodies sprawled across the floor. She glanced at me and mimed exhaling just in case I'd forgotten how to do it.

I parted my lips and air exploded from my lungs. I was just finishing up a prenatal yoga class, one of only two times I'd been out in public in the past two weeks.

I'd been an anxious wreck since the break-in. Things had been quiet, but that was just because I ran away to Southampton, to a house no one had the address to. I'd stopped posting on social media, stopped using my online calendar, stopped attending all the in-person events Emily sent me invites to. Only my closest friends and family even knew I was pregnant.

The pain was just a flickering ache in my lower back, like the start of my period. I was concerned, but not so concerned that I felt the

need to leave the class. Dr. Hill was always telling me that some discomfort during pregnancy was perfectly normal. It had gotten to the
point where the two things were linked in my mind: the discomfort
was the baby, and the more I suffered, the healthier the baby would be.

This wasn't just me being a martyr. Pregnancy books all said
women who experienced morning sickness were less likely to have a
miscarriage. It put me in the bizarre position of hoping for the pain,
the nausea.

I shifted off the bolster I was propped on and moved a hand to my
lower back, digging my knuckles into the muscles around my spine.
Part of me even wondered if this pain was a punishment for leaving
the safety of the house, no matter that I'd been going stir crazy, that I
was desperate to be around anyone other than my husband.

Think about how badly you want this, I thought, to distract myself.
It was my favorite meditation these days. Breathe in while thinking of
tiny onesies with funny sayings on them: *I'm new here* and *Mommy's
favorite.* Breathe out thinking about midnight feedings, my baby's
face nuzzled up against my chest, those warm wet lips still smelling
like my milk.

I slipped my hands under my tank top, fingers cold as death
against the soft mound of my fifteen-week belly. I'd stocked up on
roomy yoga pants and shirts with ruching up the sides the second
my jeans stopped zipping all the way. The top was still too big, extra
fabric pooling comically around my tiny bump, but whatever. I'd
grow into it.

The other women started shifting around me, their winter-dry
feet scratching against yoga mats as they moved into more comfortable positions. There were only four of us, five if you included

the instructor. That's why I'd chosen this class, because it was in the middle of the workday, little chance of a crowd. I knew it was a risk to come out in public at all, but I couldn't help it. I'd been so lonely. I needed to spend just one hour surrounded by other pregnant women, a small taste of the village I'd heard so much about, a network of mothers to hold my hand and guide me into this next stage of life. How much could one hour hurt?

After a few more minutes of shavasana, we all sat up and *om*ed and *namaste*d, and then everyone started making their way to the cubbies on the far end of the studio to chase down coats and scarves and tote bags. The other women must've known each other from outside of class because they clumped ahead of me, Jenna, 36 weeks, and Camilla, 26 weeks, talking like they were picking up a conversation they'd started earlier. That was how we'd all introduced ourselves at the beginning of class. We'd say our name and how far along we were, and the teacher would tell us what size fruit our baby was.

I'd used a fake name. According to this class, I was Monica, 15 weeks, baby the size of a pear. I was so proud of that little pear.

The women drifted away, all except for a very petite, very young woman with thick brown curls and freckles, her belly like a basketball shoved beneath her shirt.

Kylie, 38 weeks, I remembered. Baby the size of a mini watermelon. Kylie had her head down, digging through a tote bag with the yoga studio's logo on the front. She hadn't given me a second look all throughout class—none of the women had—so I didn't even bother to duck my face as I leaned past her to grab my own bag from the hooks on the back wall. Her eyes flicked up and a slow smile touched her lips. "Oh! Wow, I'm sorry. I just realized why I recognized you."

My stomach tightened, even as I felt the familiar rush of flattery and warmth I always felt when I was recognized out in public. I should've done more to alter my appearance. I'd considered shoving my hair under a baseball cap but figured that would look more conspicuous than doing nothing, so I'd settled for leaving it naturally curly, which I never did during interviews, and hoping the change of texture would be enough to keep people from looking at me twice.

"You're Anna Victoria Alcott, right?" Kylie continued, her eyes lighting up. "From *The Auteur*? God, that movie made me cry." She shook her head, like she was coming out of a trance. "I'm sorry. You probably get bombarded with people like me all the time."

"No, it's fine, I—" Another cramp lit up my lower back and I cringed, one hand curling, protectively, around my barely-there bump. *God, I hope he can't feel this.*

"Are you okay?" Kylie asked.

I nodded through the ache, waiting for my muscles to unclench. "Yeah...I've just been getting these cramps in my lower back. It's kind of freaking me out."

Frown lines appeared between Kylie's eyebrows. "I might have some Ibuprofen if you want?"

I hesitated, the pain so bad that I was considering it. But Ibuprofen wasn't on Dr. Hill's list of approved medicine, which meant that, before I could take it, I'd have to scour the internet to see what people were saying about whether it was safe. Dr. Hill once told me that no medication could ever be considered 100 percent safe for use during pregnancy—they all existed in a weird limbo where they could be anywhere from mostly safe to mostly disastrous depending on where you were getting your information.

"I...better not," I finally said, figuring it was safer for the baby for me to just deal with a little suffering.

"No worries," Kylie said. "I had so many aches and pains during my first pregnancy. But when something's really wrong, I think you just kind of...know, you know?"

"What do you mean?" I asked. "You just...know when it's a bad pain versus a normal pain?"

"Yup." Kylie closed her eyes and swayed a bit, demonstrating how I might "just know." "Trust your body and you'll be fine."

How? I wanted to ask again, but Kylie had knelt to shove her foot into a tennis shoe and she wasn't looking at me anymore. Women like her—women who were so obviously in tune with their own bodies— had always made me strangely insecure. After two years of trying to get pregnant, my body was more of a mystery to me than ever.

"Give it time," Kylie was saying, smiling at me. "You don't need to call a doctor unless the pain doesn't go away for twenty-four hours."

I smiled and thanked her, even as the muscles in my shoulders tightened. *Give it time.* I'd lost count of how many people had told me that over the last two years. And maybe there was some truth to what they were saying, maybe there were some problems you could only solve with "Let's wait and see." But that didn't stop the fear from growing inside of me, from taking root in my gut, branches stretching into my chest and shoulders, making everything tight.

=====

Outside, the sky was heavy and gray, the same color as the old snow piled up by the curb, turned dirty from car exhaust and muddy boots.

Everything felt tired and bleak. Even the thin breeze tickling the back of my neck felt like it had given up.

I pressed my hand to my belly as I walked to the car. The pain still hadn't faded. It was making me nervous now. Ironically, it was Kylie's comment I couldn't stop thinking about, her insistence that she was sure everything would be fine. Because why would she have said that unless there was a chance things wouldn't be fine?

Go away, I thought at the pain. *Please, just go away.*

I was distracted by a familiar *chirp* from my bag, a new email, probably another Google Alert telling me Io Preecher had posted to her Tumblr account again. She was posting constantly, mostly nonsense conspiracy theories about how fantasy role-playing games were corrupting the youths, and videos about "how to spot devil worshippers hiding in plain sight." I could never bring myself to watch any of them.

I'd put an alert on *number1crush's* social media accounts too, but her posts came less frequently and were a lot more concerning. She never used my real name, but instead called me The Snake and, sometimes, Snake Lady, and posted pics of me with my eyes colored in red, fangs curving out of my mouth, or else she'd distort the image so that I looked much older than I was in real life. She used to post hateful things on my social media accounts, but she didn't do that anymore. Now, she took screenshots of things I posted years ago and tore them apart on her own accounts. At one point, she dug up this ancient interview I'd done for *Teen Vogue*, where I'd (jokingly) said I thought puppies were cuter than babies, and commented, *The Snake is a legit psychopath pls keep her away from small children.*

That's what scared me, that she thought *I* was the dangerous one, that she was trying to protect other people from me. The knowledge that she might try to get to me again, that she might take it upon herself to do something to protect my own child from me was enough to convince me and Dex to pack up the dogs and everything else we couldn't stand to be away from for a few months and drive three hours east to the beach.

The Range Rover was parked just ahead. It wasn't mine. It came with the security guard I'd hired after the break-in, Kamal. Some actors had people to perform literally every chore they could think of—gardeners and closet organizers and personal chefs—but I didn't employ a lot of household staff. Kamal was different though. Necessary. Even Dex agreed. Ever since the break-in, I hadn't been able to fall asleep without remembering the feel of that woman behind me, the *smell* of her. And it wasn't just me I was worried about. Stress hormones were bad for the baby. Cortisol affected the growth of the fetus, increased the chance of premature birth and miscarriage, and I could practically feel the cortisol flooding my system whenever I closed my eyes. The only way I could sleep was if I knew there was someone standing guard outside, a physical barrier between that woman and me. For the next twenty-five weeks I was going to do everything in my power to keep my life—and body—blissfully calm. It was the only thing that mattered.

Kamal glanced out the window as I hurried up to the car. He was an Indian man in his thirties with a baby face that made him look much younger than he was. "Did you enjoy your class, ma'am?"

"Anna, Kamal," I said, climbing into the car. The other yoga moms must've all parked in some hidden lot I didn't know about because, as far as I could tell, we were the only people outside. It made Main

Street feel empty, desolate, and I shivered despite myself, feeling like I was someplace I shouldn't be. "You make me feel like I'm ninety years old. And I did enjoy my class—it was very relaxing."

"That's good to hear." Kamal put the car into drive, smoothly pulling away from the curb. "Are we heading back to the house?"

"We are," I murmured, rubbing my belly as we began crunching through the snow.

Southampton flew past the car window, full of antique shops and churches, American flags dangling off every storefront. In the summer, the town was like Disneyland for the rich. Ice cream parlors and antique shops, $27 salads loaded up with juicy bits of lobster and fresh asparagus, farmers' markets that sold tomatoes the size of your head. Occasionally you'd see a familiar face, but it was gauche to stare, so most people pretended they didn't notice.

In the winter though, the town was a completely different place. It was dead, practically a ghost town. Talia had a house out here that was vacant all season, and she offered to let us use it when Dex mentioned we were thinking of getting out of the city. I hadn't loved the idea of hiding out here for months, but Dex insisted that Southampton would be a welcome break from the city, where it seemed like everyone was watching me, judging me, even if their eyes never left their phones. So far, I wasn't so sure which was worse, the crowds or the lack of *anyone*.

Wind screamed outside my car window. Cold air was seeping through the cracks around the door, making me shiver. Half the businesses on the street were shuttered and dark, and there was only one other car parked by the side of the road, something vintage and sporty and completely inappropriate for the weather, the windshield covered in a thick layer of ice. It looked like it hadn't been driven in months, and I found myself staring as we rolled past, wondering what kind of person would leave such an expensive car outside to freeze over. But this town was full of things like that: empty swimming pools and snowed-over tennis courts and sad-looking yachts bobbing in the cold gray water, toys that were only meant to be seen during the sunnier parts of the year.

My phone buzzed in my lap, drawing my attention—it was Emily, texting to let me know that there was a box of gluten-free cookie dough coming in the mail for me. She was the only person (other than Talia, of course) who had the exact address where I was staying, and only because she'd insisted on sending me my Golden Globes gift bag when I skipped the event itself. It was truly disgusting how much free stuff you got when people thought you might be nominated for an Oscar. I donated ninety percent of it, but there was always more coming. Half of Emily's texts were to let me know that some new company was sending a gift basket of promotional material. The other half were increasingly desperate attempts to get me to come out of hiding and start campaigning again.

I started to write back, when—

"Oh." Another cramp. I braced a hand against the back door, cringing.

Shit.

The fear I'd been trying so hard to ignore was spreading through me fast now. This was bad. Pain like this could mean something was really wrong. I pressed my lips together to keep a sob from breaking across my face. I needed to think; I needed to figure out what I was supposed to do. But I couldn't think about anything other than how much it hurt, how scared I was.

I lifted my phone to my ear and held it there for a few seconds before realizing that I'd forgotten to pull up a contact. Dex. I had to call Dex.

Kamal looked up, meeting my eye in the rearview mirror. "Anna? Is everything okay?"

I nodded even as the pain intensified, my nerve endings flaring like lit matches. I stared at my phone for a second, my eyesight clouding as I clumsily tapped the screen.

It was ringing.

"Hello?" a woman answered. I frowned, confused until I glanced at the screen: I'd accidentally called Siobhan, not Dex.

"Siobhan?" I choked out. My voice sounded terrible, thick with tears and desperate.

"Siobhan can't come to the phone right now..." I must've sounded worse than I thought because after a moment, the woman added, "Honey, are you okay? Do you need help?"

Dimly, I realized I recognized her voice. Her name was...I couldn't remember. Siobhan had so many friends.

"Yes." I murmured. Or maybe I just thought it. I was having a hard time distinguishing between what I said out loud and what I'd said in my head. *Yes, I need help. I'm pregnant and this pain is wrong. Something's wrong.*

"Wrong..." I choked out. Another wave crashed over me. I closed my eyes and gritted my teeth, forcing myself to breathe through it.

I had the sensation of losing time, slipping in and out of consciousness—not for long, just a few seconds—but it left me feeling dizzy, light-headed. I think I might have screamed.

"Honey? Are you all right...?"

I'd dropped my phone, but the voice continued to echo from the floor. I didn't have the strength to pick it up again. The pain I was feeling now…I didn't realize pain could be like this. It was like someone was reaching into my body, cold fingers tightening around my uterus, squeezing…

The feeling changed. It deadened so that it didn't feel like pain—it felt like nausea. It was that feeling past pain, when everything went numb, your body shutting down to try to protect you. Something was wrong. I knew it deep in my bones.

I closed my eyes, picturing how the baby had looked during my very first ultrasound. It was no longer a distant alien planet in a petri dish—now it was a fuzzy white bean in a black ocean. It was so small, so helpless. Suddenly, I felt so scared for that bean that I couldn't breathe.

When I opened my eyes again, I saw that Kamal had stopped the car and twisted around in his seat. I could see his mouth moving, but I couldn't hear his voice.

I felt something new beneath the pain then, a sensation between my legs. Something wet.

The wet was blood. I was bleeding.

The pain began to ebb. Slowly, slowly, like water inching away from the beach, it dulled. I could breathe again.

I heard Kamal's terrified voice calling, "Ma'am? Ma'am? Anna, are you okay?"

"C-call my husband," I managed to choke out. And then, gasping, "And take me to the hospital, Southampton Hospital is the closest, I think… Something's wrong with the baby."

I didn't know this then, but it was starting.

10

DEX JERKED THE DOOR OPEN BEFORE THE CAR CAME TO A complete stop in front of Southampton Hospital. "Anna? Are you okay?" The cold had chased the blood from his lips, leaving them almost blue. "What's wrong? Is it the baby?"

He looked so scared, his face all blank and tight. It chilled me. Dex had always been the calm port in a storm, the fixer. I needed him to be calm now, for me. I wanted to shake him and tell him to be Dex, be normal.

But all I could manage was, "I–I don't know. I've been getting these cramps."

Cramps was the wrong word. The pain was stronger than that. It felt like someone was hacking through me with a chainsaw.

Dex ushered me through the hospital's automatic doors, and the strong smell of antiseptic slammed into me. The ER was chaotic. Men in papery gowns passed out on stretchers, nurses pushing screaming machines down the hall, an old woman struggling with her wheelchair.

I looked away. I wasn't usually squeamish about other people's pain, but I still felt strange, light-headed. It was too much to handle on top of my own.

Dex glanced at me, noticing my discomfort. "Why don't we drive back to the city? We could call Dr. Hill."

I shook my head. Dr. Hill was all the way in Manhattan, and it would take us at least two hours to get there. Longer, with how icy the roads had been.

"I need to talk to someone now," I explained, searching Dex's face for some assurance that I was making the right call. "I mean...this is probably nothing, right? Doesn't this kind of thing happen all the time?"

I wanted him to tell me that this was just a precaution, that everything was going to be okay, that our baby was fine. But he just swallowed. I could see the fear he was trying so hard to hide. His eyes were too wide, his lips pulled into a tight line.

The room felt suddenly, stiflingly hot. I said, "Dex..."

He took my hand and squeezed. "Let's just wait for the doctor, okay? We shouldn't jump to any conclusions."

I nodded, unable to speak.

Our baby's going to be fine, I told myself. It was a desperate thought, a tiny bullet pinging off the sides of my skull. *Fine, fine, our baby's going to be fine.*

———

We'd been there for a little over three hours when there was a screech of metal, the curtain surrounding my bed being ripped back so a short woman wearing blue scrubs could wheel in an ultrasound machine.

"I'm *so* sorry to keep you waiting." She was wearing vibrant red lipstick that looked much too cheery for that dull place, and when she smiled, I noticed a tiny bit smeared across her front tooth, like blood. "You both have been so patient. If you don't mind, I just want to do a couple quick tests."

I propped myself up on my elbows, my heartbeat speeding up. *More* tests? They'd already given me an IV and taken my blood and vitals. "Is something wrong?"

"Oh, no, this is all fairly standard. I wouldn't read anything into it. I just want to take a quick look at your uterus." Her voice had the endlessly patient quality of a nursery school teacher and I found myself relaxing at the sound of it. She didn't seem like the sort of woman you sent in after a tragedy, which I took as a good sign. "My name is Meg. I'm an ultrasound tech."

I glanced at the machine she was setting up. "I'm getting an ultrasound?" My last ultrasound had been a week ago. Despite everything, I felt a twist of raw hope.

I get to see my baby again.

Meg removed a short, stubby wand in a plastic cover and squirted a spiral of clear goo onto the tip. "Can I get you to lie back and lift up your shirt?"

I did as I was told, and Meg eased the wand over my belly. I felt the shocking cold of the jelly first, followed by a slight pressure against my skin.

At my last ultrasound, Dr. Hill had twisted the screen around so I could see my baby's heartbeat. But Meg didn't move the screen. She studied it in silence, occasionally clicking on something, tilting her head. I watched her face, waiting for her to turn to me, to smile and tell me that everything was going to be okay.

But Meg didn't look at me. She didn't say anything. The only sound in the room was the beeping of the machine.

An eternity later, Meg removed the wand and started packing up her things. "I'll see if I can find your doctor," she promised, giving us a sympathetic head tilt as she wheeled the machine out of the room.

I knew then, but I still didn't want to believe it. Tears slid down my cheeks as I turned to Dex and saw that his face was wet too. My ultra-logical, man's man husband never cried. Not when we got married, or when his mom spent a week in the hospital for pneumonia a year ago. We used to talk about it, how bad we both were at showing vulnerability, how we didn't see the point of tears. The closest I'd ever seen him get was when his company went public: his eyes clenched tight and a fist pressed to his lips, a single, elated, *yes*.

Now, he wiped his eyes with his sleeve and grabbed my fingers again. "How are you doing?" he asked, his voice gruff.

I closed my eyes, but I was too angry to cry or answer, so I just shook my head.

The pain had gotten worse. It wasn't coming in waves anymore. It just was. I tried to say something else, but the pain had surrounded me in a thick black cloud, like poison gas. I couldn't think past it or through it, and I couldn't claw my way outside of it. It was everywhere. I felt like I was choking on it.

Breathe, I told myself, but I couldn't, not without feeling like I was going to throw up. The room seemed to be getting dark around the edges. Everything was hazy, fading in and out.

I needed to do something. I couldn't just sit here anymore. I sat straight up, the muscles in my back contracting. "Something's...I think something's..."

"Stay here, I'll go find a nurse."

I shook my head to tell him that I didn't like that plan, but I couldn't bring myself to speak. The pain wasn't like it was before. There was a pressure now, a very significant pressure in my pelvis, like something inside of me was trying to get out. I felt like I had to take a shit. Didn't women do that sometimes during childbirth?

Could it happen during a miscarriage too?

The mortification of shitting myself in front of my husband was too much. I threw my legs over the side of the bed, stumbling to my feet. The IV pulled at my arm, tugging me back.

Dex was trying to grab my shoulders. "Anna? Anna, I really think you need to sit down. I'll go find a nurse."

"No, no I need to go to the bathroom. I need to go *now*." I shrugged him off and wheeled my IV around the side of the bed, using my other hand to hold my hospital gown closed. The insides of my thighs were damp, but I didn't know if it was sweat or blood or urine. And that pressure was still there, in my pelvis, twisting through me. Something was about to happen, and I wanted to be in the bathroom before it did.

"Then I'll come with you," Dex said, standing, but I shook my head, moving past him. Just before I left the room, I noticed that the bed was bright red where I'd been sitting.

There was so much blood.

My baby will never cry, I thought. *My baby is dead or else it's dying right now, inside of me. It's dying and I can't do anything. I can't protect it.*

I staggered to the bathroom, dragging my IV, frantically kicked my underwear off, and sat. There was blood everywhere, on my ankles and my hands and the floor. It looked garish under the fluorescent lights, such a deep, vibrant red, not like real blood at all but like the fake stuff they used for fight scenes on set. I grabbed a wad of toilet paper and tried to clean some of it up, but my hands were shaking too badly, and my aim was no good. I just smeared it across the tile, making it worse.

I started to cry. I didn't think I was going to shit anymore. This pressure was something else, something worse. I was scared and I was alone and this was happening; it was happening *here*, in this filthy bathroom, and there was nothing I could do to stop it.

Tears blurred my eyes. I stared at the dirty grout between two tiles and tried to breathe, *in and out*, but my breath turned into a sob, and then I was shaking all over, my mouth hanging open like I was trying to scream except there wasn't any sound coming out. I pressed my hands to my mouth and dug my fingers into my cheeks, like I was trying to hold myself together. I cried harder.

A fresh shock of pain twisted through me. I jerked forward, keeling over, my head going between my knees. There was a release, and then I felt something warm and still slide out from between my legs.

Oh God.

I closed my eyes.

That wasn't blood. It had shape to it, a form. I could *feel* it.

I tried to build a wall around that thought, to keep myself from thinking too hard about what just came out of me.

But it was no use.

I knew it was my baby. My baby wasn't inside of me anymore. I was no longer pregnant.

11

"ANNA?" DEX LEANED IN CLOSE, JOSTLING MY SHOULDER. "Hey, it's time to wake up. The doctor's here."

I groaned and shoved my face deeper into the flat hospital pillow. I wanted to stay unconscious, drift back down into the black space where none of this was happening. I wanted to sleep forever.

But I couldn't do that so, after a moment, I turned my head to the side, cringing when the fluorescent hospital lights hit my pupils.

A doctor stood inside the curtain surrounding my bed, studying a clipboard that must've held my lab results. Not Dr. Hill, my kind fairy godmother of a doctor, but a generic emergency room doctor who didn't look up until he was seated on the stool across from me, and then looked at Dex instead of at me. "Hi, hello, my name is Dr. Crawford. I'm so sorry to have kept you both waiting for so long. As you've probably noticed, we're a bit busy tonight. How is she feeling?"

I looked at Dex, half-expecting him to comment on how retro it was for the doctor to talk about me like I wasn't there, but he didn't seem to notice.

"She's doing a little better, I think." Dex didn't even look at me. Clearly he didn't feel like he needed my input to answer a question about my own body. I felt a moment of fury, followed by numbness. What did it matter? What did anything matter?

"Did I have a miscarriage?" I asked. In that moment, all I wanted was the truth, no matter how terrible. I thought I was prepared to hear the worst.

But then Dr. Crawford put his hand over mine and squeezed, and I felt the bottom fall out of my stomach. "I am truly very sorry," he said.

I wanted to bury my head in my pillow again. I wanted all of this to go away.

Tiny onesies, I thought, a sob building in my throat. *Baby hair and baby smiles*. All of it, gone.

"I–I don't understand," I said when I could find my voice again. "Was this...was this my fault? Did I...do something wrong?"

"Most miscarriages are the result of an undetected chromosomal abnormality," Dr. Crawford said.

He was being vague: "most" miscarriages, not "your" miscarriage. "Is that what happened this time?" I asked. "There was a chromosomal abnormality?"

He hesitated for a moment before saying, "We really have no way of knowing for sure."

I could feel my face heating, frustration building inside of me. Why couldn't he just answer the question? "But...but that doesn't make sense. We're in a hospital. Can't you do something to find out?"

"Anna..." Dex murmured, putting a hand on my shoulder. I could tell he thought I was overreacting, but a part of me didn't care. There had to be something they could tell me. They just did all those tests, they took my blood and my vitals and performed an ultrasound. How could they not know anything?

Or was he being cagey because this really was my fault? Dr. Hill had given me pages and pages of guidelines when I first got pregnant—foods I shouldn't eat, drugs I couldn't take, exercises I had to stop doing. I was even told to avoid certain *sleeping positions*. There'd been so many rules. Maybe I'd messed something up. Maybe I did this.

"Please," I said, feeling desperate. "I have to know why this happened. There must be something you can tell me."

Dr. Crawford let his hands fall open on his lap, as though to say, *It's just one of those things*. "The truth is, Anna, most of the time, when a woman miscarries, we never figure out why. It just...happens."

I stared at him, sure I hadn't heard correctly. "What?"

"I know that can be frustrating to hear. We all want answers."

"We understand," Dex said, squeezing my shoulder. I wanted to shrug him off of me. *I* didn't understand. I didn't understand any of this.

I cleared my throat, blinking fast to push back tears. I knew I was supposed to ask probing questions, advocate for my health and all that, but my mind was a terrifying blank. I wanted to trust my doctor to know what went wrong and how to fix it. I was tired of everything being a big question mark.

"Do you know...? Is there any way to find out the sex?" I asked finally. I was told I could find out the sex at a twelve-week ultrasound, but we'd decided to wait and be surprised.

Dex looked at me like I was crazy. "You don't really want to know that."

"I do, I want to know." I would never be able to live with not knowing.

Dr. Crawford hesitated for a moment, looking back and forth between the two of us, and when Dex nodded, he said, "Your blood test didn't show the presence of Y chromosomes, so the fetus was female. We'll need to do an ultrasound to confirm any other details, but my primary concern right now is that the majority of the fetal tissue may still be inside her uterus." Dr. Crawford had turned back to Dex, addressing him like he was the one in charge of my uterus. I wanted to grab his chin and force him to look at me, talk to *me*, but I didn't. I didn't have the energy for that.

"Is she going to be okay?" Dex was still holding my other hand, crushing my knuckles together like he was worried I might slip away.

"If she doesn't expel the fetal tissue, we'll need to perform a D and C," Dr. Crawford said. "But we can wait and see if it passes on its own—"

"Wait," I interrupted, trying to keep up. "Why would I need another ultrasound?"

Dr. Crawford was doing that sad head tilt thing people did when they felt bad for you but knew nothing they said could make it better. He glanced down at the clipboard he was holding and said, "Well... According to your chart, your last ultrasound was...let's see...a week ago?"

I shook my head. "No. I just had one tonight, half an hour ago, maybe."

Dr. Crawford shook his head. "No, that's not right..." he said, as though an ultrasound was something I might just forget.

"She had one. I was here," Dex added.

Apparently, Dr. Crawford just needed to hear a man say it because he stopped shaking his head and frowned instead, staring at Dex like he'd just added something incredibly fascinating to the conversation. I resisted the urge to snap, "Like I said."

Dex glanced at me. "What did that woman say her name was? Mary?"

"Meg," I murmured, remembering the red lipstick, the nursery school voice. "Her name was Meg."

I'd foolishly thought things couldn't get worse. The miscarriage had felt like rock bottom, the furthest I possibly could've fallen. But then Dr. Crawford stared at me with his lips very slightly parted, like he was so shocked he'd forgotten to close his mouth, and he kept his eyes on me for just long enough that I felt the beginnings of real dread building inside of me.

What? What is it? Before I could say the words out loud, he excused himself, hurrying from the room so fast there was no doubt just how bad everything truly was.

It was worse than if I'd managed to ask the question and get an answer. I felt like the floor had opened up and swallowed me whole.

———————

Over the next hour, I learned that there was no one named Meg working at Southampton Hospital. There was only one ultrasound tech on staff that night, an Asian woman in her mid-forties named Sharon Lee. At some point, Dr. Crawford paraded her in front of me: *Was this the woman who examined you?* It wasn't; Meg had been at least a decade younger.

I don't have any clear memory of what happened after that. Even now, when I think back on those strange, surreal hours in the hospital,

I have only the vague feeling of sinking down into dark water, of desperately gasping for breath. I can recall a few stray images, but they don't hold together in any logical way.

I remember Dex screaming, the sound of doors slamming. I know security was called, and then the police. People asked me questions, and someone put a blanket over my shoulders. At some point, I was sipping tea from a paper cup and then wondering where I'd gotten it, if someone could've put something into it. I spit it out.

No one knew where Meg had come from, or how she'd gotten into the hospital. When the police searched the security footage, they found a single image of a woman with dark hair darting down the hallways, but the picture was too blurry to make out anything other than a smear of red lipstick on pale skin. They asked me to describe her face in detail. *How tall was she? How much did she weigh? How dark was her hair?*

The whole time I was talking all I could think was *She touched me; that woman with the red lipstick* touched *me.* I tried to make myself feel the horror of it, like when you press down on a bruise to remember the pain, but all I felt was a terrifying blankness, the absence of horror, the absence of any emotion at all. My baby was already gone. Did anything else she might've done even matter?

As I waited for the police to finish, I went over everything that had happened to me over the last few months, cataloguing them like I might be quizzed on it all later. There were the missed calls from my doctor and the appointment times that someone had hacked into my online calendar to change. The break-in. The miscarriage. And now this.

And that wasn't all. There had been other things, things it hadn't even occurred to me to consider might be connected. Like how my medication kept getting left out on the counter overnight, even though I knew I'd put it in the fridge. We'd just assumed I was being forgetful, even though I'd never been forgetful before. I wasn't the person who was constantly running late or misplacing my wallet or forgetting people's names. I'd always been on top of things. I got things done. And this, the baby, it had been the most important thing in my life for the past two years. So why the hell did I let everyone convince me that I was suddenly forgetting things, misplacing things, *missing* things? What kind of twisted sense did that make?

That night in the hospital, for the first time, I allowed my mind to drift to a strange, dangerous place. I thought about the break-in, the medication, the appointments, and now this—some woman sneaking into my hospital room, giving me an *ultrasound*. Was it really so impossible to think that all of those terrible things could be connected? That someone really hadn't wanted me to be pregnant, and once I was, did everything to stop it?

I didn't tell the cops my theory—I didn't even tell Dex. I was somehow aware enough in that moment to realize that I was grieving and that my ability to think rationally might not be the best. But it was more than that. I thought of the doubt in Officer Gia's voice when I told her about my cyberstalker, the calm look Dex got on his face whenever he had to explain that I'd forgotten something again. There was no way they were going to believe me about this.

And if I was right, if this woman had done something to hurt my baby, then the miscarriage really was my fault. *I* was the one who'd chosen a public life. *I* was the one who'd wanted to be an actor. *I'd* taken the roles and done the interviews and allowed my photograph to be taken. I'd put myself out there, and she'd found me.

If you leave your trash outside overnight, you don't blame the bear who comes by and rips it open, drawn by the smell. You blame yourself.

I stared out the car window as we drove back to the house, listening to the distant sound of the ocean and watching the sky morph above us, turning a deeper and deeper gray, blowing snow. The colors were all wrong, like photos placed under a too-dark filter. The bark on the trees was near black, the snow piled up along the sides of the road brown and muddy. It didn't fit the Norman Rockwell image I had of Southampton. Staring out at the dirty streets, I was overwhelmed by the feeling of something rotten seeping up from beneath the sidewalks. All of this excess finally starting to spoil.

It's going to storm soon, I thought. Ice cracked beneath our tires as Dex aimed our Jeep down the straight, tree-shrouded drive that led to Talia's house, the sudden snap like brittle bones. I no longer felt numb. I felt whatever came after that. I felt dead. I felt like everything inside of me was rotting. I wanted some acknowledgment from the universe that it was sorry for what had happened to me. Blood in our tire tracks, something. It was wrong that the world should still look this beautiful. But the grounds were pristine, as untouched as if they existed inside a snow globe. The universe didn't care.

We pulled into the wide arc of the driveway, white columns and ornately arched windows appearing through the pine trees like ghosts. Talia's beach house was ridiculous, more wings and floors and rooms than should've been possible in a single home. Dex parked in the gravel drive out back, and we sat in silence for a while.

"Damn," he said, his deep voice booming through the otherwise silent car. I blinked and tore my eyes away from the pool. I hadn't even noticed that he'd already turned the engine off. The Jeep was quickly getting cold, icy air seeping in through the cracks around the windows.

I couldn't bring myself to form the question, but Dex caught my glance and explained as though I had. "I just remembered that Talia and Keagan wanted to take us to brunch tomorrow. I'll have to tell them it's not a good time."

I felt a momentary ache, imagining the day the four of us might've had if none of this had happened: Keagan telling us all about his recent work trip to Reykjavik, Talia trying to get us to share our baby names with her, insisting that I have a taste of her mimosa, that it couldn't hurt. For a second, I wanted to scream, to break something. But I knew Dex was right. I couldn't stand the thought of seeing them right now, of seeing anyone. No one felt safe.

Dex draped an arm over the back of my seat, angling himself so his entire body was facing me. "What else can I get you?"

Time, I thought. *Get me another ten years. Let's go back in time and meet when I'm in my twenties. Give me a do-over. Please.*

Or give me *her*. I hadn't been letting myself think about her, but I couldn't help the image that popped into my mind: her head on a stake, on a platter, her eyes still open, those red lips mid-scream. Anger shot up my chest, red hot and pulsing like a second heartbeat. I wanted to rip out her heart like she'd ripped out mine.

"Bourbon," I croaked instead, pushing the image away.

Dex looked at me like he was going to say something about how he didn't think booze was a good idea right now, but eventually he

nodded. "Do you want anything else? Food? You should put something in your stomach." But there was no conviction in his voice. He
was quiet for a long moment, still staring out the windshield. Then,
like he couldn't hold it back anymore, he dropped his head to one
hand and covered his eyes, shoulders slumping. Either crying or
holding back tears, I couldn't tell.

"Dex," I murmured, reaching for him. Seeing him like this felt so
wrong. My husband, who climbed mountains and swam with sharks
and took meetings with the most powerful men in Manhattan, brought
low by a few hours in the emergency room. I wanted to say something,
do something to take away his pain. But I'd left all my strength behind
at the hospital. I didn't have any emotional reserves left.

I could feel my heart beating slow and steady at the base of my
throat, tracking the seconds, foolishly keeping me alive.

"This just sucks," Dex said. He shook his head once, hard, and said
again, "This sucks."

I nodded, barely hearing him. "The doctor said we can start trying
again right after my period comes back. We should call Dr. Hill, see
how long we have to wait before starting another round."

"You really want to jump right into it all again?" Dex asked. It
might've been my imagination, but his voice sounded a touch accusatory. "After everything we just went through?"

I felt an ugly twist at the word *we*. Maybe I was being unfair—he
too had suffered through endless disappointment. But that word felt
like a stretch. He'd only had to contribute a few sperm. There'd been
no hormones, no injections, no invasive surgeries.

"Of course, it's what I want," I said. It all seemed pretty straight-
forward at that moment. What had happened was devastating, with

the potential to completely destroy both of our lives. The only way to stop that from happening was to start again, to get back some small portion of what we'd lost. "Don't *you* want to keep trying?"

"You know I want a baby more than anything. But what happened tonight was... God, Anna, it was a lot. Maybe we should wait for a little while before we throw ourselves into the whole thing all over again. Give ourselves time to grieve. Give the cops time to..." He swallowed and turned away, but I knew where he was going with that: give the cops time to find the woman messing with me and lock her up someplace where she could never touch me again.

He had a point, obviously. But I didn't want to think about her. Thinking about her would make me so angry that I wouldn't be able to see straight, and I didn't want to get distracted and lose sight of what was important.

"I don't have time to wait, Dex." It felt important to me that he understand this. Maybe this would seem strange to someone else, but I had an almost frantic desire to start trying again. It felt like time was moving too fast, slipping away. If we didn't act now, do this *now*, it was never going to happen, I could feel it. "We just lost *fifteen weeks*. Longer than that, if you include all the time before, the injections and the transfer and... And I'm turning forty in a few months. I...I..." I could hear my voice getting higher, faster, the words tripping out of my lips before I'd fully considered what I was saying. "Are you saying we should just give up?"

"No," Dex said quickly. "Of course not." He looked at me and his eyebrows went up. "Why? Is that what you want?"

I felt a chill down my spine, thinking about his ex-wife. *Addy made it clear that she wasn't interested in being pregnant.*

I wondered briefly if now was the time to ask whether that was why they'd split up, if I was pathetic enough that he might give me the full story, at last. But I couldn't do that. I couldn't think of her on top of everything else.

"No...I..." I didn't know how to finish that sentence. I didn't want to stop trying. I just didn't want it to be this hard. I didn't want it to hurt so badly. Not just emotionally, but physically. I didn't want to have to sacrifice absolutely everything else that I'd worked for, my career and my friends and my home, only for it to fail. *Again.*

I looked at Dex and I wanted, just for an instant, to switch places, to experience pregnancy and parenthood like he would, as an observer, someone who got to take part in all the joys and highs and lows of parenting, but who wasn't tasked with physically creating life with his own body. And I wanted Dex to know what it felt like for me. Not the movie version of pregnancy, some beautiful thin woman wearing a basketball under her shirt, everything magical and miraculous. But the reality. I wanted him to know how physical it was, how much it had demanded. The acne that had crawled over my chin during my first trimester—not normal, pubescent teenager acne, but hard pustules that hurt to touch and stayed under my skin for weeks. And the nausea, how it felt like someone was punching me in the gut over and over again, and the exhaustion, how it came on in a wave the second six o'clock rolled around, so powerful that the idea of keeping my eyes open for even one more minute was excruciating. And I wanted to explain the things that weren't physical, the things you would never understand unless you'd gone through it. My *personality* had changed. The second I saw that second line, half of my brain had just turned off, like a thrown breaker, the electricity on that side of my mind going dark. That part of my brain, the dark part, was focused on the baby, always. Even now that she wasn't there anymore.

I'd already gone through weeks of that. More than a year, if you counted rounds of IVF that came before. And now all of it, all that time and energy and pain, had been for nothing. Dex would never know what that felt like. He'd never have to sacrifice himself like that for anything, ever.

I didn't realize I was holding my phone until it started vibrating in my hands, making me flinch. I looked down automatically and saw that my screen was filled with missed calls. My dad, my manager, Siobhan, Emily—

Something twisted inside of me. My job had painted a bullseye on my back. It was presumably the thing that had brought this woman into our lives in the first place. But it had made other things possible. We might've still been able to afford these expensive rounds of IVF even if we just had Dex's income to work with, but—and I truly hated to admit this—my fame had opened other doors, to the best doctors with the most advanced medical care, and my flexibility was the reason I was able to put everything on hold and devote all my attention to the baby.

It was like a horrible catch-22: Keep doing the job that I loved, and I'd have to live in fear that I was a target forever. Stop doing it, and I might be sacrificing everything for nothing.

And, in the end, nothing I did or didn't do even mattered. I still lost the baby, and no one could tell me why.

The dogs swarmed as soon as we made it through the back door, like always.

"I'll get them; you just head upstairs," Dex said through the chaos. He had Peanut Butter by the collar to keep him from lunging for me, Happy sniffing around his ankles for treats.

I slipped up the stairs while they were distracted. I loved the dogs, but I couldn't face them right now. Their little trusting faces would only make me more aware of all the ways I'd failed. I wanted to be alone with my grief.

Talia's house was labyrinthine. The second floor twisted and curved, like it was trying to trick you, hallways opening into rooms that opened into yet more hallways, more rooms. I got lost the first time I walked through on my own but, this time, I found my way to the master bedroom without thinking. My bottle of prenatal vitamins was sitting on my bedside table, along with a book on pregnancy and a list of foods and medications I was supposed to avoid, which I'd saved from my very first appointment with Dr. Hill.

I stared at the vitamins for a moment, feeling sick. I'd taken them religiously. One vitamin along with a cup of hot water and lemon at the same time, every single morning for almost two years. Not that it had done me any good.

I climbed into bed and squeezed my eyes shut. For a second, I thought sleep would be kind, that it would take pity on me. But then I saw the bathroom, the bloody tile. I saw the red lipstick smeared across her front teeth. My eyes snapped back open. How was I ever supposed to close my eyes again?

Outside, the snow was getting heavier as thick wet flakes stuck to all the windows. They looked like feathers, and they made me think of down coming loose from pillows, of suffocating. That's what I felt like now, like I couldn't breathe.

I wanted my mom, I realized. I wanted someone who loved me unconditionally to hold me while I cried, and promise it would all be okay. But my mom was gone, and I'd never been close with the rest of my family, so I wrestled my phone out of my pocket and called the next closest person I could think of. The phone rang once, twice.

"Are you okay?" Siobhan said by way of answer. She sounded terrible, her voice raspy and thin. I wondered, vaguely, whether she'd been out late the night before. "Olympia told me you called. I've been so worried."

Olympia. I had a vague memory of speaking with a woman who'd answered Siobhan's phone earlier that evening. She'd called me honey and asked if I was okay. I must have scared her to death.

"Sorry," I murmured. "I mean, tell Olympia I'm sorry. I didn't mean to scare her."

"Don't worry about her; she's seen worse at the center."

The center, right. Now I remembered where I'd heard her voice before. She was one of the women from the birthing center Siobhan had told me about. I could picture her clearly, a tall woman with intensely kind eyes and a low, soothing voice. Now, I felt even worse about scaring her.

"Anna," Siobhan was saying. "What happened?"

My chest felt suddenly tight. It was the way she said *what happened* that did it. I tried to get myself under control, but it was no use. I released a sudden sharp exhale that was already halfway to a sob. And then it was all over.

I told her everything. I'd been planning to keep it short but talking felt better than I'd thought it would. As soon as the words started coming out of my mouth, I couldn't figure out how to stop them.

"What do you need?" Siobhan asked when I'd finished. "Anything. Please, Anna, let me help you."

Her voice was barely a whisper. She didn't sound capable of getting me anything. I should've told her to get some sleep, that we could talk in the morning.

Instead, I blurted, my voice choked with fresh tears, "Can you get me my baby back?"

"Oh, Anna..."

I felt guilty as soon as the words left my mouth. "I'm sorry," I said, my shoulders shaking. "I shouldn't have said that. I just...I really loved her, Siobhan. I felt like I already knew her, and I...I just can't believe she's gone. I can't believe..." I had to stop for a moment. I couldn't breathe; I was crying too hard. My mouth dropped open, a wordless scream.

Even after everything I'd been through, all the rounds of IVF, all the heartache, I'd still had hope. I'd never believed the world would be this cruel. And now, all of that was gone.

"I just feel so...so desperate," I said when I could talk again. New tears were already blurring my eyes. If I wasn't careful, I was going to lose it all over again. "I'd give anything to have her back. Anything."

"Anything," Siobhan repeated, her voice soft, like she didn't realize she'd said the word out loud. Then, clearing her throat, she said, "This is going to work out for you, Anna. I know it's hard to believe that now, but it will. I promise."

It was the reason I'd called her, because I'd desperately wanted someone to tell me it was going to be okay. I tried to make myself believe it. "Yeah."

"I'll do everything I can to make sure it does."

I cleared my throat and said, "Right. Your friends at the birthing center, Olympia and the others."

"Yes, them, and anything else you need. Just name it."

"Can you come out here?" I asked. My voice cracked. I hadn't realized how badly I wanted that until the words left my mouth. "Please? I need you."

Siobhan hesitated. I thought again of how tired she'd sounded, and I almost told her never mind, that she didn't need to reschedule her whole life because I was having a crisis, but then she said, "Of course. Give me the address and I'll come as soon as I can."

———————

I woke much later that night sweating, my muscles contracting so painfully that, for a moment, I couldn't breathe. It was another cramp, leftover pain from the miscarriage. I lurched forward, groaning, and kneaded my side with my thumbs.

Happy had been curled up at the foot of the bed and she lifted her little head, massive ears perked in concern.

"Come here." I scooped her up. She licked my chin as I dragged my heavy body out of bed and slipped into the hallway.

The hall was dark, Talia's family staring at us from the photographs lining the walls, their still eyes seeming to follow wherever I went, like the house itself was tracking my movements. I headed to the kitchen, a cavernous space with a six-burner stove, two islands, and gleaming stainless-steel appliances that never showed fingerprints. The countertops were made of some expensive stone that repelled dirt. I'd had the thought before that I could kill someone in this kitchen without leaving a trace. It was like the house itself was an accomplice.

I heard Dex's voice murmuring in some other room. It sounded like he was on the phone, probably catching up on the work he missed while we were in the ER. Peanut Butter and Oz were probably curled up with him on the couch getting head rubs. For a moment, I considered going to them, letting Dex comfort me, letting the dogs lick my face and curl up on my feet.

But then I remembered the doubt in his voice when he asked, "*Is that what you want?*" and a hollow space opened inside of my chest.

Dex had left the bourbon bottle on the counter, so I grabbed it and filled a glass one-handed, Happy still wriggling in the other. I let my eyes travel around the kitchen as I drank, taking in the farmhouse sink, the ice-covered windows, the promo basket Emily had sent earlier in the week. I'd already eaten the fruit, but there was still a box of chocolates left untouched. I ripped them open and shoved a few into my mouth. I wasn't even hungry; I just needed something to fill the hole that had opened inside of me.

I ate mindlessly for a few minutes, washing the chocolate down with a swig of bourbon, my gaze settling on the basement door on the other side of the room. Talia once mentioned that her mother had kept all her baby things, every last onesie and bib. Talia didn't have space for it in her Manhattan penthouse, so she'd stored it all out here, waiting for the day her IVF worked.

I'd been fascinated. I didn't have anything left over from when I was a baby. I stayed with my mom after my parents split up, living in a series of tiny Brooklyn apartments that didn't have enough storage space to be sentimental, even if my mom had been the type to tuck onesies and baby socks away until I became a mother. My dad hadn't been super interested in parenting, and he'd sort of left her to take care of me on her own. But then she died in a car accident when I was nine, and I'd gone to live with him and his new wife in Burbank, California. They'd never had any other kids, just a series of increasingly neurotic poodles that Nora had knitted little sweaters for. We'd gotten along okay, but it had always been pretty clear to me that I wasn't part of their plan.

I took another swig of bourbon. It was a terrible idea, going down to the basement, looking through Talia's private things, but the sudden rush of alcohol had left my brain tender and dull. I crossed the kitchen and swung the door open, thinking, *To hell with it*.

The basement was dark. I smelled oak and something dank that made my nose wrinkle. I still had all those hormones pumping through me, increasing my sense of smell. Pregnancy hormones didn't go away when your pregnancy did. It was like a really messed up parting gift.

I groped along the top of the stairs for a light switch, but I couldn't find one, so I gave up and picked my way down in the black. Happy yelped in my arms, scared. I put her down and she immediately scampered back up the stairs to the safety of the kitchen.

A musty, forgotten smell rose up from the basement. The stairs groaned with each step I took, the unfinished wood so rough that splinters pricked through the bottoms of my socks. They were the kind of stairs that didn't have backs to them, leaving gaps of space between each slab of wood. I thought of a story Talia told, how her older brother and his friends once hid beneath these stairs and grabbed her ankles when she walked down them, how it'd scared her so much she'd peed her pants. My skin prickled with fear. For a second, I felt like a little kid again, imagining hands reaching through those gaps, grabbing me. I shivered and walked faster.

The basement wasn't finished. There were shadowy beams stretching over my head, God knows what hiding in the corners, shelves of storage bins lining the walls. My footsteps echoed hollowly on the concrete as I made my way to the middle of the room, the sound strangely mournful. I felt the ice of the floor through my thin socks, shivered when the cold air touched my ankles. It didn't matter how warm we kept this place; winter kept sneaking in.

I studied the labels until I found a bin that read *baby things* in Talia's small spidery handwriting. I went to unlatch the lid, then froze. My hand was trembling, bourbon sloshing up against the sides of my glass. I felt like Pandora in the old Greek myth, like opening this box would unleash something terrible into the world, and a part of me didn't care. Maybe it would be better to let the world burn down. Maybe it was time to create something new in its place.

I let my hand drop away from the bin, fresh sobs bubbling up inside of me. *Why?* I thought. Why did this have to happen to me? Why couldn't anyone tell me what I'd done to deserve this? Why couldn't I fix it?

I just want to do a couple quick tests.

The memory hit so suddenly that I felt as though I'd tilted sharply backwards. I saw Meg, or whatever the hell her real name was, the red lipstick on her front tooth, the crack stretching across the ceiling as she slipped the ultrasound wand over my belly. In my memory, she was staring at me hungrily, her eyes a touch too wide, her teeth too sharp. A witch in a fairy tale, licking her lips.

I clenched my eyes shut. I didn't want to think about her right now. I *couldn't* think about her. It was too much; I couldn't take it. But it was too late. Her voiced echoed through my head, taunting me.

I just want to take a quick look at your uterus.

Can I get you to lie back and lift up your shirt?

The skin on my belly burned with the memory of her hands on me, *touching* me. I wanted to peel it off my body, but instead, I clenched my hands into fists, focusing on my fingernails driving into my palms until the memory of her touch faded away. This was why I hadn't wanted to let myself think about her, because it filled my body with so much anger that I didn't have any room left for sadness.

Was she the same woman who'd climbed into bed with me back in Brooklyn? I couldn't say for sure; I hadn't gotten a good enough look at that woman's face. But I knew she was small and dark-haired like Meg had been. And the idea that there might be more than one of them was too terrible to contemplate.

Why had she come to my hospital room? How had she even gotten inside? What had she done to me?

That last question was the big one. She hadn't come all the way out to the Hamptons just to scare me. She was here for a reason. *What was it?*

I couldn't stay standing any longer. I carefully placed my glass on top of one of the storage bins and sunk to the ground, curling my body into a ball on the cold concrete. From the corner of my eye I noticed a black beetle creeping up the wall, antennae twitching. I felt a tickle on my skin imagining those tiny legs creeping over my arm, up my back.

The pain that rose inside of me was different from the pain I'd felt during the miscarriage. It was different from any pain I'd ever felt. It was like someone had pulled my heart out of my chest. I wasn't a person anymore, just a shell, a body.

The room seemed to spin around me as I cried, and I had to press my hand flat against the floor to remind myself that *I* wasn't spinning. I was still.

———

Later, I stared up at the basement ceiling, studying a cobweb stretched tight across the unfinished wooden beams. Crying had left my eyes puffy, and it was getting hard to keep them open. I knew I should get up and go back upstairs to my bed, but my body felt so heavy. Also, I thought I might be a little drunk. Or very drunk. Apparently, all it took anymore was half a glass of bourbon.

My eyes closed. I didn't want to think about this anymore. I wanted to sleep. Sleep would be so good. Maybe I wouldn't ever have to wake up...

I heard a wet thumping sound somewhere in the darkness. The water heater turning on? God I hoped so. Through the haze of bourbon and drowsiness, I noticed that my left hand had started moving on its own. Twitching.

Groaning, I opened my eyes. My left hand was sitting on the soft mound of flesh between my belly button and the waistband of my pajama pants. It wasn't moving. I was drunk.

I was awake now so I stared at my belly, trying to think past the alcohol swimming through my brain. Several long minutes passed. I was just about to push myself off the floor and go back upstairs to my bed when something stirred deep inside my body. It felt like cramps or nausea at first, that strange, churning sensation of something shifting. I sat up, worried I was about to be sick...

But then the movement became sharper, clearer. I realized it wasn't nausea; it was the feeling of something turning over, a tiny body rolling and stretching inside of me.

The skin on my belly shifted from one side to the other. Staring down at it, my breath caught, a sour taste inching up the back of my throat.

It's didn't feel like a flutter, like everyone said it would.

It felt like something waking up.

ABIGAIL ROWE, 1789

ABIGAIL'S SCREAMS ECHOED THROUGHOUT THE HALLS OF Arden House for much of the evening. They were shrill, quivering things, weak and hollow sounding. Elizabeth could hardly stand them. She'd had to stuff her ears with cotton so she could focus on her work, and even then, she could still hear the sounds Abigail made. Before she came to Arden House to act as Abigail's lady's maid, Elizabeth had occasionally hunted deer with her father. Abigail's screams were just like the ones a doe made before her life was ended: pure animalistic terror, mindless wailing.

Nurses had crowded the halls outside Abigail's chambers, a gaggle of anxious geese. They were murmuring among themselves, casting glances at the closed doors. It was only when Elizabeth got closer that she saw that Abigail's physician, Dr. Frederick, was among them as well.

She stopped beside him, frowning. "Why are you not attending to Abigail?" she asked. It was unseemly for her to address a man of his station like this, but she couldn't help herself. How could he have left Abigail alone in this state?

Dr. Frederick turned at Elizabeth's voice and said, a bit snobbishly, she thought, "She sent me away."

Elizabeth's frown deepened. This made little sense. Abigail had fought to have the physician present for the birth of her first child. The "man midwives" as they were called, had become very popular among the London elite. Elizabeth thought it indecent for a man to attend to be present for a birth but, then again, she wasn't high society, so what did she know about it?

"Why would she send you away?" she asked.

Dr. Frederick said nothing but pinched his lips together tightly. Elizabeth felt a sinking in her belly as she realized what he must be thinking. There had been rumors since the very beginning of Abigail's pregnancy. She was in her thirty-ninth year, and everyone at Arden House knew it was quite rare for Mr. Rowe to visit her bed. Just the week before, Elizabeth had heard their cook joke that she thought Abigail's supposed pregnancy was more likely to "end in wind rather than anything else." And she was not the only one. Most of the staff did not believe Abigail to be with child. They whispered that she was having a hysterical pregnancy. That her childlessness had driven her mad.

But Elizabeth knew the truth. The pregnancy was quite real.

At least it had been at first.

Elizabeth liked to think that she and Abigail were more than just lady and maid. They were also companions, friends. Abigail had come to Elizabeth when she couldn't conceive, she'd begged for her help. And so Elizabeth had arranged for her to meet with a midwife she knew, a woman from the village where her family still lived. Midwives might not be in fashion among the elite, but this woman was a miracle worker; she'd helped several of Elizabeth's friends and neighbors. She was more than a midwife; she was a folk healer, an expert in the kind of old remedies these new "doctors" looked down their noses at.

Elizabeth had gone with Abigail to visit the midwife, and she'd hovered in the corner of the dimly lit room, doing her best to not to draw attention to herself as the old woman crushed herbs and murmured under her breath, insisting Abigail down a tea made of ginger root and honey. The midwife had promised Abigail that her womb would quicken in just ten days and told her to return once she was with child. Abigail had been polite to the midwife's face, grateful even. But on the way home, she'd called her a batty old witch and told Elizabeth she thought the woman's methods were nothing but superstition.

Superstition or not, the midwife's methods worked. Ten days after her visit, Abigail missed her monthly bleeding. She was with child.

It was then that things fell apart. Once she was pregnant, Abigail wanted to forget that she'd needed some silly folk healer's help. She'd refused to return and see her again. Elizabeth went back to the healer alone to tell her the good news. The old woman didn't ask why Abigail hadn't come herself but loaded Elizabeth up with teas and herbs and told her to make sure Abigail took them regularly.

"And you must promise me one thing," the woman said, grabbing Elizabeth by the arm before she could slip out the door. Her bones were thin and brittle as a bird's but her grip was firm. "She doesn't have to come back here, she doesn't have to ever see me again, but I must be in the room when that baby is born. Do you understand?" Elizabeth understood.

Abigail, unfortunately, did not. She wouldn't hear of being attended by a midwife, not when all her friends were seeing male physicians from the most respected schools in Europe. Elizabeth tried reason and, when that didn't work, she begged. It was no use. Abigail could be stubborn when she wanted to be.

Now, Elizabeth pressed an ear to Abigail's door. "My lady?" she called softly. "May I enter?"

There was no answer but a break in the screaming. Elizabeth swallowed and let herself into the chambers.

The first thing she noticed was how dark it was. The sun had long set, but Abigail had extinguished her candles. Elizabeth could still smell the smoke drifting off the wicks. The only light in the room came from the softly burning fire in the hearth, and that was not near enough light to birth a baby. Elizabeth frowned, her heart beating ever so slightly faster. Her fear that something was badly wrong grew.

A soft thud as she closed the door behind her. "Abigail?"

No answer.

The second thing Elizabeth noticed was the smell. It was putrid, animalistic. The smell of adrenaline and wrenched flesh and panting. Elizabeth felt her body respond, some deep, primal instinct whispering *run, run, run*.

"What is wrong?" Elizabeth asked, even though she thought she knew. Whatever the midwife had tried to do had failed, and now Abigail sought to hide her childlessness. She was embarrassed. She had closed herself in this stinking room with no light while she decided what to do.

But, when she came up to Abigail's bed and pulled back the curtains, she saw that she was wrong.

Oh God, so very, very wrong.

Even in the darkness Elizabeth could see sharp slashes of red splattered across the bedclothes. Blood. And the smell was worse here, a mix of sweat and sickness so thick Elizabeth could taste it.

Abigail was lying in the middle of all this, spread eagle, quite still, staring at the ceiling. She held something small and pink and squirming.

A baby, Elizabeth thought. So there was a baby.

"Abigail," she breathed, coming closer. "What is it?"

Her lady turned to her. Her eyes were crazed, rolling around in her head, the whites struck through with blood.

"It is a monster," she hissed, her chest heaving. "The baby...you must get rid of it!"

You might start to feel your baby kick

12

I STARED AT MY BELLY FOR SEVERAL LONG MOMENTS, HARDLY daring to breathe. I wanted it to happen again. I *needed* it to happen again. If it happened again, it meant it wasn't just in my head.

The basement was a mess of stark colors, black shadows oozing out of the corners and eerie yellow light drifting down from the ceiling, pale, silvery slants of moon coming in from the high window. The contrasts were suddenly too much for me, an instant headache. I closed my eyes and tried to sort through my thoughts, but everything was rocking and swaying, floating away on a sea of bourbon. I could feel the floor, hard and cold pressed against my back. So much colder and harder than it'd been a few minutes ago. I was more than a little drunk.

Just breathe, I told myself. I opened my eyes again as the breath whooshed out from between my lips. I stared down at my belly.

Nothing moved. Of course nothing moved.

It was the hormones, I realized, deflating. Like how my sense of smell was still so strong. *The majority of the fetal tissue may still be inside her uterus.* Only my body didn't know it was just tissue now.

My body didn't understand that the baby it had spent months nurturing and protecting was dead. The hormones inside of me were still working, still trying to make it grow.

I pressed a hand to my belly, feeling sick.

A door creaked open, and I heard Dex call from the kitchen, "Anna? Are you there?"

"Yeah," I said, my voice too quiet to reach him. I moved my hand, staring at my belly.

Move, I thought. And I kept staring even as my eyesight blurred and my chest began to heave. *Move, please, just move.*

Dex's feet hit the stairs a moment later, the steady groan of wood telling me he was coming to get me. But I knew it wouldn't matter. He could peel me off the floor and lead me upstairs, tuck me into our bed, and in the end, it wouldn't make any difference. There was a part of me that would never leave the basement.

———

The next morning the sound of a door opening and closing somewhere in the house roused me from sleep. I heard footsteps, soft voices in the hall.

My eyes opened. I was suddenly wide awake.

It was early, not even eight, and Dex was still snoring in bed next to me so it couldn't be him. Which meant it might be her. I rolled over and jostled Dex's shoulder, trying to wake him up. "Hey, did you hear that?"

He didn't move, didn't even seem to notice I was touching him. He'd always been impossible to wake up. He slept like he was dead.

Somewhere below, a door opened and closed. Footsteps wound their way down the hall.

I held my breath, listening, suddenly intensely aware of how big Talia's house was, how many empty rooms there were below me, around me. My stalker could've broken a window in the basement, and we never would've heard it.

I crawled out of bed and pushed the door open, listening. When I heard nothing, I crept toward the staircase, holding my breath. I wanted it to be old house noises but I had to see for myself, to know there was no one else here.

If I saw anyone, I was still close enough to the bedroom that I could run back for Dex.

Or scream.

The hallway opened up just ahead of the steps to the main floor, the wall giving way to a polished wood balcony that overlooked a marble foyer and a curving, *Gone with the Wind*–style staircase. I stopped at the balcony, fingers curling tight around the banister as I peered into the entryway.

There was just pale wood, white and gray tile, shadows stretching like dark fingers down the halls.

"Hello?" I called, feeling bolder.

My voice echoed back to me.

Ello...oh...oh.

I closed my eyes, forcing myself to breathe. I was being ridiculous. Kamal was outside. He wouldn't have let a stranger in. But I had to see for myself.

I drifted down the stairs, through the dining room (the table large enough to seat sixteen comfortably), down two long halls, and through the more formal of the two living rooms. Sweat broke out on the palms of my hands.

There's no one here, I told myself. *There's no one; it's just my imagination...*

The house was silent except for the steady tick of the grandfather clock in the living room. *Ticktock. Ticktock.* No movement, nothing out of place. My gaze settled on the powder room door—

The door was closed tightly.

But we never closed that door. It always stuck in the frame and swung back open. You had to jiggle the knob and pull hard to get it to shut right. It was left open. *Always.* Which means that someone really was here. It wasn't all in my head.

Fear flared through me. For a moment I couldn't think, couldn't move. Then, I heard the soft sound of someone swearing on the other side of the door, and it jolted me back to myself. I needed to do something. I needed to get help.

I briefly considered racing out the front door and finding Kamal. But what if she heard me? If I left now, I risked her getting away. And then I might never know who she was.

My stomach turned over at the thought. I remembered Meg, the ultrasound tech, lipstick smeared across her tooth like blood. I remembered the woman who'd crawled into my bed, touching me, whispering *baby* in my ear. My fingers curled into fists. There was no way I was letting this bitch get away again. This ended now.

I grasped the doorknob, turning slowly, slowly, until I was sure the latch wouldn't click. My heart leapt into my throat.

I yanked the door open—

A woman stood over the sink, the front of her shirt tucked into her bra. Bruises trailed across the dark brown skin of her belly like a garden of flowers. They were blue and brown and deep purple, reminding me so much of the bruises I'd gotten during IVF that, for a moment, I couldn't breathe. Some seemed old and half-healed, already fading around the edges, while others looked fresh, raw, the blood still hovering close to the surface of her skin.

I froze, thinking, *Oh God she's gotten in again; this is some sort of masochistic ritual...*

And then the woman's eyes flicked up, finding mine in the mirror, and I realized what I'd walked in on: not a stalker, but Talia, giving herself a hormone injection.

"Oh my God, Talia, you scared me to death..." I was already stepping back into the hall, pulling the door closed when she reached out to stop me.

"Anna—" Talia was still leaning against the bathroom sink, holding a chunk of her own bruised flesh between pinched fingers. "I'm so sorry! I knocked but no one answered, so I used my key to get in. I wouldn't have; it's just that if you don't do the injections at the right time..." She trailed off, letting me fill in the blanks, but I was distracted, still staring at the bruises crawling across her belly. My throat felt suddenly thick, and it took considerable effort for me to lift my eyes to her face. I remembered when my belly looked like that, evidence of the baby I was trying to make spread across my skin like a map.

"Right," I murmured.

Talia was still looking at me, seeming to take in my pajamas for the first time. "Didn't Dex tell you about brunch?"

I had a vague memory of discussing this with Dex last night. He must've forgotten to cancel our plans.

"Do you need help with that?" I asked instead of answering. It was a particularly twisted bit of masochism, even for me, but Talia's eyebrows went up gratefully.

"Really?"

"Of course." Why not help someone else get pregnant? Maybe it was the karma I needed to turn my own luck around.

Talia looked surprised but grateful. "That would be amazing. Keagan had to go into the city this morning, and I didn't realize it would be so hard to do the injections myself."

"Yeah, but you get the good sperm," I said. It was an old joke. Talia and Keegan were using a donor, and they had access to some amazing databases. We used to jokingly read through the descriptions, laughing about how silly they all were. Do you want Ivy League sperm? Six-foot-seven sperm? Sperm that speaks four languages?

I took the needle from her. I could still remember what it felt like to shove the tip of the needle through my own skin, to feel that soft *pop* as my flesh gave way beneath my hand.

Talia was still holding her belly between two fingers. I crouched, aiming the needle. My mouth felt suddenly dry. "Just...tell me when you're ready."

She gripped the sink with one hand and, closing her eyes, took a single deep breath. "Okay," she said on the exhale. "Ready."

I pushed the needle into her. It felt exactly as I remembered it, that faint *pop* as the metal tip broke through skin, disappearing inside her. I pushed the plunger down, trying not to wince as viscous liquid flowed into her belly.

Talia hissed through her teeth. "Mother*fu*..."

I told Talia what happened, and she made us cups of smoky tea that she picked up the last time she and Keagan were in Paris, and fed me buttery cookies filled with seeds and herbs.

"These are incredible," I told her, taking a third. "Where did are these come from?"

"A mutual friend gave them to me," she told me. "I couldn't keep them to myself. Here, have another."

The two of us settled in the oversized Adirondack chairs on the enclosed back porch, blankets tucked snug around our legs, mugs of tea balanced on our laps. I didn't want to talk about the miscarriage. I couldn't talk about it without crying, so instead I finished my third cookie and told Talia about the woman who'd snuck into my room to give me an illicit ultrasound. I found it easier to talk about her than the baby. Anger was so much easier to sit with than grief.

"Jesus," Talia said, her dark eyes perfectly round, unblinking. "What is wrong with people?"

I took a sip of my tea because if I tried to answer, I knew I would start screaming or crying or both. I could hear Dex bustling around in the kitchen, making coffee, but he hadn't poked his head out to say hello yet. He wasn't a morning person. He would need an hour to pull himself together before he could be expected to socialize.

"Did the cops get her?" Talia wanted to know.

"Not yet."

Talia shook her head. "Well, I hope she gets some disgusting disease. Smallpox or maybe malaria. Something *tragic*."

I peered into the dregs of my tea, smiling a little. For a second, sitting there with Talia, listening to her talk about my stalker, I almost felt normal.

And then, a twist through my insides, a reminder that I wasn't going to feel normal again for a very long time. Maybe ever.

"Do you ever wonder why we're putting ourselves through all this?" Talia asked, blowing on her tea.

I glanced at her and she ticked a finger between our bellies, mine still swollen with hormones, hers bruised, deflated: pregnancy, motherhood, IVF.

"I'm doing it because I want a baby," I said, my automatic answer.

"Yeah, but *why* do you want a baby? Like, if you think about everything we've had to go through, all the rounds of IVF and the hormones, the miscarriage... Why are we wasting our time with it all? Life is short. Why can't we just live our lives, be happy in the moment and all that crap?"

"You mean like women who don't want to have kids?" I'd always envied them a little. I'd even pretended to be one of them for a while. In interviews, there was always a reporter who asked if I wanted a family, usually throwing in something misogynistic about how the clock was ticking. Whenever that happened, I'd always let my mouth drop open and say, "Oh my God, I *knew* I was forgetting something!" As though having a baby had just, *whoops*, slipped my mind.

But Talia shook her head. "I've always hated how people separate women who want kids from women who don't, like we're two separate species. It's infuriating how people insist on defining cis women's entire lives by this one choice."

I blinked and looked away, thinking her question over. It was strange, given the amount of time I'd put into trying to get pregnant, that I'd never really thought about *why* I wanted a baby. I only knew that I did, badly. But what was it really going to add to my day-to-day life that I couldn't get from my dogs and my friends and my husband? Was there some magical, next-level love I wouldn't be able to feel until I became a mother? Or was that just something we told women so they'd keep breeding?

"I think…" I said after a long moment, "I've just always wanted to be a mother. My mom died when I was little, and I never got a chance to know her. I guess I want a do-over on the whole mother-child relationship thing." I shook my head. "I don't know, maybe that doesn't make sense."

"No, it does." There was a beat of silence, then Talia shifted in her chair, mug of tea balanced on her knee. "I always thought New York was this progressive utopia, and then I started trying to get pregnant and I realized just how stuck in the past this entire country still is. You wouldn't believe some of the stuff people have said to me and Keagan. You know a nurse actually told me I was lucky I was Black, because Black women didn't feel the same labor pain white women do?"

"That's disgusting," I said, horrified. "I'm so sorry."

"It comes with the territory, I guess. In this country, giving birth while Black is incredibly dangerous. Even Serena Williams nearly died." Talia shook her head. "And that doesn't even touch on the transphobia. It honestly makes me wonder why I want this so badly. I think too many people take it for granted that folks with uteruses are going to keep having babies."

I felt my eye twitch. "The thing I can't get over is why there is still so much confusion over really common things. People have babies all the time. It shouldn't be this big mystery anymore; it should be *biology*."

I thought of Dr. Crawford telling me that doctors didn't know why women had miscarriages, and I could feel my eyes fill. I should change the subject, but I couldn't bring myself to do it. "I don't think it's too much to ask that my doctor figure out why I can't get pregnant, or why I had a miscarriage. But it's like they're all just *guessing*! It's like I'm the first person on the planet who's ever done this."

"They really don't have any idea why it happened?" Talia asked.

I shook my head. "And now Dex is saying he doesn't want to do another round of IVF right away. He wants to wait until the cops catch this woman who's been following us first. Like it's that easy to stop and start this thing, like it's a load of laundry."

"You don't want to wait?"

"I don't want to miss my chance to be a mother because of some awful woman—" I bit off the word, resentment and anger oozing through my teeth. "But Dex...it's like he thinks we have all the time in the world."

"Yeah, well cis men can have babies into their seventies, can't they?" Talia rolled her eyes. "But look, there are other options out there. I think if this round of IVF doesn't work for me, I'm going to start talking to some midwives and doulas, come at this thing from a whole different angle." Talia reached out to take my hand. "And, if that doesn't work, there's always adoption, surrogacy."

I nodded. I could tell she was trying to be kind, let me know this didn't have to be the end. But it felt like what she was really telling me was that it was time to give up.

———

It wasn't until an hour later, when Talia was bent over her phone calling her car service to take her back to the city, that our conversation switched to anything other than the miscarriage.

"I saw Emily at Keagan's office yesterday; she told me what was going on," she said, peering out the front window to watch for her car's lights in the driveway. Keagan was a senior publicist in the NY office for the same PR firm that represented me. "Do you know whether they're reassigning you to someone new?"

Talia said this like she assumed I already knew what she was talking about, but I was completely lost. "Emily's in New York?"

Talia glanced back at me, clearly surprised that I didn't already know. "Yeah, for the past month at least. Keagan said the higher-ups are siphoning off a bunch of her clients. I just assumed you'd be one of them."

I felt a little buzz of anxiety. Some part of me was aware that this was a big deal, but it was nowhere near the top of the things I was concerned about right now. Though it was weird that Emily hadn't mentioned she was in New York. Usually she tried to get me to meet her for a drink when she was in town. "Do you know why?"

"I guess they didn't think she could handle them after Kyle Holly publicly fired her."

I recognized the name Kyle Holly but couldn't remember exactly why. He was a newer star, I think, the lead on some Netflix series. I had no idea why he'd fired Emily.

"It's weird that they didn't reassign you," Talia said as her car's headlights poured through the window, briefly illuminating her face. "You might be the last client she has left. Anyway, I'll come out again soon, I promise," she told me, kissing me on the cheek.

I forced a smile and waved goodbye. And then I stood at the window for a long time, watching the headlights disappear into the gray day, ignoring the cold that pressed in through the glass and crawled up my arms.

Once Talia's car had disappeared, I called Siobhan. I was feeling guilty about our conversation last night, how I'd asked her for favors when it was clear she hadn't been feeling well. I was going to tell her I was fine, that she didn't need to worry about coming all the way out here, but on the first ring, a woman answered. "Hello?"

I hesitated. The voice wasn't Olympia's, but it wasn't unfamiliar either. "Hi...is Siobhan available? This is her friend Anna."

There was a long silence, punctuated only by the sound of voices in the distance, machines, beeping. Whoever I was talking to, she was somewhere public. "Hello?" I asked again.

The woman on the other end of the line cleared her throat. "Anna. Hi. We haven't officially met yet, but my mom talks about you all the time. This is Gracie."

Gracie was Siobhan's adopted daughter, I remembered. She was right; we hadn't met, but Gracie Walsh's picture had been plastered all over the internet since practically the day she was born, shot after shot of a shy-looking Black girl, then a gawky teen with braces and legs that seemed too long for her body, then a beautiful woman in her early twenties, usually with long brown braids and amazing earrings, standing next to her famous mother on red carpets.

"My mother's ill," Gracie explained in a halting, pained voice. "It happened last night, very suddenly."

My heart dropped. "Oh God...Gracie...is it...is her cancer back?"

"I'm afraid so. She...her doctors think that, if she were awake, she'd be in a lot of pain, so they've put her in a medically induced coma while they try to figure out whether it's possible to continue her treatment. She's at Mount Sinai, if you'd like to visit."

I thought of how wretched Siobhan sounded on the phone, how tired. I should've guessed. "I spoke with her last night," I said, feeling horrified, numb. I couldn't make my brain believe this was happening, not on top of everything else. "She'd sounded... I should've realized..."

"You talked to her last night?" Gracie asks, surprised. "You might've been the last one, then. Her neighbor called me around midnight. They heard some big thump, I guess, and got worried when she didn't answer her door. I found her on the floor of her apartment."

Midnight, I thought, feeling a chill. That meant she'd collapsed at roughly the same time I dropped to my knees in the basement. It meant she would've been lying on her floor, fighting for her life, at the exact same moment that I was lying in the basement, willing my dead baby to move.

We'd always talked about how strange it was that going through cancer treatment and going through IVF should have so many similarities but this was too much; it was too terrible. Tears flooded my eyes. "Oh God."

"I'm going back to her room now, but let me text you a number where you can reach me. I'll let you know if there's any change."

"Thank you," I murmured. A moment later, Gracie hung up.

———

After hanging up with Gracie, I walked out of Talia's house and down toward the snow-dusted beach. I walked slowly at first, wondering if

Siobhan was going to die and, if so, how long she had left, if I would even get a chance to say goodbye.

I had to have known it might come to this. Siobhan and I had met when she was in the worst throes of chemo, when her diagnosis had been dismal. I had to have known there was a chance she could die. But even so, I never truly believed it. Siobhan wasn't just a person; she was a force. It should've taken an act of God to bring her down, not something as simple, as mundane as cancer.

Before I could stop myself, I pictured her small and quiet on the floor of her apartment, fighting for her life, and the image was so wrong that I shuddered. It was so similar to what I'd been doing at the exact same moment that it made me want to cry.

She hadn't even told me she'd gotten sick again. She'd let me talk about my own misery, promised me she'd be there for me, but she hadn't let me be there for her. It made me angry, not at her but at myself. I should've made sure she understood that she could lean on me too. I hate that she thought she had to face all that alone.

As I obsessed, I found myself walking faster, adrenaline pumping through me. After a moment, I broke into a run. The sky was flat and gray as a corpse, the wind coming off the ocean bracing. Seagulls circled overhead. Every now and then one of them released a high squawking cry before diving into the cold water. It seemed wrong that they were here, it was too cold. Did seagulls migrate in the winter?

Circling birds are bad luck, I thought. My mother told me that once, a long time ago. Maybe she was right. It was too much, everything that was happening. It was all too much.

I pushed myself faster, until I couldn't feel the cramps still raging through me. While I ran, I let my mind go perfectly, blissfully blank.

The only time I thought about Siobhan or the miscarriage or my stalker was when I caught sight of Kamal from the corner of my eye, following behind at a slow, steady jog.

There was only one other person on the beach with me, a Latine woman in her mid-forties who was inexplicably wearing a pair of motorcycle boots. She lifted a hand to wave as I ran past, but if she'd considered shouting a hello, Kamal's presence must've convinced her that wasn't a very good idea. She dropped her hand quickly and turned away.

I ran faster, kicking up sand and broken shells, the adrenaline in my blood making it easier for me to push back the grief that kept threatening to roar up. The ocean was crashing in my ears, the rhythmic noise steadying my chaotic brain. My muscles were screaming, my lungs burning. Distantly, I heard a seagull calling. It sounded like a child screaming.

I made my way down the beach to the old lighthouse. The ground got rougher, the sand rockier. This was usually where I turned back, but not today. The pain felt good. It reminded me of the burning feeling I got in my toes and fingers when they started to defrost after going numb in the cold. Sometimes being alive hurt like hell.

Suddenly my foot connected with something small and hard, sending it skittering. I stopped and doubled over, breathing hard. After I'd taken a second to catch my breath, I glanced around for whatever I'd kicked. I expected a shell or a rock, but my eyes landed on something else.

Something with a face.

Fear leapt up inside of me. It was an animal, I thought at first, a corpse. I reeled backward, hands coming up over my mouth before I'd fully processed what I was seeing.

Not a dead animal: *me*. I was looking down at my face on a doll's plastic body. Staring at her, I felt all the oxygen leave my body. It was a grotesque approximation of what I actually looked like, limbs comically large compared to a too-small face, mouth frozen in something that looked more grimace than smile, the makeup garish, dated, lips too pink, eye shadow too blue. It took me a moment to recognize that it was an action figure of Summer Day, my old character from *Spellbound*.

Another crash of ocean, saltwater spray in my face. The roaring cold jolted me back to my body. The doll hadn't been well taken care of. She was covered in some sort of green ocean slime, her long blond hair tangled with seaweed. I felt a kick of concern, the strange impulse to take care of her, pick her up and clean her off.

I didn't know how long I'd been there, frozen with fear and confusion, but I felt cold and damp, and a dark shadow bobbing just outside my field of vision told me Kamal was approaching. I looked over at him and saw that he had his hands cupped around his mouth, calling me, but I couldn't hear his voice over the crashing waves.

Hesitantly, trembling a little, I leaned over and plucked the doll out of the sand. She wasn't wearing any clothes, and there was sand crusted in her joints. I hadn't seen one of these dolls in over a decade. Not many had sold. I was pretty sure the only place you could find one was on eBay and, even then, you would've had to search for it. This wasn't some toy left here by a forgetful child. She was meant for me to find.

I heard a sharp wet sound and jerked my head up in time to see a seagull dive below the surface of the water. It reappeared a moment later clutching a dead fish, watery blood streaked across its beak.

Breathing hard now, I looked back down, my eyes moving from the doll's face to her torso. Someone had drawn an X over her belly, thick angry lines made with red Sharpie.

Staring at that X, I thought I knew what the message was: *I'm not done with you yet.*

I was wrong about so many things, but I was right about that.

13

KAMAL MARCHED ME RIGHT BACK TO THE HOUSE, ONE FIRM
hand on my elbow, the other resting on the gun he kept under his suit
jacket. I was confused, still holding the Summer Day doll by one leg,
not understanding why he was suddenly so alert until he muttered,
his voice low, "Whoever left that could still be out here. We need to
get you inside *now*."

Of course. We had no way of knowing how long the doll had been
here, if *she* was still here somewhere, watching to see my reaction to
her messed up gift. I noticed Kamal's eyes roaming the beach as we
walked, looking for her. But we saw no one else.

Once we were home, I stood in front of the sink in the kitchen
while Kamal phoned the cops, staring out the window. Outside, the
snow-covered lawn gave way to white beaches, the change so subtle it
was almost imperceptible. Spindly, leafless trees stood watch like dark
sentries as the steel-covered waves crashed into the sand over and over,
leaving frothy white bubbles behind as the ocean pulled them back.

I wasn't reacting the right way. I knew that. I should've been scared.
She'd come to where I lived, just like she had back in Brooklyn. Only

this time, she'd left me this cruel threat. I should've been terrified to be alone; I should've been huddling up next to my security guard, my husband, desperate for someone big and strong to protect me.

Instead of feeling scared, I felt angry. I wanted to hit something, I wanted to scream. She'd already taken the most important thing from me; what did I care what she did to me now? There was a part of me that wanted to draw her out from wherever she was hiding so I could hurt her like she'd hurt me. Then maybe I could figure out what she really wanted, and all of this would be over.

I got my phone out and pulled up my online calendar. I hadn't been using it lately for obvious reasons, so there weren't any new appointments this week. I made a new one:

WHY ARE YOU DOING THIS TO ME?

After I added it to my calendar, I changed my password back to the one I'd been using when she altered all my appointments, and then I spent the next few minutes staring at the screen, hoping she'd figure it out and take the bait. Nothing happened.

Dex's voice was suddenly behind me. "Hey, I called your name like three times. You didn't hear me?"

I flinched, startled. The walls in this house were all lath and plaster and old as sin. Someone could be screaming in the next room, and you'd never know. Always made me wonder what sort of things Talia's family was hiding.

"Sorry," I murmured, closing out of my calendar. "I was distracted."

"Did I hear Kamal on the phone with the cops?"

"Yeah. We found something on the beach. A doll."

Dex frowned, trying to follow along. "I don't understand... You found a *doll*?"

"It was a Summer Day action figure with an X on her stomach. I think she left it for me. Like, as a threat."

Dex frowned and scrubbed a hand over his mouth, saying nothing for a long moment.

I could feel his eyes on me, watching me. It annoyed me for a reason I couldn't quite pinpoint. "What?"

"It's just that...anyone could've left a doll on the beach. You don't know for sure that it was from the stalker, do you?" When I didn't answer, he added, "You didn't, like, see her or anything?"

"It was a doll of *me*," I snapped, my voice coming out a bit harsher than I meant for it to. "It was obviously from her."

"Okay, if you say so." Dex sighed and rubbed his chin with one hand. After a moment, he added, "Are you sure you're okay?"

I shook my head, but when I brought a hand to my mouth, I noticed that I was shaking, hard. Not just my hand, but my arm too, My whole body.

"It's not just the doll..." I said, finding it difficult to get the words out. "It's Siobhan. I just found out that she...she..."

"Shh, hey it's going to be okay," Dex said before I could explain. The words felt caught in my throat as he fitted my head beneath his chin like a puzzle piece. I didn't even realize I'd started crying until he wrapped his arms around me. "I'm here... It's going to be okay."

I followed Dex to the formal dining room, where Kamal was still on the phone with the cops.

"Let me take care of this," Dex said, putting a hand on my back. "You should go upstairs and rest."

"No, I want to talk to him too." I didn't want to be sent away, some woman verging on hysterical, too delicate for the harsh realities of life.

"Anna," Dex said, his voice low. "Are you sure you're up for it? After everything with Siobhan and... Why don't you let me handle it?"

I felt a twinge of pain at the mention of Siobhan, but I shook my head. This was happening to *me*. I had a right to know what the cops had to say about it.

When we'd left Brooklyn, Detective Wood had told us he was looking into a few leads. There'd been a neighbor who saw a strange car driving past our house at a crawl, and a print in the backyard that didn't belong to a shoe in either Dex's or my closet. I hadn't been particularly optimistic about any of it, but now I could barely breathe, thinking *Please*.

Please let it be that easy.

Kamal said into the phone, "Hey, detective, I've got Mr. Harding and Ms. Alcott here too." And he put the phone on speaker and placed it in the middle of the table.

"Mr. Harding, Ms. Alcott," Detective Wood bellowed. "I'm afraid I was just telling Kamal that we don't have much to report. The shoe print we found in your backyard belongs to a Converse sneaker, either a men's size eight or a women's ten. Unfortunately, that's a pretty common brand, so we can't say for sure whether it came from your intruder."

I was chewing my lip, nodding. Half the programmers who worked with Dex wore Converse sneakers. That print could've come from any one of them.

"We're still trying to track down the car your neighbor saw, but we only have a partial plate to go off of so that might take a while. I did speak with the hospital again this morning and they've agreed to send over their security footage. I know some officers went over it the other night, but I want to have my own guys take a look so we can be sure no one missed anything."

"What about the other names we gave you?" Dex interjected. "Leon and Ellie, and that woman Anna saw at the clinic. Io something?"

"Preecher," I said. "Her name was Io Preecher. She has a Tumblr thing. And actually, I noticed that the cyberstalker I told you about, *number1crush*, commented on a bunch of her posts so, I don't know, maybe they know each other or something."

"We spoke to Ms. Preecher and she admitted taking a photograph of you and posting it online, but she doesn't have a record and, in my opinion, she didn't seem to have an unusual level of interest in you," Detective Wood said, talking fast like he wanted to get this out of the way so he could move on. "We'll keep an eye on her moving forward, but I don't think she's our woman."

I thought about how Io hadn't blinked when she'd looked at me, the way she'd pointed that gnarled finger in my face when she'd said, *"I know you."* God, even normal fans could be creepy.

"We're still trying to track down Ellie Pratt," Detective Wood was saying when I started listening again. "But we were able to locate Leon Baker. He's been living in Berlin for the past three years, so we can safely rule him out."

Kamal leaned close to the phone, frowning slightly. "What should we do about the doll?"

"I understand why you called me about the doll, but since the beach you found it on is public, it's impossible to say for sure whether it was meant for you."

I saw Dex glance at me from the corner of my eye, like he was saying, *Told you*, but I refused to give him the satisfaction of looking back. "It was a doll *of* me." I could hear my voice getting higher, verging on hysterical, and a part of me didn't care. "It was an action figure of my old character from a television show I was on. They haven't sold those in, I don't know...like fifteen years. There's no way it was a coincidence."

"I'm with Anna on this," Kamal said, "It seems like a big coincidence."

"Do you know who could've gotten their hands on one?" Detective Wood asked, a bit of a sigh in his voice. "Do you keep a few in your basement or a storage unit that someone else might have access to?"

I was already shaking my head. I'd always thought the dolls were creepy, so I hadn't kept any of them. "No, I don't have any, but I think my old studio has a few left." I only knew this because of a conversation back when Emily first started working as my publicist. She was telling me about how she used to intern at Warner Bros and saw some of my old dolls in their warehouse.

"Sometimes this job is so surreal. I mean, how weird is it that just a few years ago I was looking at a doll of you, and now I'm here, getting a drink with real you?" she'd joked.

"I'll check with the security team at the Warner Bros warehouse to see if they've had any problems with theft," Detective Wood said. "Whoever put that doll on the beach probably got it off eBay or something, but it's worth asking just in case. And I can get some tech guys to look at it and see if we can pull any prints, but I wouldn't get my hopes up if I were you. I know this is hard, but right now you need to hold tight—we'll be sure to be in touch when we have more to go on."

"We understand," Kamal said into the phone. "Thank you for your help, detective. We'll let you know if anything else comes up." He hung up. Turning to me, he added, "Regardless of what the detective says, I'd like to up your security."

Dex folded his arms over his chest. "In what way?"

"No more unscheduled visitors, no leaving the house without me present." Kamal looked at me. "And, Ms. Alcott, with your permission, I'd like to start monitoring all incoming calls and emails."

"You think she might try to get in touch with me?" I asked. The thought made me feel sick.

"I don't know, but I don't want to take any chances. I'd like to set you both up with burner phones later today so—"

"Both of us?" Dex interrupted, frowning. "I'm sorry, why do you need my phone?"

Kamal steadied him with a look. "Is that going to be a problem?"

"Of course not," Dex said quickly. "I just take a lot of work calls on that phone."

"You can keep up with work, but I'd warn you not to give the number out to too many people. This woman could be in touch with one of your acquaintances, getting information on you from them."

I nodded, feeling suddenly cold. I'd already left the city, hidden myself away in this fortress. Now I had to start using a burner phone? When was it going to end?

Dex looked at me, concern creasing his forehead. "Hey, we're going to find her, okay? I won't let her hurt you."

Again, I thought, but didn't say. *You mean you won't let her hurt me again.*

Of course, there was still the question of how "Meg" had hurt me the first time. *If* she'd hurt me. The night it happened, I'd been convinced it was too much of a coincidence that she'd appeared in my hospital room on the same day I'd miscarried. I knew someone didn't want me to have a baby. Could she have done something to me, caused my miscarriage somehow?

According to the internet, the most common way of having a medically induced abortion was to take two pills exactly twenty-four hours apart. Doctors didn't recommend the abortion pill after you were eleven weeks pregnant—but that was just because it wasn't safe, not because it didn't work. The first pill blocked the hormone progesterone, which caused the uterus to soften and break down, and the second caused the uterus to expel the pregnancy—

After reading that, I went to the bathroom and dry-heaved for several minutes, picturing my perfect baby, the baby I'd spent two years trying for, breaking down inside my body. This Meg person could've slipped me something. That idea wasn't so unbelievable. She could've dropped a pill into my water bottle or dosed the chamomile tea I'd had in the yoga studio lobby before class maybe. But two pills exactly twenty-four hours apart? Even I had to admit that it seemed unlikely that anyone would've been able to coordinate that.

Unfortunately, the primary drug in the pills, misoprostol, metabolized so quickly that it was impossible to detect in your blood even five minutes after an oral dose. Some hospitals could perform something called an assay, which was a procedure to detect misoprostol acid, but very few facilities were even capable of doing that type of testing, and they were mostly in Europe. And even if I could find one locally, miso-prostol acid was only detectable for six hours. I would've been dosed a few hours before my miscarriage, and that was almost a week ago now.

Like so many other things to do with pregnancy, there was no way to know whether I'd ever been drugged, no way to figure out what had happened to cause this. If this woman really did do something to me, I would never, ever be able to prove it.

Kamal had my new burner phone ready within the hour. I trans-ferred Gracie's number, as well as a few contacts from my old phone, then texted my Dad, my manager, and Emily to let them know I'd be at a new number for the time being.

Emily responded immediately: Hey Anna. I just got off the phone with that reporter from The Cut. Did you forget about the interview we'd scheduled?

Buried in my brain was a vague memory of scheduling a phone interview for today, part of their *How I Get It Done* series, which I used to read religiously. A few days ago, I'd been so excited about it.

Now, I stared at Emily's text, blinking, thinking there was no way I could pull it together to talk to her today. And I definitely couldn't handle a reporter.

We're going to need to reschedule I texted back.

Emily responded instantly: Reschedule for when? Nominations are in less than a week, remember? We gotta make sure everyone's thinking about you!

I closed my eyes and tried to focus on breathing. My head was killing me. I wanted to hide. I wanted to turn off my phone and all my other devices and just pretend I didn't exist for a little while. But this was the Oscars. It was my career. Somewhere underneath all this grief I still cared about my career, didn't I?

I rubbed my temples. It didn't matter that this was terrible timing, that it sucked. This was what I'd signed up for when I decided to be an actor. Terrible hours were part of the deal, I'd always known that.

And really, how could I possibly complain about my job? I wasn't working the night shift at a twenty-four-hour diner, like my mother had after my dad had left, living off tips and a truly abysmal hourly wage. If she'd had a miscarriage, I doubt she would've been able to go to the emergency room. She hadn't had health insurance or savings. And there was no one around to watch me, no one to cover her shift at the diner.

My life couldn't be more different from that. I had the job of my dreams, and the people I worked with were understanding. If I wanted to take time off, it wouldn't be that big of a deal. That wasn't a luxury everyone—or even *most*—in this situation were afforded. I needed to stop feeling sorry for myself and handle things.

Taking a deep breath, I called Emily. As the phone rang, I thought again of what Talia had said about her career, how I might even be her last client. What I was about to do could seriously screw things up for her. The people pleaser in me even considered hanging up right then, sucking it up, and doing my job, for her sake. But I needed time, there was no way around that. I couldn't put my mental and emotional health at risk for her. I just had to hope she would understand.

When Emily answered the phone, she seemed like she was in an amazing mood. "Anna, hi! How *are* you?"

I hesitated for a second, taken aback. Emily didn't sound like someone who'd just been given a huge slap on the wrist. Maybe Keagan had gotten things wrong.

"Listen, Emily. I'm calling because..." I hesitated. *Spit it out.* "I, uh, needed to tell you that I had a...a medical thing. A miscarriage. A few days ago."

"Oh my God," Emily breathed. Her cheery tone evaporated. "Anna, I can't tell you how sorry I am to hear that."

I felt my throat getting tighter, tears threatening, and I had to swallow a few times before I said anything. "That's...thank you. I appreciate you saying that."

"Is there anything I can do for you? Anything at all?"

"Yes," I said, relieved to be getting to the point of this call. "That's actually why I was calling. I need to take some time off. No press or interviews for a few days at least."

Emily hesitated for a fraction of a second. When she spoke again, her voice was a little stiffer than it had been before. "Anna, of course you should take some time off. Take as much as you need."

My stomach tightened with guilt. "I know the timing isn't great—"

"Don't worry about it. We'll make it work. You just get some rest, enjoy that beautiful private beach, and we'll talk again soon."

I thanked her and hung up, but I didn't put the phone down right away. The conversation had gone about as well as I could have expected and yet something she'd said was bothering me. I couldn't quite put my finger on what it was.

The beach, I realized a moment later. I'd never told Emily that Talia's house was on a private beach.

14

I FOUND TALIA'S HOUSE ON GOOGLE EARTH, ZOOMED IN ON
the image until the mottled green and blue unpixellated and turned
into satellite photographs. The detail was shocking. There was the
guest house and the tennis court, the pool, the twisting, white pebble
drive. The image spun on my laptop, a perfect miniature of Talia's
house in the summer, the private white sand beach stretching out
before it.

Emily had Talia's address. It's not completely weird that she
would look the property up on Google Earth. It's the kind of thing
I would've done not that long ago. I'd always been deeply curious
about other people's lives, and the internet made invading people's
privacy so easy. One glance at these photographs and it would've
been obvious to her that the house was on a private beach. Emily
probably just forgot that I wasn't the one who'd told her about it.
Nothing suspicious, nothing creepy.

And yet I felt vaguely ill as I zoomed in on the Google Earth image
of Talia's house, closer and closer, until I could practically see through
the massive windows overlooking the ocean. Even though I wasn't

there when these pictures were taken, even though there was no possible way anyone would be able to see me, I couldn't help the chill that shot straight down my back. I imagined Emily looking through these images, perhaps wondering if I took my coffee on the covered porch at the back of the house, if I walked over the little deck that led out to the beach. Wondering which bedroom was mine, which window. It felt like she was watching me, still.

———————

Kamal drove me into the city to visit Siobhan the next morning. Gracie had already gotten her transferred from Mount Sinai to her apartment in Williamsburg. She'd hired a nurse and had what seemed like an entire hospital's worth of medical equipment set up in her apartment. I had no idea how she'd gotten it all taken care of so quickly, but I was grateful that Siobhan looked comfortable, that she was home instead of in a sterile hospital room, nothing more than a door separating her from the people who might snap her picture and sell it to some online tabloid for a few bucks.

I sat by her bed for an hour, feeling powerless and angry as I stared down at her gaunt face, her flickering eyelids. She was leaning back against her pillow, head tilted so that I could see the birthmark just below her chin, a faint dark stain on her skin in roughly the shape of a hand. *My witch's mark*, she called it, when she gave interviews. I'd always been too embarrassed to tell her I knew that, that I'd read every interview she'd given long before we ever met in real life. Now, I never would.

"This is going to work out for you," I whispered, taking her hand. "I know it's hard to believe that now, but it will. I promise."

It was the same thing she'd told me the night of my miscarriage. I wondered if she felt just as helpless saying the words to me then as I do saying them to her now.

I swallowed, and added, "I'll do everything I can to make sure you're okay, Siobhan. I promise."

Gracie stopped me before I left. "Does this mean anything to you?" She asked, holding out a scrap of paper. The words *Call Olympia* were scrawled across the bottom, along with a hastily written phone number.

"I found it next to her cell phone," Gracie explained. "And I remember you said you spoke with her the night before she collapsed. Could it have been for you?"

"I think it is," I said, taking the paper. "Thank you." My request that Siobhan put me in touch with her friends at the birthing center seemed like it'd happened so long ago to another woman in another life. I felt deeply touched, realizing it might've been one of the last things she did.

―――――――

A storm blew in later that night, snow billowing thick over the roads, the sky low and heavy. I'd never been a religious person, but this storm had a biblical, end-of-the-world feel to it. The snow flurrying outside the windows reminded me of the fuzz you used to see on old TV sets when you didn't have cable, a solid wall of white. My only clue that the rest of the world still existed was the sound of the waves crashing into the beach a few yards away. It didn't even sound like water anymore; it sounded like thunder, like cannons firing. At one point,

Dex tried to open the front door, but the snow piled outside was so high he couldn't move it more than a few inches. After pushing for ten minutes or so, he gave up. The next morning, news anchors with toothpaste commercial smiles said things like "Snowmageddon" and urged people to stay home. As if we had a choice.

Even after the blizzard passed, Dex and I found we had little desire to leave the house. It was the coldest, darkest part of the winter, barely eight hours of sun a day, and it was dim, watery light, filtered through low-hanging clouds. We got our groceries delivered and loafed around in pajamas, brewing pot after pot of coffee and eating more of Talia's cookies for dinner because neither of us cared enough to make real food. Even Talia's massive house began to feel claustrophobic with snow piled up outside the windows and nowhere to go, the air inside cold and stale.

I could tell I was getting on Dex's nerves. He kept closing himself off in other parts of the house. He claimed he had to work, but I walked in on him once and he didn't even have his computer open; he was just screwing around on his phone, either playing some dumb game or texting, I couldn't tell. When he saw me, he set the phone down, fast, guilt on his face: a little boy caught messing around when he was supposed to be doing his homework.

I couldn't blame him. Dex and I loved each other, but neither of us were used to spending *this* much time together. Back in the city we had work and friends and business trips. It was strange for us to go even a full week without a night or two apart. But now we were just here. All the time.

Early one morning, Dex leaned into our bedroom while I was on the phone with my dad. "We're completely out of food," he said.

"Are you going to be okay if I run to the grocery store to pick some stuff up?"

I told my dad to hold on a second and glanced at the window. "Are the roads okay?"

"There's no snow for the next few hours. I think it'll be fine."

It hit me that he might be looking for an excuse to spend some time alone. "Of course," I told him. "Have fun."

"Say hi to your dad for me," Dex said, and ducked out of the room.

After I got off the phone, I decided I would take a shower. Anything to keep from obsessing about my baby, my body, my friend.

A mirror took up one entire wall of my bathroom, making it impossible to miss the reflection staring back at me: greasy hair already falling out of its topknot, blotchy, discolored skin, wrinkles crawling across my forehead and bunching at the corners of my eyes. I was the very picture of an over-the-hill actor. A woman past her prime. Staring at myself, I wished I could wind the clock back and back and back. Be twenty-six again. Do it all over.

My bottle of prenatal vitamins was still sitting on the counter next to my toothbrush. I used to take them at the same time every morning, right after brushing my teeth. Seeing them now made me want to break things. I opened the bottom drawer of the vanity and went to throw the pills inside, where I wouldn't have to look at them anymore—then paused.

Talia had stuck a framed photograph down here. It was of her and Dex and Dex's ex-wife, Adeline. They must've been out to dinner somewhere, because they were sitting at a candlelit table, the room behind them dark and unfocused. Talia was turning in her seat, waving at someone outside of the photograph, but Adeline and

Dex were facing each other, laughing, and Dex had his arm casually strewn over Adeline's shoulders. Possessive, happy. He was staring at Adeline with a look of utter adoration on his face. Like he couldn't believe how lucky he was.

I felt a sharp pain in my chest, right between my breasts. No wonder Talia had hidden this photograph. Dex and Adeline looked so beautiful here. I thought of what Dex had told me, *Addy made it clear that she wasn't interested in being pregnant.* Would that really have been enough to get him to leave her? They looked so in love.

I stared at the photograph, a lump forming in my throat. What would that mean for us if I couldn't get pregnant either? The thought caused an unexpected flare of anger. Adeline deserved more than that. So did I.

I shoved the photograph back into the bottom drawer and slammed it shut, so I wouldn't have to look at it anymore. Then I stood and splashed water onto my face, trying to get myself to calm down. Steam billowed around me, filling the small room, clouding the mirror. I forced myself to breathe deep. All I had to do was breathe.

A moment passed, and I started to relax. I was inventing this drama in my head after all. Dex had never indicated that he might leave me if I couldn't give him children. Never. And I didn't know for sure that the pregnancy thing was what broke him and Adeline up. It could've been just part of a much bigger problem that he didn't want to talk about with me. I was just obsessing because of what had happened.

I shook my head and stepped into the shower, gasping as the hot water scalded my body. I waited a moment for my skin to adjust, and then I lifted my face to the spray, letting it roll over my cheeks and shoulders and chest.

I ran my hands down my water-slick body, hesitating when my fingers found the soft mound of my belly. It seemed unfair that it was still there, this pouch, that it hadn't disappeared the moment I'd miscarried. I thought about what Dr. Crawford said, about there still being fetal tissue inside of me, about how I'd have to wait to see if I passed it naturally, or else have an operation to remove it. The thought filled me with dread.

Water beaded along the curves of my skin. I moved my fingers lower, to the space just below my belly button. There was a tightness there, a pressure that was almost like a muscle contracting. It felt strange when I pressed down on it. Not painful, but sort of tender, almost like—

A tremor moved through my belly, causing my hand to shift.

I swore out loud and yanked my hand away, nerves pricking up the back of my neck.

What the...?

Something had moved. Inside of me. It wasn't like what happened in the basement, that twitch. I wasn't drunk. My belly had *moved*, all on its own, like something alive. I felt it. I *saw* it.

No, not *it*. My baby. There was still tissue inside of me. That must've been what I'd felt, that tissue. I must've imagined that I saw it move, just like in the basement. God, what was wrong with me?

For a moment, all I was aware of was the roar of water in my ears, the pressure pounding into my back. It felt like the water had gone cold, and I realized, dimly, that it wasn't the water—it was me. I was practically shivering. I swallowed, unable to pull my eyes away from my belly.

I watched it expand as I breathed in, collapse as I breathed out.

Water trailed down my skin. I let my hands travel over the underside of my belly again, searching for that ball of pressure. When I didn't find it, I pressed my fingers into my belly, gently at first, and then harder, deeper, ignoring the dull pain that spread through my stomach. Nothing happened.

And then—

My body moved all on its own. It was surreal, like watching an animal swim underwater, the ripples it left across the surface of my skin the only sign that anything had been there at all. The flesh on my belly rose and fell without asking my permission as that knot of pressure crossed to the other side of my body. I felt something like motion sickness, a sudden wave of nausea sweeping through me, following the movement. It took my breath away. I had to lean against the cold, wet tile, shivering.

I was too stunned to breathe. And then, I *laughed*. The sound shocked me so much that I pressed both hands to my mouth. Tears were streaming down my cheeks, carving warm lines down my already wet skin.

Something was happening. Something had moved. I'd watched it move. That wasn't my imagination, and it wasn't hormones. It was something inside of me. In the space of a single second, I thought of night feedings and diaper changes and bedtime stories and trips to the zoo. I laughed again, louder this time.

She was still in there. It was the only explanation that made sense, the only thing that explained the movement in my belly, not just now but that night in the basement too. Whatever that woman had tried to do to me hadn't worked.

My baby was still alive.

JUDY MARSHALL, 1957

JUDY WAS HOLDING HER CUP MUCH TOO TIGHTLY. HER HANDS trembled, causing a bit of hot tea to slosh over the rim, scalding her hand. It burned like the dickens, but she couldn't figure out how to relax her grip. Her whole body felt tense. She felt like one big spring that someone had stretched far too tightly.

"You're...pregnant?" Her neighbor Maude repeated, shocked. And why shouldn't she be shocked? Judy was forty-two. Far too old to have a baby. It was indecent.

She hushed her and quickly glanced around. It was the first warm day of spring and Maude had wanted to sit outside at the little table and chairs she'd just bought for her front porch. It was the wrong place for this conversation, much too public. Anyone could wander by and hear what they were talking about, and then where would Judy be?

"Six weeks along, I think," Judy said, lowering her voice and hoping Maude would take the hint. "I haven't been to see the doctor, yet."

"Have you told Brian?"

Had she told Brian? It wasn't a funny question, and yet Judy found herself wanting to laugh. How could she have possibly told her husband? She'd hardly ever *saw* Brian.

Brian was a police officer with Cleveland's fifth precinct. His unit had been working the night rotation for the past few weeks, which meant he had to report to the station by 7 p.m. each night and didn't return home until after seven the next morning, at which point he went directly to bed and slept for nine hours. The only time the two of them were both awake and home at the same time was between four and six thirty, which happened to be when their four children were home from school. Between science projects and book reports, driving to soccer and cheerleading practice, and making sure the casserole was in the oven and four sets of teeth had been adequately brushed, Judy and Brian rarely had the time to say two words to each other. And it took a lot more than two words to say, "Honey, I'm pregnant again and I don't know what we're going do." Honestly, it was a miracle the two of them had found the time to make the baby in the first place.

"I suppose congratulations are in order," Maude said, sipping her tea.

"Are they?" Judith asked woodenly. She didn't feel much like celebrating. It was difficult enough providing for four children with Brian's schedule and a police officer's paycheck. Most days she felt like there wasn't enough of anything—time, money, space, *her*—to go around.

And now they were going to have another. Another mouth to feed, another body to dress. Another whole person who would need to be held and loved and provided for. It was too much.

"I don't know how I'm going to do it," Judith said, her eyes filling with tears. "I don't know what to do. God, Maude, I'm desperate—"

"Hush," Maude cut her off harshly. She glanced at the sidewalk. "Don't talk like that. Someone might hear you."

Judith swallowed, chastened. She swiped a hand over her face to dry the few tears that had spilled onto her cheeks. "You're right. I know."

"No, you don't know." Now Maude was looking at Judith with a peculiar intensity. "There are people who will take that baby away from you if you aren't careful what you say, Judith."

Judith didn't know what Maude could've meant by that. People who might take her baby away from her? She'd never heard of such a thing. It sounded like superstition. Like the boogeyman.

But that very night, while Brian was at work and after she'd put the kids to bed, she could swear she heard something in the attic. Something moving. Pacing even. She told herself an animal had gotten in, a squirrel maybe or a raccoon. But the noises she heard were much too loud to be a squirrel or a raccoon. They'd sounded more like footsteps. Like a man walking across the floor directly above her head.

The next morning, Judith met Brian at the door the moment he got home from his shift, and she marched him right up to the attic. She waited at the bottom of the stairs while he searched every inch of that dusty space.

But he didn't see anyone up there. He told her it was probably just the house settling.

Judith knew it wasn't the house settling. This was different. It was a person. Someone had snuck into her attic. She couldn't help thinking of what Maude had said to her.

There are people who will take that baby away from you.

She heard the footsteps in the attic again that night, and the night after. It sounded like a person walking in slow circles, over and over.

Finally, Judith couldn't take it anymore. She dug one of Brian's golf clubs out of the back of their closet and stood at the foot of the stairs in her nightgown. Trembling.

"I know you're up there!" she called. Her voice was small and quivering and not remotely intimidating. And why should it be? Who would be intimidated by a forty-year-old mother? She gripped the golf club tighter, holding it like a weapon. "Now tell me what you want!"

She didn't expect that to work. But a shadow appeared at the door to the attic.

Judith jerked backward so quickly she collided with the wall behind her, knocking one of her and Brian's wedding pictures to the ground. She heard breaking glass and knew the frame had shattered.

Oh God, she thought, not even daring to breathe. *Oh God what have I done?*

The stairs creaked as the figure walked toward her.

Judith tightened her grip on the golf club. She couldn't waste time being afraid. She had her children to think about. Her four perfect children, sleeping just feet away, not to mention the baby growing inside of her. She had to protect them from whoever this was. *Whatever* this was.

"What are you doing here?" she said. Her voice was low and shaking, betraying her. "What do you want?"

"Don't be afraid," the figure said. It was a woman, Judith realized, a very tall woman with broad shoulders and dark hair. Her voice was deep and gravelly.

"I'm here to help," the woman told her. "I heard that you were desperate."

Is "pregnancy brain" real? Many moms experience moments of forgetfulness starting in the second trimester.

15

I JERKED THE FAUCET OFF AND STOOD UNDER THE DRIPPING showerhead, trying to catch my breath. For a long moment, I didn't move, not even to grab a towel. I just stared at my belly, desperate to feel that movement again.

Water dripped lazily down the inside of the shower door. The ancient plumbing creaked and groaned behind the walls.

Finally, when nothing happened, I stepped onto the icy bathroom tile, fingers trembling as I knotted a towel around my chest. My phone sat on the counter, where I'd left it. I grabbed it and called Dex. No answer.

"Come on, Dex, answer your phone for once in your life," I murmured. I didn't know how to process this without talking to Dex. He was always the person I turned to when something bizarre happened. And this definitely fell into the "something bizarre" category. A doctor told me my baby was gone. I'd had an ultrasound and everything. But what I'd felt just now—that was real.

And it'd happened *twice*. Three times, really. It couldn't just be my imagination. Could it mean...? Was it possible that there'd been a mistake? That I hadn't miscarried after all? I wished there was some way to know for sure now. I wanted to peel back the skin on my stomach and see what was going on inside of me.

I didn't want to let myself hope—at least not any more than I was already—until I had more information. But I couldn't think of another explanation. Something inside of me was moving. That meant something was alive.

I called Dex again. He still didn't answer, but I couldn't wait any longer. I needed to talk to someone now.

I looked up the number to Southampton Hospital on my phone and dialed with trembling fingers. It seemed to take forever to get through the automated system, and another eternity for the receptionist to transfer me to the right department and page Dr. Crawford.

"Hello, Mrs. Harding," Dr. Crawford said when he finally came onto the phone. "How are you feeling?"

"It's Ms. Alcott, actually," I corrected him. I swallowed, suddenly nervous. It was one thing to hope privately for a miracle, and another to say the words out loud to a doctor. "I...I was actually calling because I had a question about the other night. My...miscarriage."

"Of course. What's on your mind?"

"I was wondering, uh, whether it's possible for something like that to be...to be misdiagnosed? Like, could there have been a mistake?" When Dr. Crawford didn't answer right away, I rushed on before I could lose my nerve, "Because I felt something just now, in the shower. It was like a little kick, and I thought... Well, that's weird, isn't it?"

There was a pause, and then Dr. Crawford said, "It's not that weird, no. Pregnancy hormones often remain in the blood for a few months and many women claim to experience nausea or breast tenderness—"

"This wasn't nausea."

Another pause. "Right. You said you felt physical symptoms, yes? Fetal movement?"

"Yes. Fetal movement—that's exactly what I felt."

"And this just started?"

"No, I actually first felt something a few nights ago." The hope inside me flared brighter. I could feel my heart beating steadily in my throat, making it impossible to breathe. "Is there any chance at all that I could still be pregnant?"

A gaping silence opened up on the other end of the line. I crushed the phone to my ear, waiting for the words that could change everything.

Please. Please let there have been some mistake.

Finally, Dr. Crawford cleared his throat. "Ms. Alcott..." he said in a somber tone of voice. That was all I needed to hear. I knew what he was going to say before he could utter another word. Disappointment cracked me open. *No*, I thought, squeezing my eyes shut. *No, he's not listening; he doesn't believe me.*

"I *felt* movement," I said, more urgently this time. "Just now. I know I did. You have to believe me."

"It's okay; of course I believe you." Dr. Crawford sighed and there was a brief pause, a sound like maybe he was writing something down. After a long moment, he said, "Have you ever heard the term *pseudocyesis*?"

Throughout my IVF journey, I'd tried to learn all the unfamiliar medical terms so I could follow along with conversations like this one. I'd written most of them down in the Notes app on my phone, but of course, I didn't have my real phone right now. I took a moment to try to recall the jargon Dr. Hill had thrown around over the last few months, but *pseudocyesis* didn't register. "No," I admitted. "What is it?"

"It's a condition that can affect women in your situation."

"You mean people who've been through IVF?" I said pointedly.

"Yes, as well as women who've experienced pregnancy loss. I'm afraid it's not uncommon to continue having symptoms even after the fetus has expired. In your case I believe this is manifesting as physical movement."

I went still, momentarily unable to speak. "Are you saying...you think I'm imagining this?"

"Now, Ms. Alcott, I never said you were imagining anything. I think these symptoms are very real...to you. Grief can be very powerful after an experience like yours. I think it's important that we start treatment right away. Are you currently working with someone? If not, I might be able to—"

"It sounds like you're saying I'm having a hysterical pregnancy," I said, cutting him off.

There was a brief, tense silence. Dr. Crawford inhaled audibly. "I never said *hysterical*," he said in the low, even voice of someone trying to soothe a screaming child. "What I was going to say before you got so upset is that I'd be happy to help you find a psychotherapist. If you decide to pursue the pseudocyesis diagnosis once you calm down, please let me know."

I had tears in my eyes when I hung up, feeling embarrassed and disappointed, those words still circling my head. *I think these symptoms are very real...to you.*

Once, a few years ago, I got sick with a cold. The cold cleared up after a few days, but for weeks after, I had a lingering cough that I just couldn't kick. It had felt like there was something dripping down the back of my throat. I went to a doctor to see whether I'd developed an infection, but he took one look at me and said he didn't think there was anything causing the cough, and that I should just "try not coughing" for a while. I'd left his office feeling silly, like I'd been over-reacting, like the cough was all in my head.

I felt like that again now, times about a million. But Dr. Crawford didn't actually know what was happening inside of my body. He might diagnose miscarriages every single day, but unless he'd carried a life for months only to have it die, he couldn't possibly know whether what I was feeling was real or not.

I needed a second opinion. I'd spoken to Dr. Hill briefly, the morning after my miscarriage, and I dialed her number again now.

Cora answered right away. "Anna, hi, how *are* you?"

I winced at the tone of her voice. *Pity.* So she knew what had happened. "I was hoping to speak to Dr. Hill," I told her. "Could you transfer me?"

"Of course. Let me see if she's available."

Dr. Hill was slightly more encouraging than Dr. Crawford had been, but she stopped short of actually telling me there was any chance of a misdiagnosis. "Of course, we can take a look," she said. "I'll be more than happy to schedule a follow-up ultrasound for next week so we can see how things are progressing."

Next week? "Why would we wait that long? Can't we do one now?"

"It takes time to see how these things are going to evolve, I'm afraid. If I had you in now, the scans would look just like the ones you got in the ER, and that wouldn't be very helpful to either of us, would it, dear?"

I had to admit that was true. "But...how am I supposed to get through the next week?"

"Just try to take it easy," she said. "If you were my daughter, I'd tell you that the *best* thing you could do for yourself would be to try and put it out of your mind. Take a bath, make sure you're getting plenty of rest, eat lots of fruits and vegetables."

"Fruits and vegetables?" I repeated, aching a little. I wanted to ask if she was joking, only it was clear she wasn't. "Is that all?"

"Food is medicine," Dr. Hill continued. "You'd be amazed at what a healthy diet can do for you. If the discomfort gets to be too much, you're welcome to take an aspirin, but I wouldn't recommend anything stronger, just in case you decide to do another round of IVF. It's important to keep your body in tip-top shape."

The words felt like a tiny barb, like she was hinting that maybe I hadn't done as much as I could have before, that maybe I was the reason my pregnancy had failed.

"I know that," I said. I could hear the annoyance in my voice, but I didn't have enough control to tamp it down. "I've been keeping my body in tip-top shape for years. You might recall that I've been doing this for a while now."

"Of course, dear. I'm just trying to help."

After I hung up, I couldn't bring myself to get off the bathroom floor. A fresh tide of grief had washed over me, leaving my body so heavy that I could barely move.

The windows in the master bath stretched from the floor to the ceiling, perfectly framing the beach and ocean outside. A thick layer of snow stretched across the sand, the surface untouched except for where the frothy waves crashed into it, revealing a thin strip of brown. Everything else was either steel gray or so white it hurt to look at directly. Even the tall grass that grew up along the edge of the beach was tipped with frost. Cold air roared up against the window, rattling the glass.

I watched the ocean stretch across the sand and then curl back into itself. Stretch and curl, stretch and curl. After a while, snow began to fall, great flakes of it that stuck to the glass before melting into watery streams. If I squinted, I could see past the window to where the flurries drifted onto the water's surface and floated for a moment before melting into ocean.

It's quite common to experience symptoms, I thought. I rolled onto my side on the cold tile, my body curled around my belly. The belly with nothing in it after all.

———

Eventually, I peeled myself off the floor and called Dex again. He answered this time, and I told him what happened, what I'd felt, what Dr. Hill said about it being all in my head.

"God, Anna," he said once I'd finished. "That sounds awful. Are you okay?"

I swallowed and, before I could answer, he rushed on. "Of course, you're not okay. Forget I asked that. I'm still at the store. Do you want me to get you anything? Ice cream or, I don't know, pizza? Something comforting?"

It felt like he'd been gone forever, but I supposed it was only around thirty minutes or so. "I think I'm too nauseous to eat."

"Literally, name anything in the known universe and I will find a way to get it for you. You want the crown jewels? A slain bison?"

I looked down at my belly. I wanted to say, *Get me a heartbeat.*

———

It was still early after I got off the phone with Dex, just past eight. The house was bright and cold and silent. The smell of winter air seeped in through the cracks, and clear silvery light bounced off the snow, turning the windows into spotlights. I wanted to pull all the curtains closed, crawl back into bed, and pretend it was night. Instead, I crept down the stairs. I considered calling Georgia or Kyle or my dad, just to fill my head with something other than my own voice, but I couldn't imagine trying to make conversation with anyone right now.

Dex had left a Post-it for me on the kitchen counter:

I love you! Try to eat something!

He'd taken the remaining fruit out of Emily's promo basket and arranged two clementine eyes and a banana smile on the counter around my coffee mug, forming a kind of lopsided face. It was like he and Dr. Hill were in on this together. *Eat lots of fruits and vegetables! Get plenty of rest!*

The only thing I could remember eating over the last few days were the cookies I'd gotten from Talia. I considered the banana for a moment, then unpeeled it and took a few bites. As soon as I swallowed, my insides began to roil, twisting and churning and tightening. I had just enough time to throw the trash can open and lurch forward before it all came up: not just the banana but the cookies and the few sips of coffee I'd managed to choke down that morning too. It all gushed out of me, stringy and foul-tasting, splattering over the garbage.

I wiped my mouth with the back of my hand and stood up straight, blinking. In the last five years I'd never thrown up, not even during my first trimester of pregnancy, when nausea was expected. I felt another stubborn flare of hope—*what if*—followed immediately by the memory of what my doctors had said on the phone: *Pregnancy hormones often remain in the blood for a few months... Many women claim to experience nausea... Let's schedule a follow-up ultrasound for next week...*

The thing that really sucked about hope was how good it felt, like a cold drink of water on a hot day. After it was gone, everything was hard and sharp and cold. I didn't know how I was supposed to keep going. Every plan I'd made for the day seemed pointless now. All I wanted was to feel that hope again. I wanted it like an addict wanted heroin.

I took out my phone, intending to set a reminder in my calendar to follow up with Dr. Hill next week, just in case. I was using the burner phone Kamal had gotten for me, so I had to download my calendar app and log in again. As soon as it loaded, I froze, my eyes snagging on the appointment I made after finding the doll on the beach.

WHY ARE YOU DOING THIS TO ME?

? I'd written. A question for the woman screwing with me, a little bait to drag her out from wherever she'd been hiding.

It'd worked. Below, in the description, she'd responded:

I want to warn you.

They did something to your baby.

16

THEY DID SOMETHING TO YOUR BABY.

I closed my eyes, suddenly queasy with horror. There it was, written out in black and white. *They did something.*

They, not she. This wasn't just one person; it was two. At least two. And they'd done something to my baby. I wasn't being paranoid. This wasn't just grief. Someone outside of my own head had confirmed it. I pictured the woman in the hospital, her dark hair, her red lips. I imagined her following me, slipping something into my drink.

Had she written this? Maybe she'd been hired by someone to mess with me, and now she felt guilty and wanted to warn me. Or was the person who'd written this someone else, a third party who'd seen what she'd done—what *they'd* done?

I tried to remember every single thing I'd put in my mouth over the last few days. A muffin from Starbucks. A cup of chamomile tea from the pitcher at the yoga studio. And—oh God—there was all the fruit and chocolate from the last publicity basket Emily sent me. So many opportunities for someone to slip me a pill, drug me. And I never would've known.

I looked back down at my phone again, my heart beating in my ears. I had to write something back. I started to type, fingers jabbing every letter into the screen. Who are you? How do you know this? Who did you see? What did they do?

And then I paused, nerves crawling up the back of my neck. I had no way of knowing how long this person would talk to me, how many chances I was going to get to ask her what I needed to know. I couldn't leave my password unchanged forever. If she had access to my calendar, then she had access to my email account and my Google Drive, too. I needed to get whatever information I could get from her quickly.

I deleted everything I'd typed and wrote: Did someone kill my baby?

The stranger answered instantly, like she'd been waiting for this question all along:

Are you sure it's dead?

———————

She stopped writing after that. I refreshed the app again and again, but my calendar remained stubbornly blank though I typed a dozen new questions into the appointment: Who are you? What do you mean are you sure it's dead? Do you know something you're not telling me? She didn't take the bait. She'd apparently told me all she'd come here to say, and now I needed to figure out what to do with it, whether to trust it.

I tried to fill my water glass, but I was shaking so badly I couldn't work the faucet. I closed my eyes, bracing one hand against the kitchen counter.

Just breathe, I thought and inhaled through my nose.

I wanted to believe the message meant something, that whoever was writing didn't think my baby was dead either. But even if that is what they meant, how could I trust them? Dr. Crawford made it clear that there was no chance I hadn't miscarried. And the person who'd been sending these messages and messing with my calendar, could also be the one leaving me dolls and crawling into bed with me. I couldn't trust her. Not until I knew more.

But..."Meg" had been at the ER the night those labs were taken. Everything had been so hectic, so confusing. And now, I was feeling movement. Was it really such a stretch to think there could've been some mistake?

Maybe Meg had been hired to do something to my tests. For days I'd been thinking she slipped me a pill to cause my miscarriage, but what if she'd done something much simpler: switched out my labs so that it looked like I'd miscarried even though I hadn't, changed the results on my tests, messed with the ultrasound machine.

I gulped down one eight-ounce glass and then another, drinking until my belly felt like it might burst. I was suddenly very aware of the stink coming off the garbage: old milk and coffee grounds and chicken bones with the meat still attached. For a tilting moment, I thought I might hurl.

Dr. Crawford wasn't able to find a heartbeat. That was the part I still couldn't explain. If this mystery person was right, and my baby wasn't actually dead, *someone* would've been able to find his heartbeat. You couldn't sabotage a stethoscope. Could you?

There was an easy way to find out. I could buy a fetal heart rate monitor online, but there was no way I was waiting twenty-four hours for one to be delivered. I wanted to know *now* whether there was any chance that the baby inside of me was still alive. I wanted to know this second.

They sold fetal heart rate monitors at the CVS in town—I'd seen them on the shelf before. If I left now, I could settle this in about fifteen minutes.

I texted Kamal to bring the car around. And then, still pulling on my coat, I made my way out the back door and around to the side of the house. The morning was flat and gray, the cloud cover low enough that it almost felt warm. The snow from earlier had made the ground slushy, fresh snow and old snow and mud all melting together into a kind of soup. It got into my shoes and soaked through my socks, the icy sludge touching bare skin as I hurried over to the driveway, shivering.

I was watching for the Range Rover when something made me pause. The air out here smelled strange. Not like chimney smoke and pine needles like it had for the last few weeks, but like someone had been cooking over an open grill, that heavy richness of meat and fire. It smelled good.

My stomach rumbled. I actually felt hungry.

I could see the empty pool from where I stood. The cover had blown off, and I saw that snow had spilled onto the floor and piled up against the sides. Some animal had made its way around the perimeter, leaving a trail of tiny prints I didn't recognize. A fox, maybe.

Beside the pool was the hot tub and a few stacked deck chairs, all carefully tucked beneath expensive covers. Or, at least, I assumed there were covers—there was so much snow packed around and on top of them that I couldn't tell for sure. Beyond was the wide expanse of Talia's backyard, bordered in lush, hundred-year-old pine trees. The wind off the ocean had scoured the yard bare of snow, and I could see dead grass and crusty earth, everything frosted in ice and glittering.

It was a moment before I realized I was fisting my hands so tightly that my fingernails were digging into my palms. That meat smell was intoxicating. It was the first time in days that anything had smelled remotely appetizing. Was one of the neighbors grilling? I'd assumed all the other houses on our street were empty.

I drifted to the edge of the pool, following that scent. Frozen grass crunched beneath my shoes, and I tasted snow on my lips, felt it starting to flurry through the air around me. Wind blew somewhere in the trees, rattling the branches. They were so icy that the sound they made when they knocked together was solid and sharp, the sound of cracking bones and breaking glass. Wind blew overhead, a thin wail.

I stopped when I reached the pool's edge, shivering now. The smell was stronger here. Sizzling steak, juicy burgers. It filled my nostrils, leaving me dizzy and hollow and so hungry I could faint. I swayed slightly and then imagined tumbling over the side of the pool, my skull cracking as it smacked against the concrete. I swore and grabbed for the guardrail. The metal was iced over and so dry with cold that it immediately stuck to the sweat on my palms. I took a few deep breaths until I felt steady again. Then, very cautiously, I looked over the side.

There was a raccoon curled on the bottom of the pool, his eyes glassy and unfocused, fur frosted with ice.

I jerked back, fear shooting up my chest. The first thought I had was that the raccoon was sick, rabies maybe, that he was going to leap up at me, bite me. I could practically feel his claws digging into my skin. It sent tremors of fear through my body, so bad that I had to grip the guardrail with both hands to keep from losing my balance. I gulped down a few quick inhales, the icy air burning through my lungs.

A minute passed, and the raccoon didn't come at me, didn't seem to move at all, at least not that I could hear. The only sound was the distant ocean, my own raspy exhales. My breath hung in the air before me in tiny clouds.

After a moment, I found my courage and peered into the pool again.

On second glance, the raccoon was clearly dead. Its claws were worn down to bloody nubs, and I could see shallow marks it'd left on the side of the pool when it'd tried to climb out. I cringed, picturing that poor animal digging at the wall, the desperation it must've felt when it realized it couldn't get out, the increasing fear as the cold set in.

I clenched my eyes shut and forced myself to breathe through my mouth so I wouldn't smell him. But that intoxicating scent made its way into my mouth and down my throat. My stomach rumbled.

———

Kamal didn't think I should be going out in public, but there was no way I was giving up. I found a black beanie in Talia's closet, along with an oversized pair of sunglasses: a makeshift disguise. Reluctantly, he agreed.

I hunched in the back seat as we drove, replaying what had just happened by the pool. I felt disgusted with myself, disturbed. I'd *craved* that dead raccoon. I'd wanted to...

Not *eat* it. No. I would never.

Would I?

Nervous energy rocketed through me, making it impossible to sit still. I kept tapping my foot, jiggling my leg, until Kamal shot me a concerned glance in the rearview mirror, and I forced myself to stop.

There had to be a logical explanation for what had just happened. Something to do with my hormones, maybe. Maybe I'd wanted to eat something *like* the raccoon, something wild and gamey, like rabbit or lamb. Didn't pregnant women often crave strange things? I was pretty sure I'd read somewhere that craving meat was a sign of an iron deficiency, that it was normal. And a dead raccoon, while completely disgusting, was really just raw meat. I didn't normally eat meat, and we didn't have any in the house, so that raccoon would have been the only meat I'd smelled all morning.

Maybe this was another sign, another clue that I was still pregnant. I inhaled and exhaled deep, trying to get the smell of that animal out of my nose. Maybe it was a good thing?

It was already ten, but the CVS had just opened when we pulled up, and there was only one other woman inside, a clerk who looked like she was in her late fifties with steel gray hair. *Patricia*, her name tag read.

"Can I help you?" she asked.

"Yes, you can." It occurred to me that I should've called to ask if they still had a fetal heart rate monitor in stock, but I'd been so focused on getting here, on looking for myself that I hadn't even considered it. "I'm just looking for a...a fetal heart rate monitor."

I blushed as I said the words, feeling pathetic. But Patricia smiled kindly and said, "I know exactly how you feel, dear. I could never wait for my next ultrasound either."

All the air went out of me with a soft *oh*. She thought I was pregnant. Of course, she thought I was pregnant, I'd just asked her for a fetal heart rate monitor.

"How far along are you?" she asked.

I hesitated. I felt raw, vulnerable. Even with the hat and the sunglasses, she might recognize me. She could pull out her phone and tweet about where she saw me and what I'd told her the second I left the store. But I couldn't figure out how to get out of this conversation without saying something.

"Sixteen weeks," I murmured, adjusting my glasses. It was how far along I would've been.

"Second trimester. That's so exciting." Patricia smiled wider. The soft lighting in the store left her features unfocused, like a watercolor, the paints all blurring together.

"Exciting," I repeated. I felt a nervous twitch at the corner of my lips. "It is exciting, yes, but I'm trying to keep it quiet, so could I ask—?"

"I won't say a word, dear," Patricia said, nodding knowingly.

"Okay. Thanks." I needed to get out of the store and back to the car before I started crying. "I'm sorry, do you have the heart rate monitor?"

"I'm afraid we don't have any in stock at the moment, no, but I know we have them online. I could order one for you if you like?"

"No, that's okay," I said, thinking Kamal had been right; I should've just gotten it off Amazon. I felt embarrassed for wasting everyone's time, angry with myself for taking such a risk and having nothing to show for it. "Thank you."

"I'm sorry. I know this is considered rude now, but would you mind if I..." She didn't even wait for me to answer; she just reached for me, pressing both hands to my belly.

"Ma'am," Kamal said, from behind us. "I'm going to need to ask you to take a step back."

The woman looked startled, but her hands stayed on my belly a second longer, long enough that I could feel the cold of her skin through my thin cotton T-shirt. My eyes went watery, and I was about to move away, tell this woman that I really should get going, when I felt a tumbling sensation deep inside me.

I froze. It was subtle enough that it could've just been nerves, my stomach twisting like it always did when I was in a situation that made me uncomfortable. If it hadn't been for that moment in the shower, I probably wouldn't have even noticed it.

Patricia's hands were still pressed to my belly.

"Ma'am," Kamal said again, his voice firmer. "Please—"

"Wait, it's okay," I said, holding up a hand to stop him. I'd spent all morning waiting for this to happen again, desperately *hoping* it would happen again.

The next time something inside of me rolled over, Patricia and I looked up at each other, smiling. Her eyes widened.

"He's a kicker!" she said, and I went breathless.

"You *felt* that?" I asked, my voice cracking.

"Oh yes," she said, her hands still cupping my belly. "Feels like he wants out of there already."

"She," I blurted before I could stop myself. "It's a girl." I closed my eyes, worried I might start crying and be unable to stop. I didn't need the monitor anymore. I imagined feet and elbows and knees sliding against the underside of my skin—my baby, still alive, turning over. She *had* to be, or else how had this woman felt it too?

"Feel that?" Patricia asked. When I opened my eyes again, I

noticed that she had the yellowing teeth of a smoker and the store's light just made them look darker. More grimace than smile. "It's like she's trying to kick her way out of you."

17

BACK IN THE RANGE ROVER, I CLOSED MY EYES, TEARS LEAK-
ing onto my cheeks.

She felt him. That woman from the drugstore *felt* my baby. That
had to mean something. And there were the other symptoms, the
meat craving, and the nausea. This couldn't all just be in my head.

My cell started buzzing. I opened my eyes and checked the screen:
EMILY.

I had no desire to talk to her right now, but if I kept ignoring her
calls, she was going to start freaking out. Taking a breath, I brought
the phone to my ear. "Listen, Emily, I'm sorry but I need to—"

"*Anna*," boomed Emily's voice from the other end of the phone.
Her normally very cool British-tinted voice was practically giddy.

"Anna, I'm here too." It was Naomi Richardson, my director from
The Auteur. "I'm just...I can't believe this is happening. This is all so
exciting. And of course, you deserve it, Anna; it's just unbelievable—"

I pressed a finger to the skin between my eyebrows, feeling a headache coming on. "Slow down, please—what are you talking about?
What's going on?"

They started talking over each other, Emily saying "Oh my God, do you really not know?" at the same time that Naomi gushed, "But you do know what *day* it is, right? Haven't you been watching Twitter?"

What day it is? I frowned, trying to count in my head. February the fourth and then fifth, and then—

Oh.

"The Oscars," I said, feeling numb. They were supposed to announce the nominees this morning. I'd completely forgotten.

"Yes! The Oscars!" Naomi started laughing. "You've been *nominated*, Anna. Academy Award for Best Actress!"

Their voices were overlapping, Emily congratulating me, Naomi filling me in on all the other categories *The Auteur* had been nominated for. I was unable to speak.

I'd dreamt of this moment. Not just in the months since I realized *The Auteur* had a shot at nominations, but my whole life. I used to practice my speech in the shower when I was twelve, clutching a shampoo bottle as a makeshift Oscar statue, imagining how I'd try not to cry as I thanked my mother, who'd wanted to be an actor before she had me. This moment was the culmination of twenty years of hard work, a lifetime of dreams. I should've been crying, bursting with pride and happiness.

Instead, I was still thinking about how my baby had moved, how someone else had *felt* her move. How there was a chance.

I pressed a hand to my mouth, suddenly overwhelmed by the conflicting emotions rising inside of me. It felt dangerous to hope, but I couldn't help it. I needed answers. I needed to find that heartbeat. I couldn't think about my career until I did.

After a few minutes of *Congratulations!* Naomi said her goodbyes, and I heard a click that meant she'd hung up. I was about to hang up myself when Emily said, "Anna, I'm still here. I was hoping to touch base before I let you go."

"Right," I said, my mind still on the heart rate monitor. "What's up?"

"Well, I know we talked about you taking some time off, and I'm still more than happy to accommodate that in whatever way I can. But now that you've been officially nominated, I'd love to discuss which campaigning opportunities you'd be comfortable moving forward with."

"Oh, right." I cleared my throat. "I guess...I could try to do some interviews? I don't think I'm ready to travel yet, but—"

"Zooms and phone calls only for now, got it," Emily agreed immediately. "There was one other thing I wanted to run past you. I don't need an answer now, but I wanted to remind you that we were thinking of having you come to LA for a few weeks before the awards. The ceremony is scheduled for late March, so we wouldn't have to make any plans for a couple of weeks."

"Emily, I don't—"

"I wouldn't even bring it up now, not with..." She cleared her throat. "Not with everything else you have going on. But, Anna, this really is important. I've heard of campaigns being *made* by these last few weeks in LA. And winning the Oscar...well, I don't have to tell you that winning would change your entire career. It would change *both* of our careers forever. I know things are...hard right now, but maybe this could be a silver lining? Now you have a little more time to focus on awards season."

For a moment I was so stunned I couldn't speak. Did she really just tell me *Maybe this could be a silver lining?* What a thoughtless thing to say.

I pressed a hand to my mouth, feeling suddenly nauseous. The car had felt nice and warm after coming in from outside, but now it was stifling. It's not like I was getting over the flu. I'd had a *miscarriage*.

Sweat was gathering in my armpits and between my legs now. And I felt something rising in my throat, something solid.

"Anna?" Emily said hesitantly. I'd been quiet for too long. "Hey, I'm so sorry; I shouldn't have said anything. You don't need to be thinking about this right now. Anna?"

I couldn't answer her. A sour taste clung to the back of my mouth. Something was coming up, whether I wanted it to or not.

Morning sickness, I thought.

"Emily, I'm sorry...I—I've got to go. Sorry." I ended the call before she could argue with me and lurched forward, grabbing a water bottle from the console between the seats.

"Could you pull over, please?" I asked, my voice trembly as I took a deep swig.

Kamal frowned into the rearview mirror, but he didn't ask what was wrong, only nodded and pulled to the side of the street. I swished water around my mouth and opened my door to spit it out. My gums felt strangely tender, almost painful. I swallowed another mouthful of water and spit again. A pale pink froth of bubbles gathered thickly on the snow.

I grimaced.

A sharp *crack* split the air above me, the sound of something slamming into the car window.

Kamal said something I didn't hear. I was in my head, panicking. *A rock*. I thought, my throat shrinking. *She found me, she threw something—*

But when I looked up, I saw that the window wasn't broken, just smudged with something dark and red. My heartbeat steadied. *Oh*. Understanding now, I looked back down at the ground.

A seagull lay in the snow, neck broken. Its wing twitched once, twice. And then went still.

Bad omen, I thought

———

Dex still hadn't returned from the store when I got back to the house. I glanced at the time on my phone: he'd already been gone for over two hours.

I couldn't just sit around waiting for him. I needed to do something. I wanted to be outside, wind biting into my cheeks, blowing snow over my feet. The cold had always helped me think clearer.

I decided to take a walk down by the beach, Kamal trailing a few feet behind me. The gulls were out, again, flying in low circles directly above me. I tried to ignore them.

I couldn't stop thinking about that phone call, how Emily had sounded...off. And it wasn't just excitement over the nominations—there was something else too. Some emotion she'd been trying to hide.

Desperation. She *needed* me to win this Oscar. I thought of what Talia had told me, about how all her other clients had been reassigned to other publicists. Was she really in that much trouble at work? If she was, this whole situation was pretty convenient, wasn't it? She'd called my miscarriage a silver lining. And it was—for her. All of a sudden, I was free to take this trip, a trip that she said herself could make her career. But only because I wasn't pregnant anymore.

I stopped walking and looked down at the snowy sand, thinking about the doll I found on the beach. A doll I knew Emily had access to.

Emily had access to my calendar too, I realized. I gave her my password so she could add events when she needed to. I'd totally forgotten about that. She could've been messing with my appointments all along, keeping me from getting pregnant so I could campaign for her.

And there were the threats, the stalking—wasn't all of it more reason for me to run off to LA? Right where Emily wanted me.

I shivered and tried my best to push the suspicions to the back of my mind. Why would Emily mess with me and then warn me about it with ominous messages on my calendar? It didn't make sense. And Emily obviously wasn't the woman who'd climbed into bed with me—I would have recognized her. And she wasn't *Meg*, the ultrasound tech with the red lipstick, either.

Then again, said a nagging voice in the back of my head, Emily worked with plenty of actors in New York. Desperate actors. How hard would it have been for her to hire one of them, tell them she'd work a little harder to break them out if only they'd do this one thing for her?

That flare of suspicion burned a little brighter, and I had to remind myself that I didn't actually *know* anything, and that hiring an actor to follow a client was a seriously messed up thing to do.

I shook my head, pushing the paranoid thoughts away. As much as I wanted to figure out who was stalking me, I had more pressing things to deal with right now. I called Dr. Hill back and told her I wanted another ultrasound as soon as possible. I even offered to drive out to Manhattan if necessary. She was hesitant, but she agreed to take a look if it would set my mind at ease. She even offered to come to me, telling me I should stay off the icy roads if I could help it. I hesitated, because the idea of giving one more person my address—even someone I trusted—made me incredibly nervous. But, in the end, I relented. I needed clarity, one way or another.

After I hung up, I called Gracie, wandering a little farther up the beach casting anxious glances up at the gulls as I walked. Siobhan was the same, Gracie told me, no change. I thanked her for the update, my heart feeling heavy. I'd been desperately hoping she'd made a miraculous turn, that she'd woken up. She was the only person I wanted to talk to right now, the person I knew would believe me about everything I'd felt. I imagined the conversation we might've had about what Dr. Crawford had said to me, how furious Siobhan would've been on my behalf.

Tears pricked my eyes, and I wiped them away angrily, feeling selfish. I wanted Siobhan to get better for her. Not because I needed her. I thought of the phone number she'd left for me. I'd tucked it in the top drawer of my bedside table back at the house. Maybe I would dig it out when I got back, give Olympia from the birthing center a call. If my doctors weren't going to believe me about what I felt, maybe it was time to talk to a midwife.

When I looked up again, I spotted a woman farther down the beach.

I stopped walking, my heartbeat increasing. The woman seemed to be looking at me. As I watched, she lifted her hand, a half wave. Was she waving at me? I looked around. Aside from Kamal, I was the only one here. I'm pretty sure she was waving at me.

She took a slow step me toward me, stumbling like a drunk. A shot of fear went through me. It was probably because her foot had sunk into the sand, but it reminded me of old monster movies, a zombie lurching down darkened halls. It looked inhuman. Somewhere in the distance, a seagull cried, making me jump.

Kamal was suddenly behind me. In an instant, he'd angled his body between mine and the woman's, nodding to indicate that we should head back to the house.

"It's probably just a neighbor," he said. But he kept one hand on my back, and I noticed that he checked over his shoulder several times as we trudged back through the sand. As though to make sure she wasn't following us.

I walked faster, fear throbbing in the base of my spine. I didn't turn around again, but I swear I could feel her staggering after me.

———————

Dex was alone in the kitchen by the time I got back, vegetables, ice cubes, and containers of protein powder cluttering every inch of the counter in front of him: the makings of one of his protein smoothies. A massive bouquet of roses sat in the middle of the mess.

Dex looked up when I came in. "Hey, I was wondering where you went."

I saw the roses, but I had too much going on in my head to immediately acknowledge them. I glanced out the window to see whether the woman from the beach was still outside. I froze, sure I saw movement in the yard next door, a shadow moving behind a tree, something. But a moment passed and then another, and no one appeared.

I glanced back at Dex. "Do you know whether the people who live next door are in town?"

"No, hon, Talia owns the place next door."

What? "Talia owns this house *and* the one next door?"

"I know I told you about this. She wanted to update the tennis courts out back, but in order to get the permits, she needed an extra foot of property on the east side. The house next door was up for sale, and I guess she figured it'd be easier to buy it than to cross her fingers that the new owner would be willing to give up part of their property. I think she rents it out in the summer."

I frowned at him. *Had* he told me about this? I didn't think so. It was weird enough that I would've remembered. Talia wanted a new tennis court so she just up and bought the place next door? This is the Hamptons. Even if the next-door property wasn't quite as lavish as this one, I'd guess it was still a multimillion-dollar investment. And if Talia owned both properties, why would she have insisted we stay here instead of in her rental?

I was still thinking about this when, in a different tone of voice, Dex said, "Isn't there something you want to tell me, babe?"

The abrupt change of tone shook me. I pushed thoughts of Talia out of my head, thinking *How did he know*?

Had Dr. Hill called him after we'd spoken and told him what I'd said? I didn't think that was legal, doctor-patient confidentiality and all. Or did that not cover phone calls to make appointments?

I put a hand on my belly, realizing that it didn't really matter *how* Dex had found out. I'd been planning on telling him right away.

I looked out the window one last time to make sure there was no one there. There wasn't. I exhaled, relaxing a bit as I turned back to

Dex, my brain already shifting to the baby, the possibility that there *was* still a baby.

I tried out a shaky smile. "Well, actually..."

But Dex was getting something from the fridge, and he didn't seem to be listening. I faltered. I couldn't say this while his back was turned. I needed to be able to look into his eyes.

It seemed to take him forever to find what he was looking for in the fridge. I pressed my lips together, waiting. I was too aware of the way my clothes pressed into my skin, the sweat clinging to the back of my neck. Time crawled.

"If you're not going to tell me, I'll have to do this myself." Dex finally closed the door and turned around. He held up a bottle of champagne.

I frowned. What? How did he...?

And then he said, "Congratulations *Oscar* nominee!" and I blinked, understanding settling over me. Of course. This wasn't about the baby at all.

"Anna...this is huge." Dex was already fumbling with the champagne cork. "And you've worked so hard. You deserve it."

I made myself smile. This didn't feel real. It was like being on a movie set, like I was playing a character, *Anna the actor* instead of *Anna the expecting mother*. It took every acting trick I knew to shift my brain off the baby for long enough to react the way I knew I was supposed to, the way Dex wanted me to.

Then Dex popped the cork, and I jumped, my concentration breaking. I couldn't do this. I couldn't pretend right now. He pulled a crystal flute down from the cupboard. "I know it's early, but I think we should have one—"

"I–I don't think I can, actually," I said.

Dex finished pouring, champagne bubbles spilling over the side of the flute. He looked up at me, surprised. "Really?"

"Something happened... I was just about to tell you. That thing I felt earlier...the movement? Well, it happened again, at the drugstore. Only, this time, someone else felt it too."

I was holding my breath, waiting for how he would respond. Every muscle in my body felt tense.

Dex put the bottle down, frowning into the pool of champagne that'd gathered around the flute. He seemed to consider his words carefully before saying, "But it's normal to keep feeling symptoms, right? Dr. Crawford said you might feel nausea, and—"

"This wasn't nausea," I interrupted. "I felt something inside of me *moving*. It was like the baby was kicking."

"Anna..."

I cringed at the tone of his voice: *pity*. "You believe me, right?"

"I believe you." Despite what he just said, I could practically feel the doubt radiating off his skin. "I'm sure you felt *something*, Anna. I'm just saying I don't see how it could be our baby. Honey, our baby's gone."

I flinched. Tears pricked my eyes, but I blinked them back, angry with myself for explaining this so poorly. I sucked a breath in, trying again, "Listen, I know this sounds far-fetched, but I think someone made a mistake. She was there that night at the hospital, remember? She could've messed with my charts or something, and—" I'd been planning on telling him about the messages on my calendar but stopped myself, realizing at exactly that moment how strange it sounded, how desperate. I swallowed and said instead, "And, Dex, I could *see* the baby moving. It's happened like three or four times now. Someone else felt it too. A woman at the store."

Dex said, "And you're sure she felt something? She wasn't just telling you what she thought you wanted to hear?" His tone was a little cooler than it had been a minute ago. He was getting frustrated with me.

I forced myself to breathe, trying to get my heartbeat to steady. "I don't think there's any harm in checking."

"You don't think there's any harm? Really?" Dex sounded incredulous. "I can't go through another ultrasound like the one we had the night of your miscarriage, Anna. Waiting to hear the heartbeat like that..." He shook his head and said again, "I can't do it."

There was a brief, tense silence, neither of us knowing what to say. I wanted to point out that the ultrasound had been hard for me too. But if there was a chance there'd been some mistake, wasn't it worth it to at least check?

After a moment, Dex sighed. "Look, I don't want to fight. Come here."

I didn't want to be comforted but I let him pull me into his arms. I didn't want to fight either.

He kissed the top of my head. "We're both stressed. Let's just let it go."

I was quiet for a moment, staring down at the bump between us separating us. *It's gotten bigger*, I realized, moving away from my husband. I cupped the bump with both hands, feeling the heft of my body beneath my fingers. I'd gained weight over the last few days. I couldn't say exactly how much because I usually felt the extra pounds in my thighs and arms and this was all in my belly. But the ruching along the sides of my maternity shirt was straining against me. Only a few days ago, the little pouch of extra fabric hung loose around my waist.

"My bump is bigger," I said, looking up at Dex. "Why would it be bigger when I've barely even eaten anything?" My voice had gotten high and breathy, like it sometimes did when I was talking too fast, not giving myself time to think through everything that was going on in my head.

Dex heard it too. "Anna..."

I felt the movement inside of me again, the flutter of a body sliding beneath my belly, a soft thump somewhere deep inside of me.

I must've made a weird face because Dex touched my arm and said, "What is it? What's wrong?"

I pulled his hand toward my belly. "I need you to feel something."

Dex looked unsure. "I don't—"

"Just come *here*." I lifted my shirt and, suddenly, my belly was between us, a slight mound of taut white skin. Dex eyed it. I could see how badly he wanted to pull back, but then his gaze snapped up to mine, and his Adam's apple rose and fell beneath the skin of his throat as he swallowed, stopping himself.

I took his hand and pressed it to the soft curve of flesh just below my belly button. Dex didn't move—he didn't even seem to breathe. His hand was limp in my own.

Nothing happened.

After a moment, he said, "Anna..."

"Just *wait*."

Inside me, something twisted. It was subtle, subtle enough that Dex might not have felt it.

But he went still, his eyes widening. "What was that?"

"I *told* you." I moved his hand down a little and pressed it more firmly to the spot where I felt it. "Here. It's right here."

More movement, a tumbling, motion sickness–inducing motion that made me feel like I was on a roller coaster going up and down, up and down. My eyelids fluttered, and I grasped for the wall to steady myself.

Dex didn't seem to notice my discomfort. "Anna..." His voice was high-pitched, hopeful. "Anna, can you feel that?"

I swallowed. The inside of my mouth tasted sour. "I told you, it's been happening all morning. I think—"

Something inside of me flipped over. I felt a sharp jab to my bladder and gasped out loud.

Dex looked at me. "What's wrong?"

"It's nothing, just—" I inhaled, sharp.

"Anna? Listen, I'm really starting to get freaked out. Maybe I should call someone..."

A quick prod upward, followed by intense pressure to my ribs. A hitch of breath escaped me as the pressure sharpened into a pain so clean that every muscle inside of me clenched at the same time and refused to release.

The sensation stunned me so completely that I forgot to breathe. I pictured something inside of me snapping in half. That's what it felt like, like something breaking. *Bone?*

No, I thought, practically swooning with horror. Whatever was inside of me was thrashing, or at least that's what it felt like. I curled around myself, trying to hold my body together using my bare hands.

"Anna!"

My mouth fell open, but I couldn't answer. I tried to breathe, and it was like inhaling broken glass, so many sharp edges pricking my insides. My eyes felt wet. I couldn't see anything, just black stars and sudden bursts of light.

The pain was blinding.

"Anna? What's wrong? What's happening?"

"I...think..." I managed to choke out. Then, gasping, "I think the baby broke my rib."

18

WE TOOK DEX'S CAR TO THE HOSPITAL. I DIDN'T REMEMBER climbing inside or the treacherous drive over, the car's tires sliding over all that snow and ice. There was only that swift kick to my ribs, that all-encompassing pain, and then, as if the two moments had happened one right after the other, the screech of automatic doors sliding open, a blast of recycled air, and the sharp, antiseptic smell of cleaning products layered over the scents of sweat and sickness and dozens of bodies too close together.

Dread inched up my throat like bile. That smell, it was attached to some animal deep instinct inside of me. I felt every fear impulse inside my body switch on. I was a rabbit suddenly attuned to the scent of a predator. I wanted to run.

"No." I froze in the doorway, my knees locking. I couldn't go into this building again, not after she'd gotten to me so easily last time. And this baby, this...whatever was happening inside of me, I couldn't let that woman anywhere near her. Not again.

I felt Dex's hand on my back, that gentle pressure trying to coax me forward. "Come on, Anna," he said. The doors started to slide shut and he jerked an arm out, stopping them. "We need to see the doctor."

The muscles in my shoulders knotted up. "Please, I don't want to..."

"You're hurt. We have to—"

"I *can't.*"

Dex exhaled, hard. He must not have seen how scared I was because he said in a lower voice, "Anna, you have to go inside—we need someone to look at your ribs."

I closed my eyes for a moment, trying to steady myself. I felt very strange. Light-headed. My thoughts weren't totally making sense. I knew there was a reason I was supposed to be here—it wasn't just the pain in my ribs; it was something else. I needed to see the doctor to find out what was going on inside of my body. Being at the hospital, it was a good thing, like Dex said. Everything was going to be okay.

But, when I blinked, I saw the woman with the red lipstick smeared across her teeth and the dirty tile in the bathroom and the blood running down my legs. Even after I opened my eyes again, those images were still there, burned into the back of my brain like I'd been branded with them. My doctors never knew what was going on inside my body. And I hated this place. Actually *hated* it, in a way that felt more physical than emotional.

I heard phones ringing in the distance and the mechanical sound of someone speaking over an intercom, but everything faded in and out, like someone messing with a dial on a radio.

A nurse was suddenly standing in front of me. "...feeling okay... pale..."

I stared at her, trying to pull the rest of her question out of the fog of my head. I didn't realize I was tilting backwards until I felt the hands pressed into my back, holding me up. There were more voices around me, muffled and distant. They didn't seem real.

Dex was shouting, "Somebody help! Somebody...please, we need some help over here!"

The nurse was hovering over me again. "She's dehydrated...need to get her hooked up to an IV right away—"

And then, as suddenly as if someone switched the radio off, there was nothing.

———

I woke with the sound of screaming still echoing in my head. My eyes were closed, but I could tell that I was lying on something. There was a stiff, cool pressure beneath me, and the faint weight of a blanket draped over my body. Behind me, the sound of steadily beeping machines. I inhaled, and my nose filled with the smell of lemony chemicals.

The hospital.

I bolted upright, feeling a shot of pain through my ribs. I didn't care. I needed to get out of here. Light burst across my retinas as I forced my eyes open, but the brightness was overwhelming, pain shooting straight through my skull, and I had to blink a few times before everything adjusted and I could see again.

"Anna?" Dex leaned over me, one hand pressed to my shoulder to keep me from getting out of the bed. I noticed his eyes were hooded, and there was a sallow gray cast to his skin. He looked so worried. I could see it in the lines around his mouth, the way he kept chewing on his lip.

Why was he worried? What happened this time? What did they find?

"Can you hear me?" he asked. "I need you to stay still, okay?"

"Why?" My throat was scratchy. There were guardrails on either side of my bed, and I realized that I couldn't actually go anywhere because there were tubes snaking into the blue veins at the crooks of my elbows, holding me in place.

I grabbed one, intending to pull it out of my arm, when my eyes fell on the ultrasound monitor set up next to my bed. I froze. "Did you do an ultrasound?"

"Anna, you need to calm down," Dex was saying.

"Is the baby okay? Did you see her?"

"The doctor's here." Dex shifted to the side, and that's when I noticed that we weren't alone. But it wasn't Dr. Crawford like last time—it was Dr. Hill. She'd already gotten in from the city.

How long had I been asleep?

The harsh hospital lights brought out the creases around Dr. Hill's eyes and mouth, the white streaking through her hair. "I'm so glad to see you're awake, dear. How are you feeling?"

I barely registered that she'd asked me a question. My entire brain was focused on my baby. "Did you do an ultrasound?" I choked out. "What did you see?"

Dex lowered himself to the edge of my bed, his weight making the mattress shift beneath me. "I was so worried... You passed out and the nurse thought it was because you were dehydrated—that's why she got you hooked up to the IV."

An IV? My eyes dropped to the needle taped into the crook of my arm, the one I'd been trying to pull out. I followed it up, to a pouch of clear liquid hanging beside me. I had no way of knowing what was in that liquid, what they were pumping inside of me. I watched it drip for a moment, my breath hitching.

"Please," I choked out. "Just tell me what you saw. Please. I *have* to know."

Dr. Hill said, "Of course, Ms. Alcott."

Her voice sounded far too cheery for the situation, which immediately put me on edge. Something had to be really badly wrong if she was forcing herself to put on a happy face for me.

She tilted the screen to face me. I braced myself.

"Let's just take another look, shall we?" Dr. Hill said. Again, that too-happy voice. She leaned over me, pressing the ultrasound wand to my belly. I felt the cold shiver through my body.

Static buzzed around us, perfect, unbroken. The green-lit display on the ultrasound machine stayed blank, three horizontal dashes telling me there was no heart beating inside of me, that nothing was moving. I felt my shoulders drop, all the hope leaving my body.

Oh God, I can't go through this again.

The plastic slid around in the gel coating my skin as Dr. Hill moved the wand to the underside of my belly, just above my pelvic bone.

Dex squeezed my hand. I felt a cold finger tracing my spine. I suddenly realized what this was, why they were doing this. Dex wanted to prove something to me, show me that there was nothing inside of my body, once and for all. To make me realize all that movement had been in my head, just like they'd been saying all along.

My hands started to shake. Any moment now, I was going to see my uterus fill that screen, I was going to see the dead tissue that used to be my baby floating around inside of me. I couldn't do it. I couldn't watch. It all felt suddenly, unbearably cruel. I didn't want to look anymore. I wanted to squeeze my eyes shut. I wanted to turn away.

And then numbers jumped onto the screen. 110 at first, and then 111, 124. Black and white static surrounded a kidney bean–shaped blotch of clear black that I recognized as my uterus. Inside, there was a mass of cloudy white tissue. I saw the profile of a face—tiny nose, tiny chin, kicking legs.

Kicking.

Time stopped. Dex, the doctor, the hospital, even the women following me—all of it fell away. There was just the two of us. Just me and the baby.

And then I inhaled a sharp breath, and everything jerked into life again. The static took on a *swish swish* sound, almost like a siren, and Dex squeezed my hand. He was crying, I saw. Big fat crocodile tears that rolled down his cheeks. And Dr. Hill was smiling at us, a wide toothy grin.

"I–I don't understand," I said, my voice shaking so badly I could barely get it out. "What happened?"

"That, Ms. Alcott, is your baby," Dr. Hill said, beaming like she was the one who'd conjured the baby back from the dead. Like she'd believed all along.

She angled the wand down, held it steady. The baby kept kicking and the numbers climbed higher, 149, 152, and the *swish* sound grew clearer, louder, transforming into a familiar *ba-du-ba-du-ba-du*. "It looks like she's still in there. What you're hearing right now is a very strong, very healthy heartbeat."

LUCY WASHINGTON, 2007

LUCY WENT WITH JOSIE TO HIDE THE DOLLS. THEY PLACED THE first on Waverly Avenue, in the parking lot under the BQE, and the second on the Pratt campus, tucked into one of the art students' over-sized sculptures. The third went behind the packs of adult diapers in Walgreens because Josie said she no one ever bought those, and a fourth was on Myrtle Avenue, hidden up a tree where passersby wouldn't be able to get to it. Finally, they chucked the last one onto the subway tracks at the Clinton Washington stop. No one ever went on those tracks.

"That's important," Josie said. "Once we put the dolls in place, no one can move them until the baby is born."

"And this will keep the baby safe?" Lucy asked, absently running a hand over her close-cropped curls. The hair was her trademark. She always wore it short against her scalp, her deep widow's peak making it look like someone had drawn a heart around her face.

She smiled, pretending she still thought the whole thing was silly.

"It'll keep all of you safe," Josie promised. "Nellie and Erin too."

"Nothing like a little mystical protection," Lucy joked. But secretly, she couldn't help being relieved. Before Nellie, she might've rolled her eyes when some lady she met at a prenatal yoga class suggested a "protection spell" to help ease the pain of pregnancy, but this time around, she was willing to try anything. Magic, midwives, medication, literally *anything* that might make pregnancy a little bit easier.

She'd cried when she first found out about the baby, great gulping sobs that she'd had to muffle with the bathroom sink turned up high so her wife and daughter wouldn't hear her. Erin was supposed to be the one getting pregnant with their second child, but Erin was 42 and her body wasn't cooperating, so it fell to Lucy again, which had seemed just so incredibly unfair after how badly things had gone with Nellie. But who said motherhood was fair? Nobody, that's who.

She knew she should be grateful. A child was a blessing, that's what her mother always said. But her first pregnancy had felt more like an actual nightmare, nine months filled with excruciating, debilitating pain, and none of her doctors—not one—had believed her when she'd tried to tell them how bad it was. They insisted there was nothing physically wrong with her, that she must be exaggerating. They told her to try taking a Tylenol—Tylenol!—when the pain felt like someone tying her insides into knots. Lucy couldn't help wondering if that's what they told all the women who came in complaining about being in pain. But there was another part of her, a small shameful part, that wondered if maybe she wasn't strong enough, if she was unworthy.

Then, during her C-section, her doctors opened her up to find that her uterus was filled with scar tissue and adhesions, an inflamed bladder, and a uterine window so thin they could see through it—all complications of a bladder infection she'd had in her twenties. How had they missed that? So much for the pain "not being that bad." All that scar tissue made the surgery take so much longer than they'd expected. The spinal block only lasted two hours. After that, they'd used anesthesia, but Lucy had always metabolized anesthesia really quickly, and they didn't use enough (another thing they didn't listen to her about).

She felt it all, the whole operation. She felt fingers moving inside her, and she felt the exact moment when the doctor pushed her uterus back into her body, and she felt each prick of the stitches they put in her. All of it. She felt all of it.

She'd had to disassociate from the pain while it happened. It was the only way she could make it through. She'd sent her mind far, far away. She didn't even remember the moment they put Nellie on her chest for the first time, though she had a photograph of it. She didn't remember anything.

So, yeah, when Josie, a skinny blond woman with hair so long she could sit on it came at her talking about spells and protection and dolls, Lucy had been like, *Sign me* up. Anything that might help. Anything. She'd drank the teas Josie told her about, and she'd eaten the herbs and seeds she'd told her would make the nausea better, and she'd said sure, why not hide some creepy dolls? Modern medicine hadn't done anything for her.

And the weird thing was that the tea and the dolls and the herbs had worked, for a little while. But then...well.

Then, things got a little strange.

==== **WEEK 20** ====

Congratulations!
You're halfway through
your pregnancy!

19

DR. HILL EXPLAINED THAT MY RIB WAS BRUISED, NOT BROKEN, which was apparently not unusual during pregnancy. It was called "rib flare," and it was more common during the third trimester, but it could happen at any time. Nothing to worry about. Just put some ice on it. Take it easy.

"Have you tried prenatal yoga?" she asked. "Many expecting mothers find that gentle stretching helps prevent pain like this. And, of course, if the pain gets worse—"

"Aspirin," I interrupted, already knowing what she was going to say. I didn't even care that there wasn't anything stronger that I could take for the pain. I would've done absolutely anything Dr. Hill told me to do in that moment. If she'd said that lighting my hair on fire could guarantee a healthy pregnancy, I would've asked to borrow a match.

Her theory was that I'd experienced something called "vanishing twin syndrome," which was a type of miscarriage that could occur when you were pregnant with multiples. One of the fetuses miscarried, but the other survived.

"You think I was pregnant with twins?" I asked, dubious. No one had mentioned twins to me before.

"I think it may be possible," Dr. Hill said, "and it would explain the pain and bleeding you experienced, though I still want to take some blood and urine for testing."

I wanted her to do more than that. I wanted every prenatal test they had. I asked to schedule an amniocentesis, and a chorionic villus sampling, as well as anything else that might show me what was going on inside of my body. Now that I knew my baby was still alive, I wanted to be absolutely positive she was healthy.

Dr. Hill nodded at me, smiling slightly. "Of course, my dear," she said, patting my hand. "We'll do whatever you like." But she spoke in the tone of voice you used with an exasperating child, one who will not run off and play and leave the grown-ups to their work. And I thought I saw her catch Dex's eye over the top of my head when she thought I wasn't looking, her eyebrow twitching skeptically. My phone screen was crowded with missed calls and texts when we finally left the hospital, words that seemed to fade in and out the longer I stared down at them. My favorite makeup artist, Molly, wanted to schedule a trial run for a week before the awards ceremony, my dad had texted his congratulations on the nomination, and Gracie had sent a group text letting everyone know that Siobhan was still hanging in there, that there hadn't been any change. Emily had called at least three times and texted twice, wanting to see if I'd given any more thought to LA.

I read through every message, but they left no lasting impression on my brain. My head was too full of that *ba-du-ba-du-ba-du*—proof of life. I felt like I was floating above our car, hovering in the sky outside and watching as it slowly crunched up the snowy drive, the Range Rover looking a bit like a black beetle in the middle of all this white, leaking exhaust.

I felt a little tap inside my belly and lowered my hand to my bump, a giddy electrical current of joy running through me, lighting me up. My baby was alive. She was alive and she was inside of me right now. I'd been right all along—she was there; she was really there.

I double-checked that my seat belt was buckled, that the strap wasn't pressing into my bump. The only thing in the world that mattered now was keeping the heartbeat inside of me safe. Everything else could wait.

Dex turned the radio on and spent a second trying to find music in the static. He switched it off again.

"You're sure you're feeling all right?" It was the third time he'd asked since we left the hospital. I could tell he was feeling guilty for not believing me sooner.

"I'm good, really," I said, checking my seat belt, again. "Do you know whether this car has passenger side airbags?"

"Probably. Are you hungry? I could stop and get you some...ice cream and pickles? Or, I don't know, pizza and bologna? Whatever pregnant women crave these days."

I smiled, listening to the slushy sound of tires over melting snow, the beep of our turn signal. I wanted this moment to last for the rest of my pregnancy. For four more months, I wanted to think about nothing more serious than pizza and bologna.

I didn't think there was a single thing in the world that could kill my good mood. But then a notification popped up on my phone screen—and I went cold.

It was the appointment I'd made, the one I'd called WHY ARE YOU DOING THIS TO ME? Someone had updated it.

You can't trust them. You can't trust anyone.

20

I SHOWED DEX AND KAMAL THE MESSAGE AS SOON AS WE GOT back to the house.

Kamal was furious with me. "The point of having a disposable phone is that it limits who can get in touch with you," he pointed out. "I told you I wanted to screen your incoming messages. I can't protect you if you go behind my back like this."

"I'm sorry," I murmured, chastened. I took an uneasy breath. "I wasn't thinking."

"You're going to need to change your password again. We can't let this woman have access to any of your other accounts."

"Of course. Anything."

"Her timing is interesting though," Kamal added. "Does anyone else know about your doctor's visit?"

I started to shake my head—I hadn't spoken to anyone since we'd left the hospital—but Dex surprised me by saying, "Actually Emily, Anna's publicist, she knows." He glanced at me, a little apologetically. "She kept calling your cell. I finally answered and told her it wasn't a good time."

I felt a skip of panic in my stomach and said, in a more accusatory voice than I might normally have used, "What exactly did you say?"

"Nothing." Dex scratched the back of his head, looking taken aback by my tone. "Just that it wasn't a good time because we were at the hospital. She asked if you were okay, and I told her we had a scare with the baby, but that it was all fine now."

My chest felt tight. "You told her everything was fine with the baby?"

Dex shrugged. "Yeah? Was that bad?"

And, immediately afterward, I got that threatening message.

Kamal was watching me, eyes narrowed. "Are you suspicious of this woman, Anna?"

"I don't know," I said, hedging. "Maybe a little." It felt strange to admit it. This was *Emily*. I'd known her for years. Did I really think she was capable of something like this? "Maybe I'm being paranoid; it's just... She's said some strange things over the past few weeks."

I could feel Dex's eyes on me, and I knew he wanted me to look back at him, but I couldn't bring myself to do it. I didn't want to see the judgment on his face. After a moment, he let out a laugh. "Come on, Anna, you don't really think this could be *Emily*?"

I bristled at his doubt. "She's been acting really weird about all this Oscars stuff," I explained. I didn't want Kamal to think I was jumping to conclusions without any proof, being paranoid, but I couldn't ignore this feeling in my gut that something was going on with her. And Dex's skepticism made me want to double down, prove that I had real reasons for my suspicion. "And Keagan said she's in major trouble at work. It's like...if I don't win this award, her entire career's going to fall apart. And she keeps trying to get me to go to LA to campaign even though I've told her I can't because of the baby—"

Kamal was nodding, getting it. "So she figures, if she gets rid of the baby..."

I relaxed a little, relieved to be taken seriously. "She wouldn't have even had to go that far. Maybe she thought that, if I had a stalker in New York, someone threatening the baby, trying to hurt it, that I'd be freaked out enough to want to get out of town. Which, by the way, I was; I just didn't go all the way to LA. It was only when that didn't work that she did something to make me think I'd lost the baby."

"You mean your miscarriage?" Dex frowned. "But we know Emily couldn't have had anything to do with that. Dr. Hill said it was vanishing twin syndrome—"

"She said *maybe* it was. She doesn't know for sure. And Dr. Hill still doesn't know why no one could find a heartbeat the night I went to the ER," I pointed out. "We know someone was at the hospital with me. That woman could've messed with my charts or done something to Dr. Crawford's equipment. Maybe I never had this vanishing twin thing at all. Maybe someone made it seem like I lost the baby even though I didn't."

Dex pinched the bridge of his nose between two fingers. It looked like it was taking an enormous amount of effort for him to accept this line of thinking. "Okay, but the woman at the hospital wasn't Emily. It was that ultrasound tech, Meg—"

I could feel the frustration building inside of me. I just wanted him to tell me I wasn't being paranoid. Was it really so hard for him to be on my side about this?

"Look, I'm not saying I know it's Emily for sure," I said, working hard to keep my voice calm. "I know I don't have any proof, and I know it's far-fetched. All I'm saying is she's been acting strange, and there are reasons she might've wanted this to happen. As for Meg... Emily works with actors in New York all the time. Talia said she was just in town. Maybe she got in touch with someone then."

"You think she hired an *actor* to give you an ultrasound?" Dex asked, making sure I could tell from the tone of his voice how ludicrous the idea was even before he added, "Anna...come on, that's not possible."

"You'd be surprised what people will do when they feel like they don't have another choice," Kamal interjected. "And I've said before that whoever's been following you could be working with someone. It could explain why nothing's adding up."

In that moment I could've cried, I was so grateful to Kamal for backing me up. "And Emily would've known where to get that *Spellbound* doll," I added. "She's one of the only people I know who has access to them."

"Okay," Kamal said, nodding. "Emily's at the top of our list. Does anyone else know about the baby?"

I looked at Dex. "Did you tell anyone else?"

"Just Talia. The woman who owns this house," he added for Kamal. "I had to call and let her know we were going to be staying for a while longer."

"Talia and Emily," Kamal said. "We can work with that. Anna, I don't want you giving this publicist any more personal details about your life, okay? In fact, I think we should talk to whoever does your PR and get you reassigned. If this Emily person really is coming after you, I doubt that will be the end, but I can talk to Detective Wood in the meantime, and we'll check her out. Moving forward, let's keep the number of people who know about your pregnancy as small as possible. No posting online, no interviews. For now, we're going to keep this a secret baby. Got it?"

"Of course," I said.

But I felt a chill worm its way down my spine as soon as the word left my mouth. It suddenly occurred to me that my baby might've been safer when everyone thought she was dead.

———

Days later, I was half asleep, half dreaming when I heard something moving in the ceiling. There were the sounds of groaning and creaking wood, shifting beams, moving floorboards. And then—nothing. It was like the walls were breathing.

In my mind, I saw a dark gaping mouth open up on the side of the house. It inhaled, and the siding bulged outward like cheeks, windows squinting like eyes. It exhaled, and everything constricted.

Groaning, creaking wood. Soft, pitter-pattery movement.

Before the house could inhale again, I blinked my eyes open, suddenly wide awake. It took me a few minutes to remember that it was early morning, a few weeks after that last hospital visit. Watery gray sunlight spilled through the windows, draining the room of color. A storm had rolled in last night, and I could still see the thick shadow of snowflakes dropping from the sky outside my curtained windows, hear the wind howling through the trees. Burying me, Dex, and the baby inside this house. Hiding us from the rest of the world.

I was still for long moments, staring up at the ceiling, listening for the sound of creaking wood. But the sound had stopped. I don't know how long I stayed there listening, but I didn't hear it again.

Had it been a dream? Or had someone really been up there moving around?

I glanced over at Happy, still curled up at my feet, fast asleep. She hadn't moved or lifted her head. If there had really been something up on the third floor, Happy would've been dancing in circles around me and barking.

And I didn't have any new reason to be nervous. I'd fired Emily, like Kamal had suggested and, over the last few weeks, he'd been taking my concerns very seriously. After speaking with Detective Wood, he'd gotten in touch with a colleague of his in LA, a private detective, who'd agreed to take a look at Emily's activity and see whether she'd been doing anything strange. Nothing had turned up yet, but Kamal upped my security here just in case. He changed all the codes on our security system nightly, and he'd searched the house and the grounds once a day since we'd come back from the hospital, but he hadn't found any sign that someone had ever been here. In fact, ever since I'd stopped working with Emily, things had almost returned to normal. There hadn't been any new dolls on the beach, no neighbors following too closely. The sounds I'd heard could've been a million other things—old house sounds or an animal skittering across the roof. If Emily had been the one behind this, maybe it was over now.

Still, I stared at the ceiling for a moment longer. I didn't like the way the sounds had just stopped. If it was old house noises or an animal on the roof, wouldn't I have kept hearing them?

There were footsteps in the hall outside my room. I tensed. But it was Dex.

"Smoothie delivery," he announced, coming into the room to set my smoothie on my bedside table. He'd spent hours researching which superfoods mama and baby needed during pregnancy to grow big and strong, and now he was making kale smoothies for me for every meal.

I didn't want to tell him this, but I didn't see how he could know that kale was good for the baby. Leafy greens were more likely to give you listeria than ham, and yet deli meat was forbidden. Who had decided kale was okay? But everything was like that. Medications and foods were deemed fine or dangerous, seemingly at random. I'd learned to stop questioning it.

Unfortunately, the smoothies were truly awful, full of wilted kale and flax seeds and all sorts of other things that were apparently super healthy but tasted like grass. And there was something else about them, a chalky flavor that I couldn't quite place, even when I made Dex tell me every single ingredient he'd used.

I eased myself up against my pillows, grimacing at the effort. My belly had doubled since I came home from the hospital, or it seemed to have. It was a little mound beneath my breasts, half a basketball.

"I don't think I can choke another one of those down," I said.

"Dr. Hill said you're supposed to be eating something like *twenty-four hundred* calories a day, and you're not getting anywhere near that much." Dex's phone vibrated in his pocket. He took it out and frowned at the screen.

"Who's that?" I wanted to know.

"Office," he murmured, shoving the phone back into his pocket without answering. "I'll call them back later. Now, drink that and I'll make you pancakes."

I grimaced. My belly didn't want pancakes. "I'll settle for more cookies." Talia had sent us a few more boxes of those buttery, herby cookies she'd brought when she came to visit me. They were the only things that settled my stomach.

"You can't live off cookies, Anna," Dex said, stern. "You have the baby to think about. Come on, drink up."

I could tell he wasn't going to let this go. He was being a stickler about the baby's health. Sometimes I felt like I was on the world's strictest diet, every morsel of food I ate considered and analyzed for its nutritional value.

I picked up the smoothie and took a small drink, trying not to cringe at that awful chalky aftertaste. "There," I said, forcing myself to swallow. "Happy?"

"Ecstatic." He didn't look ecstatic. He looked like he was thinking about something else.

"Were you upstairs a minute ago?" I asked, grimacing as I hauled myself out of bed. The extra weight was starting to make it hard to move, but that was such a small price for my baby growing big and strong.

"No," Dex said, reaching for my elbow to help me. "But Talia's housekeepers got here about an hour ago. Maybe one of them went upstairs?"

"They're here now?" I could hear the nerves creeping into my voice. If Emily could hire an actor to play an ultrasound tech, she could hire one to one to play a housekeeper. "I thought we weren't going to let anyone else inside."

"These are the same housekeepers Talia's had for years—they aren't going to do anything. And her one condition of our staying here was that we let the housekeepers come once a week to keep things fresh. Remember?"

I made myself breathe deep. He was right; Talia knew these women, even if I didn't.

The sound came again: one long soft creak of the floorboards directly above my head. A chill crawled over my skin.

I looked up, my heart stopping. "Did you hear that?"

"You mean that creak?" Dex raised an eyebrow at me. "I'm pretty sure it was just the house settling."

I nodded, but my mouth had gone dry, and my blood was thumping thickly in my ears. Things had been good for the past few weeks, quiet. But I couldn't stop thinking about that last message: You can't trust anyone.

After a moment, Dex said, like he wasn't sure whether it was a good idea to even bring it up, "I've been thinking...what if this whole thing's just some really messed-up joke?"

"What do you mean?"

"The message said someone did something to your baby, right? But all your tests have come back normal. We know the baby's healthy and growing. So what if they were never warnings at all? What if this whole time someone's just been trying to scare you?"

I gave him a look, and he rushed on, like he was worried I was going to shoot him down before he'd made his point, "No, think about it. It makes sense, in a twisted way. All this woman has really done is left weird dolls for you to find on the beach."

"And snuck into my bed and my *hospital* room—"

"Even you've admitted that you don't know for sure whether it was the same woman who did that. I know you think this is all Emily but...I don't know, Anna. Even you have to admit that theory is a little far-fetched. You're a public person. Isn't it way more likely that those women were just fans with incredibly bad timing? Maybe they hadn't actually wanted to hurt the baby, and all of this was just meant to...I don't know, freak you out?"

"What about the miscarriage?"

Dex winced. I knew he hated talking about it. "But you *didn't* miscarry. Dr. Hill said it was vanishing twin syndrome and, well, she would know."

I bit my lip. I'd looked up vanishing twin syndrome when I got back from the hospital. And while, yes, some of the symptoms do fit with what happened to me, many of them just didn't. The people who'd gone through vanishing twin syndrome all knew they were pregnant with multiples. None of my doctors had ever heard two heartbeats or seen two fetuses on my ultrasound. And maybe this wouldn't be enough evidence for someone like Dex or Dr. Hill, but I never felt like I was pregnant with two babies. From the moment I saw that positive pregnancy test, I felt a very real connection to one baby, not two.

I lifted my eyes to the ceiling. I still didn't think that creak had sounded like it was just the house. It sounded like someone moving, someone trying desperately not to make any noise. A cold chill went down my spine. I didn't care if Dex thought I was overreacting; I needed to know no one was up there. "Could you please go upstairs and look?"

"Anna—"

"You said it's probably just the housekeepers, right? So go upstairs and see if any of them are up there."

He got an annoyed look on his face. "I'm not going to go spy on Talia's housekeepers. I don't want to be that guy."

"You don't have to spy. I just want to know if that's who's in the attic."
Dex sighed.

"Please," I said, cutting him off before he could keep arguing. "Can you just look? If it's the housekeepers, then I'll let it go, all right?"

A pause as he considered it. Then, "Okay, fine, I'll look. Just drink that while I'm gone, okay?" He pointed to the smoothie.

I picked up the smoothie and took the smallest drink I could manage.

Dex shook his head to show he was doing this under protest and left the room.

I curled myself around my belly, listening. I tried to make myself believe Dex's theory. Maybe he was right, and some fan—*fans*—were just trying to scare me. Maybe the only people in the attic were Talia's housekeepers. Maybe my theory about Emily was paranoia.

I heard his footsteps in the hall and then on the stairs. I could feel my heart beating in my throat, even as I thought, *There's no one up there, no one, everything's fine.*

The door to the third floor creaked open, and then Dex was walking across my ceiling, his footsteps much heavier than the ones I'd heard before. I held my breath, listening. After a while, I began to wish I *would* hear the footsteps again, just so I knew I wasn't going crazy. They'd been softer, lighter, someone trying to move without making too much noise. Housekeepers didn't move like that, like they were sneaking around.

Then a terrible thought occurred to me. Maybe *this* is what she'd wanted to happen. Whoever was up there, maybe she'd wanted me to send Dex upstairs alone. Maybe she had a weapon, and she wanted to take him out so she could get to me.

It would be so easy for her to do. Dex wasn't taking this seriously. He wouldn't be on alert for the sound of someone creeping up behind him. I pictured him standing in one of the spare rooms, annoyed as he looked around the furniture, under the bed. I imagined a closet door silently opening behind him, like in a horror film, Dex completely oblivious as a figure approached him from behind, holding a baseball bat, a butcher knife—

I clenched my eyes shut. My heart was beating so loud that I couldn't hear anything over the bass drum pounding in my ears. I never should have let him go up alone. I should have gone after him now just in case, but I felt like I was frozen in bed. I couldn't move, couldn't even open my mouth to call out to him—

"Hey," Dex said, his voice startling me so much that I flinched and released a short choked scream. I hadn't heard him come back down the stairs.

"Whoa, it's okay," Dex said, coming to sit next to me. "There's no one up there, like I said."

"You're sure?" My heart was still pounding, my breath short. "You checked every room? And all the closets?"

"I checked everywhere. There was no one." He gave me a kiss on the forehead. "I know this is stressful, but just try to calm down and relax, okay? For the baby?"

I tensed at that. I hated when he told me to calm down.

"How about I go get you some more of those cookies?" he offered. I could tell it was a concession, his way of trying to keep the peace. I softened a little and nodded.

"I can't stop eating them either," he admitted with a smile. "You really need to figure out where your firm got them."

My firm? "My firm didn't send those, Talia did."

But Dex was shaking his head. "Talia hasn't sent us anything in a while, babe."

I swallowed, a sharp sour taste hitting the back of my throat. "She must've sent something. She brought these cookies when she came to see me. I know they came to her."

"You don't think it's possible that someone else bought the same cookies?" Dex asked. When I shook my head he sighed and added, "I can check and see if Talia sent something I missed, but I know she didn't. And I'm pretty sure I found these right next to one of those gift baskets lying around downstairs, the ones your PR firm keeps sending."

A cold feeling shot down my spine. Talia said a *mutual friend* had given her those cookies. And she saw Emily when Emily was in the New York office.

My stomach was a hard lump. Emily could've slipped something into the cookies before I'd let her go, done something to them. How many had I eaten?

"Throw them out," I said.

Dex scoffed. "You can't be serious—"

"Dex, please, just throw them out," I shot back. "Throw away everything she sent me."

My stomach didn't feel hard anymore. Now it was churning. I felt acid crawling up my chest, the taste of blood on my tongue. It was as though there was something alive inside of me, clinging to the insides of my throat, curled in my belly.

The next time I heard the sound was the following night, when I was in the bathroom getting ready for bed.

The floor above my head creaked and I froze, nerves buzzing over my skin.

I waited one long moment, and then another, my ears pricked. But the sound didn't come again.

"Old house noises," I muttered out loud.

I really, really wanted to believe that.

I stared at my reflection in the mirror as I fumbled with my toothbrush and toothpaste. My appearance had...altered over the past few weeks. Deep shadows colored the area beneath my cheekbones, and there were purple bruises under my eyes. If it weren't for my growing belly, I'd think I'd actually lost weight. I looked ghastly, skeletal.

I opened a drawer in Talia's vanity, idly looking through her products, wondering if she had anything that might help bring me back to life. A rose quartz crystal tumbled around the bottom of the drawer, along with a bottle of something called "star water," whatever that was, and a few tubes of expensive-looking skin care. I checked the labels, groaning when I saw the big red **ASK A DOCTOR BEFORE USING WHILE PREGNANT** warnings on the back. The last I heard there was very little proof that any active ingredients in products like this could seep into your blood through your skin, but—like everything else—the evidence wasn't conclusive. I closed the drawer with my hip, sighing. It was better to be safe.

My eyes drifted to the bottom drawer of the vanity. I wondered if the framed photograph of Dex and Talia and Adeline was still there. Before I could talk myself out of it, I leaned over (groaning, one hand pressed to my growing bump) and pulled the drawer open.

There it was. Talia looking over her shoulder to wave at someone not pictured, Dex and his ex-wife sitting in some forgotten restaurant, laughing at a joke I'd never hear. I pulled the photograph out, chewing my lip, unable to quell the curiosity inside of me. *Who was Adeline, really? Did Dex miss her? Why didn't he mention her, ever?*

I knew it wasn't that unusual to want a clean break after a marriage fell apart. Siobhan had a (rather famous) ex, and when I asked if they still spoke, she looked at me like I'd asked whether she was still in touch with her third-grade teacher and said, "Now why would I want to do that, honey?" So no, it wasn't strange that Dex wasn't in touch with Adeline. Why was I doing this to myself? I had no reason to feel threatened by her. Dex and I were having a baby. We were happier than ever. And this woman was just a part of his past. She had nothing to do with us.

I went to shove the photograph back into its drawer, shaking my head, but the frame slipped from my hands and fell to the floor, shattering.

"Damn it," I muttered. The frame was broken in half, the glass split into three sections.

I groaned as I eased my heavy body to the floor. The photograph was mostly okay, thank God. That would've been a lot harder to replace than the broken frame. I gingerly pulled it out from beneath the shattered glass. I hadn't been able to tell when the photograph was in the frame, but now I could see that it had been folded over.

Curious, I straightened the photograph against my leg. Talia had turned to wave at someone else in the restaurant, but the person hadn't been left out of the image like I'd assumed they had. The photographer had managed to capture them, but Talia had carefully cropped them out. I examined the image, half-expecting to see some ex of hers. I knew of a few of the men Talia had dated before Keagan.

But Talia was waving to a woman. I blinked a few times, waiting for my eyesight to focus. I was sure I wasn't seeing correctly, that the image before me would break apart and reform into something that made more sense. But it didn't. The woman was in the background of the photograph, her face slightly unfocused, but I could clearly make out her dark hair and pale skin, the bright red slash of her lipstick.

For a moment, I forgot to breathe. My skin felt like it was vibrating, my blood thumping too fast. That woman...it looked just like Meg, the woman who gave me the illicit ultrasound. But did that mean...

Did Talia *know* Meg?

I dug my fingers into my scalp, pulling at my hair a little as I forced myself to breathe, to calm down. I had to be imagining things. I had to be seeing Meg in this stranger's face. But (*You can't trust anyone*) if I wasn't imagining things...had Talia cropped Meg out of this photograph on purpose? In case I found it?

My eyes moved from the photo to the drawer it'd been shoved in. She'd hidden it beneath a towel. I'd assumed she'd done that because she hadn't wanted me to see a picture of Dex and Adeline looking so happy together. But maybe she hadn't wanted me to see *Meg*, hadn't wanted me to realize that the two of them knew each other.

I was pulling too hard on my hair, I realized absently. My head felt strangely tender, everything pricking and stinging, like lemon juice in a paper cut. I forced myself to let go, drop my hands—

And then I bit back a cry.

There was something on my knuckles, little flecks of red.

Blood. Had I pricked myself on the glass without realizing? I wiped the blood on a piece of tissue and stared at my finger, waiting for fresh blood to bubble up, again. It didn't.

Had the blood come from my head?

I ran my fingers over my head, gasping a little as I searched for the raw spot on my scalp.

Then...a strange sensation, a sharp sting of pressure. It felt like something moving beneath my skin, like a little worm wriggling around between my skull and the outside of my head, pushing up against the roots of my hair.

I jerked my hands away from my head and saw that there was hair woven between my fingers. Thick clumps of it. More hair than I'd ever lost at one time.

"Oh God," I murmured, shaking the hair loose of my hands. It floated across the countertop and to the floor. I reached for my head again, hands trembling badly now, desperate to prove that this was nothing, that the rest of my hair was still exactly where it was supposed to be.

I inhaled deep, telling myself to calm down, that it was probably just a weird hormonal thing, yet another pregnancy symptom no one ever talked about.

But, when I pulled my hands away from my head, there was an even bigger chunk of hair caught between my fingers. This time, the roots were still bloody.

21

DEX BURST INTO THE BATHROOM SECONDS AFTER I STARTED screaming. "Anna? Jesus...what is it?"

I couldn't speak so I just pointed at the hair. It was everywhere, in the sink and the counter, strewn across the broken picture and frame still littering the floor.

"What the—" Dex's eyes skated over the hair, the picture, and the skin between his eyes creased. He sucked in a breath. "Did that all just fall out?"

He looked at me for an explanation, but I didn't know what to say. I felt unbalanced and, try as I might, I couldn't get my voice to work the way it was supposed to. My hair was falling out. I wasn't hallucinating and I wasn't dreaming. My *hair* was falling out.

Dex suddenly had me by the shoulders and was telling me to calm down, to breathe.

"It's going to be okay," he was saying. "This is okay, it's normal. Hair falling out can have something to do with pregnancy hormone shifts. It's okay."

It took me a second to focus on his face. "What? How could you possibly know that?"

He shocked me by saying, "Adeline's sister had it."

My breath caught. I wasn't prepared to hear Adeline's name in this context, and it took me a second to shift my focus away from the hair strewn across the floor and respond. "What?"

"Her younger sister had this horrible pregnancy—she was sick the entire time and, even afterward, she was never really the same." Dex blinked. He was staring at the photograph on the floor now. He and Adeline were still visible beneath the broken frame. "Addy told me the whole story right after we got married. It was why she hadn't wanted kids."

I paused, giving him the chance to keep going. It was the most he'd ever said about his ex-wife. Before this moment I hadn't even known Adeline had a sister.

I could feel my horror slowly fading, replaced with fascination. Adeline's sister had a bad pregnancy. That's why she hadn't wanted kids. It was so odd, how those few details shifted the picture I had of her, turning the composed, smiling woman from social media into a fuller person. A concerned sister, someone who was a little terrified by what her body could and couldn't do. The details were like catnip. I wanted to keep pressing him until I got the whole story.

"What do you mean she told you after you got married?" I asked, hesitantly, not wanting to break the spell. "You guys didn't talk about kids while you were dating?"

Dex's eyebrows drew together. "No," he said, a little darkly. "She waited to drop that bomb on me until after we said, *I do.*"

Something flashed across his face, pain or anger, I couldn't tell, but it made me flinch, shocked. I'd never heard him talk like this before, like a baby was something he was owed.

Before I could call him on it, he'd leaned over and slid the photograph from beneath the shards of broken glass. "What's this?"

He looked at me, frowning slightly, and I understood that the moment had passed. If I kept asking about Adeline, I was just going to get the same vague, half answers I always did.

I glanced at the photograph instead, Talia waving at a blurry Meg—or at least, someone who looked a hell of a lot like Meg. "Look," I said, pointing at her. "See, right there? Who does that look like to you?"

Dex squinted down at it. "Uh...are you talking about the woman in the background? I can't really see her."

"Look closer. Doesn't that look like the woman who snuck into the hospital and gave me an ultrasound?"

Dex looked up, giving me a long, unsettled gaze. "Anna..."

"Look," I said, pointing. I needed him to believe me on this. "See the red lipstick? It's her."

He barely glanced down. "Lots of women wear lipstick."

"I remember her face, Dex." I blinked against tears. How could I ever forget it? "It's her, Meg or whatever her real name is. And Talia's waving at her. She *knows* her."

I could see a tangle of emotions playing out on Dex's face, the desire to comfort me mixed with an inability to hear—or believe— what I was telling him. After a moment, the disbelief won out, and he sighed deeply and said, "First you get Emily fired, and now you want me to question one of my best friends? Can you hear yourself?"

I was taken aback. The comment about Emily stung. "Talia is

waving at the woman who—who violated me." My voice cracked, and I had to pause and take a slow, deep breath to steady myself. "I can't believe you won't back me up on this."

"Okay," Dex said. His voice was dull and flat. "Fine, I'll ask Talia who she is, if it'll get you to calm down." He pulled out his cell phone. "First I'm going to call Dr. Hill and let her know what's going on with your hair."

———

Dr. Hill agreed with Dex that the hair loss was normal, though she thought it had something to do with my stress levels. She recommended that I try to take things easy for a while. Nap. Yoga. Bath. And, if things got really bad, I could take a low-dose aspirin.

Of course that was my only option.

"I asked Talia about the photograph," Dex told me later that evening. We were sitting at the dining room table, eating dinner. Or Dex was eating. I was mostly pushing food around my plate, feeling nauseated.

I looked up, surprised. I assumed he'd take forever to talk to her, that I'd have to remind him a few times before he finally gave her a call. I felt my shoulders tighten as I said, "You did?"

"I said I would, didn't I?" He pulled out his phone, frowning down at something on the screen before tapping it a few times and handing it to me. "Look, you can read our whole conversation if you like. Talia said the woman she was waving to was someone she'd met at a fertility testing place in the city a few years ago, back when she was considering freezing her eggs... Anyway, the woman's name is Margaret, but Talia doesn't remember her last name."

I took the phone from him. "Meg's a nickname for Margaret," I said, scanning the exchange.

Dex had been reaching for his water glass, but he stopped and looked at me. "Yeah...it's also a nickname for Megan and Margery and Margo and probably a million other incredibly common women's names. And you thought it was an alias anyway."

"I'm just saying we can't rule her out."

"We can't rule out this Margaret woman? Or Talia?" I didn't say anything, didn't even look up from the phone, and Dex dropped his hands back onto the table, hard. "Jesus, Anna, you wanted me to ask Talia about the picture and I did. Even if this woman was the woman you saw in the hospital—and that's a *big* if—Talia said she barely knows her."

"But how do we know that's true?" I asked. Dex threw his hands up as though to say *what more do you want?* and I kept going, "Think about it, Dex—*of course* Talia would've lied about how well she knew Meg. We need to hand this over to Kamal, and maybe Detective Wood too, and see what they think about it."

"Whatever you say." Dex stood, shaking his head. "I need a drink."

I felt a wave of anger rising inside of me as I watched him leave the room. He was acting like I had some vendetta against Talia. But I liked Talia; I wanted to believe she didn't have anything to do what was happening to me. The problem was, this wasn't just about me anymore.

You can't trust anyone, I thought, my skin prickling. I rested a hand on my bump and forced myself to breathe. That message wasn't some idle threat—it was a warning. I'd almost lost my baby once. And if I wasn't careful, I was going to lose her again. For real.

It was 3 a.m. when I couldn't take the creaking any longer.

Dex hadn't come to bed. He was locked away in his office, doing God only knows what. Sulking, probably. I'd tried to sleep, but the creaking had started up again sometime after midnight. I crawled out of bed and went upstairs to the third floor myself. I needed to see with my own eyes that there wasn't anyone up there. Otherwise, I'd never believe it.

The stairs to the third floor were shallower than they were in other parts of the house, and it got colder the farther up I climbed. I was shaking a little, overheated and keyed up with adrenaline. The cold felt nice against my sweaty skin. I figured it was a good sign, that it would be harder for someone to stay up here if it wasn't heated. It got so cold at night that my teeth sometimes chattered, and that was downstairs, with the heat blasting and a duvet pulled up to my chin.

I reached the top of the stairs and fumbled with the door. I took a second to catch my breath, one hand braced against my back, gasping like I'd just run a mile. I caught myself fantasizing that I might find Meg waiting on the other side of the door, just standing there, dumbfounded. And then I could...

What? Scream? Run away? *Attack her?* None of those answers seemed right. I had the distant thought that I should've made a plan before tearing after this woman on my own. That I should go back downstairs and get Dex and make him come up here with me. But then I thought about how he'd looked at me when we'd been talking about Talia over dinner, how he'd gotten so frustrated that he'd thrown up his hands and stomped out of the room to get a drink.

We'd barely spoken since then. I knew I didn't have the luxury of bringing him another unfounded suspicion. I had to do this myself. Maybe she wouldn't want to hurt me. Maybe I could just talk to her, ask her who'd hired her.

I pushed the door open, hinges creaking.

The twin scents of mildew and dust filled my nose, making me take a step back. Such strange scents in this pristine place. They made me think of neglect, of rot. I coughed, eyes squinting.

"Hello?" The sound of my voice was flat, dull, the rooms up here too small for an echo.

I shuffled forward slowly, not wanting to jostle the baby.

It was clear immediately that there wasn't anyone up here. The beds were all so low to the ground that there was no way someone could crawl underneath them, and there wasn't enough furniture to hide behind. All the closet doors hung open, revealing boxes and water-skiing equipment and punch bowls. Not enough room for a person.

I wasn't disappointed. That was the wrong word. I hadn't wanted her to be hiding out up here. But, as the adrenaline that had been racing through my veins began to drain away, it left me feeling strangely deflated. I felt, suddenly, very tired.

The wind rattled the windows, cold air pinging off glass. I turned back toward the door, and I was about to go back downstairs when I saw something out of the corner of my eye—

My body understood first. My hands tightened into fists, and I went cold all over. I staggered backward, suddenly light-headed, and I would've fallen if the wall wasn't right there. I pressed a hand against it to steady myself. For long moments, I found it impossible to breathe.

She'd been here. My stalker had been *here*, in this room, right above where I'd been sleeping. I'd been right all along.

I knew this because there was another Summer Day action figure sitting on top of the dresser. It was naked, just like the last one had been, but this one didn't have a red X drawn over her belly. Instead, someone had pulled every last hair out of its head.

22

KAMAL PUT THE DOLL IN A ZIPLOC BAG, JUST LIKE HE'D DONE with the first one, and he called Detective Wood, but he didn't think the doll was cause for alarm, even when I pointed out—hysterical, sobbing, snot running down my face as I struggled to get the words out—that *my* hair was coming out just like the doll's, that it had to mean something, that she had to have *done* something to me.

"No one has come into this house without my knowledge for months," Kamal said. "I can promise you that."

"Except for Talia's housekeepers," I pointed out, tugging on the ends of my hair to make sure it was still attached to my scalp.

Out of the corner of my eye, I saw Dex's shoulders slump. He brought his hand up to his face, slowly shaking his head.

"Those housekeepers have all been thoroughly vetted," Kamal said, glancing at Dex as though to confirm. "They've had background checks—"

"The housekeepers didn't leave this in the attic," Dex cut in, nodding at the doll. His tone was low and even, the long-suffering voice of reason. He didn't look at me as he added, "I told you, Anna, they've been working for Talia for years. They're trustworthy."

I drove my teeth into my lower lip as I stared back at him.

But how trustworthy is Talia?

———

Talia knew I was still pregnant. *She could have accessed the house through the housekeepers;* she even had a conveniently empty house right next door. The perfect place to hide and watch us. Watch *me*.

But why? *Why?* That was still the unanswerable question. Talia had always been kind to me. We'd always been friends. So why do this? It didn't make sense.

I thought about the photograph again. Not about how Talia appeared to be waving to someone who looked like Meg, but how Talia and Dex and Adeline had been huddled together, happy. It felt like a clue, a piece of the puzzle I wasn't getting. Was Talia mad that I was with him instead of Adeline? That I was having a baby with him?

"I think we should leave," I told Dex after I'd spent a few days obsessing. "We can go stay somewhere else until the baby comes."

"You want to go back to Brooklyn?" He looked hopeful, but the thought of returning to the brownstone made my stomach turn over.

"I can't...she's already gotten to me there." I hesitated, chewing my lip. "What about a hotel?"

"You know what Kamal's going to say about security at a hotel," Dex pointed out. He was right. Making arrangements to travel to LA for the awards had meant hours on the phone with hotel staff in California to set up my security. And we'd had weeks to deal with that. I couldn't imagine what Kamal would say if I asked him to do the same thing in a matter of days. He hadn't even okayed me taking another day trip back to Brooklyn to visit Siobhan, insisting that the beach house, with its alarm system and cameras and privacy fences, was the safest place for me.

"Look, we'll be in LA soon." Dex pulled me toward him, rubbing my arms. "She's not going to follow us across the country, right?"

I'd swallowed. I wasn't so sure.

I ended up by the side of the pool again late one night on my way to take a trash bag out to the dumpster. Shivering.

The dead raccoon was still lying at the bottom of the pool, half covered in snow and dead leaves. He'd been out here for weeks now. Staring. Frozen. I was amazed some other animal hadn't gotten to him yet. There were bears and foxes up here. Weren't they hungry too?

I tilted my head to the side, my eyes traveling over the swell of his belly, the heft of his legs. I noticed, absently, that my mouth was filling with saliva.

My phone buzzed in my pocket, startling me so much I nearly dropped my trash bag. I pulled it out and checked the screen: Detective Wood. My stomach seized. I felt like I'd been caught doing something shameful.

"Anna, good, I'm glad I was able to catch you," Detective Wood said when I answered. It sounded like he was eating something. Chips, maybe? I could hear a wrapper crinkling, the sound of chewing. "I wanted to let you know that we were able to track down that username you were interested in... Let's see... *Number1crush*, is that right?"

I swallowed and turned my back on the raccoon. My mouth was suddenly very dry. "And? What did you find?"

"*Number1crush* is the handle of a seventeen-year-old girl living in Havertown, Pennsylvania, named Amelia Davies. I checked Ms. Davies's schedule for the day of your break-in and the day of your hospital visit. On both days, she left school at three p.m. and went straight to a shift at a Cenzo's Pizzeria, which is where she was until approximately nine p.m. on both evenings. I confirmed her alibi with her teachers, as well as the manager at Cenzo's, and several coworkers. It's pretty tight. I think we can safely rule her out."

I only really understood maybe a third of what he'd said. *Number1crush* was only seventeen? *Seventeen?* And she couldn't have been the same woman who broke into our house and climbed into bed with me because she'd been at her after-school job at a pizza place?

I thought back on all those cruel messages she'd sent, the emails and the pictures and the threats. It didn't seem possible that they'd all come from a teenager.

"I...I don't understand," I said when I could find my voice again. "I think you might have the wrong person... You haven't seen the messages she's sent me—they're awful." *That baby would be better off never being born.* For a moment I felt so queasy that I thought I might need to sit down. "I don't think a child would've sent those. Could they have come from someone else in the house? Her mother, maybe?"

"We've seen the messages, Ms. Alcott. Miss Davies never deleted them from her outgoing messages, so it wasn't difficult to find them. I understand why you would've been upset. When we spoke to Miss Davies, she said they were just a joke. Apparently a lot of her friends send stuff like that to celebrities. It's a game."

A *game?* For a moment I was so angry that I couldn't see straight. I couldn't think or speak. *A game?* I imagined snapping at her. *You think this is a game? This is my life you're messing with.*

"Is that all?" I asked, feeling deflated.

"Not quite. I got in touch with the head of security over at Warner Bros and, according to them, there was a break-in at their warehouse a few months ago."

I blinked fast, the sudden change in subject taking me a second to process. "There was?"

"They can't say for sure whether any *Spellbound* dolls were taken, but they sent me the security footage from the night of, and based on a very rough, preliminary visual ID, I feel comfortable saying it was very likely the same woman who broke into your hospital room."

I felt my mouth open but said nothing.

"I'm going to be straight with you," Detective Wood continued when I didn't respond right away. "We still don't have any way of identifying her. It's impossible to get prints from a warehouse or a hospital, and she doesn't appear to be affiliated with Warner Bros in any way. Unless you have some other lead—"

"I think maybe I do," I said, my heart beating faster. I gave him Emily's name and information, and then I glanced over my shoulder to make sure Dex hadn't followed me outside. Lowering my voice I said, "And there's one other person I want you to look into. Her name is…uhm, Talia Donovan? She's a friend; she actually owns the house we're staying at right now."

Silence, just the sound of Detective Wood chewing, a piece of paper getting flipped over. And then, "Has she given you a reason to be believe she might want to scare you?"

"Sort of..." I told him about the photograph of the woman who looked like Meg, how Talia seemed to be waving at her, and how she'd mentioned they'd met at a fertility place. Then, feeling a stab of guilt for suspecting Talia, I added quickly, "I don't want it to be her, but a lot of the stuff that's happened around the house, the dolls and stuff, Talia's really the only person who could get close enough to do that."

"I'll take a look and let you know if anything unusual comes up," Detective Wood said. "It would help if you could you send me a copy of the photograph. And the name of the fertility place where Talia met her."

I told him I would and hung up the phone. And then I turned back around, casting one last glance at the raccoon at the bottom of the pool. Glassy eyes. Full belly.

I didn't realize I'd been licking my lips until they started to chap.

─────────

I couldn't sleep that night. I couldn't stop thinking about Talia and the housekeepers and the doll in the attic, the woman in the photograph, the chunks of hair that kept coming loose in my hands. The raccoon that still smelled so appetizing, no matter how much other meat I let myself eat.

I finally gave up and pulled up Instagram on my phone, desperate for something to distract me from memories of the raccoon, how my stomach still rumbled when I thought of it.

Hormones, I told myself, and forced the memory of the raccoon out of my head. I didn't want to think about it anymore. It was just hormones. Pregnancy hormones were strange.

I began scrolling through my Instagram posts, back and back, to one from September two years ago, the night Talia and I first met. Dex and I had gotten dinner with Talia, Keagan, Frank, and Bianca, and we'd all taken a photo together right outside the restaurant, arms draped around each other's shoulders, grinning big. Talia was the only one of us not looking at the camera. Instead, she was staring at me.

I zoomed in on the shot, studying Talia's face. Her eyes were slightly narrowed, and there was a lock of dark brown hair hanging over her face. Was that frustration in her expression? Resentment? Had she hated me all this time?

I realized I honestly didn't know.

When I finally slept, I dreamt I was outside, next to the pool. My baby wasn't in my belly anymore, I realized—she was lying curled on the pool floor, surrounded by rotting leaves and mounds of dirty gray snow. She didn't cry, which surprised me. I thought all babies cried.

My heart lurched. I wanted to hold her, to help her. I lowered myself to the bottom of the pool and reached for her—and then I reeled backward.

The creature at the bottom of the pool wasn't my baby. It had a feathered, birdlike body, and there was a mouth where its eyes should've been, beak parting like it was looking for food. I imagined that beak clamping down on my nipple, and a shudder of horror went through me.

"What are you?" I muttered, staring at the creature on the pool floor. "What did you do to my baby?"

The smell of the pool rose around me, then old mulchy leaves and snow and the faint whiff of chlorine.

It was so strange; I didn't remember ever noticing scent in a dream before.

It woke me up, the smell. I opened my eyes, blinking into darkness.

I wasn't in my bedroom anymore, I saw. I wasn't inside at all. I was standing at the bottom of the pool. This wasn't a dream—I could feel the slimy chill of rotting leaves beneath my bare feet, the snow sludge crusted between my toes. The air around me was bitter, bitter cold. It pressed into my skin like a sheet of solid ice, so intense that I felt it sink down into my bones. Wind moved through the trees, rattling the branches like chains.

I lurched backward, horrified. Icy air spiked down my throat, and my feet were so, so cold. I felt weird, light-headed, my eyes refusing to focus. The night was still around me. No animals, no snow. The silence was perfect.

I'm still dreaming, I thought, panic rising in my chest. I turned in place, the strength threatening to leave my legs and send me sprawling to the ground. I was clearly not dreaming. I was outside, in the pool. This was real.

What happened? I thought desperately. *How did I get here?*

The kitchen light was on back in the house, a trickle of gold spilling across the yard, the back door hanging open. I could see my own footprints in the snow, marking my trail across the grass and over to the pool, down the steps.

Cold fear filled me. I'd walked out here on my own. I'd left the warmth of my bed and walked outside and climbed down here, into the pool, in the middle of the night, in the snow.

Why?

My breath grew short and labored. Of course, I already knew why. Somewhere in my mind, I knew. There was only one reason I would've come out here to the snow-filled pool. I didn't want to think about the reason, but it was there, hidden in the corner of my mind like a naughty child. Some part of me had been thinking about the thing lying at the bottom of the pool ever since I followed its scent across the backyard. And now, while I was sleeping, my subconscious had done something about it.

My chest was tight, and there was a film of something sour on my tongue. I cringed as I looked down, blinking in the darkness, a wave of fresh disgust rising inside of me.

No. I didn't. Please tell me I didn't.

I expected to see the raccoon's mangled corpse. My body had stiffened, preparing to see limbs torn from its torso, chunks of meat gnawed off bones, patches of fur ripped away from skin and muscle. Proof that I'd given in to my urges, that I'd snuck out here in the middle of the night to eat a dead animal. I'd half convinced myself that I could feel something warm and tacky beneath my fingernails, that I could still taste the gamey flavor of its meat on my tongue.

But the raccoon was gone. I was standing in the pool alone, surrounded by my own footprints. Perhaps some predator had snuck down here and gotten to him finally, eaten him and dragged him off into the woods. It would've had to have been something big—a wolf or a bear, maybe—because there was no sign of a body anywhere.

My fingers twitched. My stomach turned, and I realized, distantly, that some part of me was disappointed.

23

I SNUCK BACK INTO THE HOUSE THROUGH THE SIDE ENTRANCE, barely daring to breathe as I eased the door open and closed. I couldn't let Dex hear me. I needed to be quiet. But my heart was beating so hard it was making my chest hurt. I couldn't stop obsessing:

How had I gotten outside without tripping the alarm? How had I made it across the grounds without the motion sensors going off?

And how had I'd gotten past *Kamal*, the *security guard* stationed in the mudroom just beside the front door with a *gun*, whose entire job was to watch the grounds for strange people doing strange things? It was like I'd teleported outside as soon as I'd fallen asleep. It wasn't possible.

I swallowed. It didn't matter how I'd gotten outside. The only thing that mattered now was making sure no one heard me come back. Because then I'd have to try to explain why I'd been out there in the first place.

There is nothing to explain! I told myself, a little giddy. I'd been sleepwalking, that was all. I'd wandered outside. I woke up when I got to the pool. *Nothing happened.*

Years later, I would think back at that moment and marvel at the mental gymnastics I was able to perform, the sheer force of will it had taken for me to push the memory of the raccoon—of what I'd wanted to *do* to that raccoon—out of my head. But I'd had to. I wouldn't have been able to live with myself if I'd accepted what had just happened, what I'd tried to do.

I met my eyes in the mirror and took a deep breath and said it again, out loud, "Nothing happened."

There was a sound like a twig breaking outside, and I jerked my head around, frowning. All I saw was my own reflection staring back at me from the windows.

Still, I felt a tingle of exposure. Anyone could be outside looking in. Watching me.

I crossed the room and fumbled along the wall for the switch to turn the back-porch lights on. It was a moment before I found the right one, flipped it—

Snow had begun to fall. The flakes were mushy and wet, the kind that were almost rain. I squinted trying to see past them, but whenever I exhaled, clouds of condensation exploded across the glass.

There was movement in the darkness. I shaded my eyes and now I could make out something—

A woman. I could see the outline of her figure, her dark hair, but the fog and darkness obscured the rest of her.

Everything inside of me constricted in fear. I couldn't see her face; I couldn't be totally sure whether it was the same woman from the hospital, whether it was Emily or Talia, but there was *something* about the way she tilted her head to the side like a bird that I recognized.

I stumbled backward, wanting to get far away from the window, far away from *her*. But before I could scream, before I could do *any-thing*, I heard footsteps slamming down the hall, and then Kamal was bursting through the bathroom door.

"Something tripped the motion sensor, ma'am," he explained calmly. "I need you to step away from the window while I secure the grounds."

"I just saw...she was *outside*, just now." I motioned to the window, pointing, but the woman was already gone. "She was just there."

"All right, stay here," Kamal told me, already reaching for the gun at his hip. "Do *not* leave the bathroom, do you understand? Stay away from the windows and lock the door."

"But—"

It was too late. He was already gone.

I had to call the police. I didn't have my cell with me, but Talia still had a landline. I grabbed the cordless phone from the hall and locked myself in the bathroom again, just like Kamal told me to. I dialed 9-1-1, and a dispatcher informed me that someone would be at my property as soon as possible. Thank God.

I tried Dex's cell after I hung up, but of course he didn't answer. He never answered.

I closed my eyes, trying to calm myself down. Stress was bad for the baby. I needed to try and stay calm.

But what if she was already inside the house? What if she'd climbed the stairs to the second floor and Dex didn't hear her and she found him, alone and sleeping—

There was a sound outside, a soft rustle, like wind in the leaves. I jerked my head back to the window.

"Kamal?" My voice was barely a whisper. No one outside would've been able to hear me. I cleared my throat and tried again, louder this time, "Kamal? Is that you?"

No answer.

I heard Kamal's voice in my head as I curled my hand around the bathroom door. *Do not leave the bathroom, do you understand?* It took everything I had to push that voice away. I was on the first floor, just a few feet away from the side entrance. I was exposed and alone. Kamal was wrong; I wasn't safe here. I needed to get upstairs, with Dex. I would feel safe if I was with Dex.

My heart was beating in my throat, and my ears were filled with static. I pushed the bathroom door open and exhaled unevenly, my breath releasing in two ragged sobs.

The hall was dark, empty. I looked to one side and then the other.

The side door, the door I'd just *snuck in through*, was hanging open, moonlight spilling in from outside.

I stopped breathing. Did I leave it open like that? Did Kamal? Or was she inside with me now, hiding somewhere in the shadows?

My hands were trembling. I noticed this in a detached way, like they didn't actually belong to me. I crept down the hall, away from the door, my movements jerky with fear. I thought I heard something outside, the shuffling sound of movement, and I flinched and looked over my shoulder. I'd pictured her coming out from around the other side of the door, creeping up behind me. But there was no one there.

Fear roared up inside of me. I almost ran back to the bathroom right then and locked myself inside, but my need to get my baby somewhere safe was stronger. I had to keep going. I had to get up the stairs.

The floor was cold beneath my bare feet. I shivered. The stairs were just ahead. I was almost there.

And then a hand dropped onto my shoulder.

I screamed, or I tried to. The sound never actually made it to my lips. Instead, I felt it reverberate inside of me, like a rock skidding through a cave, the sound of something small echoing through the darkness. I took a single clumsy step backward, nearly losing my balance.

Dex was the one who grabbed my arms, steadying me. It took a long moment for me to focus on his face. Dex. He was the one who'd touched my shoulder. *Dex*, not her, not the woman out in the yard. She hadn't gotten to me. I was safe. I could've cried.

Oh thank God.

"Anna?" Dex said, frowning. "What are you doing out here?"

"Dex," I murmured, exhaling. "I thought... Oh God, I thought..."

"What's going on? I heard something, and then I thought I saw Kamal running across the backyard."

I glanced over my shoulder. "She's here," I said. I could feel my pulse fluttering in my palms, quick and fast. "Or, she was."

Dex looked skeptical. "Did you *see* her?"

"No. I mean *yes*, but I didn't get a good look at her. She was outside the bathroom window, but it was so dark." I tried to move, but Dex still had me by the arms.

His grip tightened. "Anna..."

For a second, I was certain that he somehow knew what I'd been doing sneaking around in the dark. The pool, the raccoon. The bottom dropped out of my stomach.

Nothing happened, that voice inside of me hissed. I swallowed.

But Dex just exhaled. "Okay," he said. "Okay, why don't we go back inside and—" His eyes fixed on something behind me, and he stumbled backward, hands raised. "Hey, hey, it's just *me*."

I turned, fear flaring inside of my chest. But it wasn't her; it was Kamal, both hands wrapped around a gun aimed at the ground.

"I thought I told you to stay in the bathroom," he said to me.

I ignored him. "Where is she? Did you find her?" God, I hoped I sounded calmer than I felt.

Kamal wiped his nose. The skin on his hands was already red from the cold. "No. I'm going to do another full sweep before the police get here, but I think that whoever was here is already long gone."

―――

Two police officers showed up less than an hour later.

I waited inside with Dex and Kamal, watching the yellow beams of their flashlights dance through the trees like ghosts, listening to their scratchy, mechanical sounding voices echo through the glass. *"No luck on the east side...over..."*

They didn't find any sign of the woman I'd seen. The security cameras didn't pick anything up, and there weren't any fresh footprints in the snow or tire tracks in the driveway. Nothing. It was like she hadn't been there at all.

"But *I* saw someone," I insisted. I could hear the desperation in my voice. I couldn't help it; I badly wanted to be believed. "I know I saw someone."

Dex's eyes lingered on me for a long moment, and then he turned to Kamal, talking to him instead of me. "She could've seen a shadow. Or maybe it was a reflection in the window, like some weird trick of the light?"

"It wasn't a reflection; it was a *woman*," I insisted, my voice rising. I wasn't yelling; I just wanted my husband to talk to *me* about what *I'd* seen. But Dex put a hand on the back of my arm, as though telling me to calm me down, and I knew I was making everyone uncomfortable. I could feel the energy in the room shifting, everyone dismissing me as some hysterical woman, some hysterical *pregnant* woman.

"Why would I lie about this?" I asked, struggling to keep my voice calm. "What could I possibly gain?"

"No one thinks you're lying, honey," Dex said, squeezing my arm. "We believe you, we do."

But the way he looked at me with his forehead all crinkled, I could tell he didn't mean that.

VIVIANA TORRES, 1978

VIV USED TO THINK SHE WANTED BREASTS. BACK WHEN SHE was younger, like eleven or twelve years old, she thought of them as adult and feminine and sexy, things to be coveted, a sign that she was starting to become a woman finally. Now, she knew better.

Hers had first appeared when she was only thirteen. She'd looked like she was about nine until, seemingly overnight, her breasts *erupted*. That was the only way Viv could think to describe it. One day there was nothing but the fleshy buds all her friends had. And the next they were very much there. Not a teenage girl's boobs, but a woman's *breasts*. At thirteen.

They made high school impossible. Girls hated her. Boys teased her. Viv's parents were deeply religious and insisted she attend St. Mary's Catholic School, and all her teachers seemed to be deeply offended by her body. They were constantly telling her to put on more clothes, to button up or add a sweater, or even once, *horrifyingly*, to buy a better bra.

Anyway. That's why she'd gone all the way at that party a few months ago. She'd known it was a mistake. Hell, she couldn't even remember the guy's name, just that he had good eyes and he was nice to her. She'd needed that. She'd needed to believe, just for one night, that her body could be what she'd always hoped it would be, adult and feminine and sexy. That it could make her feel good instead of terrible.

Then, not even three weeks later, came the nausea, the exhaustion, the crazy sensitivity to smells. Viv suspected what was happening long before she took a test. Pregnant at sixteen. Her Catholic parents and teachers were going to love that.

Viv wanted an abortion, but she lived right smack in the middle of Texas, hours away from any clinic that would give her one, and she didn't have access to a car or money or the kinds of parents who would give their permission, which was what all the clinics seemed to require. She knew of a couple of girls who'd gotten them illegally, and she considered it, but the risks were so terrifying, so dangerous.

Her friend Sofia said she had another idea, something safer. She knew of a ritual that could take care of it. Sofia's parents had come to the United States from Mexico, just like Viv's had, but they weren't Catholic. In fact, Sofia's great-aunt was Isabella Navarro, the famous bruja. Any ritual Sofia knew about would've come from her. And it was probably legit.

Sofia had Viv ingest herbs and seeds to "prepare her body for the spell." She made her lie on her back on the floor, and she traced a star on her forehead with something sticky. Viv thought it might be blood, but she couldn't figure out where Sofia would've gotten it. She decided she didn't want to know. Sofia said some spooky-sounding words and that was it. The ritual was over.

But two months after the spell, Viv felt something moving inside of her. And she started craving things. *Weird* things. The ground-up hamburger in the supermarket meat aisle. The raw chicken her mother was seasoning for dinner. Her neighbor's dog. And she'd gained weight. A lot of it, right around her belly. She figured the ritual Sofia had performed hadn't worked after all. She must still be pregnant.

"That doesn't sound like a normal pregnancy," Sofia said when Viv told her. She was staring at Viv's stomach, and she looked…scared. It took her a long moment to pull her eyes away. "I think I did it wrong. I think we need to talk to my aunt."

Viv felt suddenly cold. Pregnancy was bad enough. But a pregnancy that wasn't "normal?" What did that even mean?

They called Isabella and told her everything. "Mijitas," Isabella said, her voice grave and shaky over the phone. "What have you done?" She wasn't in the country, but she told them she would come as soon as possible. In the meantime, they weren't to speak with any doctors or take any medication or tell anyone else about what was happening to Viv. "I can fix this," Isabella promised, "but only if you do exactly as I say."

Viv really hoped that was true. Because this "pregnancy"—or whatever it was—had progressed. It wasn't just nausea and strange cravings anymore. Viv was starting to…to *see* things. *Impossible* things.

Sometimes, when Viv was alone in the dark, staring at the soft mound of her stomach, she could swear that whatever was inside of her could feel her watching it. She imagined she could see the shape of a hand pressed up against the underside of her skin. Except the hand…it wasn't a normal hand.

At least not a normal human hand.

WEEK 27

Welcome to the last week of your second trimester—get ready, the end is in sight!

24

IT WAS TWO DAYS BEFORE THE OSCARS. LATER THAT NIGHT, Dex and I were going to take a private plane out to LA. Kamal had strongly advised against giving my favorite designer access to the house, so I'd done a few virtual fittings over Zoom, and now my gown and Dex's tux were being sent ahead and were waiting for us at Chateau Marmont. I hadn't packed anything else yet—I hadn't even gotten my suitcases down from the closet. I was having a hard time thinking about the Academy Awards as a real thing that was happening. The part of my life where I was an actor preparing for the awards felt far away, something happening to a character I was reading about in a book, not something that was happening in real life.

I wasn't Anna the actor anymore. No, I was the Anna whose hair was falling out, the Anna who snuck out of bed in the middle of the night to find dead animal carcasses in the pool.

I was running late for a virtual training session when I finally dragged myself out of bed. Dex and I had debated whether it was a good idea for me to continue personal training, but decided it was necessary to my mental health that I get some physical activity. We were still trying to limit the number of people who knew I was pregnant, but in the end, we figured it would be fine as long as I kept my camera off so my trainer, Mila, wouldn't see my belly. It wasn't as effective this way, but it was better than nothing.

"I'm going to have you start with some yoga stretches," Mila said once I'd finally logged in. "Why don't you get into a wide-legged child's pose for me?"

I did as I was told, unfurling my yoga mat and dropping to my knees, pressing my hips back and down, my forehead going to the floor. I couldn't seem to get comfortable. In this position it was impossible to ignore how huge my belly had gotten. It pressed into the floor beneath me, causing odd aches along the sides of my body, like strained muscles. I tried to breathe, but I couldn't manage to fill my lungs.

Mila told me to lift into downward dog.

I raised my hips, struggling to get my knees underneath me. My body felt foreign, like someone had switched it out with another woman's while I was sleeping. I couldn't make it do the things it normally did. I felt dizzy, off balance. My knees shook, struggling to hold up my weight.

"Remember to breathe, Anna..."

I inhaled slowly, through my nose, but I still couldn't manage to get a full breath of air. It felt like there was something lodged in my throat, something small and sharp.

I held my breath because I knew that any sound I made would turn into a sob. Something was wrong, something bad. My arms trembled, struggling to hold me up. I had a perfect view of my belly from my position upside down, and I watched it shift and distort beneath my tank top.

It's just gas, I told myself. It had to be.

But I clenched my eyes shut, feeling sick.

Mila told me to come to a standing position at the front of my mat.

I raised my hands over my own head, feeling awkward as I tried to follow along. My legs, my arms, everything was shaking. I couldn't hold myself together, couldn't keep my balance. My breath was coming in short, shallow bursts.

Still, I tried to push through, tried to let my spine curve like it used to curve, even as I felt dizzier. I closed my eyes, swaying on my feet.

The thing in my throat shifted. It felt exactly like eating fish and accidentally swallowing one of their tiny bones, that too-long, too-sharp feeling of something stuck in my throat, poking me. I forced myself to swallow again and again, but the thing didn't move. It *pierced*.

Mila was saying something about my core, how I needed to use my core, but I couldn't hear her. I started to cough. I dug my toes into my yoga mat, but I couldn't keep my balance. I listed to the right, stopped myself from falling by putting a hand down—so hard I felt the bones in my wrist shudder.

And that's when I felt it: the thinnest trickle down the back of my throat, the taste of copper on my tongue.

I started coughing. And then I wasn't just coughing, I was gagging, choking, deep phlegmy sounds that echoed through the studio. I was on all fours, hunched over, *hacking*.

Mila's voice blared from my computer's speakers, "Anna? Anna, oh my God, are you okay?"

I tried to wave at her but of course she couldn't see me with the camera off, and I couldn't say anything, I was coughing much, much too hard. I clawed at my neck, my eyes blurry with tears.

I could feel it, the shape of it inside of me, hard and small and so, so sharp. Whatever it was, it didn't belong and my mind spun, trying to come up with an explanation that wasn't completely terrible. Was it a piece of food I hadn't digested properly? It didn't feel like food. It felt dangerous. A paper clip. A nail.

I doubled over and *spat*.

It landed on the floor in a spray of blood, something small, and even with all the blood I immediately clocked the color: the eerie white-yellow of bone.

Bone. How could I have swallowed a bone?

I reeled backward, choking. It took me a moment to catch my breath, to blink the tears from my eyes.

A few seconds passed. Mila was shouting from my computer, asking what was going on, if I was okay. I ignored her. I could see again, and my breathing had steadied, and I knew it was time to examine the thing on the floor. The thing I'd just coughed up. It took all of my willpower to lean over to pick it up, let it roll to the palm of my hand.

It wasn't a bone, though the color was the same. It was a tiny tooth.

25

THIS TOOTH WASN'T ONE OF MINE. I KNEW THAT, AND YET I counted the teeth in my own head, my tongue moving swiftly across the lower row, and then the top, lingering on the sore, still-bloody gap on my gums.

But I could tell just by looking at the tooth resting in my palm that it wasn't human. It was far too small to fit comfortably inside of my own mouth, and the shape was all wrong: smooth and long and yellow, a flat surface that tapered to a finer edge on one end, a single long root on the other. It was bloody.

Oh God.

I blinked, suddenly aware that Mila was shouting from my computer. "Are you okay? Anna? I thought I heard choking..."

I curled my hand around the strange tooth, feeling sick. "I'm fine, I'm sorry. I–I'm just...I'm not feeling well. I should go."

Mila was still talking, asking me if I was sure I was okay, if she could do anything, if I needed anything, when I snapped my computer shut, cutting her off.

It was rude, but I couldn't bring myself to care. I was too focused on the small, sharp tooth in my hand, the way it bit into my skin.

I couldn't ignore this. I had to figure out what it was, how it had gotten into my throat. I took one breath, then another, and then I opened my hand.

The tooth wasn't there. I could see a tiny prick of red on my palm where I'd squeezed too tightly, and it had pierced my skin. But the tooth itself was gone.

I'd dropped it. I looked all over the floor, under my shoes, and then I checked the corners, certain it had skittered to the edge of the room. But I didn't find it again.

I found an air vent in the corner of the room, half-hidden behind an armchair. The tooth must've slipped between my fingers, bounced across the carpet, and dropped into the vent. That was the only explanation.

I opened my hand again, studying that tiny prick of red to remind myself that it had really been there, that I had felt it.

Watching that small mark fade, taking with it all my certainty.

———

Dex was working at the dining room table, but he looked up when I walked past, and asked how I was feeling, if I needed anything. I hesitated for a moment, considering telling him what had just happened. But,\ if I told him about the tooth, he'd want to see it, and then I'd have to explain that it'd disappeared. And I already knew how he'd respond to my story about the vent, how he'd look at me. No, I was keeping this to myself.

I hurried upstairs, locked myself in the master bath. Sweat had broken out on the back of my neck. I couldn't breathe, couldn't think past the sound of blood pumping in my ears. I felt frozen.

"I dropped it," I said out loud, my voice not even a whisper. "I dropped it and it fell down the vent."

Of course, that didn't make me feel any better. I still needed to explain how I'd swallowed it in the first place.

You can't trust anyone.

Could someone have snuck something into my food? Was that where the tooth had come from? If they did, I needed to know for sure. Certain types of raw meat contained bacteria that could be fatal to an unborn child. It was why doctors told women to be careful around undercooked steak and deli meat. Toxoplasmosis, for example, could cause miscarriage, stillbirth, brain defects. Could I have a parasite inside of my body even now, getting closer to my baby, closer to infecting her, hurting her?

I pulled out my phone and dialed Dr. Hill's number with shaking fingers. Cora answered and told me that Dr. Hill was on a call and couldn't speak right now.

I told her that I needed Dr. Hill to call me back immediately, but I could hear that my voice had gotten high, verging on hysterical.

"Is this an emergency?" Cora asked. To my relief, it sounded like she was taking me seriously. "Because if it's an emergency, you really should go to the emergency room—"

There was no way in hell I was going back there. "It's not an emergency," I said as calmly as I could. "It's just important."

"I'll let Dr. Hill know," Cora said. "In the meantime, try to take it easy. Take a nap, maybe, or have a bath?"

A bath. After I hung up, I switched the bathtub faucet on, deciding to take her advice. I did need to try to calm down. Stress was bad for the baby. And there could still be some other gross but perfectly rational explanation for the tooth. How many times had I heard horror stories of people finding disgusting things in their takeout? A dead mouse at the bottom of a salad, or a cockroach wrapped in the folds of a burrito. The tooth could've been in something I'd eaten, and I swallowed it and then coughed it back up.

Or it could've been in my head, I thought. A sign that something was wrong with my brain instead of my body.

My fingers curled toward my palms. I couldn't decide which was more terrifying. I vowed to look for the tooth again after my bath. I would get into the vent. I would dig up the floorboards if I had to.

Water thundered into the copper tub, steam rising all around me. As I waited for the tub to fill, I closed my eyes and tried to tell myself that everything was going to be okay, that I'd get to the bottom of what had just happened, that I wouldn't let anyone hurt my baby.

But I couldn't stop imagining some parasite winding its way through my body. Closer, closer.

A mirror hung above the double vanity, taking up nearly the whole wall. I studied my reflection as I peeled off my yoga clothes. My collarbone jutted out from my chest, and my hip bones protruded unnaturally from below my skin. But my belly seemed to have gotten even bigger. It was a tight round mound that dwarfed the rest of my body, odd looking and strange. I felt heavy, bloated.

I tried out a smile, tried to be happy—no matter what else, I was still pregnant, my baby was still here, still growing—but I was too rattled.

The tub was full now. Heat steamed up the room, fogging the mirror. I switched the faucet off and slipped in, letting water rush over my thighs and belly. The room was very quiet, only the sound of water dripping from the faucet and the creak of glass from the sky-light overhead.

My belly was an island rising from the water. I felt a flicker of movement and then again, another little twitch. It was incredible how much the baby moved now, kicking and turning over inside of me.

I smiled and touched my belly just as a bulge formed below the surface of my skin. The bulge surprised me, and I jerked my hand back. God, I was jumpy. I'd heard other pregnant people talk about this, how they sometimes saw the shape of a tiny foot or hand pressed just below the skin of their belly. It was strange, but perfectly normal. Like the baby saying hi.

I stared at the bulge, feeling my smile flicker. It didn't look like a hand or a foot. It was too long, too thin. I tilted my head, nerves fluttering through me as I examined it. The shape didn't actually look like a part of the human anatomy that I could think of. So what was it?

I thought of the tooth and curled my fingers into the bottom of the tub, anxious now. I was starting to feel light-headed. I stared at the bulge below my skin and tried to figure out what it might be. It was too thin to be an elbow or a knee. Too sharp-looking to be a hand.

A horrible thought occurred to me: if there'd been some strange tooth inside of me, then what else? A bone? An entire jaw?

Sweat broke out on my forehead and along the back of my neck. I exhaled through my nose and my eyelids fluttered. But I didn't dare move. I had the strange thought that, whatever it was, I didn't want to upset it.

Without warning, the bulge moved. I felt something sharp radiate through my torso and cried out, curling around my belly. It hurt more than it usually did when the baby moved. Not like a dull ache, but like a splinter, like a paper cut on the wrong side of my skin. I pushed my body up against the very back of the tub, whimpering slightly. Despite the hot water, I was suddenly cold.

What is happening? Is the baby okay? Is something wrong?

The bulge turned, shifting to the side before disappearing below my skin. I felt a moment of relief before it twisted inside of me and then I gasped, water rolling into my mouth over my tongue. I came dangerously close to inhaling a mouthful but scooted up a little at the last second and spit it out. What the hell was going on?

I watched, numb with fear, as something new jutted up from beneath my skin. It was small and sharp-edged, like a fingernail pressing at the underside of my belly. It was like the baby was *poking* me. I released my breath in a little burst of panic. God, it hurt. I felt the bite of it against me, not cutting yet but *close*, like when you pushed a knife into the pad of your finger to test the blade. It was like the baby was doing something to me intentionally. Like she was trying to hurt me.

Something's wrong, I thought, horrified. Whatever this feeling inside of me was, it was definitely *wrong*. Pregnancy wasn't supposed to feel like this; it wasn't supposed to hurt like *this*.

The pressure to the underside of my skin increased, subtly at first, and then all at once, that press of something sharp hardening to a jab. It was...it was *cutting* me. I gasped out loud and bolted upright, water sloshing over the sides and hitting the floor in great sloppy splashes.

My belly bulged, and then I felt a blistering pierce of something barbed splitting my flesh. Something black appeared, small and burrowing out of my skin like an insect. I stared in horror, not quite believing what I was seeing. This couldn't be happening. It wasn't possible.

Blood seeped into the water and spread, blossoming like a flower. The small, pointed thing grew bigger until it curved out of me.

I was aware, distantly, that my body was cold and shaking badly, my spine jerking against the side of the tub. I couldn't hold myself steady. My fingers kept slipping against the porcelain.

There was a creak of wood just outside the bathroom door, a footstep maybe, or just the house settling. I ignored it, focusing all my attention on the small sharp curve jutting out of my skin. It was black and smooth, not even a quarter of an inch long and tapered at one end, the other end still disappearing inside of me.

The hair on the back of my neck stood straight up.

It was a talon. A nasty, sharp one, like something that belonged to a large, predatory bird. It twitched, the movement feral, an animal trying to pull herself free.

It was too much. I couldn't handle it. I was shuddering all over, my muscles jerking against the sides of the tub. I felt like a little kid, that desperate fear you only felt when you were young and small and scared. I needed someone to hold me and tell me it was all going to be all right. This was a nightmare, a living nightmare. I desperately wanted to wake up.

My eyes blurred. I felt my breath hitch. I was properly sobbing now. Tears fell freely down my cheeks, making it impossible to see. I wiped my eyes with the back of my hand, and—

And the talon wasn't there anymore. I stared, frozen for a moment, trying to understand. It wasn't just that it wasn't there—it's that it never seemed to have *been* there. The skin I'd saw it curl out of was unbroken—no cut on my belly, no blood in the water. I lowered a trembling hand to my belly, cringing a little when I touched the place where I'd seen it. It was deeply bruised, like something had pushed too hard against the underside of my skin. But it was clear that nothing had come out.

The talon—whatever it was—was gone.

26

DEX KNELT IN FRONT OF ME, THE DAMP MARBLE LEAVING FAINT wet spots on his jeans. "I still don't understand why you were screaming like that."

I was sitting at the side of the tub, still shaking even though I was dry now, a bathrobe draped around my shoulders, and it took a second for his comment to work its way through the fog in my brain.

"I told you," I murmured, hugging my arms around myself. "I thought I saw...something. It scared me."

He frowned. I could tell he didn't believe me, but he didn't press it either. For that, at least, I was grateful. I had no idea how I was supposed to explain what I'd just seen—what I'd just thought I'd seen. I didn't even know how to explain it to myself.

I looked down at my stomach, where the only sign of what had happened were the bruises now standing out in stark contrast against my pale skin. They looked so similar to the bruises I used to get from my IVF injections, like smears of mud that I should be able to wipe off.

Bruising could be a symptom of inflammation, I thought, remembering some random fact I'd picked up in my pregnancy reading.

It could also be a sign of vitamin deficiency. But I'd always bruised easily. I'd tell Dr. Hill about them, of course. But I was more worried about my mind.

First the raccoon, and then the tooth, and now I was having full-on hallucinations. What was wrong with me?

I swallowed. I had no explanation. And the worst part was that it made me doubt everything else I'd experienced. Not just the tooth that I was so sure I'd coughed up, but everything I'd blamed on my stalker. The drugs and parasites and the woman sneaking around outside, the creaking I kept hearing, like there was someone moving through the house—

What if none of it had happened? Or, if it had happened, what if it hadn't happened like I'd thought it had? What if my brain was tricking me, making things seem different than they were in reality?

Staring at those bruises, I felt a sudden rush of shame. I realized I had no idea what was real and what wasn't. How did I expect Dex and my doctors to trust me when I couldn't trust myself?

Dex was looking at the bruises too. He traced them with one finger, carefully, like he was afraid I might break if he pressed too hard. "Did you bump up against something?" he asked, looking up at me.

"I–I don't remember," I lied. I felt light-headed. I kept seeing movement in the corner of my eyes, zipping shadows and flickering lights that had me glancing back down at my belly. Something rustled above us, some animal scurrying across the roof. *A raccoon*, I thought and flinched, my fingers wrapping tight around the sides of the tub. My heartbeat was loud in my ears.

Dex flicked a sideways glance at me. "Why don't you come downstairs? We can make some dinner."

When he touched my shoulder, I jerked away, my skin crawling and he looked so surprised, so hurt. I should've explained, told him that it wasn't him, that I didn't want to be touched right now, not by anyone. I wanted to peel the skin off my body so I could see what the hell was happening inside of me.

But all I said was, "Actually, I...I think I need a second. I'll come down in a minute, okay?"

"Yeah, okay," Dex said, frowning. "Of course. If that's what you want." And he headed into the hall, dejected, leaving the bathroom door open for me to follow.

I waited until he left to try to stand. My knees knocked together so badly that I stumbled and had to grab onto the edge of the vanity to steady myself, accidentally sending my bottle of prenatal vitamins to the ground. The bottle exploded, cap flying off, tiny capsules shooting everywhere.

I stared at the spilled capsules for long moments, my chest heaving. My eyesight seemed to double, so that I couldn't tell which were real and which were tricks of my head.

Was I going crazy? I'd *felt* that tooth, first in my throat and then in the palm of my hand. And the claw...I'd *watched* it curve out of me like a fishing hook, slicked with blood. And then both had just...vanished.

How? What other explanation was there if I wasn't losing my mind?

I tried to hold on to the memories of those things, the way the tooth had bit into the palm of my hand, the hot pain as the claw curved out of my belly. It was as if, by remembering them, I could prove that they'd been real, that I wasn't sick. But they kept slipping away from me, until I couldn't say for sure what I'd felt, what I'd seen.

I knelt, cringing as I tried to reach past my belly to scoop the pills back into the bottle.

The door to the hall moved all of a sudden, hinges releasing a slow creak. I looked up, breathing hard. It was probably nothing. I forced myself to stay still, to keep calm.

Footsteps approached.

No, not footsteps. It was like the tooth and the talon. It was all in my head. Or maybe it was my own heartbeat echoing in my ears?

A few vitamins dropped from my hands, rattling as they hit the tile. My fingers felt suddenly thick, much too clumsy to hold them.

"No," I whimpered. I felt suddenly small and helpless, like a child. "Please," I murmured to myself, "please, I can't take anymore." As if I could convince my mind to go a little easier on me.

But when I looked up again, I saw a woman reflected in the mirror. She had dark hair and red lipstick. She smiled at me, a strange, stiff smile that didn't seem to reach her eyes.

Meg.

There was lipstick streaked across her front tooth, a bright red stain like blood. She was holding a *Spellbound* doll by the leg. There was a tiny blindfold tied around the doll's face, covering its eyes.

I heard a roaring sound in my ears. I tried to stand too fast and lost my balance, clipping my shoulder into the bottom of the sink, which caused me to slam right back down onto my knees. The pain was immediate and nauseating, tile hitting both kneecaps at the exact same moment and in the exact right spot to send twin daggers radiating up my bones. Tears leapt to my eyes and, for a moment, the room blinked out. I released a choked scream.

"Anna." It was Dex's voice, I realized. Dex was speaking directly into my ear. If I concentrated, I could feel his hand on my back, rubbing in slow circles "Anna, can you hear me?"

Slowly, slowly, I came back into my body. I was crouched on the floor in a weak pool of moonlight, curled around my bump, prenatal vitamins scattered around me. Meg wasn't there. She'd already gone.

If she'd even been here at all.

I gasped, sweating. My throat was raw. There was hair sticking to my face and cheeks. I had no idea whether she'd really been there, or it was another hallucination. There was no sign of her, no clue. I was disoriented, my knees and shoulder still aching.

I sucked a breath through my lips. My eyelids fluttered.

"What-what happened?" I murmured.

"You collapsed, baby. I heard you scream, and by the time I ran back up here, you were already on the ground."

BETTY ANDERSON, 1833

IT WAS A DEPRESSING PLACE, THIS HOUSE. WILD-LOOKING trees had grown up over the windows, letting in hardly any light, and the dreary rooms and thick plaster walls muffled all outside noises. Frances wanted to leave, but she had come here with a purpose: she needed to see her dear friend Betty. She'd been trying to see her for weeks, but Betty had been struggling since the birth of her child, and her husband and doctors had made it impossible. Frances was determined to comfort Betty, to have tea and cookies and find a way to get her through this. It was only once the door had closed behind her that she felt her first real trickles of unease.

It was the baby's screams that weren't quite right. Shirley, her name was. Her low, terrible wails echoed from some upstairs room. They sounded too thin and oddly...

Animalistic. *Unnatural.*

Frances turned to Betty's husband, Charles, and said, "Where is she?"

Charles hesitated. "I am not sure it is...wise for you to see her just now. She needs more time."

"She's *had* time, Charles. Weeks and weeks of it." Betty had been placed on Dr. Weir Mitchell's famous "rest cure." That meant isolation and bed rest, no going outside, no company.

It had been six weeks of this already. Surely these men couldn't mean to keep her locked up forever?

"She is different than you remember, Frances," Charles explained. "She is half mad. She won't see the baby, or me. She won't *sleep*. She says—" he paused, glancing up the stairs, as though expecting to see his wife standing behind him. When he spoke again, his voice was much lower. "She says there are people who want to steal the baby from her."

Frances felt a chill, listening to this. It did not sound like the Betty she knew at all.

"Is she going out at all?" she asked Charles. "Taking walks in the garden?"

He shook his head. "No. Weir Mitchell said she is not to overexert herself."

Of course he did, Frances thought. These doctors always seemed to think women's emotions were things to be hidden and locked away and fixed. But Frances knew better. More likely than not this so called "cure" for Betty's madness was the cause of it. Which meant Betty needed her more than she thought. She couldn't let them destroy her friend any more than they had already.

"I will be quick," she told Charles. "I promise. Just a few minutes."

Frances slipped past Charles, climbing the stairs despite his weak protestations. Six weeks was too long for anyone to be alone.

The air in the house was stagnant, foul smelling. It made Frances's nose itch to breathe it in. The halls were filled with creeping shadows, creaking floorboards. Frances had always said she did not believe in haunted houses, but here she could almost think she'd stepped beyond the veil and into the other world. It felt as though she herself were a ghost, her body no longer entirely solid, but a specter moving through these darkened halls. The thought made her shiver.

Then she reached the second floor, and her body become real to her once more. She was suddenly aware of her sweating palms and her pounding heart, her fear growing and spreading like a disease below her skin.

The wails she'd assumed belonged to the baby were not coming from the nursery. They were coming from Betty's room, most likely from Betty herself, and they sounded...

Wretched. Like the keening of an animal in pain.

Frances's fear grew. What had these men done?

Steeling herself for what she was about to see, she tapped softly on Betty's doors. The wails quieted at once. Somehow, the silence was worse than the howling had been. It didn't seem natural that whatever had been making those noises was capable of following directions. If it was, it meant the howling had been a choice.

"Betty?" Frances called through the door. Her voice quavered. "It is Frances; I've come to help you."

When Betty did not answer, Frances tried the door and found it unlocked. She pushed it open.

Betty was kneeling on the floor, one shoulder pressed into the wall, hair hanging over her face in unwashed clumps, dark gaps in her scalp where it seemed to be missing. Her dress was torn and hanging open at the chest, her breasts exposed and pale in the darkness. The dress had ripped open at the knees, and Betty's skin was bleeding from where she'd been crawling on the floor. She'd left a trail of blood all around the room, a gruesome path.

Frances threw her hands over her mouth. She didn't dare breathe or speak. How long had they left her in this room alone? How could they have thought this might help? She could still fix this, but she needed to act now.

Betty looked up, one eye staring from beneath that hair. "They took her!" she said in a voice that sounded raspy and inhuman, nothing like her normal voice. "They took my baby, just like you told me they would. They took her!"

You may feel some
Braxton-Hicks contractions
as your body practices
for the big day

27

STRESS IS BAD FOR THE BABY. EVERY PREGNANCY BOOK THERE
is will tell you that. Cortisol, the stress hormone, can damage a developing fetus. It can increase risk of miscarriage, hypertension, premature birth, and postnatal development delays. I had to stay calm, no matter what was happening to me. My baby was depending on it.

And so I let Dex lead me back to my bed and wrap me in blankets. I drank mug after mug of chamomile tea.

But in my head, where no one could see me, I couldn't stop screaming.

Dr. Hill didn't want me traveling and insisted on coming to me instead. She was at our house within hours, unpacking ultrasound equipment in my bedroom, telling me to undress below the waist, to try and relax.

I stared at her. *Relax?* How could she possibly expect me to relax? I wanted to cry. I wanted to throw things. For a moment, I felt like my body had been taken hostage, like all of my actions were being controlled—not by the baby inside of me, but by the people tasked with keeping her healthy.

Dr. Hill didn't seem to notice this battle going on inside my head. She slathered gel over my belly and ran the wand across my skin. I closed my eyes and tried to focus on my breathing.

When I opened my eyes again, I saw that my baby had appeared on the ultrasound screen, a tiny little sea monkey squirming around in outer space, the sound of her heartbeat like a bass drum. Dr. Hill smiled and told me everything was healthy, that I was overstressed, that I should take a nap, a bath, another aspirin.

I dug my fingernails into my palms. *Breathe*, I told myself. *Just breathe; it's all going to be okay.*

But I could feel my heart beating faster, my chest seizing, like I was about to have a heart attack, cortisol flooding through me even as I did everything I could to make myself calm. It wasn't enough to drink tea and practice deep breathing. The only way I was going to be able to relax was by getting answers. Either I was losing my mind, or something truly horrifying was happening to my body. It seemed ridiculous that all anyone ever told me was that I needed to take another damn aspirin.

Bed rest, Dr. Hill decided. Not for the rest of my pregnancy, she promised, but for a few weeks, at least until I was feeling better.

"I'd like you to try and limit stimuli," she told me with a wan smile. "We don't want you getting overexcited."

"But...what about the Oscars?" I asked, and no one said a word because it was obvious: I wouldn't be going to LA tonight. I wouldn't be going anywhere for a while.

———

I found out the morning after that I didn't win—Gugu Mbatha-Raw won for her role as Ophelia in *Hamlet*. I tried to watch her speech online, but I got as far as, "I'd like to thank the Academy," and had to turn it off.

I was bombarded with phone calls and texts in the days afterward, Kevin and Georgia telling me I was robbed, asking if they could come out to see me, my dad saying that every important actor needed to lose the Oscar a few times before getting her big win, my new manager offering her condolences, telling me that it didn't matter whether I'd won or not, the offers were still pouring in—

I hung up on her then and stopped answering the phone. Maybe Dr. Hill was right, maybe I needed to limit my external stimuli. Or maybe I just didn't want to deal with the outside world. In either case, I rarely left my room after that, and I avoided contact with almost everyone. Dex didn't even sleep in the same bed with me, opting instead for the spare bedroom. He said he didn't want to disturb me. But sometimes, I noticed that his light was still on when I got up to use the restroom at two or three in the morning. Once, I heard his voice murmuring on the other side of the door, seeming to talk to someone. But when I knocked and asked if he was on the phone, he told me it was just a show he was watching on his computer.

I thought he might be lying, but I didn't trust myself enough to call him on it. I was having a hard time telling what was real and what wasn't, which thoughts I should trust and which I needed to ignore. It wasn't just paranoia; it was everything. Things had started sounding strange to me. It was mostly small things. I'd pull the curtains in my bedroom closed and the sound of the rings sliding over the rod was too soft, like I was hearing it through layers and layers of plastic.

Once, I closed my bathroom door and the sound of wood hitting wood was so loud I jumped.

I knew what it meant. Or I thought I did. I was going to have another hallucination. The only way I could think to stop it from happening was to completely close myself off. I kept the blackout curtains in the bedroom shut at all hours and set up the white noise machine we'd bought for the nursery on my bedside table. My room had begun to feel like a sensory deprivation tank: perfectly dark, the only sound the soft crackle of the white noise. It was almost like being in the womb.

Time behaved strangely. That was the nature of bed rest, I guess. Some days would last forever, hours stretching like taffy. On those days, I found myself thinking of fresh meat. Steak that was still pink in the center, blood pooling beneath the bone, and rabbit that tasted gamey and woodsy, like it had just been caught. On those days it took everything in me to ignore the churning in my stomach, the way the meat seemed to call to me. Other days seemed to end before I'd even had a chance to sit up, to get dressed, to brush my teeth.

I turned the white noise up as far as it would go, but even then I could never block the thoughts in my own head. They were there in the dark and through the white noise. They followed me when I slept.

Who was the woman Talia had been waving to in that photograph? Was it Meg? Did they know each other? I didn't know her last name, so I couldn't Google her. All I could do was think about it. *Obsess* about it. Could Talia have slipped me something? Was that why this was happening to me? Could she have done something to me? *Hurt* me? Or was I fooling myself thinking that any of this was really happening? Was it just paranoia? Another sign that I was losing what remained of my sanity?

My sensory deprivation tank stopped feeling warm and womb-like and began to feel more like a casket. It was as though I'd been buried alive. The darkness that had once seemed so safe was heavy, filled with things that flickered and vanished when I turned to look at them more closely. Sometimes I would swear I heard the shadows whispering to me. It sounded like they were saying my name over and over. *Anna. Anna. Anna.*

Suddenly, it was mid-April, and then June, and I swear it was like no time had passed at all. It was supposed to be spring, but it was still so cold, the weather predicting rain every other day. It was impossible that my due date was hovering just a month away, that all of this was nearly over. I just had to make it through four more weeks of bed rest. Just four more weeks of darkness and whispering and cravings that were getting harder to ignore. Four more weeks of questions.

And then I would have my baby. Finally.

—————

One day an alert from my phone split the soft crackle of my white noise: Io Preecher had released a new video.

I'd been getting alerts for Io's videos for months, but I'd never actually watched any of them. This was different. I went still when I saw it, my heart beating hard in my throat.

The thumbnail was a blurry shot of a woman with dark hair and red lipstick. It looked like Meg or Margaret or whoever she was, but

I wasn't sure. I looked from the thumbnail to the headline: *Is this the face of a witch?*

I felt a churn of disappointment. This was why I hadn't bothered watching anything Io posted before. She'd always seemed a little...off, the kind of person willing to believe baseless theories about satanic cults. It seemed unlikely that this had anything to do with what was going on with my body, my stalker. But this was the first lead I'd gotten, even if it was shaky. I hesitated, but my curiosity got the best of me. I hit Play.

The video started with a series of blurry photographs flashing across the screen. They'd been taken only seconds apart, and the effect was similar to watching an old flip-book, one still image after another, so fast it seemed as though the images themselves were moving. I watched the woman that could have been Meg walk into a fertility clinic, speak with someone behind the counter, then turn and walk out again.

Io spoke over the flashing images, her voice low and firm. "These photographs were taken the first week of May 2022 at the New Hope Fertility Clinic in Forest Hills, Queens. I was able to confirm that, of all the people who came to the clinic that week, this was the only woman who wasn't there for an appointment and who didn't—"

I quickly paused the video, cutting Io off. Then, holding my breath, I clicked back a few frames, paused it again.

This was the clearest image yet. The woman had looked over her shoulder, directly at whoever was taking her photograph. Her mouth was half open, a look of shock on her face.

My stomach gave a sick twist. It was her, the woman who'd given me the illicit ultrasound. I was absolutely sure.

I exhaled shakily and hit Play again.

The photograph was only on-screen for a moment before Io's face appeared, replacing it. She looked just as I remembered, her dark hair streaked through with gray, and faint lines around her wide unblinking eyes.

"I was able to confirm that, of all the people who came to the clinic that week, this was the only woman who wasn't there for an appointment and who didn't leave her name," Io was saying. "No one can say why she was at the clinic. She had no reason to be there. But just one week later, a pregnant woman who'd been treated at the same clinic was admitted to the emergency room, complaining of intense pain and hallucinations. Coincidence? I don't think so."

"As longtime followers of this channel already know, I believe there is a satanic cult operating in North America and the UK. I've been searching for its members for over twenty years and this, *this* photograph might the closest I've gotten to finding one."

The photo of Meg popped back onto the screen again. The clear one, where she was looking over her shoulder, seeming to look directly at the camera aimed at her.

"No," I murmured. What Io was talking about sounded like nonsense, like a throwback 80s Satanic Panic conspiracy theory. But in the darkness of my room, I couldn't help thinking of the claw I'd seen curve out of my belly, the tooth nestled in my palm, the dead raccoon lying at the bottom of the pool. Cold sweat broke out on my neck.

"This woman isn't working alone," Io continued. "These people are everywhere. You must be vigilant! Through my research, I've been able to trace members of her cult to New York, LA, even London."

My hands clamped into tight fists. I felt a jolt move through me with each new city she named. New York City, where Talia lived. LA, where Emily lived.

And London—where Adeline lived.

———————

I watched five of Io's videos in a row. From what I could tell, she seemed to be an old-school, Satanic Panic truther. She believed in satanic cults stealing babies and unborn fetuses for use in depraved rituals. She thought there were normal people—doctors and nurses, men and women—selling information on pregnant people in exchange for protection from these cults. She seemed to spend all her time trying to track these cultists down. Halfway through one video she explained that she traveled to clinics across New York and photographed the women who went in for appointments, hoping to catch another of these "witches" on camera.

I was deeply skeptical. Back when *Spellbound* was on the air, I used to get hate mail from people saying the show was glorifying the occult, that I was participating in satanic worship. I'd read up on the history of the Satanic Panic back then, and it was beyond clear that these theories had all been thoroughly debunked many times over. For one thing, real pagans and Wiccans existed, and they had nothing to do with Satan or child abuse. Many of them had been fans of the show and were actually very sweet. But Io still believed there were evil witches out there. It was enough to make me want to dismiss everything she said out of hand.

The thing that stopped me was that photograph of Meg—that, and the things Io said the witches *did*. Overall, her videos were infuriatingly vague. She spoke obliquely about strange cravings, weird symptoms, ER visits. She called the pregnancies "wrong" and would give an ominous shake of her head. But few details.

"This has been happening to us for decades," she said in one video. I wanted to grab her and scream, *What? What's been happening?*

She never said. She claimed the "information" she had was too sensitive to reveal online, that she couldn't risk it "getting into the wrong hands." She invited anyone who was curious to get in touch with her directly.

I didn't think Meg was a witch. But that didn't mean she wasn't involved in something deeply disturbing, something that affected me and my unborn child. And Io seemed to have information related to it. If I could sort through all the Satan worship nonsense, I might come away with something useful. And I was desperate. This was the first solid lead I had.

I wasn't going to be able to do anything about it from here. I opened my email account in a different browser and typed in the address she posted beneath every one of her videos.

Io, you don't know me, but I'm pregnant, and I think you might have some information about some disturbing symptoms I've been experiencing. I need to speak with you as soon as possible.

I considered the message. Then I deleted I need to speak with you as soon as possible and wrote instead, Can we meet?

All the while I was thinking *Please. Please, I'll go anywhere, do anything.* To hell with bed rest. I had to know what was happening to me.

28

I WOKE UP LATE THAT NIGHT, WHEN DEX CRAWLED INTO BED
behind me and sleepily kissed my neck.

"Babe?" I whispered, trying to turn my massive body over.

"Hmm?" he murmured, but I could already tell he was half asleep.
He was snoring before I managed to roll onto my back.

I gave up and fell onto my side, waiting to feel drowsy. But it was
no use. I was awake now, thinking of Io's videos, of the email I'd sent
her, the photograph of Meg walking into another fertility clinic.

Out of nowhere, my stomach rumbled.

The dogs were curled up at our feet like always. Three warm bodies.
I watched their bellies rise and fall in the dark, listened to the raspy
sound of their breathing.

Oz's leg twitched. He let out a soft, excited *yip*.

I wondered if he was dreaming of running. Chasing down a rabbit,
maybe. For a second, I imagined what that would be like: to feel the
warmth of the ground beneath my paws, all that adrenaline running
through my blood. God, it would be nice to desire such simple, easy
things. Running, chasing. *Food.*

My mouth watered. I thought I smelled something in the air, something rich, and twisted my fingers around my sheets, frustrated and hungry.

Happy shifted in her sleep, burying her nose deeper into the duvet. In an instant, all my attention was focused on her. I watched her little body move, muscles and fat rippling beneath fur, bones shifting. That's all she was, just meat wrapped in skin and fur. It was so strange to think about.

I could smell her, I realized. Not the normal dog scent she always had, kibble breath and sweat, but something deeper than that. She had a musk, the smell of meat and blood.

She smelled like food.

I inhaled sharply and bolted upright, feeling shaken. That thought...that was a seriously messed–up thought. Happy was my pet. She was my friend.

I couldn't understand why my mind had gone there. It was psychotic. It was *sick*.

I was just hungry, I told myself. It was making me think things I never thought, *want* things I'd never wanted. I'd read somewhere that when pregnant women didn't get enough calories, their bodies automatically fed the baby first, leaving the mother to starve. If that wasn't the perfect metaphor for pregnancy, I didn't know what was. I hadn't eaten enough today. These strange thoughts, they were just my body telling me I needed to feed myself.

Happy had lifted her head to watch me. Her ears were monstrous in the dark, pricked in that way that made her look half bat.

"Go," I told her, my voice low. I didn't want her anywhere near me, not when I felt like this. She tilted her head, confused, so I slapped the mattress and said it again, louder. "*Go.*"

With a yelp, she hopped off the bed and darted into the bathroom. My muscles tensed and tightened, wanting to follow her. To *hunt* her.

I needed to eat something. Now.

I climbed out of bed—carefully, carefully—and headed downstairs to the kitchen. I wanted to get away from the dogs, to redirect my hunger toward something reasonable. A sandwich, maybe.

I pulled the refrigerator open, and the light clicked on, illuminating my bump, my feet, spilling chilled air all over my bare legs. I was wearing a pair of underwear and one of Dex's T-shirts that didn't quite cover my bump, nothing else. Goose bumps climbed my calves, but I didn't feel cold. I'd never been so hungry in my life.

I scanned the first two shelves of the fridge: cheese and grapes and plastic containers filled with spinach and kale, a loaf of multigrain bread, baby carrots. I grimaced. *No.*

There was an open baggie of sliced turkey on the next shelf. Deli meat was bad for you when you were pregnant; it could hurt the baby. I felt my mouth water and I knew I should eat something else, that the meat was risky, but I couldn't help myself. I grabbed it and shoved a piece into my mouth without thinking twice.

It was slimy, cold, a little dry, the smell terrible. I didn't care. I chewed mindlessly, already knowing that this wasn't going to cut it. My stomach was twisting and aching. My baby was hungry. I needed to feed her.

Two raw pork chops sat on a plastic cutting board on the bottom shelf, salted and still on the bone, waiting to be cooked for tomorrow's dinner. Dex bought them after I'd told him the baby was craving meat, wanting to make me happy.

I stared at them as I chewed my turkey.

No. I couldn't.

The meat was pink and glistening, blood pooling between the bone and the cutting board. Deep in my belly, the baby turned over, awake. Excited.

The turkey dropped from my hands and fell to the floor at my feet with a wet splat. I reached into the fridge automatically, my fingers curling around the pork chop. I lifted it to my mouth and dug my teeth into the chilled, salty meat. Blood dripped over my lower lip and down my chin. God, it tasted good, rich and nourishing. The baby *needed* this. I could feel it.

I polished off the meat in just a few bites, and then I was gnawing at the bone, licking it, savoring it...

There was a sudden thump behind me, movement outside. My body tensed, and I spun around up in time to see a face pressed up against the glass, eyes black and reflective.

No.

I was already looking around for something heavy, something I could throw—

But then my eyes adjusted, and I saw that it was just an animal sniffing around in the night for food, drawn to the light.

My shoulders relaxed. Everything inside of me went very still. I didn't move, didn't breathe. It felt like some long-dormant instinct had risen up and taken control of my body. I was no longer a woman standing in her kitchen, looking for a midnight snack; I was a predator tracking her prey. A mother hunting down food for her young.

The animal came closer to the window, its breath fogging the glass. Its eyes were reflective in the night, two pinpricks of light.

I moved away from the fridge on instinct, so it wouldn't see me. My movements were light and fluid despite the awkwardness of my heavy body. I knew, somehow, to keep my weight on the balls of my feet, to leave a slight bend in my knees, to move slowly, carefully, breathing in and out, every muscle tense.

Around the edges of the kitchen, keeping to the shadows. One hand reaching for the back door. Kamal usually spent the night out front in the Range Rover. If I went through the back door he wouldn't see me.

The animal was still there at the window, its eyes trained on the light from the fridge.

I kept my fingers curled around the doorknob until I was sure the latch wouldn't click when I pushed it open, but the animal still jerked toward the noise, suddenly alert. It was going to run now, and I was going to have to chase it. My legs trembled in anticipation.

Carefully, carefully, I stepped outside. Grass crunched beneath my bare toes.

The animal rose to its feet, back arching, and I saw that it wasn't a raccoon like I'd thought. It was a fat gray and brown house cat. There was a collar around its neck.

"What are you doing out here?" I whispered, my breath ghosting in the dark. I felt suddenly sickened with myself, truly aware of what I was doing for the first time since I saw the eyes outside my kitchen window. *What was I planning to do? What was I thinking? Oh God...*

The cat took a step closer to me, paws silent on the ground. It wasn't afraid. Just curious. Those eyes shifted from my face to my hand, looking at the bone I was still holding, a few bits of meat still clinging. Its ears pricked.

"You want this?" I asked, holding out the bone.

The cat trotted right up to my hand, tail lifted. It sniffed the bone, licked it. For a moment, the only sound in the yard was the soft smack of its tongue on the meat.

An owl hooted somewhere in the dark. It began to rain, sleety, half frozen rain that made the ground soggy. The shadows around us were close and heavy, hiding us.

No one else was around. No one would see.

I started breathing heavier, the scent of the cat filling my nose. The blood pumping through her, warming her, it was like the smell of the richest stew boiling on the stove, all simmering onions and meat and tomato sauce. I felt my body responding to it, so aware of it. The baby in my belly moved, hungry, so hungry, always hungry. I needed to take care of her, to feed her. I was her mother.

Saliva filled my mouth. My heart started beating faster.

As though sensing it was in danger the cat looked up at me, tensing. It knew something was wrong finally.

But it was too late.

29

I SLEPT DEEPLY THAT NIGHT, THE KIND OF ALL-CONSUMING sleep that I hadn't experienced since I was a little kid on Christmas day, my belly full of ham and mashed potatoes. When I woke the next morning, sunlight drifting through my bedroom window, it felt like only a few minutes had passed.

I burrowed deeper into my pillow, wanting to linger longer in this half-asleep state where I didn't have to think about what happened last night, what I'd done, but a knock on my door told me that Dex was already here with another smoothie I had no intention of drinking. It was later than I'd thought.

"Morning, baby," he said, putting the smoothie down on my bedside table. "How did you sleep?"

"Good, thanks," I murmured, grimacing as I sat up. My body was sore from my excursion last night, and my bump seemed, somehow, impossibly, even larger than it'd been when I'd gone to sleep. I put a hand to either side of it, trying to figure out how big it was. Beach ball sized, maybe bigger. Dex's T-shirt was pulling at the seams.

Dex glanced at my belly. "You look like you are having twins."

"I know; aren't I huge?" I adjusted the duvet over my bare legs. There was a stain near the hem of my T-shirt but Dex hadn't seemed to notice.

"I think it's great; it means the baby's healthy. Keep eating."

His voice sounded strained. I glanced at him, wondering if that was a pointed remark. I'd tried to clean up after myself last night, but maybe I'd left some sign behind. A stray piece of turkey in the kitchen? Footsteps in the mud? Maybe Kamal had seen me after all; maybe he'd left the car and walked around back; maybe he'd been watching? And there was the missing pork chop. Had Dex opened the fridge and seen that it was gone? Put two and two together?

Seen the trail of blood and juices leading outside?

"You haven't been eating much lately," Dex added.

I felt my shoulders drop, relief spreading through me. He hadn't seen anything. This was just a little dig to remind me that he was always watching me, making sure I did everything right, that every choice I made had the potential to hurt our baby.

"I'll drink it in a minute," I said, pushing my duvet cover back. "Right now I—"

I stopped talking abruptly and jerked backward, my heart slamming into my throat at the sight of curving shapes, of *scales*.

My first thought was that there was something in bed with me, a massive, birdlike creature. I scrambled out of bed with a scream lodged in my throat, my sudden fear blotting out everything else. It wasn't until I was standing that I realized the creature wasn't a creature at all. It was *me*.

There were no scales, that had been a trick of the light. A rash covered my legs. The skin was sunburn red and raised, as thick as a callus, and it was everywhere, covering my legs from just above the ankles all the way up my thigh. It was patchy around my knees but thick everywhere else, so thick I could barely see my skin below.

I could feel my entire body beginning to shake, horror and disgust and horror again. *No, no, no.*

I yanked my T-shirt up over my belly, frantically moving my hands over my bump, checking for the rash. The skin on my torso was still smooth and pink. *Thank God.*

"*Anna,*" Dex said, his voice firm in a way that told me he'd already said my name a few times now. I felt a second of pure undiluted horror, thinking that he couldn't see the rash, that it was in my head, like the tooth and the claw—

And then he caught me by the shoulders, making sure I was looking him in the eye and said, emphasizing each word very carefully, "You need to tell me what you did."

I stared at him, confused. "What?"

"What did you do to your legs?" he repeated slowly, as if to make sure I caught every accusing word.

"You-you think *I* did this? To *myself*?"

"This is clearly some sort of...of allergic reaction. What about that lotion you've been using? Could it have had something strange in it? Essential oils, maybe? I've heard they can cause rashes."

I was crying now, my chest heaving, my fingers slow and clumsy. I released another desperate sob, my legs suddenly feeling weak.

"I didn't do this," I snapped, pulling away from him.

Something in Dex's expression hardened. "Anna, this is important. Whatever this is could be seeping through your skin. It could hurt the baby."

For a moment I was breathless with rage. I couldn't believe he'd just said that, *It could hurt the baby*, as if I didn't already know, as if I hadn't spent every *second* of the last eight months worried that some small innocent thing I did would hurt her.

For a moment I actually wanted to laugh.

No—I didn't want to laugh. I wanted to scream in his face. I wanted him to feel, for just a second, what it was like to have your body taken away from you, to be treated like a vessel, a *thing*.

"I–I want to be alone." I pushed past him, hurrying to the bathroom. Dex followed, telling me to calm down, to talk to him, but I closed the door in his face, twisted the lock.

He rattled the doorknob. "Anna. Come on, open up."

I ignored him. The sink made it tricky to see the lower half of my body in the mirror hanging over the vanity, so I had to maneuver one of my legs up onto the countertop, cringing as I pretzeled it in front of me, uncomfortably wedged against my bump. I held my breath, leaning closer.

The skin on my legs looked nothing like skin was supposed to look. It was deeply strange, bright red and thick. It didn't itch, but when I ran my hand over it, it felt coarse as sandpaper, bits of skin flaking away. The feeling of my hand brushing over skin felt muffled, as if that red-scaled leg belonged to someone else. As if all of me (my skin, my cravings, my thoughts) had somewhere along the line slipped out of my control. My own body had become completely alien to me.

Dex was pounding at the door now, furious. "Anna? Anna, open up, please!" The door shuddered in the frame.

I lifted my eyes to my reflection, taking in my pale skin, my bloodless lips. My mind flashed to last night. How I'd crouched in the mud with that cat, bloodlust thumping in my chest. The memory disgusted me so much that I had to look away from myself. *Don't think about it*, I told myself. *Think about anything else...*

"Anna! Don't make me break down this door!"

And all at once, I had to know.

Acting on impulse, I jerked open the vanity drawer and snagged the first thing that came to hand: my cuticle scissors. Bracing myself, I caught the edge of a patch of red, flaking skin with the tip of the scissors and wedged it up, up, cringing at the sensation. I had to stop for a moment, to catch my breath. The muffled sensation of being outside my own body was gone now, pain so bright it was like a shock. I wasn't sure I could do this.

But I had to know if *my* skin was still there, hiding underneath the flaking rash. If any of me was left at all, or if it had vanished. If *I* was vanishing.

"Anna!"

I took another deep breath, and then I slid the scissors below the peeling skin, ripping a strip of it off before I could stop to think about it. Fast, like pulling off a Band-Aid.

The pain was stunning: it was skin splitting open, followed by a sudden shudder I could feel all the way in my bones.

I hunched over the sink, heaving.

Behind me, the bathroom door slammed open, and Dex stumbled into the room, swearing. He took one look at me and tore across the room, ripping the scissors from my hand. "What are you doing?"

"I just wanted to see what was underneath." I stared down at the spot on my leg where I'd removed the rough skin. It looked scraped-knee fresh, and it burned where it hit the air—but at least I could feel it. At least I *knew* I was still in command of my own body. I sucked a breath in through my teeth.

"Jesus, Anna, you're being..." He stopped talking so quickly that I knew the next word out of his mouth was going to be *hysterical*. He closed his eyes, pinching the bridge of his nose. "I'm going to step out for a minute to call Dr. Hill. Can you just...stay here for a moment? I want to know if I can trust you to stay here on your own?"

I glared at him. "Why wouldn't you *trust* me?"

Dex gave me a pointed look, and then yanked the vanity drawer open and swept his hand around the contents. He pulled out a glass nail file that was pointed at one end, a pair of tweezers, some finger-nail clippers. He put them in his pocket, not looking at me. "Just stay here, okay? I'll be right back."

"I want to hear what Dr. Hill says."

"Maybe you should try to rest. Why don't you have a glass of water and try to calm down?" He gave my legs one final glance and then, shaking his head, walked out of the bathroom.

I stumbled back into the bedroom, wondering if a woman has ever calmed down after a man told her to. My phone was lying on my bed, screen lit up with a new message. I grabbed it and clicked, my hands shaking.

It was Io.

I'm in Huntington. Can you meet?

It felt like a life raft, and I grasped at it desperately. Here was a solution, the promise of answers. Huntington was only about forty minutes from Southampton. I would've driven dozens of times as long to find to what was going on with me. I would've gone anywhere.

Yes, I wrote back. When?

I'd only just hit Send when, outside the window, something shrieked.

My heart leapt into my throat. I stumbled backward, colliding with the side of the bed. The room felt suddenly airless.

The shrieking stopped abruptly, and in its wake the silence around me seemed to pulse. A moment passed, but there was only the raspy sound of my own breath in my throat, the thud of my heartbeat.

I held my breath as I inched over to the window. Closer, closer. When I was close enough to reach the curtains, I grabbed a handful of cloth and pulled them back—fast—before I could lose my nerve. The rings gave a hard, metal on metal scrape over the rod.

I was so ready to see someone outside—Meg in the flesh finally— that it took me a long moment to make sense of what was actually there: tree branches and moonlight and an icy curtain of snow.

I waited, feeling feverish, sweating and shivering at the same time. She was out there. I knew she was out here. I didn't imagine that sound.

The wind rattled the windows, cold air pinging off glass. My breath was just starting to return to normal when something twitched in the corner of my eye, some flicker.

I jerked my head around as a dark shadow loomed up outside of the window and the shrieking started again. It was high and shrill and sounded like it was coming from right outside the glass.

This time, I could just make out the yellow of wide unblinking eyes nestled in the tree branches, the shape of a small furry body.

It was the brown house cat from last night.

But...I could remember how it felt under my fingers, its soft fur, the brittleness of its bones. I could remember digging my teeth into its flesh, the taste of its blood on my tongue.

But obviously I couldn't really remember any of those things. Because the cat was *there*, perched in the tree outside of my window. It was alive and watching me with its head cocked, accusatory. I stared back, barely breathing.

The cat tilted its head back and yowled into the night, its entire body seeming to vibrate with the sound.

30

I HAD TO GET OUT OF HERE. I CROSSED THE MASTER BEDROOM and pressed my ear to the door, listening.

There was no sound out in the hall. But I hesitated a moment longer, just to be sure, and then I eased the door open, peering out.

Dex was gone.

It was dark, dark like a cloud had slid over the sun, blocking all the light from the windows, but I didn't dare turn anything on. Dex might see and come looking for me. I couldn't risk that. I had to go now, before he could question me or stop me.

I crept past Dex's office, down the stairs. I glanced over my shoulder, expecting him to step into the hallway and see me, call for me to come back, restrain me even. But he didn't. I could hear the muffled sound of his voice on the phone with Dr. Hill.

And then I was down the stairs, in the entryway, the front door just feet away. I pushed it open and blustery wind whipped through my paper-thin leggings, the only pants I could manage to tug up over the rash that covered my legs. My shoelaces trailed along through the mud, immediately soaked. I hadn't been able to tie my shoes; my feet were too swollen, my belly too large. I couldn't even reach them.

The Range Rover was waiting in the driveway, exhaust leaking from its tailpipe. I climbed inside, shivering as I pulled the door shut.

"I need you to take me to Huntington," I told Kamal.

———

Forty-five minutes later, we pulled up in front of a rundown roadside bar. Io had wanted me to meet her at home, but I told her I wanted someplace public but discreet enough that I wouldn't be recognized. We'd decided on a bar called Grey Meers about twenty minutes outside Huntington. It was open all day, and Io had assured me there were never more than two or three other people there before five, and they weren't the type who'd notice anything other than the drink in front of them.

I sat in the car for a moment after we'd pulled to a stop, watching the crows circling the parking lot adjacent to the bar. *Bad omen.*

I shivered and looked away, fumbling with my "disguise," the same beanie-and-oversized-sunglasses combo I'd worn to go to CVS. With my hair pulled back and the sunglasses hiding my face, I doubted anyone would recognize me. They probably wouldn't have recognized me without them either. I was so gaunt, so sick looking. Not at all like the photographs circulating the internet. I was a ghost of the woman I'd been.

Kamal glanced at me. "You want me to come inside with you?"

I thought about it, then shook my head. It would be safer to have Kamal next to me, but Io might not talk in front of someone else. "No, that's okay. I don't think I'll be very long."

I gave the crows a wide berth as I made my way across the parking lot and into the bar. Io was already there, sitting at a table in the back of the room, hands cupped around a glass of what looked like water. She must've been in her late fifties or sixties, and she was smaller and stockier than I remembered, the lines of lean muscles just visible beneath gauzy peasant-blouse sleeves. She looked like someone's grandmother.

"You," she said, eyes widening in shock. She flashed me an anxious smile. "I saw you. Outside the fertility clinic."

You took a photo of me and put it on the internet, I thought. But out loud, I said, "Thank you for talking to me."

"Of course, of course." Her eyes flicked down to my belly and she swallowed hard. "How far along are you?"

"Almost thirty-six weeks."

"You're getting close." She stared for a moment longer, giving me the strange feeling that she could see through my leggings to the rash covering my skin below. "I guess congratulations are in order." She didn't sound very congratulatory.

"Thank you." I curled my hands around my belly, feeling protective.

"Do you want to get something to drink? I think they have coffee."

I shook my head. Doctors still couldn't decide whether it was safe to have caffeine during pregnancy, so I'd avoided it. I sat and knotted my hands in my lap, reminding myself to breathe.

"In your message, you said you've had some strange symptoms." Io leaned forward in her seat, hands cupped around her glass.

I was relieved. I'd been worried I was going to have to sit through long painful minutes of small talk before we got to this. "I have, yes."

Io aimed those weird unblinking eyes at me, saying nothing. I got the feeling she was just as anxious to hear what I had to say as I was to say it.

"I've...been having these cravings," I admitted, testing the waters. Io didn't move, still didn't blink, so I kept going. "It's like you said in your videos, I get really disturbing cravings and want to eat...strange things. And...when I was in the bathtub a few days ago, it felt like something was stabbing me, but from...from inside of my body. It was this little claw poking through my skin. Right here."

I touched the spot below my ribs where I'd seen the claw curve out of me, cringing as a spike of pain moved through my body. "It was a hallucination," I said quickly, "but it felt so real. And that's not all. I've been losing my hair, and my skin has gotten..." I trailed off, noticing that Io was looking at my leg. I followed her gaze and saw that my legging had rolled up, revealing a patch of mottled red skin. I hurriedly yanked it down again. "I feel like I'm losing my mind. My husband, my doctors, everyone thinks I'm crazy."

The lines around Io's eyes and mouth were more pronounced in the dim light. She let out a whoosh of breath and murmured, "Jesus."

I stared back at her, suddenly worried I'd misjudged this situation, that I'd said far, far too much. "Oh God...you think I'm crazy too, don't you?"

"No," Io said immediately. There was a brief pause, as she tried to come up with the right thing to say, and then, "For me, it was road-kill. Every time I drove past some poor animal on the highway, I'd think about stopping and..." She looked away, shuddering. "It was the only thing I wanted to eat. Everything else made me sick."

I stared back at her, mouth hanging open. This took me completely off guard. I'd been prepared to doubt everything she told me, but then again, I hadn't expected her to tell me *this*, that she'd been through the same thing, that I wasn't the only one. "For...for *you?* This happened to you?"

Io nodded, staring down at her hands. "Almost forty years ago now. I was twenty years old, poor as you can imagine, just truly desperate for money. I had this friend who'd made a couple thousand dollars being a surrogate—or at least I'd *thought* she was a friend— and I thought, *Why not?*" She shook her head. "Ten grand... Well, that was a fortune back then. To me, at least."

I was leaning forward in my chair, listening hard, my heartbeat lodged in my throat.

"So you agreed to do it." I was glad to hear that my voice sounded almost normal.

Io nodded. "I know that sort of thing is a lot more common now, but this was back in the eighties, remember. Surrogacy was virtually unheard of back then. The whole thing seemed like something from science fiction to me, and it was all very hush-hush. I never even met the couple I was supposed to be having this baby *for*. Everything went through my doctor."

Somewhere in the back of my head I heard something click, but I didn't know what it meant, not yet. I swallowed. "When did you figure out that something was wrong?"

"When the cravings started." Io's eyes seemed to go unfocused, like she was seeing something I couldn't. "I used to sneak out in the middle of the night and peel the dead animals off the road... I can still taste them in my mouth, even after all these years. It was richer than other kinds of meat. *Gamier*." She shuddered, like she was coming out of a trance. "There were other symptoms too, like I said on my video. Hallucinations. And I got this strange...rash all over my arms." Again, her eyes darted to my leg.

Before I could say a word, I felt a shift of movement inside of me, the feeling of something turning over, and I looked down, my back suddenly rigid. Io released a breath through her teeth.

The two of us watched as a long thin shape appeared beneath the skin of my belly, then quickly vanished.

"What happened after the baby came?" I asked, still watching my belly. "Was he...she...were they okay?"

Io stared at me for a moment, something blank in her eyes. It occurred to me that she might not really know. She'd been a surrogate, after all. She'd never intended to be that baby's mother.

"I never saw the baby," she admitted. "I hadn't wanted to see her. I made them take her immediately after she was born."

Them. I looked up quickly, my heart was beating loud and fast in my ears. This was the part I still didn't know how to believe, satanists and ritual sacrifices and spells. I wanted her to tell me that it wasn't true, that she'd made it all up for her YouTube followers. "You mean the people you keep talking about in your videos? This...this cult you keep mentioning..."

Io stared at me, unmoving, a smug trace of pleasure on her lips. "I assure you the cult is very real, Anna," she said. "*Very* real. But that's not who I'm talking about. I was kept away from the cult members during my pregnancy. They'd wanted to meet me after, but I knew what was going on by then, so I refused. Everything went through my doctor. She's the one who took the baby."

"Your doctor?" I felt my shoulders tense up, realizing this was the reason I was here. This was why she'd wanted to speak with me so badly. "Who was your doctor?"

Io's eyes came up, meeting mine. She only paused for a fraction of a second but, to me, it seemed to last forever. Because suddenly, I knew what she was going to say.

Unblinking, she said, "It was Dr. Carla Hill."

31

DR. HILL. *MY* DR. HILL.

"That's why I wanted to see you," Io continued. "Dr. Hill's in deep with these people, and now she's doing the same thing to you that she did to me."

"No," I murmured. "No, I don't believe in any of that."

Io continued as though I hadn't spoken. "I think that all of this, your whole pregnancy, it was set up so Dr. Hill could take your baby and give it to them. I think she trades it for something, protection or wealth; I'm not totally sure."

"No," I said. But my voice was shaking so badly I sounded drunk. Dr. Hill has had more access to me than anyone other than Dex. She knew my address in Brooklyn and in Southampton, she'd prescribed medication, she'd read all of my labs. *She* was the one who kept saying everything was fine, even as I told her that something was wrong, that I could *feel* that something was wrong.

But cults? Ritual sacrifices?

"No," I said again. But the light in the bar seemed to dim suddenly, the walls and the floor all falling away until there was only me and Io in the circle of yellow light, surrounded by black nothingness, just the two of us in a void at the end of the world, spinning through space. I had a feeling of vertigo, like there was a gravity reaching out from the nothingness around us, and I had to lean forward and put my head in my hands, clenching my eyes tight just to get everything to stop *spinning*.

Dr. Hill. Dr. Hill, who knew how badly I wanted this, how I'd suffered for it, how I'd *prayed* for it. Could Dr. Hill have been planning all this time to—what?

Kidnap my baby?

"...water..." Io was saying when I finally managed to start listening again. "You need some water. Here." And she pressed something cold and hard into my hand. I blinked at it, frowning: her water glass.

She was right; I did need water. My head was pounding, and my throat was suddenly unbearably dry, so dry that swallowing was painful. I really should ask the bartender for something to drink. But I'd promised myself that I wouldn't eat or drink anything once I got here just in case Io wasn't as trustworthy as I was hoping she was.

Instead, I swallowed a few times, trying to wet the inside of my mouth, to convince myself I wasn't actually thirsty. "You said online... You made it sound like there were others..."

Io was nodding. "Oh yes. This sort of thing happens much more frequently than you would think. Satanic cults *need* children for their depraved rituals. That's why they work with doctors like Dr. Hill, because they discovered they can pay them for unborn babies and children. It's *sick*."

I gripped the arms of my chair, trying to steady myself. "Okay... let's say I believe you about Dr. Hill. Is there some other reason she might be doing all this? Something that doesn't have anything to do with cults or Satan?" I still couldn't make myself believe this was a ritualistic sacrifice. There had to be another explanation.

But Io leaned closer to me, licking her lips, lowering her voice like she was worried she'd be overheard. "I've spent the last forty years looking into this, dear. It might seem far–fetched to you, but when you've done as much research as I have, the signs are all very clear. Dr. Hill is one of many doctors working with a very small, very powerful Satanic cult. She does something to the pregnant mothers, and then she delivers the babies to them. I believe they need the babies for a ritual of some sort, or a spell maybe?" Io laughed once, the sound short and brittle and entirely unamused. "Believe me, I know how all of this sounds. I used to be a skeptic too. But there has to be a reason they need babies. There *has* to be. It's why I keep looking for others, because I have to know..." Io trailed off, her face grave.

I thought she was going to say something about her baby, the one she carried. But she just added, a little more quietly, "I have to know what happened to me."

I closed my eyes, thinking of the baby inside of me, tiny arms and legs, tiny fingers, tiny nose. Skin softer than a puppy's belly. Midnight feedings and milk-warmed breath. My baby's face nuzzled against my chest. For nine months I'd been dreaming of her, planning for her.

Could what Io was saying be true? After all this time, could my own doctor, the person I'd trusted the most, be planning to take her away from me? I didn't believe in Satan, but maybe I didn't have to. It was enough that Dr. Hill did, that she thought she was engaging in some horrible ritual, that she was going to do something to my baby.

I wasn't going to let her. Not after I'd come this far.

"Thank you for talking to me," I said. "This has helped, really."

"I hope it has." Io watched me push myself out of my chair. Her expression had gone blank, unreadable. Before I could step away from the table she added, like an afterthought.

"Did you see the birds circling outside?"

I felt a chill straight through to my spine. "I did."

"It's a sign of bad luck." Then her eyes flicked to my belly and I saw disgust pass over her in a shiver.

———

"Back home?" Kamal asked once I'd climbed into the car. I nodded, too numb for words, and turned to watch out the window as that god-awful bar slowly grew smaller behind me, those birds still flying in a low, tight circle. We made it out of the parking lot and down the street before I had to bend over, head between my knees. Breathing hard.

I was having a hard time sorting through my own thoughts. Dr. Hill. The claw I thought I'd seen. The cat I'd wanted to eat. The rash still covering my legs.

And Io's voice, repeating on a loop, *She does something...she delivers the babies to them.*

I wanted to curl into a fetal position, I wanted to breathe into a bag. My thoughts were thick, chaotic: *This can't be happening, there has to be some other explanation, there has to be.*

And, at the same time, *She can't have my baby, I won't let her...*

My phone pinged. For the first time in hours, I thought about my husband. I imagined him going into our shared bedroom, finding me gone. I hadn't even sent him a text to let him know where I was going, that I was safe, that I was coming back.

I pulled my phone out and stared down at the screen. There were dozens of messages from Dex, new ones popping up every few seconds:

Where did you go?

Anna come back, please.

I'm really scared here.

Think about what you're doing! This isn't safe for the baby!

I'm calling Kamal and if he doesn't answer I'm going to call the police...

Anna please don't do this.

I reread his messages twice, but when I saw the little gray dots that meant he was typing something new, I flipped my phone over in my lap. I didn't want to read whatever he was about to send. I'd be home soon enough. He could yell at me all he wanted then.

I settled back in my seat, my arms curled protectively around my bump as the car's heat settled over me. Something about Io's story was still bothering me. I stared at the back of Kamal's head, sorting through everything she'd told me, everything I already knew. Sweat gathered under my arms and thighs, but I didn't tell Kamal to turn the heat off. It felt good. I hadn't realized how cold I'd been for the last few weeks. Cold down through my skin, cold all the way to my bones.

The warnings, I realized, after several long moments of quiet. They were the one piece of this puzzle that didn't fit. And not just the warnings, but the altered appointment times and the sabotaged meds. I pulled my phone out and read the warnings in my calendar, just to be sure I was remembering them correctly.

They did something to your baby.

Are you sure it's dead?

You can't trust anyone.

Headlights passed through the car, the sudden flare of light making me cringe. I realized I hadn't taken a breath for several long moments and forced myself to inhale, one hand braced against the car door to hold myself steady.

I'd suspected for a while now that these messages might've been coming from someone other than my stalker, maybe even someone trying to help me. But now that I knew about Dr. Hill, I felt stupid for not putting it together sooner. All this time playing amateur detective, trying to narrow down my pathetic list of suspects, and at the end of the day, there was only one person I could think of who knew my schedule at the clinic almost as well as Dr. Hill, who would know exactly which appointments I couldn't afford to be late to, which meds couldn't be left out overnight without going bad. I felt like an idiot for not seeing it before.

I dialed the number to Dr. Hill's office with stiff fingers and she answered halfway through the first ring, "Riverside Clinic, this is Cora."

"Cora, hi, it's Anna Alcott."

"Good afternoon, Ms. Alcott. Dr. Hill's attending a labor at the moment, but I'd be happy—"

"No," I said, cutting her off. I could barely hear my own voice, my heart was beating so loud. "Actually I'm calling to speak with you."

There was a long uncomfortable pause. A *knowing* pause. And then finally, Cora cleared her throat and said, "Uhm. Yeah, okay. Hold on a second."

I heard the squeak of a door and then a muffled walking sound, distant voices.

Finally, Cora brought the phone back to her ear, exhaling loudly. "Okay. I can talk now."

If I'd had any doubt about Cora's involvement, it left me then. It was the way she'd taken the call somewhere private before she even knew what it was about, the caution in her voice when she spoke to me. She was nervous. I could feel it vibrating through the phone.

"You've been messing with my calendar," I said. Not a question. "You've been leaving me weird messages."

There was another long deliberate silence. I couldn't tell if she was trying to figure out whether there was any point in denying my accusation, or she just didn't know what to say. It took forever for her to speak again.

"You had to create a password for your online account through Riverside," she said finally. "The assistants can see what one you use. I figured you probably used the same one for everything. Lots of people do."

And there it was, the answer to the riddle that had been plaguing me for months.

"Did you do the meds too?" I asked when I could trust myself to speak. I thought I was calm; I really did. It wasn't until I heard how badly my voice was shaking that I realized how furious I was. Whatever her motives, what she'd done to me was unforgivable. "We found medication left on the counter all night, even though I know I put it away."

A pause, and then—

"I had to," Cora said, her voice thick with tears. "I couldn't let her hurt you."

"What about my miscarriage? Did you—?"

"No," Cora said firmly. "I swear, the second I found out you were pregnant, I stopped, you have to believe me—"

"Why?" I snapped, cutting her off. "Why would you do that to me? I thought I was losing my mind. If you wanted to warn me about something, why not just *talk* to me?"

"I couldn't." Cora sniffed on the other end of the phone, and I realized that she must've started crying. "It was awful, I'm sorry. I just...I really didn't want you to find out who I was. I couldn't think of another way."

"I still don't understand how," I said. "Did you—? Were you the one who broke into my *house?*"

"I didn't break in." Cora said, too quickly. "I mean, I..." and she trailed off, swearing under her breath like she'd said too much, which didn't make sense. Of all the things she'd just admitted, the fact that she didn't have to break in was what bothered her?

"What do you mean?" I asked. "Was the door open or something?"

"No, I...I had a key."

"You had a key to my house? How?"

"He gave it to me."

That's when it hit me, right then. I felt the word like a bullet, and everything inside of me went still.

He.

"You mean...you mean *she* gave it to you, you mean Dr. Hill?" But of course that's not who she meant. Dr. Hill didn't have a key to my house.

"Anna," Cora said. Her voice was different now. It was lower, raspy. *Familiar.* It was the same voice that had whispered the word *baby* to me in the dark, the voice that had haunted me for nine months. "Anna...I'm sorry. I *never* wanted you to find out."

"No," I said. I was beginning to understand. I didn't want to, but it was too late. I was replaying the night she broke in, how it had been dark, so dark that I hadn't even been able to see her face. So dark that she hadn't been able to see *my* face. I thought of the whispered rasp. *Baby.*

I thought she'd meant *my* baby. But she hadn't.

She'd meant Dex.

Cora started talking faster now, words tumbling over words in her rush to get them out before I hung up the phone. "He said it was over between you two, that you'd been trying to get pregnant for two years, but you both knew it wasn't going to work, that you wanted to try one last time, just in case. He said he was going to leave you once this round of IVF was done. That's why I told myself it was okay...that sleeping with him was okay. I'm so sorry, Anna. You have to believe me. I was stupid, so, so stupid."

I stared straight ahead, feeling like I was walking through gunfire. I'd barely registered the first bullet when the next one came and the next.

Dex had slept with someone else. He'd given her a *key* to our *house*. And he told her it was over between us. He was going to leave me after that last round of IVF.

He had to know she was the one who'd broken in. He had to at least suspect. But he let me believe I had a stalker. He let me live in fear for *months*.

I felt a twist in my gut and doubled over, worried I was going be sick.

Cora was still talking, her horribly familiar voice echoing from my phone. "It's over between us, Anna; you have to believe me. Over this last year, with you coming into the clinic all the time, I—I got to know you so much better, and I realized how horrible it was, what I was doing to you. I only came to your house that night to break it off and...and to say goodbye, I swear. I didn't think you'd be there. You'd stopped putting your appointments in your online calendar and I had the day off, so I didn't know about your procedure. I waited outside your house until I saw you leave, but I was pretty far away, and I didn't get a good look; I just saw someone walk out the door wearing this pink hat. You know that pink stocking hat you always wear?"

I had a sudden flash of memory: Dex putting on my hat. Dex leaving to get the dogs after my surgery. She saw Dex leave and she was far enough away that she thought he was me. She thought he was alone. She'd thought she was climbing into bed with him.

I remembered, suddenly, how long Dex had been gone that night. So much longer than it usually took to go get the dogs. Had he been looking for her?

That wasn't the only time he'd disappeared for hours with no explanation. Now, it made sense. I couldn't believe I'd been so naïve.

My breathing hitched, my eyes clouding. There were things I

wanted to ask Cora, of course. There was so much I still wanted to know. *How long did it last? How many times were you in my house? Did he tell you he loved you?*

But I also wanted to undo this moment. I wanted to go back to two minutes ago, before I picked up my phone and called this woman. But I couldn't undo it. I would know this for the rest of my life.

I thought about of all those weeks of injections, my hand trembling as I went to jab myself again and again, my belly so bruised and bloated that I couldn't zip up my pants. I thought of hours spent waiting for the phone to ring, feeling so nervous that I collapsed over the toilet, dry heaving. All the things I'd done to give Dex a baby. All the ways I'd suffered, so that we could build a family together.

And he...he'd done this.

I felt a sinking as I realized why she'd been trying to keep me from getting pregnant. I'd thought she'd been trying to protect me from whatever Dr. Hill was doing to me, but that wasn't it.

I thought of the message she'd left in my calendar. Are you sure it's dead? I thought she'd been trying to give me hope, so I'd keep fighting. But she was just making sure it was gone.

"Did you think Dex would leave me for you if I couldn't get pregnant?" I asked her. "Because it didn't work. I'm having a baby."

"You...you are?" Cora breathed, horrified.

"If you ever come near my family again, I'll kill you."

I lowered the phone from my ear, my thumb moving automatically over the power button.

She called again, a moment later. I hit Ignore. She called *again*, right after that. I blocked her number. I was done talking to her. I didn't want to hear her voice ever again.

The taste of something sour crawled up my throat, leaving a film at the back of my mouth.

I forced myself to breathe and pulled my sleeve over my hand to wipe the fog off the windows. I felt the moment the ground below the car changed from concrete to white gravel, how it crunched under the Range Rover's tires as we crawled down the straight, tree-lined drive toward Talia's house. Toward Dex.

I balled a hand near my mouth, my stomach churning. My breaths were shallow, labored. My head felt staticky.

"Ma'am?" Kamal said. "Do you need some help?"

We were parked, I realized. He was waiting for me to get out of the car.

I shook my head and pushed the car door open, my legs buckling when I tried to ease my weight onto them. "You can go, Kamal,"

Kamal frowned. "Ma'am?"

"I'll be fine on my own now," I explained. Now that I knew who my "stalker" was and that she wasn't a threat, I didn't need Kamal sticking around. And I didn't want him to see what was coming next.

"I'm not sure that's a good idea, ma'am," Kamal said.

I could see that he wasn't going to leave quite so easily, and I didn't want to stretch this out any further than necessary. I pulled out my wallet and shuffled through the bills inside, finding a fifty. I hesitated for just a moment, then grabbed another.

"Really, I insist." I said, thrusting my hand toward him.

"If you're sure," he said, taking the bills.

"I am. Thank you for everything," I said, smiling weakly. "I won't forget it."

I shut the car door and turned toward the house. I wasn't ready for this. I would never be ready for this. But it didn't matter. I heard the door slamming open, footsteps on the porch.

"Anna? Anna...oh God...where were you? Is it the baby? Are you okay?" Dex's voice.

I could feel his hands on me, one braced against my back, the other just below my elbow, helping me up the steps. I pulled away from him.

"I spoke to Cora," I said.

"What—?" Dex blinked, and then he sucked a breath in through his teeth, steadying himself like he was about to go into battle. "Cora? Why? I mean, what about?"

I closed my eyes. It was the familiarity in his voice when he said her name—not like he was talking about a receptionist he'd said hello to a few times at the clinic, but like he *knew* her. I felt the sting of it in my cheek, in my eyes, as strongly as if he'd slapped me. Any doubt I had that Cora had been telling me the truth vanished with that one word.

I brought a trembling hand to my mouth. Angry tears filled my eyes. "Oh my God."

His expression broke. "Anna...please, you have to let me explain."

I shook my head. I needed a moment to sort out what was happening, to make sense of this new reality. The porch seemed to revolve beneath me, making me dizzy.

"You have to understand," he was saying. "This all...it started when things were really tense between us...right after *The Auteur*, when you were so busy with all those meetings and premiers, and the IVF wasn't working, and we were fighting—"

"Are you trying to say it's *my* fault?"

"*No.*" Dex looked at me, pleading, and I stared back at him hard, trying to get him to flinch. "I–I love you," he said, faltering. "I broke things off with her as soon as I found out about the baby, I swear."

"She said *she* broke things off with you."

"She's lying! After we broke up, she went crazy. You can't believe a word she says."

I ignored him. All this time I thought we were happy, that we were starting a family together. I thought we were in *love*.

And then I thought of all the times I'd asked him about Adeline, how he never wanted to tell my why they'd gotten a divorce.

I thought of Talia, standing beside me in the restaurant bathroom, her words careful, cautious. *I never talk about their past, not ever... We all deserve a second chance.*

Something sick twisted through my stomach. "Oh my God...*this* is why you and Adeline split up? *This* is why you never want to talk about her. Did you cheat on her too?"

Dex dragged a hand over his mouth and said nothing. Which, of course, was all the answer I needed. I thought about what Dex said when I found the photograph of them together, how in love they'd seemed, followed by the bitter tone in his voice when he'd said *she waited to drop that bomb on me until after we said,* I do. And Cora telling me that he'd justified what he was doing by saying the IVF wasn't working.

"Adeline wouldn't have a baby with you, so you cheated on her," I said, the realization settling over me like something heavy. "And then, when I couldn't have a baby, you cheated on me too." And there it was. The truth was obvious, once I had the courage to face it. I thought of all the times Dex hadn't answered his phone in front of me, the late-night phone calls, the nights he'd left without an explanation, disappearing for hours sometimes. The heavy feeling moved to my gut. "Cora wasn't the last, was she?" I said slowly. It added up, all of it. I was an idiot for not seeing it before. But I supposed I hadn't wanted to. "There's someone else, isn't there? Someone new?"

Dex blinked fast. It looked like he was trying to come up with an explanation. I kept talking, not wanting to give him the time to think of a lie. "Did you start cheating again the day after my miscarriage? Or did you wait a few weeks?"

His expression hardened. "That's not fair."

"*Fair?*" I had to lean against the porch rail to catch my breath. Any second, I was going to start sobbing or screaming, but I couldn't figure out which. I pressed the heels of my hands into my eyes. "Do you love me at all? Or am I just a means to an end to you? An incubator for the baby you're so desperate to have?"

"Anna, of course I love you. I don't want to lose you," Dex said. "I know I made mistakes but...you have to believe that I'm sorry. I *love* you. I want to be with you more than anything."

I kept my gaze trained straight ahead, at the rain falling on the yard. I tried to breathe, but my blood was racing hard and fast through my veins. It made me feel like a live wire, one spark and I'd explode.

He...he *cheated* on me. I still couldn't make myself believe it. My husband cheated on me. He was a cheater. And it wasn't a one-time thing. He *really* cheated. He brought her into our *home*.

And then, when she climbed into bed with me, thinking I was him, when she scared me so badly that I couldn't walk into my own home again, he let me believe that I had a stalker, that I was being followed, *targeted*. He let me live in a state of fear for weeks. All because he didn't want to get caught.

I felt like I was going to be sick.

"Anna?" Dex's voice is quieter now, desperate. "Come on, say something. Please."

I blinked a few times, stunned.

Say something?

I remembered the talon I thought had ripped out of my belly, the way it had felt when the skin on my torso split open. I thought of my dream: the baby with the feathered, birdlike body, a beak where its eyes should be. I thought of coughing up teeth.

I felt a shift in my belly, a quick twitch like an animal suddenly jerking awake, and I glanced down. But for the first time since this all started, I wasn't scared. I wasn't afraid of what the thing inside of me might do, what it might make *me* do. I wanted something to happen, I realized.

I wanted the monster inside me to devour him.

32

I WAS DONE TALKING. I'D HEARD ALL I COULD STAND, AND NOW the only thing I wanted to do was get as far away from Dex as possible. His voice, his face, everything about him made me want to scream. If I stayed with him for even one more second, I didn't know what I would do to him.

I left him standing on the porch and stumbled inside. Dimly, I had the thought that I would throw my things into a duffel bag and head to some hotel. Anywhere but this house.

I made it to our bedroom and locked the door, and I'd just pulled the duffel out of my closet when the muscles in my uterus tightened, pain rising inside me like a wave. I doubled over, gasping, tears gathering in my eyes.

The feeling was just like menstrual cramps, and it reminded me, horrifyingly, of my miscarriage. I had to remind myself to breathe. The edges of my eyesight pulsed sickeningly in time with my heart.

The tightening only lasted for a few seconds, and then, slowly, slowly, it faded away. It was gone.

Gradually, I became aware that I was kneeling on the floor and

I was drenched with sweat, and that my heart was beating so fast I could actually see it vibrating beneath my T-shirt, causing the fabric on my chest to flutter. There was a sound like wind in my ears, like static. I couldn't hear anything outside of my own head.

This pain... I knew this pain. I knew it down in my muscles, instinctively, like it was lodged in some primitive, long-forgotten part of my brain.

It was a contraction.

———

Real labor doesn't happen like it does in the movies. For one thing, it takes so much longer than you think it will. You don't rush to the hospital the moment you feel your first contraction, already pushing, screaming for drugs while an angry nurse tells you it's too late, the baby's already coming. That's all fiction. In reality, there are hours of prelabor that come before that—sometimes even days. When you hear stories of women laboring for thirty-six or forty-seven or fifty-three hours, this is often what they're talking about. The dark, long, confusing hours before you even go to the hospital.

A month ago, Dr. Hill and I had talked through my birth plan, figuring out which hospital she was going to meet me at, and what music I wanted playing, whether or not I would use drugs. Dex and I were supposed to pack a go bag, we were supposed to plan a route. But we hadn't done any of that yet. In fact, no part of the birth plan we'd so carefully designed was possible anymore. I couldn't call Dr. Hill or my husband, and I didn't want to go to any hospital where Dr. Hill might be able to find me.

Even after all I'd been through, I couldn't think of anything more terrifying than giving birth without my husband, without my doctor. The fear was so strong it felt like nothing, like going numb, and for a moment, I wanted nothing more than to give up, to lay my head down in my hands and quit. But there wasn't any way to quit. I'd never felt so lonely in my life.

I tried to breathe and a sob escaped, sounding wretched in the quiet. I clenched my hands into fists, fighting hard against the fear. I had to do this, even I had to do it alone.

I got my purse and shuffled through my wallet until I found the scrap of paper Gracie had given me months ago.

I found it next to her cell phone... Could it have been for you?

It was Siobhan's handwriting: *Call Olympia.* And below, there was a phone number. I got my phone out and dialed, feeling a rush of warmth so strong it brought tears to my eyes. It was as though Siobhan had known I would need this. My friend was still taking care of me, even though she couldn't do it physically.

"Anna?" Olympia said when I told her who I was. She sounded astonished. "We've been trying to get in touch with you for months!"

Of course they had. That was the kind of person Siobhan was. It made sense that she would've told the other women from the birth center about me, that she would've asked them to check in on me if I lost my nerve, but I didn't have time to explain to Olympia about the burner phone and the stalker, how I'd had to live in near isolation for the last eight months.

"I'm in labor," I told her instead. I waited for her disbelief, waited for her to ask if I was sure.

But she just said, "What do you need, honey? Can I call someone? Your husband or your doctor?"

"No," I said, breathing hard. "I don't trust anyone anymore. Please, can you come get me?"

———

It took hours for her headlights to appear in the driveway. The clock on Talia's table said 8:42 p.m. when I finally jerked to the window, a bright light flashing behind the curtains. Blood pounded in my ears. *Thank God she's here.*

I stood. Everything ached, but I somehow managed to pull my legs underneath my body and push myself off the bed.

I opened the door, waddling, clutching my belly so tightly you'd think my hands were the only things holding it up. It was getting hard to breathe again, but I had to keep going. Down the hall and around the corner. Through the living rooms. I spotted Dex in the dining room, crouched over Talia's massive table, his head resting on folded arms. A drink sat on the table beside him, brown liquid in a cut crystal tumbler. If I listened, I could hear the soft sound of snoring.

I held my breath as I crept past him. If he woke up, he would have questions about where I was going, and I couldn't stand the thought of trying to explain that I wanted to have this baby without him. It was better if he stayed sleeping. I would call him later. After.

It took every bit of strength I had left to ignore the ache in my back, the creaky feeling in my knees and my ankles, the weight of my belly pulling me down. Everything in me rusting and breaking. One foot in front of the other until I stepped onto the cold black and white tile in the entryway. I grasped the front door latch, fumbled with the lock.

Dex's groggy voice followed me down the hall, "Anna? That you?"

I flinched but didn't answer him. There was a click as the lock slid open. I turned the knob and a gust of cold winter air blew into the house, nearly knocking me over. I stepped outside and the door fell shut behind me.

I didn't know what kind of car Olympia drove. I'd expected to see a taxi or an Uber waiting in the driveway, the back door swinging open as she climbed out to help me down the stairs. But the woman climbing out of the back seat wasn't Olympia—

It was Cora.

I stiffened. "What are you doing here?"

Cora slammed the cab door shut and started toward me, her eyes lowering to my belly. "I tried to call you, but you weren't answering your phone."

I could hear Dex's voice echoing through the house behind me, shouting for me, but I ignored it. "I blocked your number."

"I need to talk to you." Cora looked desperate, panicky. "I have to warn you. I owe you that much after...after everything I did. *Please.*"

I cringed and doubled over, bracing myself as another contraction started. It was a pressure, a wave of nausea. I made myself breathe.

"Oh God...you should sit down." Cora hurried to my side and reached for my arm. I felt a sick twist of disgust where she'd touched me and jerked away.

"Please," she said, "please...just sit down, and I swear I'll tell you everything."

This time, when she reached for my arm, I let her take it and lead me to the top of the stairs. My legs burned as I crouched down.

The pain was fading now, easing back like the tide drawing away from the beach. I looked at her and, breathing deep, said, "What could you possibly have to say to me?"

"I didn't realize you were still pregnant. Dr. Hill—she didn't tell anyone at the clinic exactly what happened. I thought you'd miscarried and then, the next morning, you called Dr. Hill, you wanted to know if there was a chance the baby was still okay, remember? That's why I sent that message asking if it was gone, because I had to be sure. And you said someone killed your baby. I thought this was all over."

"No." I frowned, my brain struggling to catch up with what she was saying. "No, that can't be right. You've been following me."

"I haven't been following you, Anna. I had to break into Dr. Hill's office and go through her files just to find your address so I could come here now."

Something strange was happening to my breath. "I don't understand. You sent me all those warnings."

Cora closed her eyes for a moment. In the moonlight, her skin looked impossibly pale, deeply shadowed bags under her eyes, like she hadn't slept for weeks. "There's a woman who calls the office sometimes. She's been calling since before I started. I don't know her name. She always says for me to tell Dr. Hill that her old friend is on the phone, and then Dr. Hill takes the call in her office with the door closed." Cora blinked twice. "She doesn't do that with anyone else—just her. But the thing is, the phone at the receptionist's desk is connected to the line in her office, so it's really easy to listen in to calls. All you have to do is hit the mute button."

"I was just going to listen once, just for a few minutes. I figured she was a celebrity, and all the secrecy was because she didn't want the press finding out she was doing IVF. It's kind of an open secret that Dr. Hill takes jobs under the table sometimes."

"And I guess I was just sort of...curious about who it was. It gets so boring sitting at the front desk all day. But then I started listening, and Dr. Hill wasn't talking about IVF; she was telling this woman about all our clients. She was going through them like she was going down a list, sort of...describing them."

"Describing them?"

"Like, saying how old they were and what their names were, what they did for a living, what IVF cycle they were on. *Personal* details." Cora frowned. "She's not supposed to do that. It's unethical. So the next time this woman called, I listened in again. And that's when I realized she wasn't just giving out personal information. This woman on the phone, she was *looking* for someone. She had specific characteristics she was looking for. Sometimes, Dr. Hill would tell her where she could meet these women in person, things like that. She said, 'I know you like to vet them yourself,' so I knew this wasn't the first time. That's when I started messing with your appointments and meds. When that didn't work, I changed your phone number in our system. I thought that maybe if you missed a few calls, you'd get frustrated with Dr. Hill and try another clinic."

I thought back on the night at the restaurant, how I'd waited for Dr. Hill's office to call for hours. "That was you?"

Cora swallowed. "After everything else I was doing to you, I didn't think I should stand by while Dr. Hill did...whatever she was doing."

It was exactly like Io said, every detail. A cult paying for babies. Doing *something* to the fetuses.

I felt another tightening in my lower back, the muscles between my hips constricting. I groped for the stair rail to hold myself steady.

The tightening only lasted for a few seconds and then, slowly, slowly, it faded away. It was gone.

"She called again the day before I snuck into your house," Cora was saying. "I heard Dr. Hill tell her on the phone that she had a woman scheduled for an embryo transfer the next morning, but she didn't put your name on your appointment. She just blocked the time off on her schedule, and you'd stopped putting your appointments on your calendar by then, so I had no idea it was you. I didn't realize until... well, until I saw this." Cora pulled her hand out of her jacket pocket, and I saw that she was holding a folded piece of paper. She flattened it against her leg, and I felt a flutter in my chest, recognizing it.

It was the picture I'd printed out, the photograph of my embryo in a petri dish. The creases across the page were deeply worn, like Cora had folded and unfolded it many times in the months since she'd stolen it, but it was still instantly familiar: the first time I ever saw my baby.

Cora glanced at my face to make sure I was watching, and then she pointed to a date at the bottom of the piece of paper. "See? See the time stamp right there? That's how I knew that Dr. Hill was talking about you. When I figured it out, I knew I had to warn you that there was something wrong with your pregnancy."

I felt a chill. "Let me get this straight... You knew Dr. Hill was doing something to these babies?"

But Cora was shaking her head. "No, Dr. Hill was just a...a what do you call it? A middleman. She wasn't supposed to do anything other than give this woman your name. I got the sense she was only in it for the money, sort of like the under-the-table IVF stuff she'd do for celebrities, only way, way shadier. She made that very clear on the phone. She said something like, 'This is the same deal as last time. I'll help you find someone desperate enough, and I'll let you know whether the pregnancy takes, and then, I'm out.' That was how she'd put it. *I'll help you find someone desperate enough.*"

The breath went out of me. It was true. Everything Io had told me was true. "Desperate enough for what?"

"She didn't say but I..." Cora lifted her eyes to my face and said very carefully, "I think she meant desperate enough that you wouldn't terminate the pregnancy when it became obvious that something was wrong. That's why I came out here tonight, Anna. Because you can't let this baby be born." Her eyes flicked to my belly again. "It's a monster. You have to get rid of it."

ALICE PARSONS, 1648

ALICE'S HIPS AND KNEES HAD GROWN SORE FROM THE ADDI-
tional weight around her midsection, and she desperately needed to
sit, but there were people hemming her in on all sides, making that
impossible. The crowd was restless, buffeting and jostling her, no one
seeming to care that she was with child, that she was having a hard
time keeping upright. Alice had never seen anything like it. They
were angry, screaming. *Bloodthirsty*.

"Witch! Witch!" their voices rose to a single chant that vibrated
through Alice's body. "*Witch!*"

Alice pressed her palms to her belly and tried to focus on the
steady thrum of heartbeat through her thin cotton dress. There it
was, that slight, faint *bomp bomp bomp*. She let her eyes close just for
a moment, exhaustion and fear overtaking her.

Breathe, she told herself, *just breathe*.

This would all be over soon.

Like everyone else in Massachusetts Bay, she had come to the city
square to see Margaret Jones tried for witchcraft. Margaret had been
taken away two days ago and held in prison, where her jailer was said

to have found the mark of the devil—a deep red stain like a little handprint just below her chin. A near certain sign of a witch.

Alice could see that mark now when Margaret—tied to a stake outside the jailhouse—lifted her face to the heavens, as though she expected God to intervene on her behalf. It looked like a birthmark except for its dark color, the uncanny shape of it.

Staring at that mark, Alice felt something cold and sour spread through her like disease. How had she never noticed it before? She'd known Margaret her entire life. She'd *trusted* her.

The heartbeat at her fingertips seemed faster. It seemed ominous.

Before Margaret had been put on trial for witchcraft, she'd been a midwife. Not three months ago, she'd given Alice a jarful of anise seeds when Alice had started bleeding in the night and worried she would lose the baby. Her Thomas had warned her not to speak with Margaret, but Alice had been desperate. Thomas was the town pastor, and the people were already whispering amongst themselves, saying it was strange that he and Alice had been married some three years and still without child. And here Alice was, nearing the end of her child-bearing years. She worried it was already too late. She would've given up everything she had, every single possession, for just a little more time.

And so Alice had seen Margaret, and she'd taken the anise seeds with honey every morning. And the bleeding had stopped. She'd thought it was a miracle. At first.

But then...other things started happening. Just small things. Alice's gums and her fingernail beds had bled a little. And then some of her hair and fingernails had fallen off. And it wasn't just that. Her cravings had gotten...unnatural. Beastly. And just last week, Alice had found dolls made of corn husks in the woods around her house.

Alice had destroyed the dolls and hid the evidence of the rest as best she could. She'd told no one. But she couldn't help wondering.

Alice felt a heavy gaze upon her and looked up to find Margaret staring at her. Her scraggly black hair blew over a deeply wrinkled face, and her eyes were gray as the sea and unblinking.

The witch didn't look frightened. She looked...defiant.

And Alice knew. She knew it in her soul.

That witch had done something to her baby.

= REMEMBER THE 411 RULE =

Go to the hospital when your contractions are 4 minutes apart and last 1 minute and they've been coming for 1 hour

33

THE PAIN HAD BEEN COMING ON GRADUALLY, BUT NOW IT HIT all at once. I felt a tightening in my lower back, the muscles between my hips constricting. Then my heart began to race, and I couldn't breathe, couldn't think.

Whatever was inside of me was ready to come out.

I groped for the porch rail to hold myself steady, but my palm slipped off.

The pain... Oh God...

It was so bad that I couldn't breathe, couldn't speak. I closed my eyes and waited for it to pass.

I remembered reading in one of my pregnancy books that contractions were only supposed to last between sixty and ninety seconds. A minute to a minute and a half. I remembered feeling so relieved when I read that, thinking sixty seconds wasn't so long. I could deal with anything for a minute.

That little factoid popped into my head when the next contraction began. I tried to hold onto it, to remind myself that this pain might feel intense, but that it was going to end very soon. Less than sixty seconds to go. I even tried to count.

One Mississippi, two...

I made it to four, and then I couldn't count anymore. I couldn't remember what came after four or what came before it. There was only the pain. Growing, multiplying, beating against my spine like drums...

I heard the door slamming open, footsteps on the porch.

"Anna? Anna...oh God...is it the baby? Are you okay?" Dex's voice. I could feel his hands on me, one braced against my back, the other just below my elbow, probably the only things keeping me from collapsing. I tried to force my eyes open, to look at him, but all I could see was black.

"...need to get her to the hospital," I heard Cora saying, somewhere above me. "She's in labor." And then there was a shuffling sound and a shadow fell over me.

"Anna?" Dex said. "Just breathe, okay? All you have to do is breathe."

I felt my jaw clench together, teeth grinding. I wanted to tell him that I *couldn't* breathe. If I tried to breathe, I was going to throw up. I wanted to hurt him, to shove him away from me, watch him fall down the stairs.

But I wanted him to hold me too. I wanted him to tell me that everything was going to be okay, that I was safe, and our baby was safe. I was so mad but, more than that, I was scared. I reached for him, my fingers wrapping around his sleeve. "Dex..."

Cora was talking again. I heard, "...you should leave now...get through...storm..." and then her voice faded out, a radio station lost beneath the static. I tried to listen for her, but I couldn't get far enough outside of my body. It felt like I was being turned inside out. It felt like there was something inside of me, something *thrashing*.

Dex swore, and I felt his hands leave me just for a second. And then, something hard slammed into my knees, something wet. I reached out and there was a cold feeling beneath my fingers.

Mud, I realized. I was touching mud and grass and the ground.

I must've fallen.

Dex was beside me again. "Anna? Jesus...I've got you now. It's okay, I've got you. We're going to the hospital."

How long had it been?

An hour? A day?

Sixty seconds. Contractions were only supposed to last for around sixty seconds.

"Dex?" I gasped. Even as the word left my mouth, the pain intensified. My eyelids fluttered.

"We're going to the car, okay baby? Keep breathing." Dex's voice was coming in more clearly now. I forced my eyes open and—

And the bottom dropped out of my stomach.

There was blood everywhere. Great swirls of it splashed across the yard, splattered on the porch, the dead grass, the trees.

It was coming from me.

Dex was still looking at me, his eyes glistening like he was trying to hold back tears. "Anna, we have to get into the car, okay? Do you think you can make it?"

No, I wanted to scream. Of course I couldn't make it to the car. I couldn't make it up to my own feet.

"Please let me help," I heard Cora say.

And Dex snarled back, "Haven't you done enough? Just *go*."

There was a shuffling sound, footsteps, and then Cora was kneeling next to me. She didn't say a word, just grabbed my arm.

"Anna?" Dex's voice was quieter now, closer. "Come on, let's try standing, okay? Just one leg, then the other."

I blinked a few times. *Standing?*

"That's it," Cora was saying. And Dex added, "Okay, now let's try to walk. Do you think you can make it to the car?"

"Y-yeah." I was barely able to force the word from my mouth before another contraction knifed through me. I released a sharp cry and bent in half, my belly resting on my thighs, one arm curling around myself, trying to hold my broken body together.

Nonononono.

I brace a hand against the ground, breathing hard. It was all I could do to stay upright. Everything inside of me wanted to keel over, curl into a ball on the floor, and let the pain take me.

It'll pass, I told myself through the blinding shimmer of pain. It always passed.

It seemed like a very long time before the pain began to ebb away. I felt dizzy, but it was a long moment before I realized it was because I was holding my breath. I propped one hand against the ground to keep myself steady and sucked down a lungful of air, waiting for the world to snap back into focus.

Grass. Mud. Night. I straightened again, gasping. It seemed impossible that it was still night. Hadn't I been in pain for hours? It felt like I had. It felt like this pain had ripped me in two.

I touched my belly, and it steadied me somehow, the knowledge that I was still in one piece, that the pain hadn't split me open, even if that's what it felt like. I was stronger than I thought. I could do this. My body knew how to do this. It was going to be okay.

I was still repeating these words in my head, trying to steady my breathing, when my eyes fell on something lying a few feet away, a doll twisted in the dead grass, her long blond hair fanned behind her like a veil, lifeless eyes gazing back at me. Her head was cranked at an impossible angle, and one of her arms had broken off and was lying on the earth beside her.

I let my breath out in a little burst. I had the sensation that I was staring into a distorted mirror, that it wasn't a doll lying in the grass; it was *me*, that we'd switched places.

Then the world jolted back into place and I saw it for what it was: another *Spellbound* doll left for me to find.

This one's mouth had been painted red with blood.

34

DEX AND CORA HELPED ME INTO THE CAR, AND THEN WE LEFT Cora behind so Dex could drive me to the hospital.

His knuckles were white around the steering wheel, and his skin still looked pale in the soft glow of the dashboard. He gazed dead ahead, squinting to see past the falling rain. It was coming down fast and heavy now, our headlights illuminating all the silver so that the night seemed strangely bright, almost glowing. The windshield wipers jerked and stuck, unable to keep up.

We took a turn too fast, our tires giving an angry squeal on the wet pavement. I propped a hand against the dashboard as a fresh wave of pain tightened the muscles in my pelvis. The world around me flickered, the edges of my eyesight fading to black. I couldn't breathe, didn't even remember how.

Twiggy hedges and skeletal trees whipped past my window, the sound reminding me of tapping fingers. I wrapped myself around my belly, my head going to my hands, my bump pressed against my knees. My seat belt cut into my neck and belly, but I didn't bother undoing it, I was shaking too badly.

Dex's eyes flicked to me. "Hang in there, okay? We'll be to the hospital soon."

I nodded through the pain, unable to find my voice. This felt exactly like it did the night I almost miscarried, wave after wave of pain crashing into me, sweeping me out to sea.

And then, just when I couldn't take it anymore, just when I thought that this was it, that no human person could be able to withstand that amount of pain, the waves stopped coming and I could breathe again.

"How much farther?" I asked. My lips felt thick.

"We're close," Dex said, glancing at me. "Hold on."

I took deep breath after deep breath, trying to focus on the car growling below me, the headlights illuminating the slick, wet road ahead.

Breathe, I thought.

In.

One, two, three, four five...

Out.

One, two, three...

"Anna?" Dex asked. "How are you doing?"

I shook my head, unable to speak. Dimly, I noticed he was driving faster. The car surged forward, engine moaning. I opened my eyes, trying to figure out where exactly we were. The hospital couldn't be far, but the rain was making it impossible. It was coming down so heavily that I couldn't see anything, and the headlights were much too bright, reflecting off all that water. I blinked hard. Sweat broke out on my palms, my lower back, under my thighs.

"Dex—" I moaned.

"Hold on, baby, we're almost there."

Baby. The way he said that word made me think of the horrible rasp of Cora's voice in the darkness of my bedroom.

I swallowed, but my mouth was too dry, and I couldn't work up enough saliva to wet my throat. Outside, I saw nothing but dark gray sky and the fuzz of rain against the glass.

How can he see the road? I wondered, dazed. I glanced at him, studying the line of his jaw, the intent set of his eyes. He was concentrating so hard that he seemed like he was in physical pain, every muscle in his body pulled tight enough to snap.

"Dex..." My eyelids sunk as another wave of pain threatened to wash over me. I curled my hands around my knees and tried to breathe, but my chest was drum tight and my fingers were trembling too badly to work properly. I couldn't quite grasp my legs. "Something's...wrong..." I managed to choke out before I was hit with another blast of pain.

If Dex answered me, I didn't hear it. I couldn't see anything in the dark, couldn't focus on anything past the pain.

Breathe, I thought. *Breathe.*

Tears sprung to my eyes. The writhing and twisting inside of me... it was too much. It felt like something squeezing and stretching. I thought of tiny white teeth. Long curved black claws. I started to cry.

Please be okay. Please, please, just let her be okay.

Dimly, I realized we'd pulled to a stop. I stared blearily out the window, hoping to see the bright lights of the hospital. But we were stopped at a red light on some residential road that was so narrow I could've reached out and touched the stop sign at the corner. There were fewer houses here, and they sat farther back, half hidden by old oak trees with bare branches, manicured bushes white with frost.

Dex had twisted around to face me. "Anna? Talk to me. Are you okay?"

Was I okay? There was a pain between my legs, sharp, rough pain down the insides of my thighs that felt like burning. My hands trembled as I moved them down, past my belly, to the soreness below, the tops of my rash-covered legs. I felt something wet. My body went still, panic moving through me like wind over a field.

Dex followed the movement of my hands. He let out a sharp gasp.

"Oh my God...you're bleeding," Dex said. He yanked open the glove compartment, pulling out a wad of fast-food napkins. "Here," he said, leaning closer, "this will help."

He trailed off, but I was barely listening. His wedding band had caught the light while he was mopping up the blood on the insides of my thighs, drawing my eye. It made me think of Cora, how he'd told Cora he was going to leave me if the IVF didn't work, how he'd left Adeline because she hadn't agreed to bear his children. We were just wombs to him, just things. He didn't love us. He didn't even see us as people.

Despite everything, all my pain and fear and horror, I felt anger roar up inside of me. He didn't deserve to wear that ring anymore, not after what he'd done.

"Get away from me," I moaned.

Dex's expression darkened. "Anna."

"I don't want you touching me."

"Honey...don't you think you're being a little unreasonable?"

I was suddenly aware of something inside of me, a dark presence that wasn't me exactly, but wasn't separate from me either. I wondered vaguely whether I should be afraid of it, but the presence had a dreamlike quality that made me question whether it was real or whether it was another trick of my mind, a delusion.

My eyesight wavered. I blinked, and when the car came back into clearer focus, Dex was staring at me. He didn't seem to have noticed the change in me, the darkness that was rising, even now.

He was frowning. "Anna...I think you need to calm down, you need to listen to me..."

My lips formed a smile, but it wasn't *me* smiling, it was that thing inside of me. I couldn't stop thinking about that ring. I couldn't stand seeing Dex wear it, not after what he'd done. I wanted to rip it off him. I wanted—

I was looking at Dex's face, so I saw the exact moment everything changed. He seemed confused, at first, and then his expression shifted, his mouth going slack with horror, his eyes white and staring, pupils dilating fast. There was an emptiness to him, like there was nothing behind the mask of his face but a hollow space and blowing air.

A fraction of a second after his face transformed, Dex's arm jerked. I felt a spray of blood on my cheeks.

And then...and then...oh God, there was the *sound*. It was the sound of teeth snapping open and closed, ripping meat and flesh. It was the sound of an animal, feeding. I wanted to look around, to see where the sound was coming from, but I was helpless, frozen in place.

In my dreamlike state, I assumed it was the thing inside of me, the monster. She must've gotten out of me, somehow. I didn't comprehend the physics of it, how she could be outside of my body even as I was still pregnant with her. All I knew was that I had done this, I had unleashed this dangerous creature into the world. *I'd* been the one to let her grow, I'd been the one to nurture and take care of her. I'd known that something was wrong, and there had been a part of me that hadn't cared, as long as she was safe, as long as she was growing. I let this happen.

And here was the worst of it: *I still didn't want to hurt her.* Even now, I only wanted to protect her. She was my baby. Whatever happened to her, whatever she became, I was her mother, and I wanted—no, it was more than that, I *needed*—to keep her safe.

Dex began to scream mindlessly, his voice a howling echo through the car. It didn't sound human, that scream. It was hollow, deadened. I knew in that moment that I would remember that sound for the rest of my life.

There was a sudden snap, like breaking bone, and Dex finally wrenched away from me. At that moment, I snapped back into my body. The world around me became bright and hard and real. I pressed my lips together and there was something warm and wet on my tongue.

Blood.

I looked down, blinking in the darkness. I noticed my hands first. They felt strangely detached from my body, almost as though they belonged to someone else, and my fingers, my knuckles, everything up to my wrists was covered in blood. Nausea crawled up my throat, my stomach clenching painfully.

My eyesight blurred as my gaze moved past my hands to Dex. He was cradling his arm to his chest. I stared at him, trying not to gag. Everything past his left wrist had turned bright red, everything except for the jagged knob of bone protruding from his hand: his ring finger. It was broken, bone gleaming horribly bright against the ragged remains of his skin, his finger still gushing blood. His wedding ring was gone.

Dex's eyes went wild as he took in his ruined hand. He looked back up at me. "You...you bit me! You *psycho!*"

I shook my head, *no, I didn't do that, I couldn't have done that, it wasn't me.* But all at once, I remembered, I remembered everything. How I'd brought his hand to my mouth, how he'd screamed when I dug my teeth into the flesh. How the blood had tasted strangely comforting, all warm and wet.

I leaned over and spit Dex's wedding ring into the center console. It bounced against the plastic, scattering blood. I sat for a moment in the cold, my breath ghosting before me, staring down.

And then, slowly, I looked back up at him, the taste of his blood bright on my tongue. My stomach rumbled in what felt like *hunger.*

Dex jerked and twitched, panic flooding through him at whatever he saw in my eyes, his elbow smacking into the gear shift, knocking us out of Park.

The car began to roll, then slide, faster and faster over the wet road. I could feel it beneath us, the sudden transfer of weight, the way we went from fine to out of control in a split second.

I looked away just in time to see that the road had vanished. The only thing before us was trees and dark and slanting, silvery rain. It was like a scene from a dream or a nightmare, everything too fast, too bright, too close. Like so much of my life these last nine months, it didn't seem real.

35

BLOOD COATED MY LIPS AND POOLED ON THE ROOF OF MY mouth. I tried to inhale and started coughing instead, the blood trailing down the back of my throat, blocking my windpipe. Pain shot straight through my skull, shocking me so much that I closed my eyes on instinct, grimacing.

I blinked once, twice. The inside of the car was very dark. Even the dashboard lights had died.

"Dex..." The word was a sharp rasp in my throat, making me cringe. The storm inside of me had gone still for the moment, but I knew another contraction would hit any second. I didn't have much time.

I lifted my hands, fumbling for something to grab hold of. My head was crunched up against the roof of the car, and the hard fabric of my seat belt dug into my throat and belly, holding me in place, the edges biting into my skin. It took me a long slow moment to realize that this was because I was upside down. The car had flipped.

A hum rose in my skull, the sound blocking out all other noise. My confusion hardened into fear.

"Dex?" I said again, my voice stronger this time. I could make out the shape of him beside me, not moving. I shifted my hands to my lap, fumbling with my seat belt.

There was a rumbling sound, a distant light. I cranked my head around and squinted at the rain-covered windows, heart hammering as the light crept closer, closer. It must've been a car driving along the road just above us. I felt a lift of hope, thinking that the car would see us, that he'd have to stop—

But he moved slowly past, driving carefully because of the rain, those bright headlights momentarily illuminating the space around me.

For a moment I took it all in, stunned.

We seemed to have skidded off the road, flipped over, and hit a tree. Our windshield was shattered, tree branches reaching into the car like skeletal hands, glass glinting from the dashboard and car seats, airbags surrounding us like deflated balloons. I noticed those details in a detached way, and then I turned my head to the side and saw Dex.

Oh God, Dex.

He hung from the seat belt beside me. His head was slammed up against the roof of the car, his neck jerked at an unnatural angle, and his skin so, so pale. Practically white. His mouth hung open, a dribble of blood leaking onto his chin.

I managed to slide my elbows beneath my torso and awkwardly prop the top half of my body up, struggling against the horrifying weight of my bump. "Dex? Dex, can you hear me?"

His eyes were empty, vacant. He still had his mangled hand cradled to his chest.

"Dex?" I grabbed for his shoulder and shook but he just swayed back and forth, held aloft by the seat belt, his head rolling on his shoulders. Panic roared up inside of me. My fingers found his cheek.

His skin was ice.

I jerked my hand away, my heart thudding.

No, I thought, fumbling with my seat belt. *No no no no.*

My hands felt clumsy and too large, but I managed to find the release button. My seat belt slithered away, and my body slammed into the roof. Electric shocks shot down my spine, and for a moment, I was blinded by bright bursts of white light, a sudden wave of pain. The car spun around me. My eyelids fluttered closed...

Pull it together, I thought through the pain.

I forced my eyes open, forced them to *stay* open. I waited for my vision to stop swimming, and then I gathered myself, pulled my hands and knees beneath my body, and crawled over to Dex, shaking him. "Dex?" I said, but my voice wasn't working like it was supposed to. "Wake up...."

I kept shaking, but Dex's body was limp, unresponsive. I unclipped his seat belt and he slumped against the roof of the car in a tangle of limbs, not moving.

No, I thought, fear choking up my throat. No, he couldn't die, not like this. He couldn't leave me to deal with this alone, not after everything else he'd put me through.

"Wake up." I tried to swallow and a sound like a sob formed deep in my chest. I pulled Dex's head into my lap and pushed my fingers to his neck, checking him for a pulse.

For a long moment, there was only cold skin and nothing. I closed my eyes. I could feel my own heart beating at my temples, see the blood pulsing through my lids.

Come on, Dex. Come on...

I wanted to punch something. I wanted to scream again. I pressed my fingers deeper into his neck, holding my breath.

And then—

There. A faint flicker. A heartbeat.

A sob broke me in half. I collapsed over Dex's still body, crying hard. He was still alive. The relief made me so dizzy, I could barely see.

"Dex?" I said, my voice hoarse. It might've been my imagination, but I thought I heard a soft groan in the darkness, a raspy intake of breath. I kept talking, my words tumbling over each other in their rush to get out of my mouth. "Dex, I'm going to get out of the car and see how close we are to the hospital, okay? I have to leave you here, but I'll be back."

Dex didn't move, didn't say a word. His breath was a faint, labored rasp. He was running out of time, and I wasn't sure how long I'd have before the next contraction. Not nearly long enough. I was never going to make it.

Phone, I thought out of nowhere. I needed to find my phone.

I crawled around the car, frantically moving my hands through the darkness. Dread rose inside of me as I searched. My phone wasn't here.

Dex will have his, I thought. I started patting him down, searching his pockets until I felt the hard shape of his cell through the fabric of his jeans. Hands trembling, I dug it out and swiped my thumb across the screen. The battery was already on red.

I dialed 911 and lifted it to my ear, holding my breath as I waited for it to ring.

Nothing. I frowned and checked the screen: No Service.

I tried again. Still nothing. I curled my hand around the useless piece of metal and glass, fighting the urge to throw it. Instead, I shoved it into my pocket. We couldn't be far from the hospital. I was just going to have to walk until I could get a signal.

I scooted to the other side of the car and fumbled for the door handle. It felt thick and cold beneath my fingers, like a solid hunk of ice. I fumbled the damn thing twice before I heard the latch snap, the soft creak of the door swinging open.

I pushed my body forward, gasping when I brought my palms down on wet. I was outside. In my excitement to be out of the car, I lurched forward too fast, landing face first on the icy ground, my arms giving out beneath me. Soft cold flakes stuck to my cheeks, my forehead, my neck.

There were no other lights puncturing the rainy night. We could've been in the middle of nowhere.

"Help," I moaned, but my voice felt insubstantial, the words weightless as feathers. The entire world was muffled, quiet.

I stretched my fingers across the ground, cringing at the cold bite of mud. I fumbled until my hands found the edge of the car, and then I let them travel up, up, to the door. I sucked in a deep lungful of damp air. Using what little strength I had left, I pulled.

The contraction began as pressure building low in my pelvis, like there was someone inside of my body pushing down. I froze, forcing myself to inhale, exhale, as the pressure tightened, *tightened*.

And then it wasn't just pressure, it was an explosion. Pain radiated through my torso and into my arms and legs, the suddenness of it taking my breath away. I curled around myself, and a scream clawed out of me like a beast, splitting the night in half, ripping at the insides of my throat.

For a long time, that's all there was: pain, and screaming. I screamed until my voice gave out, and then I sucked down a fresh breath and screamed again.

Please, somebody hear me, I thought. *Please, somebody come.*

The scream echoed through the night air and ricocheted inside of my skull, making my head throb. It seemed to merge with my pain so that, for a dizzy moment, I thought they were the same thing. If I could remember how to stop screaming, the pain would stop too. But I couldn't, I couldn't.

I don't know how long this lasted. But slowly, so slowly I was sure I was imagining it, the pain began to fade, and my scream weakened to a ragged, desperate sob.

My body swayed, unsteady. I was afraid to let go of the door. I was never going to make it to the hospital, I realized. Not like this. My contractions were coming too fast, and they were too strong. I needed help.

I fumbled for Dex's cell and dialed 911 with frozen fingers. I waited. It didn't ring, but I noticed a single bar of service on the screen. Hope.

I hit speaker and lifted the phone up, above my head, murmuring, "Come on...come on..."

Nothing.

I waited until I was sure that the last bits of pain had gone, and then I took a single step away from the car. Two. Another bar appeared. My legs felt steady enough and so I allowed my hands to dance away from the metal, playing with letting go.

A third bar appeared, then vanished.

"Come on," I said out loud.

I let go of the car and, for a moment, I was standing on my own, swaying in the rain. I stared at the phone screen, holding my breath, waiting for it to connect.

And then another contraction hit and washed everything—the rain, the phone, Dex—away.

———

I must've lost consciousness for a while. The next thing I was aware of was lights flashing in the trees, and a familiar crunching noise that meant tires on pavement.

I opened my eyes groggily. Closed them again.

A car door slammed open. And then there were footsteps, the sound of someone breathing.

"Anna? Anna, honey, I'm here. Can you hear me?"

"Siobhan?" I murmured. Now, I knew I was hallucinating. Siobhan couldn't be here. She was back in Brooklyn, in a coma—she might even be dying.

Did that mean I was dying too?

The pain inside of me intensified. I sucked a breath through my lips.

Siobhan was saying something else, but I couldn't quite make out what it was. My eyes were still closed, and I was trying to steady my breathing, but every inhale clawed up my throat, leaving my head cloudy, unfocused. There was still an ache in my pelvis, but it wasn't as bad as it had been a second ago, when the world around me dropped away and I couldn't even manage to speak.

A cold hand wrapped around mine. "Anna? Anna, can you hear me? Just try to breathe, okay? Everything's going to be okay."

"Please...my baby...I need...hospital."

"We can't go to the hospital, Anna. Just keep breathing."

I inhaled through my nose, and when I opened my eyes again,

Siobhan had me by the shoulders, crouching a little so she could look me in the eyes. She was hard to make out in the dark, her face half hidden beneath the bill of the baseball cap pulled low over her forehead.

How had she found me? For a second, I worried I was hallucinating. I squeezed my eyes shut but, when I opened them again, Siobhan was still there, crouching over me. I stared.

"How did you know...? How...?"

"Shh...it's okay; don't try to talk," she murmured. She smiled at me, just a flick of her lips, there and then gone. I looked from her face to the baseball cap she was wearing. And then I frowned, staring.

The *blue* baseball hat.

All at once, the world went soundless. The rain was still falling, but it didn't make any noise as it hit the earth. It was like there was something wrong with my ears, like I'd punctured an eardrum, gone momentarily deaf.

In my mind, I remembered seeing a woman in a blue baseball cap standing on my curb back in Brooklyn. I remembered how she'd pulled the cap low over her face, hid her eyes behind oversized sunglasses. Hadn't I thought that she'd looked like an actor? Hadn't I wondered if I'd recognized her, even then?

"No," I said, swallowing hard. I felt numb all over. I didn't want this to be true. I didn't want to believe it. "No...Siobhan..."

"Don't try to talk," Siobhan said.

But I had to get this out. I had to know. "It couldn't have been you. Tell me you weren't the one who was following me."

But even as I said the words, I could see that I'd finally, finally guessed right. The truth was written all over Siobhan's face, in the downward tilt of her eyes and the way her lips pressed together, the sudden tension in her jaw. I felt a blaze of embarrassment, so hot it caused sweat to prick along my forehead. How could I have missed this? How could I have been so trusting, so stupid?

"It wasn't always me," Siobhan admitted, after a long moment. "We took turns."

I dug my hands into the ground below me, felt the soft earth give way beneath my fingernails. *We?*

There was an apology in her voice, as though she knew how much it was going to hurt me to learn that she'd not only been keeping things from me, but that she'd been conspiring with others behind my back, plotting against me. Something in her face told me to let it go, that I wouldn't like anything else I learned. But I couldn't do that. Not when I might finally get some answers.

"Emily?" I guessed.

Siobhan shook her head. "Emily isn't one of ours. She's just an ambitious young woman who didn't realize how hard she was making things for you."

"Talia, then? I found a picture of her and Meg."

"I believe Meg knows Talia, yes," Siobhan explained. "They met at a fertility clinic ages ago, back when we were vetting Talia. But she's not part of what's happening to you, Anna."

My mouth went dry. *One of ours? Vetting?*

I was still playing her words over in my head when I felt her trace something on my forehead.

A star?

I was staring right at her face when something twitched in the trees behind her, some quick movement. My stomach jerked with pure terror. "What was that?"

"Don't worry about them," Siobhan said. "They're friends. Sisters."

Them? I looked harder at the darkness. This time, I saw women standing around us. Women arranged in a loose circle, swaying, the edges of their bodies bleeding into the shadows around them. Meg was with them, still wearing that bright red lipstick. She caught my eye and gave me a small nod.

And there were others, women from all walks of life. A Latine woman I remembered seeing on the beach and a Black woman with short, tightly curled hair, her widow's peak so low that it looked like someone had drawn a heart around her face. A tall blond woman I recognized from the birth center was there—*Olympia* I thought—and beside her was a woman I'm pretty sure worked the cash register at my grocery store. Women I'd never seen before and women I saw every day; women much, much older than I was, and a few who were younger, barely in their teens.

"Siobhan..." I moaned. "What's happening...?"

The women standing in the trees drew closer. They held candles, the fragile flames flickering in the cold. If I listened, I could hear their voices weaving together. Chanting something in a language I didn't understand.

Siobhan released a sharp breath, and then she pressed her palm to my forehead. It was sticky and warm with...something.

Blood?

My eyelids fluttered. My baby twitched, just a small shift. I had to help her, protect her. But I couldn't move. My face, my hands, my mouth, everything felt numb.

"Keep breathing, Anna," Siobhan said, her voice low. "You don't have much longer now. It's almost time. I need you to listen to me now. I know you're scared, but this isn't a curse."

"It's a gift."

36

A LONG TIME LATER, SOMETHING COLD BRUSHED MY CHEEK.

Fingertips? A hand?

My eyes were closed, heavy, but I imagined someone was leaning over me. I thought I could still smell the Ivory soap scent of her skin. But when I opened my eyes, that memory slipped out of reach, leaving my mind perfectly black, perfectly blank. I had no idea where I was or what had just happened.

White light hit my eyelids, making me cringe.

"Ma'am?" The voice was unfamiliar, male. "I'm going to need to ask you to stay still for me, okay? Try not to move."

My eyelids fluttered. There was the sound of boots in the grass, low voices, and something else, a grinding, motor sound that I couldn't quite place.

Car, I thought, remembering the accident. I forced my eyes the rest of the way open, breathing hard. The sky spun above me, clouds and rain swirling together. Everything was so, so cold.

I was lying on my back on the side of the hill, rain coming down heavily around me. I blinked slowly, thinking of how I'd stepped away from the car, how I'd lifted my phone to see if I could get my call to go through. That was...a while ago. An hour? Longer? There was an ambulance idling at the side of the street now, red lights flashing, a team of paramedics swarming me.

I heard clanging metal, more footsteps, and then that same male voice said, "Okay, ma'am, we're going to need to lift you onto the stretcher here."

"I...I'm in labor..." I managed to choke out.

"I can see that, ma'am. I'm just going to ask you to hold tight. We're going to get you to the hospital as soon as we can."

Pain roared up inside of me. The world went black. I let out a choked moan and somehow managed a weak nod, my chin jerking up and down. Distantly, I heard the paramedic counting, and then three sets of sturdy hands were lifting me off the ground, placing me onto something hard and flat.

"Who's your doctor?" the paramedic was asking me. "We can call them and have them meet you at the hospital."

"No," I choked out. There was no way I was letting Dr. Hill know where I was, but I couldn't stomach the thought of letting a stranger deliver my baby. There was only one other option, as much as I didn't like it. "Call...call Dr. Crawford at Southampton," I said through the pain. "He knows me."

The paramedic was nodding. "Got it."

"My...husband." I sucked in a breath and forced the words past my lips. "You have to...my husband..."

"You want us to call your husband?" the paramedic asked.

"No...my husband...he's...he's still in the car... He's... You have to help him... He's hurt..."

I heard distant, panicked voices, more shuffling, car doors opening and slamming shut. Someone swore loudly. I didn't know if it was
because it was so quiet out here, or if it was the rain making everything echo, but it sounded like the paramedic was speaking directly
into my ear.

And then there was a sound like footsteps. Someone running
down the hill. The stretcher rocked beneath me, and I realized that
I wasn't on the ground any longer but floating through the air, the
paramedics carrying me the rest of the way up the hill. I grasped in
the darkness, trying to grab hold of someone's arm or hand, but I
found nothing.

Dex was supposed to be with me. He was supposed to be holding
my hand, telling me what a good job I was doing, to keep going, keep
pushing. It wasn't supposed to happen like this. I shouldn't be alone.

"No..." I moaned, but that was the only word I managed to force
out of my mouth before another contraction tightened through me.
I had to tell them that I didn't want to go up the hill, I couldn't do
this alone.

But once the contraction passed, I realized that I was somewhere
different. Inside of the ambulance, I thought. The room was small,
and the walls were close. Everything was white and crowded with
beeping, blinking machines.

A woman with short dark hair leaned over me. "I'm going to need
to get you on your left side, okay? And then we can get you and your
baby hooked up to our monitors. Does that sound good?"

I nodded, unable to speak through the pain. The woman turned
away from me, and I thought I heard her say, "Dehydrated..." and
then another paramedic was wrapping something around my bicep,

and I felt the cold prick of a needle sliding into my skin, right at the bend of my arm.

The sound of another person climbing into the ambulance. The door slammed shut. I could feel that we'd started to roll.

"Dex..." I moaned, struggling to lift my head to look down. "Where...where is he?"

The dark-haired paramedic leaned over me again. "Don't worry, honey. They're getting him out of the car now, but we can't wait. We have to get you to the hospital."

I seized her hands, moaning, "No...no, we can't...I need him...I—"

Another contraction lit me up. Everything around me faded to gray.

———

I didn't remember the ambulance ride. I was vaguely aware of being moved, transferred from a stretcher to a cot, surrounded by people in scrubs pressing cold tools to my skin, speaking to each other in shorthand I didn't understand.

At some point, the pain faded long enough for me to peel my eyes open. I was staring up at plaster instead of the tin ambulance ceiling, and there was a hard white shine everywhere: the metal of an operating table, the brightness of lights. The air stunk of chemicals and lemons, and strange people hovered around me, blue masks covering their faces. Everything was so loud, so close.

"Where am I?" I moaned.

"Shh..." someone said, and a cold plastic cup was pressed up against my mouth, air filling my lungs like balloons.

Someone else said, "You're at Southampton Hospital, in the OR," but I couldn't tell who it was. The surgical masks covering everyone's mouths made it impossible to figure out who was speaking. "Dr. Crawford will be with you shortly."

I found myself nodding, fading. Another contraction was coming, and I could feel my body preparing itself, tightening and coiling, a soldier getting ready for battle. The contractions felt different than they did before. They were no longer rising and ebbing but piling one on top of the other—not waves but tsunamis, hurricanes. Unreal, unrelenting. I was drowning in them.

My eyes flickered. With the last of my strength, I grabbed the nurse's arm and held her in place beside me, forcing my eyes back open. The oxygen mask was still pressed to my mouth, so I couldn't speak. I tried to communicate with her silently, with just my eyes.

You can't let this happen.

The nurse's eyes were kind. I imagined she was smiling behind her mask. "That's it, dear," she told me, patting my hand. I was sure she meant for this gesture to be comforting, but she was wearing thin plastic gloves, and so it felt sterile instead. "You're doing great."

No, I tried to say. I told my fingers to squeeze tighter, but there was no strength left in my hand. *You don't understand...*

It was no use. The pain dragged me under again.

Distantly, I heard someone say, "...*so* much blood..."

And then, "Looks like the heart rate is dropping."

No. I thought, woozily. *No...*

I could feel my baby inside of me, pressing, pushing, trying to fight her way out. But it was hard to separate the reality of her from the pain. For a little while at least, they were the same thing. The baby *was* the pain. She was the one splitting my bones in two and ripping my muscles apart. She was making me scream.

Somewhere in the swimming, blistering pain, I found myself thinking that I didn't know how women ever forgave their children for this. For ripping their bodies apart, destroying them.

Or maybe, I was just too afraid to let my mind wander. Because if it did, I might have to think about how I couldn't explain what happened to Dex's hand or the tooth or the claw or so many other things. I'd have to think about what Dr. Hill did to me—what Siobhan and those women wanted from me—and how I knew this wasn't just a baby. She was something else, something more.

What is it? I thought. *What does* it *want?*

———

I could mark the exact second Dr. Crawford arrived. There was a sound like a door slamming open, followed by a flurry of movement. A new energy filled the room as the nurses and orderlies crowded around me.

Something's wrong, I thought, panic rising in my throat like bile. Women died during labor all the time. Doctors didn't listen when they said they were in pain, that they couldn't do it. I remembered what the nurse said just a few minutes ago—*so much blood.* My body must not have been responding the way it was supposed to be. I wasn't able to keep up with the pain.

My chest clenched as I realized this was the only explanation that made any sense. These people must have seen what was growing inside of me; they must've known she wasn't human.

I started to shake, to buck, and it took three sets of hands to hold me in place. The corners of my eyes were wet, but the oxygen mask was still strapped to my mouth, making it impossible for me to scream.

And then Dr. Crawford was beside me, leaning over me. He held a mask up to his mouth, covering his lips. "Mrs. Alcott, I'm going to need to ask you to hold still. You're having what's called a precipitous birth."

I stopped bucking as my brain tried to work out what he was telling me. This wasn't what I expected him to say. I didn't know what a precipitous birth was. The words meant nothing to me.

"A precipitous birth is when labor is progressing too quickly for the mother and baby," he continued. "It's too hard on your body, so we need to get the baby out as soon as possible."

I was crying harder now, tears thick on my cheeks.

"No," I said, my voice lost in the swirl of oxygen and plastic. "I can't...I...I...."

I was too terrified to look down, to see what monstrous thing was trying to claw its way out of me. I pictured gnashing teeth, claws digging into my skin...

"You can do this." Dr. Crawford's voice faded in and out, sounding very far away. "You're almost there, I promise. We're going to count to three, and then we're going to push."

I shook my head, even as that word pulsed neon in my brain. *Push.*

"One..." Dr. Crawford said. "Two..."

I clenched my eyes shut. Reality flickered.

For a moment I was in another hospital room—no, not even a hospital room, but a curtained-off space. There was blood running down my legs, pain roaring through me. I was miscarrying—

"We're losing her," someone said. Was it a memory?

Or did someone just say that now, here?

Another pain, massive and everywhere. I could feel my body start to shake, my shoulders and hips shuddering up and down on the table.

"Come on, Anna," Dr. Crawford said. "We're almost there. You're only three pushes away. I need you to be strong for me. *Push*."

It was a command and my body responded, clenching with its new purpose. It felt good to have a job to do, so much better than lying with the pain, doing nothing. I gritted my teeth and my entire body tightened—

Push, I thought again. *Push*.

I closed my eyes and clenched and—

It was just like before, just like the night of my miscarriage. There was a release, and then I felt something warm slide out from between my legs. Something *moving*.

I pictured black animal eyes, thick talons, teeth.

Fear tightened through my chest.

I wanted to scream. I wanted to sob.

And then...she was out.

For a moment, the room went perfectly, utterly still. No one congratulated me or told me how beautiful she was. No one said a word. But no one screamed either.

I pressed my lips together, holding my breath even as the mask spit cold oxygen at my face. Tears glued my eyelids shut.

I don't want to know, don't want to see....

I was still holding my breath, when the tiny, choked cry split the quiet of the room. It didn't sound like I thought it would, that cry.

Dr. Crawford was turning toward me now, holding the baby. Something inside of me still stiffened with fear—*no, I can't I don't want to know*—but then I saw...she was small, so small. A normal human baby.

Dr. Crawford held my baby in outstretched arms. He said, "It's a girl."

37

IT WAS A GIRL.

Not some birdlike monster with a gaping beak where her eyes should be. She was a crying baby girl with ten tiny fingers and ten tiny toes. She had a cap of dark hair streaked through with blood, a nose that looked a little flat and swollen from coming through the birth canal. A normal baby.

I moved the oxygen mask away from my mouth and said, "Give her to me."

I wanted to check her for feathers, for talons. I wanted to feel her small shaking body against my chest, to know that she was warm, that she was alive. And perhaps even more than that, I wanted to smell her head and curl my hands around those tiny fists to keep her from trembling.

The revulsion I'd felt only moments ago was quickly fading. She wasn't a monster; she was a baby. She was *my* baby. She looked so small and blue and afraid. She needed her mother.

But Dr. Crawford didn't give her to me. He turned and handed her to a nurse who took her all the way to the other side of the room, so far away from me that I had to crane my neck to even see her.

Panic fluttered through me. *I was wrong,* I thought instantly. She wasn't a normal baby after all; there was something they could see, something that I couldn't.

"What's wrong?" I tried to sit up. "Where are they taking her?"

In that moment I didn't care what was wrong with her. I just wanted her *back*.

Someone, another nurse, came up beside me and coaxed me back down. "You need to rest. You're very tired."

I didn't want to let her out of my sight, but I didn't have the energy to fight. My baby girl. I wanted to count her fingers and her toes. I wanted to trace the whorls of her hair. I wanted to feel the static electric buzz of her skin pressed against my skin. I wanted to examine every inch of her body until I was absolutely sure she was real, that she was *mine*.

"Just a few more minutes now," the nurse was telling me, her voice low and soothing. "All of this is routine. We're just going to give her a vitamin K shot and clean her up a bit, and then we're going to do a few tests to make sure that everything's working properly. She got here a little earlier than we expected, didn't she?"

Early? I thought, blinking. Yes, that was true. She was early. Technically, I was only...thirty-five weeks along? Was that right?

And then Dr. Crawford was there, handing me my daughter, and my arms curled around her, protecting her.

She wasn't too small. She was beautiful. Perfect. She was still crying. Her eyes got lost in the crumpled folds of her face, and her tiny fists were waving around her temples, so angry. I smiled down at her and poked my finger into her fist.

It worked like a spell. Her hand tightened around my finger and she stopped crying. She blinked up at me, those tiny dark eyes not yet able to focus.

"Hi, baby," I whispered, my arms tightening around her. "I'm your mama. Hi."

She puckered her lips and stuck out her tongue. *Rooting*, I thought, remembering the word from a book I read weeks and weeks ago. She was hungry. I reached for my breast.

My daughter lifted her head to search for my nipple, and that's when I saw the faintest hint of a birthmark just below her chin in the shape of a hand.

———

The next eight hours were a blur of too-short periods of intense, dreamless sleep interrupted by sudden flurries of activity: nurses waking me up to check my temperature, my blood pressure, my hydration levels, white lights and noise as strangers strapped a breast pump to my chest and encouraged me to pump.

I found out, somewhere in the middle of this, that Dex had died. The blood loss and the accident were too much for him, and he passed the same night our daughter was born. I wasn't in a good frame of mind when they told me. There's this thing that happens after you give birth that people don't talk about, or at least they don't talk about enough: all the hormones that have been building in your body for nine months come crashing down at the same time, and it makes you feel like you're in the darkest, most intense depression of your life. People call this "the baby blues," which is just so condescending I could scream. The point is, I wasn't feeling like myself when they told me about Dex, and on top of that, I was numbed out from the exhaustion and the painkillers. I hadn't known how to make sense of my emotions—it was too much information to take in all at once. I was still so angry with Dex for cheating on me and lying to me and gaslighting me, but he was my husband. I'd thought I was going to spend the next sixty years of my life with him. I'd thought we were going to raise our daughter together. And just like that, he was gone. He hadn't deserved that, no matter what he did.

And then, of course, there was the baby. My baby. This brand-new life, this enormous responsibility. I still don't have the words to explain how different I felt, how it was as though my DNA had changed the night my daughter came into this world. And it wasn't just me I'd needed to explain; it was *her*. It was the impossible puzzle of her birth. I thought about it constantly, obsessively, trying to find any kind of sense in what happened.

I could still make out the faint imprint of a rash on my legs, but it had mostly faded after I gave birth, its color changing to a muted orange, then a faint, bruised brown. I traced what was left with the tip of my finger, studying it like it was a road map to some distant foreign country.

My doctors all said I must've had an allergic reaction to something in my lotion. They said that Dex hurt his hand in the car crash that had killed him. They said my baby was fine. Everything was fine.

I wanted to believe them. There was a part of me that wanted to believe I'd imagined everything, that Dex had been right all along. There are so many hormones in your body when you're pregnant. They make you think impossible things, *believe* impossible things. I wanted to believe that I'd gone crazy for a little while, and now that the baby was here, things would go back to normal. And maybe I could've made myself believe those things, if I hadn't started to remember.

A blue baseball cap in the darkness. Rain falling all around me. Flickering candlelight. A bloody hand pressed to my forehead.

I found out later that Siobhan had died the night I gave birth to my daughter too. She'd been rushed to the ER minutes after I'd gone into labor. At the exact moment I was bringing my baby into this world, she'd been taking her last breaths.

Only she hadn't been in Brooklyn. I didn't learn this until days later, when the news hit the internet. I was reading an in memoriam piece in *Vanity Fair*, a gushing account of Siobhan's incredible career beneath a stunning black and white photograph of her at age twenty-three, when she'd won her first Oscar, when I reached a line that made me pause.

Siobhan passed away at Southampton Hospital, according to a statement released by her family.

I stared, wondering how that could be. Siobhan had died *here*, just a few halls away from where I'd given birth? How? Why?

I was shaking my head, reading that line again, when I heard Siobhan say, as clearly as though she'd spoken directly into my ear, "I need you to listen to me now."

The words shuddered through me. I went still, hair rising on the back of my neck. The memory was there, but it was fragile, a single thread that, if tugged too hard, would break and be gone forever.

I remembered rain hitting my face, earth beneath my back. And there'd been chanting. The far-off sound of women chanting.

Then the memory blinked out and I was in the recovery room

again. The hospital was quiet around me, nothing but the murmur of distant voices, tennis shoes hitting the hall outside my room at a fast clip. Somewhere, a machine beeped.

Then, to my left, a quick knock, a woman's voice. "Anna?"

The suddenness shocked me, and some fear response kicked in. I clamped my hand around the threadbare blanket stretched across my lap, my shoulders tightening. But it was Siobhan's friend from the birthing center, Olympia. She stood outside my room in black jeans and a black sweatshirt, blond hair falling over her forehead and shoulders in soft waves.

"I'm sorry... Is it weird that I came?" Her voice was deep and soothing, the voice of yoga studio teachers and meditation apps. "I was in town, so I brought you something."

She held up a teddy bear.

I stared, my eyes blurry with exhaustion. It was odd, but I could swear I'd seen her somewhere else very recently. I had this perfect image in my head of her standing in the dark, outside maybe, tucked between trees and shadow, swaying. Then, I blinked, dazed, and the image broke apart.

"I'm sorry," Olympia said, wrinkling her nose. "It's probably too early for you to have visitors. I shouldn't have come."

"No," I said, remembering my manners. "No, it's fine. Come in."

Olympia entered my room and closed the door behind her. She was a tall woman with narrow shoulders and hips and a finely boned, angular face. She didn't appear to be wearing a lot of makeup, but her eyebrows were very thick and dark, and she'd lined her lips in a deep brownish mauve. It made her look arresting and dramatic. Her fingernails were long, pointed, painted a very pale pink.

She put the teddy bear she'd brought down on a table with a few of my other gifts and settled herself in the stiff polyester armchair beside my bed. Her movements were languid, like a house cat.

"How are you feeling?" she asked.

I felt like I'd sat cross-legged on a stick of dynamite. The good painkillers had worn off, and I was back to Tylenol which—as far as I could tell—did nothing. I was terrified to use the bathroom, to sit up, to try to put on pants. The only thing that had helped at all was a cooling spray that came in a small aerosol can, like hairspray. I'd already used up half the bottle.

But that's not the answer you're supposed to give when you've just had a baby, so I said, "I'm good. Tired. It's hard to sleep in a hospital, with the nurses checking in every hour. Not that I'm expecting to get much sleep for the next few months."

"No, I don't imagine you will." Olympia offered me a small smile. "All those night feedings, just you and her." She looked around, her smile wavering. "Where is...?"

"A nurse took her for a bath. She'll be back soon." I sat up straighter, accidently knocking a pillow off my bed. "Oh—"

"I got it." Olympia plucked the pillow from the floor, and as she leaned past me, I caught a scent off her hair. It was dark and woodsy, cool night air and smoke.

I stiffened, remembering the sound of women's voices weaving through the trees. A palm, warm and wet, pressed to my forehead. And something else. Siobhan's voice, saying something.

What had she said?

My mouth felt suddenly dry. I closed my eyes, my brain struggling to put it all together.

When I opened them again, Olympia was looking at me, an intense look tinged with something else. Curiosity? Expectation?

She said, "You're starting to remember, aren't you?"

Candles with fragile, flickering flames. Voices in the trees.

"Something happened that night..." I said, hesitant. It was all so jumbled in my head, half dream, half memory, none of it remotely possible. "The night my baby was born...You...you did something to me."

Olympia said nothing for a long time. I wondered if she was going to make me beg her for the truth. But then she steepled her fingers and pressed them to her lips and said, her eyes cast toward the floor, "You don't have to remember if you don't want to. I can give you something to make sure it all stays forgotten. A lot of women find it easier that way. It's your choice."

I felt a tumbling inside of me, a feeling like one domino knocking into another and then another. "Find *what* easier?" I asked. I'd meant for my voice to sound calm, but a note of anger slipped in. "What did you do to me?"

Olympia lifted her eyes to mine and stared for a moment. I stared right back, wondering what memories were playing in her head, what she could recall of that night that I still could not.

Eventually she said, her words slow and careful, "Siobhan came to us a while ago. She wanted to help you."

"Help me do what?"

"Conceive."

The word shuddered through me. I felt like I'd been kicked. "But... *how*?" I asked. Olympia didn't answer so I said the thing I'd been thinking for a while, the thing that couldn't be possible, except for the chanting and candlelight in my memory, the women swaying in the dark. "She wanted you to do a spell."

A beat, then Olympia nodded.

"You're witches," I murmured. My heart was beating fast. "Does that mean you worship the devil?"

"No" Olympia met my eyes. "Our practice is much older than the Christian idea of Satan. Fertility spells are simple. We do small spells like that for women who want that sort of help whenever we can, to make things a little less painful, a little easier. We consider it a public service. We were happy to help you too. But then you miscarried. I answered the phone that night of your miscarriage. I don't know if you remember, but we spoke for a few minutes. Siobhan was sick. Do you?"

"I remember."

Olympia scanned my face, her gaze heavy. The harsh overhead lights turned her skin translucent. She looked very young to me all of a sudden, a teenager wearing her mother's lipstick. "You sounded so scared on the phone, so desperate. I felt for you, and so I authorized another member of our coven to go to you, to perform an ultrasound, to see if there was anything we could do to save the baby."

I saw a flash of red lipstick, dark hair. My stomach clenched. "Meg."

"Yes. Meg's our ultrasound tech; she would've told us if the fetus was still viable. But by the time she reached you, we were already too late and the baby was gone. There was nothing that could be done." Olympia paused. "Not medically, at least. But then you called Siobhan again later that night. You begged her for help. Do you remember? You said you'd do anything."

Snow flurrying outside my window, and Siobhan's voice on the other end of the line, raspy and weak.

"Fertility spells are easy," Olympia continued, "but the kind of spell you were asking for, a spell to bring back someone who died, well, that's a much different thing."

That night on the phone, Siobhan asking if there was anything she could do. And me, blurting, my voice choked with tears, *Can you get me my baby back?*

"But she did it," I whispered. My voice was a croak. I slid my eyes out of focus until Olympia was just a blur of gold and mauve. I couldn't look at her, but her voice in my ears was clear and calm.

"We don't do spells like that for just anyone, you understand," she said. "Normally, you would've had to be vetted and inducted as member of our coven. There's a process. But Siobhan didn't think there was time. If she was going to bring your baby back, then the spell would've had to be done that very night, as close to the miscarriage as possible. And Siobhan wanted to help you." Olympia's voice softened. "She loved you, you know. She thought of you like a sister, like family. I think that's why she decided to do it, knowing it was against our rules, knowing what it was going to cost her."

My head came up. "Cost her?"

"It took an enormous amount of energy to work that spell. And Siobhan was already sick. She collapsed immediately after she was done."

I saw it. Siobhan curled on the floor of her apartment, fighting for her life, at the exact same moment that I was lying on my back in the basement, watching my belly move. It hadn't been a coincidence at all.

"We all knew what she had done immediately," Olympia continued. "A spell leaves a trace, and the whole coven felt it. We tried to reach you, but you'd changed your number, moved away. We knew you were staying out here at Talia's, which was why we were able to get the dolls in place in time, but we couldn't get close enough to speak to you, not with that bodyguard around."

I was still struggling to catch up. "The dolls...*you* put them there?"

"I'm sorry if they scared you. They weren't meant to. They're part of a protection spell meant to draw the pain out of your body and tie it to them instead. But then you found them, moved them." Something in Olympia's eyes flickered. "I can't imagine your pregnancy was easy after that. The dolls would've helped, just like the herbs in the cookies would've helped."

"You sent the cookies too?" But that didn't make sense. Emily had sent me those cookies. Dex told me he'd found them in one of her baskets.

Only...he hadn't said *in*, had he? He'd said *next to*. And before that, I thought the cookies had come from Talia. We'd eaten the same ones with her the morning after my miscarriage, and she'd told me a friend had given them to her.

I looked back up at Olympia. "You were the friend who gave Talia those cookies?"

Olympia nodded. "We've been vetting Talia for a while now. We plan to invite her into the coven soon. She knows bits and pieces about who we are, what we do, but I'd appreciate if you didn't say anything until we were ready to offer her a space with us."

"But you asked her to bring me those cookies? Why?"

"The cookies contained herbs to still your stomach and keep some of the more horrifying hallucinations at bay. Midwives and herb witches have known about remedies like that for hundreds of years, since long before modern medicine stole the practice away from us. If you'd kept eating them your pregnancy would've been easier." Olympia leaned forward, taking my hand. "It never should've been this painful, Anna. I'm so sorry. I wish you hadn't gone through it alone. The rest of us should've been there to help you."

I pulled my hand away. I wasn't quite ready to be best friends yet. There was still so much I didn't understand. "What about Dr. Hill? Cora said she was working with you, that she sold my baby to you. And Io said you do rituals, satanic rituals."

Olympia's face darkened. "Io's beliefs are the reason she was never asked to join us. For forty years she's spread harmful propaganda on that channel of hers. She tells lies, saying we worship Satan when Satan has no place in what we do or believe. Her words incite violence against us."

"As for Dr. Hill...we pay her for information, yes, but she's just a means to an end. She helps us find people who might need us, desperate people, people who the medical system ignores. But I'm afraid we could never allow her to join us either."

"But she tried to help me."

Olympia blinked at me. "Did she? Or did she ignore you when what you were saying wasn't convenient? Dr. Hill might have personally meant you no harm, but she's part of a system that regularly ignores women and other marginalized people. Think about it, Anna. Did Dr. Hill listen to you when you told her you were in pain? Have any of your doctors listened to you?"

I swallowed and looked away from her, worried I might start to cry. All this time, I'd felt betrayed by the doctors who'd insisted they could find no medical reason I shouldn't be able to get pregnant, the doctors who'd made me feel like *I* was the one who'd failed because I'd waited too long. I thought of my miscarriage, blood on the tile, my baby leaving my body, and I heard Dr. Crawford telling me he had no idea why it had happened. I remembered all the times I'd gone to Dr. Hill looking for something to help alleviate the pain of IVF, only to be told to take an aspirin, to be strong, that it wouldn't be so bad. Even as the pain made it so I couldn't stand, couldn't walk, couldn't think.

No, none of my doctors had listened to me. Not when I'd needed them to.

I heard footsteps in the hall outside of my room and blinked away the tears that had gathered in my eyes. A moment later, the door creaked open, and a woman with wiry hair and pale pink scrubs appeared.

My eyes drifted down to the tiny bundle in her arms, and I felt my entire being go still.

My baby. My daughter.

"Look who's back from her bath." The nurse walked into the room and eased my daughter's warm, wriggly body into my arms. "I thought you might want to try breastfeeding her."

I blinked, tears gathering in the corners of my eyes as I stared down at her tiny pink face, her skinny, folded legs. Her skin was electric. My arms hummed as I wrestled my breast from my bra with one hand, not caring that Olympia was in the room, that the hospital door was wide open and anyone could've seen me.

The gray-haired nurse helped me get into the right position and showed me how to move my nipple into my daughter's mouth so she'd latch.

"There you go," she said, taking a step back. "You're already a natural."

I wasn't sure if it was the hormones, but I was suddenly, over-whelmingly grateful for the compliment. "Really?"

"Oh yeah. Not all moms have it so easy." The nurse smiled at us. "I'll leave you to it," she told me. "Hit the call button if you need anything."

Olympia waited until the nurse left the room, and then she drifted over to the side of my bed. "Anna, she's beautiful," she murmured, kneeling to get a closer look. "Do you have a name picked out?"

"Not yet." The baby grew drowsy as she ate, her eyes slowly drift-ing closed. Her face already had so much personality, almost like she wasn't a baby at all but a tiny, fully formed person with thoughts and feelings and opinions.

I pressed my lips to her forehead, reveling in how silky her skin was, how downy soft. She didn't open her eyes, but she shifted in my arms, making a slight, soft sound that was almost a cry. When she lifted her chin, I saw that little handprint birthmark, just like Siobhan's.

My witch's mark.

I swallowed. I didn't want to ask. But I had to. I had to know. I touched my daughter's tiny hand, prying her curled fingers apart. I would love her no matter what, but I had to know.

I lifted my eyes to Olympia's. "Is she...?" How did I even ask this?

Is she a monster? A demon?

Is any part of her *human*?

I licked my lips. "Is she going to be okay?"

Olympia's dark eyes were on me, unblinking. "You have to under-stand...what Siobhan did, bringing your baby back like that, it was against the natural order of things. That's part of the reason your pregnancy was so difficult. The magic can interfere with your mind; it can make you see things that aren't there, experience things that never happened."

I curled my arms around my baby. "But is she going to be okay?"

"There's always a price when you take life into your own hands. If we hadn't found you when we did, if we hadn't finished the spell, it could've been much worse."

"What does that mean? What's wrong with her?"

"You don't have to remember if you don't want to. I can make you forget again."

Just for a second, I considered saying okay. I thought about what it would be like to live the rest of my life in blissful ignorance, never knowing what I'd traded to get my daughter back. Never knowing what she was.

But I knew it wouldn't work. Even if Olympia made me forget, I'd know. Somewhere in my bones, I'd know that something was wrong.

Two women walked past the hall just outside my room, laughing and talking, their shoes clicking the linoleum. By the time they'd passed, I'd made my decision.

"I have to know," I said.

Olympia nodded. Without preamble, she leaned toward me, her hand outstretched. I flinched.

"It's okay," she murmured. "We placed a little spell on you the night of the birth, to keep your memories from surfacing. All I'm doing now is lifting it."

She pressed a warm palm to my forehead and murmured something under her breath.

The memories stirred inside of me. I could feel them moving, like smoke inside my skull. My eyelids fluttered.

———

Siobhan and I were huddled in the mud, trees casting deep shadows all around us. If I listened, I could hear a distant murmur. Women chanting. It was the night I'd given birth. I was in the throes of labor.

"This isn't a curse," Siobhan was saying to me. "It's a gift."

I'd reached for my belly. I was weak, and it took all the strength I had left just to force words from between my clenched lips. "What... do you want?"

There was a beat of quiet, and Siobhan said simply, "I'm dying, Anna. I'll be gone before your baby gets here. But I'm not ready. There's still so much I want to do, so much I never got a chance to do." She smiled, a little twitch at the corner of her lips. "But the women in my coven don't have to die. When our bodies give out, we can create a new body for ourselves in the womb of another. This wouldn't have to be the end for me. I could get another chance to live again."

She pressed her hand to my belly, and I felt a wave of horror and understanding crash over me.

"You did something to her?" I choked out.

"No," Siobhan said. "Not yet. The transfer of my soul into her body is only possible with your consent. You would have to tell me it was okay."

"And she'll become...you?"

"Not right away. It takes years for the transfer to complete. She would still be her, but all my memories and experiences would grow within her. The experience is like gradually remembering a past life." Siobhan smiled. "I've done it a few times now. It's quite beautiful."

She was dressed in dark colors, some wool coat I didn't recognize, and her head was bare and pale in the darkness. She looked timeless. In the soft silvery glow of the moon, she looked just like she had twenty years ago.

I felt something harden in my throat. I had watched her for so many years, wondering what she was like, wishing I could know her. Meeting her had been like a wish granted. I felt so stupid.

"Is this why you wanted to be my friend?" I wondered if she could tell how much it hurt to ask this. "Was it all a lie? So you could...*use* me?"

Siobhan was shaking her head before the words left my mouth. "Anna, *no*. Your friendship has meant more to me than you could ever know." Her voice was suddenly thick, wavering. She pressed a finger to her cheeks to stop a tear. "No matter what happens, I need you to know that. I'd never intended to use you. That day at the acupuncturist, I'd been waiting for Talia. I was planning to ask her originally. Rayna, another member of the coven, she's friends with Talia, and we've been slowly bringing her into the coven for months now, and she wants to carry a child. We had planned to approach her. Everything was in place. But then you miscarried, and you asked me for my help, and you sounded so..." She shook her head, trailing off. "I couldn't tell you no, not when I knew how to help. And then..."

She didn't have to finish. *And then it was too late*. She'd fallen into a coma after she'd performed the spell to save my baby. She'd given up her chance to live—possibly even her few remaining days of good health—for me. Because I had meant that much to her.

It made the next thing I had to ask so much harder.

"What happens if I say no?" I pressed my hands into my belly as the question left my lips. I loved Siobhan, I did. But this was my *daughter*. This was her whole life. How could I make this choice for her?

Siobhan said, a little sadly, "If you refuse, then my soul won't be able to transfer into your baby's body, and I will die."

"And my baby—"

"She'll be born just like any other baby is born, and you'll raise her just like any other mother would." Only here Siobhan paused, as though considering her next words very carefully. "But...I won't be able to promise that she won't be affected by the spell."

"Affected?" My heart was beating hard. "What does that mean?"

"Magic isn't intended to bring people back from the dead, Anna. There are consequences. I never would've gone through with it if you weren't so desperate, if there were any other way. But a witch's soul is a powerful force, a stabilizing force. If you allowed me to perform the transfer, I could assure you that the consequences would be minimal. But without it..." Siobhan faltered. "Your baby could be completely human. Or she could be...off."

"No." The word came straight from my gut. I didn't know what else to say. I couldn't find the words to tell her how unbearably cruel this was, how *unspeakably* cruel. I wanted to rage at her, to scream.

I closed my eyes, fresh tears gluing my lids together. When I asked her to bring my baby back, she should have told me no. If this was the cost, if these were the stakes, she should have told me no. I almost asked why she didn't—the words were on my tongue—but I couldn't bring myself to say them.

The truth was, I knew why. I could see it so clearly. How the IVF would've kept failing, how even one more miscarriage would've broken me. What Siobhan had done was unnatural, and maybe it was even cruel. But it was also the only way I was ever going to be a mother. Siobhan had seen that, and she'd done everything she could to give me what I'd wanted.

Siobhan grabbed my hand and held tight. "Anna...think about this. How many mothers have any kind of assurance that their children will be healthy or successful or happy? What doctor could offer that? If you allow me to perform the transfer, then I could guarantee those things. Your doctors couldn't even tell you why you'd *miscarried*. They tried to convince you that your suffering was fine, that it was normal. They tried to control your body because they were afraid of what your body could do."

"I can offer you so much more than they can, an entire village of women to hold your hand and guide you, women who know how to heal you. You could join us, Anna. I *want* you to join us. Years from now, when your body breaks down, we could bring you back! Imagine what could we do together, if we had the time, if we weren't beholden to the laws of mankind."

I closed my eyes. I was having a hard time focusing. Pain was building somewhere inside of me. It felt like my last contraction had only just ended and already I could feel another coming. Every muscle in my body tensed. I didn't know how to fight anymore. I didn't know how to keep my baby safe. I didn't know how to hold on to myself. Everything I'd done throughout my pregnancy felt insufficient in the face of this pain. I was scared and I was hurt, and I wasn't strong enough to do this alone.

Come on, you're okay, whispered a familiar voice in my head. It sounded like Dex, like Dr. Hill. *This isn't so bad; calm down...*

With all the willpower I had left, I forced that voice to just shut up. I was tired of pretending I wasn't in pain. I was tired of being strong just because it made things easier for everyone else. I was tired of calming down.

This pain was like nothing I'd ever experienced in my life. I felt like I was sinking far inside of myself, past the point of consciousness, past the point where I could be reached by any other person. I knew that the only way through was to dig down, to confront the pain head on, to grab it by the root and pull.

To surrender.

I opened my mouth and released a deep, guttural scream.

LENA KAYNE, MANY, MANY YEARS LATER

THE INFERTILITY SUPPORT GROUP MET IN THE BASEMENT OF A church on the corner of Willow and Clark in Brooklyn Heights. Think brownstones, leafy trees surrounded by wrought iron fences, bumper-to-bumper electric BMWs and Lexus SUVs, kids riding scooters down bumpy sidewalks. Morning light streamed in through the basement's thin, high windows, painting the walls a dusty gold.

Lena Kayne didn't want to be there. It was drafty and cold, and the coffee tasted terrible. And why were they even serving coffee anyway? Half the women here had already given up caffeine and alcohol and red meat and anything else their doctors told them had even the slightest, most miniscule chance of messing with fertility. They should be serving Clomid.

Lena sat on a metal folding chair in the back of the room, beside a much older woman wearing a huge scarf and sunglasses, and she watched the minute hand on the clock on the wall above the door, tick-tick-ticking through the minutes until finally (*finally*) the woman who'd been leading the group—Tara—stood up and clapped her hands together once.

"I want to sincerely thank you all for coming today." Tara had an asymmetrical haircut and fantastic earrings, and she made eye contact with every single wannabe mommy (as she'd been calling them in her head) gathered in their lopsided circle. For some reason, this made Lena think of cult leaders and youth pastors and people who ran MLMs. Which sort of made sense. The women who showed up to these groups had always felt slightly cult-like to her. Only instead of shapeless white tunics, they were all dressed in throwback 2020s-style chunky clogs and oversized army jackets, their hair intentionally messy, faces scrubbed free of makeup.

Lena didn't know why she was so critical of them. She was just like them after all, right down to the vintage clogs. She was here because she'd been diagnosed with polycystic ovarian syndrome—a diagnosis she'd had to fight for, considering her previous doctor was convinced she couldn't get pregnant because of her weight. It hadn't helped that her husband had backed him up, encouraging Lena to eat less and exercise more, as if all their fertility problems could be solved with a salad and a jog around the block.

Lena had known there was more to it than that, but she couldn't get anyone to listen to her. It wasn't until she found her third doctor in a row that anyone even mentioned the words *polycystic ovarian syndrome* to her. It was true; the new doctor hadn't advised Lena to lose weight, but she had insisted that she come to these meetings and try a few techniques for managing stress—things like "movement therapy" and "mindful eating," which even Lena had to admit sounded a lot like her previous doctor's advice to jog around the block and eat a salad. But she was desperate.

She made her way to the back of the room when the meeting was over, keeping her head ducked so she wouldn't make eye contact with the other wannabe mommies. She just wanted to do her time and get out of here. She was reaching out to grab her jacket from the cubbies when a voice from behind her said, "Is this your first session?"

Lena looked up. It was the older woman in the scarf and the sunglasses. Only now, when Lena studied her, frowning, she realized there was something very familiar about the shape of the woman's mouth and the way her hair was styled. The woman took off her sunglasses and Lena released a little breath.

"Oh my God," she said, stunned. "You're Anna Victoria Alcott."

Anna Victoria Alcott, as in the Academy Award–winning actor turned director turned *icon*. One of the most beautiful, accomplished, talented women in the entire country. Of her entire *generation*.

And she was here. Talking to *her*.

"Guilty," Anna said, smiling a little shyly. "And here I was thinking I might not be recognized."

"But—but what are you doing here?" Lena blushed as soon as the words were out of her mouth, feeling embarrassed. She hadn't meant to be so blunt; it's just that Anna clearly wasn't trying to have a baby. For one thing, she was much too old. Her age was (famously) impossible to guess, but Lena figured she had to be pushing sixty.

And there was the fact that Anna already had a daughter of her own, a young woman who was all grown up now, an actor in her own right. Siobhan Alcott. Lena had read somewhere that Anna named her after another famous actor who'd died of breast cancer decades ago.

"I'm working on a film about infertility," Anna explained. She was leaning over her tote bag, and she dug around inside for a while before producing a small box of cookies. "But it's been a long time since I've been through this whole thing, I'm afraid. I'm not sure I remember all the ins and outs." Then, holding out the cookies, "These are amazing. Anise seed and honey. Here, please try one."

"Oh, uh, thank you." Normally, Lena didn't like to eat in public, especially not cookies, or anything else that could be considered decadent. She always worried there'd be people watching, judging her body, judging *her*.

But this was *Anna Victoria Alcott*. She took the cookie.

"Do you mind if I ask why you're here?" Anna asked, nibbling her own cookie.

Lena hesitated. Just as she didn't often take food from strangers, she didn't usually go around telling just anyone her infertility story. It was private. She only really felt comfortable talking about it with her closest friends.

But she'd been watching Anna on-screen her whole life. Her voice, her smile, her laugh—all of it was intimately familiar to her. She *felt* like a close friend.

"It was actually my doctor's idea," Lena explained, taking a bite of cookie. "It's part of my PCOS treatment." And then Lena said something she'd never even said to her closest friends, something that she'd barely admitted to herself. She didn't even know why she said it. It's just that Anna looked so interested, so concerned. It was like she was really listening, like she cared.

"To be honest, I...don't really buy any of this. How is sitting in a room filled with a bunch of other sad people going to help me? I don't need to *talk* about how I can't have a baby. I need...I don't know. Maybe I need a new body, one that works the way it's supposed to." She could feel tears in her eyes and quickly blinked them away, embarrassed for admitting so much. "I'm sorry to unload that on you. It's just been really stressful. Sometimes I feel like no one knows what's happening inside of my body."

"I understand," Anna said, nodding. "But you might be surprised by what finding the right support can do. I found an amazing group of women right after the birth of my daughter, and they've become lifelong friends. Maybe something similar can happen to you."

She held out her hand. "Here, have another cookie."

AUTHOR'S NOTE

AT DELICATE CONDITION'S INCEPTION, I WAS SEVEN MONTHS pregnant with my first child. This was my second pregnancy, my first had ended in a devastating miscarriage but, otherwise, I had no major complications, no genetic testing scares, and my daughter arrived within a day of her due date, healthy and perfect, after a mere ten minutes of pushing. Even my miscarriage was about as standard as it was possible to be, occurring early in my first trimester, the symptoms textbook. I'm, perhaps, the last person who has a right to complain about pregnancy.

And yet, I was shocked by how difficult miscarriage was, both mentally and physically, not to mention how difficult a perfectly average pregnancy could be. Of course, I'd heard people talk, and I'd seen on TV and in movies that pregnancy could be uncomfortable and inconvenient, but the way it was spoken about or depicted was always adorable, or even slightly humorous. Here was a woman waddling across a room while gripping her belly, a single instance of morning sickness, the weight gain entirely in her stomach, like she'd shoved a basketball under her shirt. As soon as she gave birth, that belly—and all her symptoms—disappeared without a trace.

It should surprise no one that real pregnancy is nothing like this. Take morning sickness, for instance. Real morning sickness is like a low-level hangover that you have all day, every day. It often comes with exhaustion so great that you find it hard to get out of bed in the morning, and it doesn't go away, even if you manage to throw up. Oh, and it lasts for three months—at least. Women with hyperemesis gravidarum deal with it every day of their pregnancies (which is a lot closer to ten months than nine, despite what your health class may have led you to believe.)

Morning sickness is the most obviously terrible symptom to point to, but it's by no means the only one. No one tells you that, by the time you're around five months pregnant, your baby will get so big that there won't be enough room for both the baby and your internal organs, and it will become difficult to breathe as a tiny head pushes into your lung. No one tells you your skin can get so dry it cracks. Your gums can bleed for no reason. Your teeth can feel loose. Your fingernails can split. You can develop hemorrhoids and skin tags and melasma and nosebleeds. I once spoke with a woman who experienced something called "ptyalism" during her third pregnancy. Never heard of it? It's when your mouth fills with an excessive amount of saliva, and you can't stop drooling. This woman went through two towels a day, just mopping the excess drool from her mouth. Why don't doctors tell women about these symptoms? Is it because they think we'll stop having babies?

And then there's miscarriage. It's more common knowledge now that 10 to 20 percent of known pregnancies end in miscarriage, but we still don't talk enough about how it feels. I'm not talking about the grief, though that can be devastating. I'm talking about the physical and mental pain of actually going through a miscarriage. If so many women experience them, shouldn't we know what to expect? It's often excruciatingly slow, confusing, and can be as painful as birth itself. It can last for days or even weeks, and during that time, doctors often can't say for sure what's happening or why.

This part in particular seemed ludicrous to me. How could my doctor not know what was happening? When I first got pregnant, I was given pages of foods and medications to avoid, activities that were no longer deemed safe, even forbidden *sleeping positions*—all with the warning that avoiding these things would make miscarriage less likely. With all these restrictions in place, doctors must have *some* idea of what causes miscarriage. It turns out that's not the case.

Unfortunately, confusion is a common theme throughout pregnancy. Despite the fact that women have been giving birth for hundreds of thousands of years, there's still a lot we don't know. In fact, one report notes that more than 90 percent of the medications approved by the FDA from 1980 to 2000 had insufficient data to determine safety. The general consensus is that it's unethical to study the effects of drugs on a pregnant woman. But lack of progress into alternative methods of testing means there's little research to go on.

Doctors are mostly guessing at how drugs affect unborn babies and the women carrying them. This bias isn't limited to people who have or are planning to get pregnant. Throughout the history of medicine, women have been included in far fewer medical studies, less research and fewer drug trials than men have been. This is true even during studies and drugs for things that solely or mostly affect cis women, like breast and ovarian cancer. It's absolutely unacceptable. And yet it still continues, to this day.

My hope is that women who've been through pregnancy

themselves will find something they recognize in the pages of this book, that it might help them to open up about their own experiences and to know that they're not alone. Anna's experience with pregnancy is intended to be hyperbolic, but all of her symptoms have their roots in real things that happen to women's bodies during their pregnancies: odd cravings and unusual fetal movements, not to mention the very real, very strange feeling of knowing there's something you can't entirely control or understand growing inside of you.

But, in my opinion, the most horrifying part of Anna's experience isn't what happens to her physically, but how the people around her react: how her doctors dismiss and ignore her, expecting her to suffer through her pain for the good of her baby without any concern for whether her body can handle it; how her husband assumes she's either making up or exaggerating her symptoms. I'm afraid I didn't have to exaggerate these reactions at all. They're all too real. The tendency to assume that women can't be trusted to accurately convey their symptoms comes from the historical diagnosis of "hysteria," which was once thought to be a medical condition said to only affect women. Doctors were taught that women were inherently liars, unreliable, or hysterical hypochondriacs. In some cases, they were even believed to be possessed. And these beliefs have persisted, even after the diagnosis of hysteria was proven to be nonsense. To this day doctors prescribe less pain medication to women than they do to men, they take longer to diagnose us with illness, and they're more likely to send us home in the middle of a medical emergency like a heart attack. Unfortunately, all these prejudices disproportionately affect women of color. If you're ever curious about why the maternal mortality rate in the United States is so high—particularly among

Black women—these are good places to start. Doctors don't understand our bodies, they don't believe us about our symptoms, and they ignore us when we try to tell them we're in pain.

Is it really any surprise then that women look for answers elsewhere? Faith in alternative and homeopathic medicines, such as acupuncture and aromatherapy is at an all-time high, particularly among women. And while such remedies can, in many cases, be beneficial, we're not always so lucky. Women are more likely to be drawn in by dangerous MLM schemes, like selling essential oils that claim to cure everything from weight gain to eczema to cancer, and women and mothers have been leaders in the anti-vaccination movement, a movement that puts children and unvaccinated adults in danger. These things are not harmless, and they don't just affect women. But when the blowback comes, women are often the ones blamed. Silly women believing snake-oil salesmen and ignorant women who don't understand how vaccinations work. People conveniently forgot the medical system that abandoned them. But would women turn to these things so frequently if they felt they were being listened to?

As I wrote *Delicate Condition*, I felt myself ruminating on these questions again and again. What would it take for our husbands and doctors to take our pain seriously? How bad would pregnancy have to get? How many women would have to die? Drafting this book has been a cathartic experience for me, allowing me to put all my fears on the page, but there's not an easy or even a clear solution. The idea that women *should* suffer during childbirth is so deeply engrained in our society that even when we do have medication that could help ease their pain, like an epidural, we're discouraged from using it.

I don't have any answers here. I wish I did. But I hope that all pregnant people will read this book and feel seen. I hope that men will read this book and feel a little less comfortable with women's suffering. I hope we stop assuming that pain is a woman's birthright and start trying to find a way to ease the burden, just a little. Childbirth is not, after all, something that only affects women—it affects us all.

READING GROUP GUIDE

1. Anna had been considering taking a break from work to focus on her health and IVF treatments when her career suddenly took off in a new way. Have you ever been in a position where one part of your life demanded more of you just as you had begun to shift your attention away? How did you handle juggling the competing priorities? What would you have done in Anna's situation?

2. Many child-bearing people struggle with the question of fertility and undergo difficult and expensive IVF treatments in order to conceive. Do you or anyone you know have a similar story? If so, do you feel you were treated any differently than friends or family who did not experience the same kind of struggle?

3. *Delicate Condition* is threaded through with interstitials from different points in history. What do you think the author's intentions were when including these interstitials? What did they tell you about pregnancy and childbirth through the ages?

4. When Anna's supposed stalker breaks into her Brooklyn brownstone, Anna no longer feels safe in her home. Instead, she flees to the ghost town that is the Hamptons in winter where she and Dex are all but alone. Do you agree with her decision to leave? In her position, would you feel safer in a relatively small space in the city or in a sprawling house with few neighbors around?

5. After her miscarriage, Anna is convinced she can still feel the fetus moving—but at first, nobody (including her doctors) believes her. Have you or anyone you've known been in a situation where your doctor either downplays or disbelieves your symptoms? What happened and how did you resolve the issue? What would you do now if you could go back and change how the interaction went?

6. As her pregnancy progresses, Anna experiences increasingly horrific physical and psychological symptoms—some of which she can't be sure ever truly happened. Which of her symptoms do you believe were real (the cravings, the raw meat, the roadkill, the tooth, the claw, the scarred legs) and which were a result of the spell making her believe something that wasn't truly there? What would you have done if you began experiencing similar symptoms? Would you tell someone, knowing what they might think?

7. Siobhan used the last of her power to help revive Anna's baby— but because Siobhan was immediately taken out of commission and Anna became so difficult to reach, nobody in the coven was able to warn Anna of the potential consequences. Did Siobhan make the right decision to help Anna even though Anna hadn't

been fully informed about what was being done to her? Would you have been able to forgive the coven for putting you through such an intense experience if it meant saving the life of your loved one?

8. Did Dex deserve what happened to him? How did you react when he met his ultimate fate? How do you think Anna felt about him after the initial rage and panic subsided?

9. Ultimately, Anna chooses to forgive the coven for what they unintentionally put her through and allow Siobhan to be reborn as her daughter. In the epilogue, it suggests that Anna is now a full member of the coven and has every intention of being reborn herself—giving her the "time" that always seems to be missing from our lives. What do you think of this decision? In Anna's position, would you make the same call?

ACKNOWLEDGMENTS

I was seven months pregnant when I came up with the idea for *Delicate Condition*. I had just made the excruciating decision to put aside another book, an adult thriller that felt neither thrilling nor particularly "adult," and I was depressed and deeply disappointed with myself. I thought maybe I wasn't a talented enough writer to tackle difficult topics for adult audiences. I felt like I'd failed. When the idea for *Delicate Condition* came to me, it was a gift. I could see the entire story in my head, as clearly as if it were dropped there by a muse. I wrote the first draft in a kind of fever dream, racing against my pregnancy, convinced that the only way I would ever finish is if I wrote the last words before my baby was born.

That did not happen. Rather, I spent three years and at least twelve different drafts trying to figure out this story, going back and forth with my agent, my beta readers and myself to figure out what was and wasn't working. I nearly quit at least a dozen times. I was convinced I would never finish or, if I did, that it would be so weird no one would want it. I've never been so grateful to be so wrong. This is the hardest book I've ever written. It's also my favorite.

Writing a book is always a team effort, and I could not have completed this one without the support, encouragement, and hard work of so many people. First, there are truly no words to express my gratitude to my agent, Hillary Jacobson. From the moment I shared the idea for *Delicate Condition*, she has been my unwavering champion, a source of encouragement and inspiration, and a true partner in every sense of the word. Hillary, you have been there for me every step of the way, through the highs and the lows, the doubts and the fears. You read countless versions of this book, offering your expert feedback and guidance with every single one. You never gave up on me, even when I thought I could not go on. You believed in me and in this book with a fervor that I can only describe as awe-inspiring. Your unwavering dedication to my success is a testament to your character, your professionalism, and your heart. You have worked tirelessly to ensure that this book found the right home, and I am forever grateful for your hard work, your advocacy, and your faith in me.

Next, I'd like to thank to Mary Altman, my editor at Sourcebooks. Mary, your editorial guidance and feedback have been invaluable. Because of you, *Delicate Condition* became a much stronger and more compelling story than I ever could have written on my own. You have truly gone above and beyond, and I am deeply grateful for the hard work and dedication that you have shown in bringing this book to life. You have challenged me to push beyond my limits, and I am so proud of what we accomplished together. Thank you.

To my team at Sourcebooks, I want to express my deepest thanks for the incredible work that you've done to bring this book to readers. To Cristina Arreola, Ashlyn Keil, and Molly Waxman, for your outstanding work promoting this book, and to Paula Amendolaro, Brian Grogan, Sean Murray, Liz Otte, Shawn Abraham, Margaret Coffee, Rachel Latko, and Tracy Nelson, who tirelessly championed this book to bookstores and retailers around the country. Also, to my copy and production editors: India Hunter, Aimee Alker, and Susan Barnett. I am deeply grateful to all of you for your creativity, your expertise, and your passion for books and storytelling. It has been an honor to work with each and every one of you.

I would also like to take a moment to express my heartfelt gratitude to my team abroad. To my UK agent, Lucy Morris, your guidance and feedback have been instrumental in helping me shape this story into its final form. Your understanding of the UK market blew me away, and you have been an invaluable part of my publishing team, and I am deeply grateful. To my UK editor, Miranda Jewess, your enthusiasm for this project was infectious and your entire team at Viper is truly something special. I feel so lucky to have such talented and committed people behind me, and I am excited to continue working with you on future projects.

To Josie Freedman, Randie Adler, and the rest of my film team at CAA, your expertise and connections in the entertainment world have opened doors I never thought possible. I do not know how to put into words how in awe I am of what you were able to pull together for this book. I am honored to have you on my team.

I am also deeply grateful to my beta readers, who took the time to read so many early versions of this book and offer their honest feedback. Thank you Leah Konen and Andrea Bartz for your invaluable contributions. Your insights and suggestions have helped shape the final product, and I appreciate your generosity and support. I am so grateful for the time and energy you put into reading and analyzing this work.

Finally, I want to thank my family and friends for their unwavering support, encouragement, and love throughout this process. You have been my cheerleaders, my sounding boards, and my inspiration, and I could not have done this without you. A special thanks to Ron Williams, my husband, for everything. Thank you for believing in me and this book.

Last but not least, I want to thank all the readers who have picked up this book, thank you for giving it a chance. I hope it scares you in all the best ways.

About the Author

Danielle Valentine is a pseudonym for bestselling YA horror novelist Danielle Vega. Her work, which includes the Merciless series, *Survive the Night*, *The Haunted* and *The Unleashed*, has been optioned for film and television by Lionsgate and Warner Bros., and has been translated into dozens of languages worldwide. Her latest YA horror novel, *How to Survive Your Murder*, was published in 2022. *Delicate Condition* is Danielle's adult debut. She lives in New Jersey with her husband and daughter.